Planet of the Orange-red Sun

Series Volume 12

The Voyage of the Eagle's Seed

Planet of the Orange-red Sun Series

Volume 12
The Voyage of the Eagle's Seed

by Vic Broquard

For Morgan and L. Ron Hubbard

Table of Contents

Part I Opening Salvos

Chapter 1 Mission Beginning

Hi. Nia Elain Compton-Jereni here, owner and Captain of the exploration ship the Eagle's Seed. I've been asked to relay what happened on our Secret Exploration Mission given to us by Emperor Bino Sanguro, the ruler of the Ataro Empire of the Twelve Sacred Planets of the Wasps. First, I should be accurate. There are now forty planets in the empire and most are located in the middle of our spiral arm, though a few are in the outer rim. None lies in the densely populated hub sector. That fact becomes important later on.

As I think this whole thing over, I'm convinced that first I must describe my crew, as boring as this may seem to you. They are fundamental to this entire mission, especially if you are to make much sense of what happened to us. Initially, there were twenty of us, including myself, plus three children, one robot assistant, a border collie named Jen, and a black cat named Hermes. Perhaps the most significant thing to grasp is that the twenty adults are all very highly educated, specialists in specific fields. Indeed, we picked up the nickname of the "brainiac crew" just before we departed Ashford-5 on our mission. While most exploration ships carry several specialists, such as a geologist or a linguist, none on record has ever had every crew member this well-educated, which suited seven of us just fine, as we were ravenous for learning everything we could. We believe knowledge is the true power, which I might add would be proven repeatedly on this lengthy trip.

The fact that the crew was all highly educated men and women is but the very least reason why I simply must describe my crew here at the start. Far from it. In fact, only the Cho family had "normal" human bodies. The other eighteen of us had hermaphrodite bodies, children of past victims of the genetic bio agent. This detail is an important one. I purposely chose my crew this way so we would have companionship of like-oriented people, but the emperor insisted the Cho family be part of my crew.

Lin and Dao Cho, thirty and twenty-nine respectively, are from Winno-3, and are the pair of engineers, who built the prototype hydrogen engine based on the mathematician Alexandra's theory and design specifications. So part of this mission was obviously theirs. Lin had built the actual engines, while his wife, Dao, had built the vital hydrogen collection mechanism needed to refuel the engines. If Alexandra's theory and design were correct, this relatively simple engine would revolutionize exploration of the galaxy at sub-light cruising speeds, because their range was virtually unlimited, as long as the ship stayed within the galactic spiral arms, where sources of hydrogen fuel were everywhere, that is, assuming the collection system worked as planned. Both had dark brown hair, but unlike Lin who kept his cut quite short, Dao allowed hers to flow to her waist, as did most women onboard, the current style in fashion within the Imperium. Their skin color had a distinctive olive hue. They had a nine year old daughter, Mai, who became our babysitter.

The other eighteen of us were hermaphrodites, but with quite different situations. Only Alexandra Khristos, twenty-three, of Aquila Prime was the most limited, from our viewpoint, not hers. As you probably recall, Aquila Prime was the dumping ground for all the horribly genetically modified humans, cast off from normal societies around the Imperium. Almost none of them had received any of the genetic cures that had been developed over the years, which means they were virtually helpless without the constant assistance of their many robots.

Alexandra was typical. Her body had no arms. Her feet were malformed, forcing her to wear the tiny toe shoes. That is, only her toes lay flat on the ground because of the incredibly high arch of her feet. A tiny spiked heel touched the ground just behind the back of her toes, making walking rather precarious. Her rich, lovely blonde hair fell to her ankles and could not be trimmed any shorter. Doing so caused excruciating pain, and besides, the shortened hair quickly regained its former length. Her breasts were each larger than her head, giving her the appearance of having three heads. (Note: teasing one of these people as being "three-headed" is about the worst insult possible.) Finally, like many of us, her lips were slit, forcing her to wear twelve inch in diameter, golden lip plates.

Since nine of us wear them, I should tell you a bit more about them, since this is also an important detail. When not wearing them, we sport two large, dangling lip loops, which are quite sensitive to touch. Rather erotic, if I do say so. Since they can easily be caught on things, we wear the decorative lip plates. A mouthpiece attaches to our upper and lower jaws, held in place by four pegs, which fit into four holes in our upper and lower gum lines. The large, but light weight, gold disks attach to these two supports, which have a tiny mechanism that allows the plates either to be locked into a horizontal position, or released and dangling down to our chests. When eating or drinking, we lock the upper plates in their horizontal position. We drink by using a spoon. Normally, we remove the plates and supports while we sleep. On Ashford-5, both men and women were these plates as a status symbol, which is why so many of us still choose to wear them and not have this genetic cure performed. (Note: without the genetic cure, using a medical machine to heal the damage fails. The body merely quickly returns to its previous state via its genetic programming. Yes, the genetic biological agent is exceedingly nasty stuff.)

These lip plates are important for two other reasons. Since we are unable to make any speech sounds involving the lips, we're forced to speak in IS, Imperium Standard. Either that language, which has none of those sounds, or use my native click language of Descartes-3, which only eight of us know. The other detail is that on the top surface of the upper disk are embossed designs, chosen by each of us. Most are unique. For example, mine shows an etching of my Eagle's Seed. Yes, we know; these are wholly not practical, but they are decorative and the height of fashion on Ashford-5, the home world for most of my crew.

As physically limited as Alexandra is, she needs to have her personal assistant with her at all times. That is, her robot, a humaniform robot called Minta, an HRM7 model. Minta looks like a normal human being who is the same age as

Alexandra, twenty-two. The robot has short curly blonde hair and olive colored eyes, most peculiar. Both Minta and Alexandra are my height, five-nine.

Another aspect all genetically modified hermaphrodites share is a tiny waist. However, Alexandra is forced to wear a heavily steel-boned corset to help her back support the weight of her massive breasts. A byproduct of this physical alteration is that we can't really gain weight around our waists. You'll never see an obese hermaphrodite, except perhaps around their hips and legs. Our unique genetic modifications simply don't allow for fat buildup in this location any longer. Some like this aspect, while others grumble about it.

A number of genetic cures have been found and my crew reflects this. Nine of us still wear the lip plates, but nine have had their lips genetically cured. Note: those are mostly the men in our crew. Seventeen of us have had the "hair cure," that is, the neurons in our hair are gone, allowing us to cut our hair as we desire. Waist length hair is the current style on Ashford-5, and most of us keep ours trimmed that long. Yes, we women like to be fashionable, but the men keep theirs short.

Seventeen of us have had some cures done on our feet. Eight of us have only had our feet partially repaired, forcing us to wear six inch heels, which are also the height of fashion on our world. Nine others have had their feet fully repaired and are able to wear normal shoes and boots. Again, those are mostly the men onboard.

What cannot be undone are the dual sexual organs and of course the requisite breasts, which, for reasons I don't fully understand, are quite large and perky. All Ashford-5 women and the hermaphrodite men have H-cup sizes, whether they wish them that large or not. Even if they are reduced via the medical machines, they quickly regain their former size and shapes. Strange. Similarly afflicted women and men from other worlds are able to have theirs reduced to more practical sizes, but not those of us who live on Ashford-5. From personal experience, I can tell you that our babies never want from hunger!

However, the men bear the brunt of this factor. You

can't hide such giant bosoms. While many of the men wear specially designed suits that attempt to look like normal men's suits, it's obvious they are not. Some men wear their hair waist length and don't try to look like a normal human male. While at first glance those men appear to be women, their deeper voices give them away. I'm thankful I don't have the problems the hermaphrodite men do.

With this said, I'm the Captain and pilot. I'm a competent Med Tech and a physicist. I have a rich, thick, wavy, waist length, black hair. My daughter is Zorina. My mate is Danika Jereni-Compton. A year older than me, she's over six feet tall with raven hair with the cutest bangs over her forehead and a rounded nose. She is my co-pilot — perhaps a better pilot than me — and my navigator. Plus, she can competently handle any piece of equipment on the ship. She's learned quite a lot these past few years. Besides this, she's a fighter. When we first met, she was a Ranger and a superb swords-woman. Now, she is mastering the d-gun. Her daughter is Nadia, two and a half. Her lip plate shows a female fighter brandishing a large sword.

I purposely chose married couples to form the crew. Next, are Martina Wells and her new mate Tesla Niko-Wells. Martina has recently used the Rejuvenation machine and appears to be twenty-two, like Tesla, but she really is ninety-two! She used to be the Hub Sector ID Minister, wielding incredible powers within the intelligence gathering community of the vast Imperium. She's been retired for some years, but moved from her home world of Descartes-3 to be with Tesla, helping her and the others get valuable educations. She has long blonde hair and blue eyes, and she always dresses like a "professional woman," with a dark skirt and white blouse. Her lip plate shows two women holding hands. Her new mate, Tesla, is also blonde with pale blue eyes. She's our electronics expert, who is also keenly interested in political science and governmental history.

Anya Pavel-Bellweather and Thomas Bellweather come next. She has raven hair and matching eyes. She is an expert with communications centers, both their use and repair. I swear she can build a new comm network from spare parts!

She has brought along her black cat, Hermes. Tom is a General Engineer, who claims he can build or repair anything. His short hair is brown, as are his eyes. Like many men, his feet are fully repaired, as are his lips. Anya has an etching of a comm center on her top lip plate.

Jovanna Darvin-Gervasi-Jones and Diego Gervasi-Jones are an unlikely pair. She has light brown hair, quite wavy. She and her twin, Jana, are both quite attractive, perhaps the prettiest women onboard. Both she and her sister are into ancient history, botany, and cooking. They can make nearly any meal into a culinary delight, something the whole crew will soon be appreciating. Her lip plate depicts an ancient volume of history, as does Jana's. Diego is a mechanical engineer with short brown hair and eyes. He's had his feet and lips fully repaired.

Jana Darvin-Childa and Len Childa come next. Jana is just like her identical twin sister in most ways. It's rather hard to tell the two apart. Len is our chemist. Like Diego, he is two years older than Jana and Jovanna, and has had his feet and lips repaired.

Dr. Leann Hamel-Valen and Hans Valen are very important to this expedition. She is our resident medical doctor, but has had some training as a geneticist as well. Hence, she has also had her lips and feet fully repaired, so she can perform her medical duties more efficiently. Hans is part of the reason for this voyage. He's a physicist and a particle physics expert. He invented a major improvement to our hyperdrive propulsion system, which we are going to test. If it pans out, he anticipates a revolution in distances traveled by this means. For example, the usual simple transport ship can travel in hyperspace about halfway across the spiral arm of the galaxy before needing to refuel. His proposed modifications suggest the range could well be five times greater. Also, we are to begin explorations in the halo of our galaxy, an area of uncharted hyperspace. It will fall to Hans, Alexandra, and me to begin to work out the needed coordinates for navigation in this new region of space.

Marisol Gervasi-Hammil and Beth Hammil come next. Both are twenty-four with brown hair and eyes. Marisol has had her lips and feet fully repaired, primarily because of her specialties. She is a *mentales* gift trainer from the Imperial Tower of the two queens of Ashford-5, and a very competent Basic Therapy giver. Plus, she is our top linguist, a protegee of Nadia's, perhaps the most famous linguist in the Imperium, though she is now a retired school teacher in Exchange City. Marisol is also a very good seamstress and has promised to keep all our clothing in good repair. Her mate, Beth, is our zoologist and also a botanist. She is well versed on all animals found throughout the Imperium. She brought along her border collie named Jen, a short haired, black and white dog that is extremely intelligent.

Next, I was extremely pleased to be able to hire a pair of gypsies. They are from the Braith Clan, Anwyn and Dylan Braith, both twenty-five. A pair of red heads, both have had their lips and feet repaired, but she wears hers waist length like the rest of us. They are observational astronomers and superb sub-light speed navigators, having spent their childhoods traveling slowly around the uninhabited regions of our spiral arm with their gypsy clan. We need their expertise with Alexandra's hydrogen engine test runs. Both have promised to show us some incredible sights, but I've secretly convinced them to take us to some of the more spectacular gaseous nebulae, which I'm particularly fond of seeing — always have been. Okay, it's a perk of being the captain on this ship.

Like Alexandra, the last member of our crew is single. Zarita Laag, named after one of her grandmothers, has raven hair and wears the six inch heels like many of us do. Her lip plate shows a mountain range. Why? She is our resident geologist, but she is also a competent Med Tech and skilled in delivering Basic Therapy, as well as Marisol. I figured we might encounter some "accidents," and having someone able to help us erase the trauma would be invaluable. Besides, they have proven if one is injured, erasing the physical and emotional trauma associated with it drastically speeds the person's recovery. You see — I wanted all eventualities covered in some way.

I picked Zarita because she and Alexandra took a liking

to each other. Alexandra arrived on Ashford-5 on the first of June, a month before our scheduled departure, so she could become familiar with everyone. When I first met Alexandra, I spotted her lip plate design: a half of a circle. "Wow, you have the definition of PI on your lip plate," I commented to her as we met and were introduced.

"Incredible! Nia Elain, you're right. That's PI. You're the first person to see it. Usually, I have to explain it to those who ask me what it is. Clever," Alexandra replied. I sensed she was very pleased and began to feel more at ease among us, who had arms and didn't need a robot to help us with everything.

Actually, I'll admit up front here I thought Alexandra was going to have a very hard time adapting to the situation. Besides being off Aquila Prime, where everything was setup for their unique needs with robots and mechanical machines, she was being plopped among "normal" people, who had arms and no robots. I expected a good deal of culture shock, and I wasn't wrong.

However, we all got a shock at the modifications made to the Eagle's Seed. While we had our working and living quarters in my ship, four more modules were added. Each was roughly cylindrical, and the four were attached together forming roughly a square in cross-section. Each module was detachable from the others. The group was attached to the rear of the Eagle's Seed, using its rear docking port as the main entrance into the four modules.

Module A contained our voluminous supplies, such as clothing and food. Module B contained a large living room with four smaller workshops. Module C contained the new hydrogen propulsion system and the hydrogen collection machine, un-deployed. Module D contained more workshops, extra fuel cylinders, a Fabrication Machine that allowed us to manufacture any replacement part we might need, and more raw materials and supplies. In this Module D, Hans would assemble his modified hyperdrive engine, and when ready, swap his for mine. That way, if something didn't work out right, we could re-install my original hyperdrive and continue on our way.

All told, we twenty adults now had nearly three times the spatial area we normally would have in just the Eagle's Seed proper. Since we anticipated being in space for quite some time, the extra room would allow us greater freedom to move around, as well as handle whatever work and developmental changes were needed to achieve our goals.

Before I signed anyone up, I carefully discussed with them the four objectives of the mission. Our first objective was to do everything possible to perfect Alexandra's new hydrogen propulsion system. The entire concept was untested, as well as her novel ideas for refueling while in space. Initially, this was the province of Lin and Dao Cho, assisted by Alexandra. However, once we departed, Alexandra was to fully brief our two physicists on her theories, namely Hans and me. That way, if something didn't work quite right, there would be five minds ready to make it right. We anticipated many months would be required to meet this first objective.

Once that one was finished, our second objective was to test out Hans' new hyperdrive modifications, using his modified engine. Again, when we were to get to his tests, he was to fully brief Alexandra and me on its operation and principles, again in case problems arose. In both cases, if we did run into problems, we had quite a number of engineers to assist in fabricating remedies.

If we got the modified hyperdrive operational, we would be using it to accomplish our third objective. If it failed, then we would use our normal hyperdrive and the extra fuel cells to achieve what we could of this third objective: explore the northern halo of our galaxy, mapping out hyperspace coordinates for future travelers, and searching for the Ceri or other alien life forms. Precisely what we were to do if we discovered the Ceri world or worlds was not entirely clear, but certainly we wanted to establish some kind of relationship with them. My guess was this portion of our mission would take the most amount of time, assuming we could even find them.

Our fourth objective was definitely minor and low-key: discover the planet of origin of us humans who had settled all the worlds within the Imperium. That we could achieve this one was dubious at best, since the Federation of Planets controlled the other spiral arm of the galaxy. While the war with them was long over, few Imperium ships ever ventured into their sectors. I had no idea if we could get official permission to wander around their spiral arm or not. Further, the Imperium knew next to nothing about the many inhabited worlds of theirs. I didn't hold much hope of achieving this last objective, but Jana and Jovanna were rather excited about this one — they being our ancient historians.

In addition to all of these activities, six of us were still learning all we could using the comprehensive computer-assisted learning courses — namely, me, Danika, Tesla, Anya, Jovanna, and Jana. In fact, our constant attempts to learn about nearly every topic imaginable soon caught on with the others. As captain, I decided to devote every Friday night to a group brainstorming of ideas session, carrying on our favorite pastime.

I should also explain one other detail before launching into my narrative: the *mentales* gifts. The only head-blind crew members were Dao and Lin Cho and Alexandra. The other seventeen had the gift, telepathy being the very least of our skills. Further, we wore psi-crystals around our necks at all times. They amplify our powers some hundredfold, except for Zarita Laag, who had one of her grandmother's super-crystals, which amplified her powers nearly ten thousandfold, though none of us knew about that at the start. She also carried along four of the giant psi-crystals, polished into "balls," nearly a foot across. With these, she hoped to be able to make a telepathic connection across vast distances, in case we ran into some severe emergency and had no other way to communicate back.

By June 1378, I had my crew picked out just in time for Alexandra's arrival. As I said before, we wanted to meet her and give her time to adjust to living among us, hoping to minimize any culture shock she might have. After all, this was her first trip off-world and her first ever trip into space, discounting her deep space transport flight to Ashford-5. Without *mentales* power, many of us knew just how helpless she would be. Similarly, we had no real idea just how her robot assistant operated, and what special needs Alexandra might need us to handle for her. Both sides had a month to learn about the other.

Queens Rael and Linda Valen-Gervasi, Governor Misty Childa-Bellweather, and I stood on the tarmac watching the deep space transport touch down. The ship bore the wasp emblem of the Ataro Empire. Emperor Bino had sent one of his official transports to bring Alexandra Khristos from Aquila Prime to Ashford-5, a rather nice touch I thought, saving her the hassle of dealing with commercial transports. I noticed five light cruisers had also accompanied the transport, though they didn't land. Well, she was the mathematician who had just invented the hydrogen propulsion system. She deserved top security measures in my playbook.

We watched a short brown haired woman helping the blonde Alexandra down the transport's ramp. She had her hair tied up in a bun giving an illusion of quite a large head, which helped balance the size of her bosom. She wore a blue satin gown, and even from this distance, her tiny waist really did set off her curvaceous form. I realized the shorthaired woman wasn't a woman at all, but her robot assistant. Yes, I admit I was quite surprised with the appearance of Minta. I'd expected some kind of metal contraption, gleaming steel or chrome.

"Oh look, Minta. There are two others like me here. What's with the pale reddish sky? I thought it was about noontime. The pilot must have been mistaken," Alexandra barked in a somewhat annoyed tone. "And the smell. What *is* that odor?"

"My Lady, I believe those are the two Ataro Empire queens who run this world. And it is noon here. Remember. Ashford-5 has a dim orange-red sun. Gloomy is right. My sensors suggest some form of tree pollen is in the air," Minta replied, her arm still supporting Alexandra, as the woman took small, carefully measured steps towards us. I sensed Alexandra was grateful for the flatness of the tarmac. "Ah, my sensors are detecting all four are homo sapiens nova. You can relax some."

"Oh. Right. I remember now. There were a lot of terrorist victims of those genetic bio agent attacks brought to this world ages ago. Still, I can't imagine having to live on this gloomy, chilly, and smelly world!"

"Quite true. But remember My Lady, there are supposed to be a lot of Class V telepaths around. Exercise caution," Minta replied, as the two drew close to us.

"Welcome to Ashford-5 or Tierra as we locals call our world," Queen Rael spoke up. "I'm Queen Rael, my mate Queen Linda, our Governor Misty, and Captain Nia Elain. I trust that your flight was uneventful."

"Hello. Alexandra Khristos of Aquila Prime. This is my personal assistant robot, Minta. Yes, quite. It would have been nice to see some other worlds, but there is time enough for that later. I have quite a few shipping crates. Will they be brought to wherever I am going?"

"Oh yes. Don't worry about your things," Governor Misty answered. "They'll be brought to your quarters shortly. You'll be staying in a guest suite at the queen's Imperial Castle next to the spaceport at the edge of Exchange City. We have an underground transport system between my Admin building here and their castle. Quite convenient."

"Yes," Queen Rael took over, "we've arranged for you to be with your other crew members in adjacent suites so you all can make your preparations and plans. Everyone dines together at meal times, so I expect we'll be seeing you at those times. If you need anything, you only need to ask us. We're quite honored to have you as our guest for the coming month."

"I expect you are at that," Alexandra barked haughtily. "I'm told the two engineers, who are building my hydrogen propulsion engine, are also here. I should like to visit with them as soon as possible."

I spoke up. "Yes, they're most anxious to meet with you as well. Once we get you to your room and unpacked, the whole crew wants to meet you too." This is when I noticed her lip plate design: a half of a circle. "Wow, you have the definition of PI on your lip plate," I commented to her.

She lightened up and exclaimed, "Incredible! Nia Elain, you're right. That's PI. You're the first person to see it. Usually, I have to explain it to those who ask me what it is. Clever. But then you are a Homo sapiens nova." I sensed she was very pleased and began to feel more at ease among us, who had arms and didn't need a robot to help us with everything. I was wrong.

Alexandra commented, "I don't see why you had all the genetic cures done on yourself, Nia Elain. We're perfect in all ways, but now you have to do all the things a HIFR does. Must be a real bummer for you now to have to do everything for yourself, unlike your queens. Say, where are your HIFR's?" Alexandra asked the two queens.

Queen Rael answered, "We do most everything ourselves, but we do use human assistants with some things, like dressing. Come, this way please."

I held the doors open for everyone, as we entered the Admin building. "Imperium consistency," Alexandra commented, as though she had seen thousands of identical spaceports before. Well, I figured she'd at least evidently recognized the same layout as the spaceport on Aquila Prime or perhaps had looked up images of them on the Net. We headed for the elevators and went down to the basement where the electric cars were parked and the long tunnel began.

"You are welcome to come by and have a tour anytime," Governor Misty suggested. Alexandra didn't reply however. I picked up her surface thoughts though. *One spaceport is identical to the next one. See one; see them all.* Not very complimentary, I thought.

As we sped along the tunnel in several cars, Alexandra whispered to me. I was driving her and her robot. "Where are the personal assistants of the queens? How can they be driving the cars? Are these fully automated cars?"

"No, they've what we call the *mentales* gifts. You know them only as telepaths, but we've far more powerful abilities. They use telekinesis to move things. I think Queen Rael is driving theirs. She tends to like to hog the controls," I whispered back.

"Oh right! The yellow eyes. I forgot. Minta told me about them. I'm supposed to be alert for anyone who has yellow eyes. They are the telepaths," she whispered to me.

I chuckled. "That's not always true. Well, that was true years ago, but not any longer. You see, many of us have used the medical machines to alter our eye color to what we prefer. Actually, nearly everyone you'll be seeing at the Imperial Castle has the gift. There are twenty of us in our crew, and only three of you don't have the *mentales* gifts, that is, a Class V telepath. You and the two Cho engineers, Dao and Lin. Everyone else on this trip has the gifts, but not all of us have the same mental powers, though everyone is a highly competent telepath."

I sensed her increasing rigidness and fears. "Don't worry, Alexandra; no one is going to eavesdrop on your thoughts."

"But why not? If they have telepathy, can't they just always know what I'm thinking?" she asked, expressing what had obviously been bothering her for quite some time.

"Because doing that to another person without their consent is akin to mental rape. It's highly unethical of us to do that, and there are strictly enforced laws against any telepath doing that to another. So you don't have to worry about all of us knowing your every thought or probing your mind."

"Really? Well, that's a relief. Still, you have to understand my position. I carry many secrets in my head," she declared. "I do change my laptop's password frequently as well."

"Of course you do. We all have our own private thoughts. No one is going to pry on you. As far as the crew goes, I've chosen married couples, since each room sleeps two people. However, I admit I didn't know what, if any, special requirements you might have. So I took the liberty of adding one woman who isn't married, Miss Zarita Laag. She'll be bunking with you, and is to assist you with anything you might need, though I suspect your robot will probably help you with most things. Still, on a cramped spaceship, you might have some needs that Zarita can help you with."

"Well, I suppose if she is a homo sapiens nova, she can't be all that bad. Still, I'm having an awful time accepting that all of you have to do all these mundane things for yourself. I suppose it is hard to import some of our robots here. There's a shortage of them on Aquila Prime or so I'm told. We don't have any to export. Still, it must be really awful for you and the others to be forced to have to do so much for yourself! I do feel sorry for all of you. I'm very fortunate to have Minta. I can see that now. It's quite plain."

I didn't know how to respond to her unexpected viewpoint, so I decided to tell her a bit more about our crew. "You see, only Dao and Lin Cho are normal. The rest of the entire crew are hermaphrodites, like ourselves, though most have had quite a number of the available genetic cures — some more than others. Me, I love my lip plates. They are the height of fashion on this world. However, the fellows don't like them or our high heels, and thus they got those genetic cures as well. You'll see; we're quite diverse."

"Well, I don't see why you needed to get arms. Our robots are very efficient and do everything that we need done," Alexandra said rather condescendingly.

I chuckled. "I know what you mean. I was born without arms and lived that way for eighteen years. How can you miss what you never had, eh?"

"I suppose you have a point there," she admitted. However, she did relax some, and I smiled invisibly.

A half hour later, the queens led her to her new suite, which she was sharing with Zarita Laag. Like the other suites, it had a large common living area with attached bath and three bedrooms, one of which Zarita occupied. I introduced them. "This is Zarita Laag, our resident geologist and a Med tech like me. Zarita, this is Alexandra Khristos and her assistant, Minta." She saw a shorter woman with waist length, wavy raven hair and light blue eyes. Zarita had a roundish face and a small nose, but thick eyebrows and angular cheekbones. She took after the Laag side of her genealogy. She wore a light red satin pencil gown with matching red patent, six inch heels.

"Very pleased to meet you at last, Alexandra. I'm in that bedroom. I saved the master bedroom for you and your robot. If you need anything, just holler. Over the years, I've had a lot of experience helping other terrorist attack victims. Just ask. We're all dying to meet you. So boss, what's next?" she said to me.

"Get Alexandra settled in, give her a quick orientation tour, and then we'll have a crew meeting. Everyone wants to meet our final crew member. After that, she and the Cho's need to meet privately," I suggested. "I'll see what's keeping her shipping crates." I left the two alone.

"Wow, your robot is — well, not quite what I was expecting. She looks so real," Zarita said, as I left them. I smiled. Everyone in the crew wanted to see her robot. None of us was expecting to see a humaniform robot. She looked like a normal human being! However, as I left them, I felt for Minta's mind and didn't find it. That was the only way I could easily tell Minta wasn't a person. She looked normal in every way. How curious I thought. Minta wore a simple day dress and flats, just like any other normal woman might wear.

"Well, of course she does. All Model 5 Personal Assistants look like normal people. Well, I admit originally the Model 1 Assistants were metal monsters, but we have improved the technology enormously since those founding days," Alexandra replied somewhat hostilely or perhaps haughtily. "She is expert at handling my needs, all of them," she added pointedly. "She's even got working sexual organs. Please, call her Minta and not my robot."

"Got it. Minta it is. That's a good idea. She looks like a normal person anyway. No offense, Minta. We've just not seen you before," Zarita mollified the pair. "Ah, here come your crates. Let me know if I can help you with anything."

Unexpectedly, Alexandra barked, "Well, I think you have it all backwards. Let me and Minta know if there's anything that we can do for you. Honestly, I can't imagine how awful it must be for you to have to do everything for yourself, Zarita. At least, you still have the magnificent lip plates. That's something. Your mountain image is appropriate for a geologist. Still, it must be really hard on you to have to do all the work yourself without a robot to help you out. You have my sympathies."

Around two, the twenty of us assembled in the dining room, where everyone was introduced to Alexandra. I also emailed her a list of us and our specialties. Of course, everyone was keenly interested in seeing Minta. We were dutifully impressed with her humaniform robot. We'd not realized just how far their evolution had come. Impressive to say the least.

However, I began to realize with all of the millions of on Aquila Prime, many having some of the brightest minds in the Imperium, they were very likely to put their talents to work on building more suitable personal assistants, their robots.

After that, Alexandra, Dao, and Lin Cho spent the rest of the afternoon in their own private meeting. I suspected they were going over the details of the Cho's implementation of her hydrogen propulsion system. When they joined everyone else in the Great Hall for dinner, Alexandra looked satisfied with their work thus far.

Naturally, with the hundreds all dining together, all eyes were focused on Minta, watching her feed Alexandra, while Alexandra stared at Queens Linda and Rael, whose spoons seemed to be working by magic. It was a fair trade of stares, if you ask me. Still, I could not get the feeling that Alexandra definitely felt sympathy for the many hermaphrodites dining here and having to serve themselves, quite the opposite from the hundreds of us who felt sympathy for her. Culture shock went both ways, I observed.

The next day, Alexandra spent in personally examining the new hydrogen propulsion engines and the hydrogen refueling apparatus. Finally, on the following day, Alexandra gave a detailed briefing to the physicists, namely Hans and me. I'll spare you the technical details. Suffice it to say, her new theory of propulsion was revolutionary. Very little could go wrong with the engines. They were the essence of simplicity, and their fuel was the most common element in the Universe. Her unique refueling or collection system was what really got my attention. I'll explain more about that later when we finally deployed it. The idea was to refuel in space by collecting up interstellar hydrogen, a novel idea, which if it worked, would make ships powered by hydrogen virtually unlimited in range, as long as they stayed within the galactic disk, where there was plenty of gas and dust around. It would revolutionize planetary explorations. No need for the periodic refueling stops, which my parents always had to do with the Eagle's Seed.

Later in the week, we began shuttling back and forth to Eagle's Seed, spending the days onboard the ship and its four modules. Besides becoming familiar with everything, we were also slowly storing our supplies and getting a real feel for what we would need on this voyage, which promised to be quite lengthy compared to all other such exploration flights.

A week before our scheduled departure, Alexandra finally asked me, "So how are we supposed to fight the incredible boredom of this long trip? Have we got a supply of flicks onboard?"

"Education. Some of us are learning freaks. We want to learn everything we can on nearly every subject. Knowledge is power. Never has there been a flight like this one. All twenty of us are highly educated, and I hope we all will share knowledge and learn vastly more things. We've ten learning computers onboard and nearly every computer-assisted educational course in the Imperium on the ship. That's what one of the computers is doing — it's a database of all the courses, a dedicated server system. I don't think anyone will be bored on this trip. Heck, we might be asking you to teach us some advanced mathematics, Alexandra." She chuckled at that idea.

As our departure date of July 1st approached, I found myself going down extensive checklists, verifying we had everything imaginable stowed on the ship. I wisely put many of the crew to work helping me out on this one. Hey, it took quite a lot of man-hours to verify a fifty page checklist of items. I couldn't imagine the time and effort the emperor and his associates had put into working out what we had to bring along with us. It was almost incomprehensible to me. Further, I insisted each crew member have a good idea what we had with us and where it was generally located, specifically which module.

Finally, our departure date arrived. The queens and the governor gave each of us a hug and their best wishes. All the crew's relatives were there to say their farewells and wish us the best of luck and a safe journey. I was a bit daunted by the sheer number who saw us off from the Imperial Castle. Only Governor Misty accompanied us to the spaceport and the small transport, which would take us up to the Eagle's Seed, in high orbit around Ashford-5. A half hour later, we climbed aboard the shuttle and sat back for the short ride. Yes, I was a bit nervous. Who wouldn't be? There was a whole lot riding on this venture. A zillion things could go wrong. Somehow, we had to surmount all obstacles and make these two engines work properly.

I suspected others had similar thoughts, though we all sat silently, watching the planet receding from view. On the other hand, I felt a surge of pride in my crew. We had the best minds onboard. Further, with three exceptions, everyone one of us had Basic Therapy and felt alive and vigorous. Our reaction times were excellent. Still, I was anxious. Would this be enough to handle whatever we would ultimately face?

As we approached the very unconventional looking contraption that was the modified Eagle's Seed, I could see the four small deep space, emergency transport ships tethered to the sides of each of the four modules. If things went terribly wrong, we could cram onboard these emergency shuttles and hopefully get to safety. Still, my Eagle's Seed sure looked strange with the four cylindrical modules appended to its rear docking station.

After attaching to the forward, smaller docking bay, everyone headed to their quarters and stowed the few last minute things they'd brought with them. A bit later, we rendezvoused in the central meeting room, midship. "Okay, is everyone ready for departure?" I asked formally. I waited a second and then said, "All right. Let's get this voyage started." Interesting, we were now wearing pants and tops. Gone were all our elegant gowns, except for Alexandra, who still wore her satin gown. It was time for real work or so Danika claimed.

Chapter 2 Clouds

"Here's the initial coordinates," Dylan Braith said, handing Danika a paper scrap. "Anwyn and I know of three very likely candidates that should meet Alexandra's requirements. The first one is the Orion Nebula. However, that one might be too hot, so we want to try the Eagle Nebula first. It's a region that has dense gas and dust clouds, along with new star formation. Proto stars. That's what they are called. Small red ones, at least right now."

Danika frowned. "I don't recognize these coordinates. They seem very odd. Way out of range."

Anwyn laughed. "Of course, silly. It's in Federation space."

"Oh. But we're not allowed to enter the Federation of Planets' space, are we? The war and all?" I asked, catching on to the location and its significance.

Having been around during that war as an ID Minister, Martina spoke up. "Of course not. Part of the peace treaty dictated they stay in their spiral arm, and we stay in ours. It's illegal for us to go there."

"We gypsies go there all the time," Dylan countered. "No one owns the galaxy. We go to appreciate the beauty of God's Creations. If we are stopped, we're gypsies. They won't bother us unless we try to land on one of their planets. As long as we stay close to the interstellar gas and dust clouds, it should be just fine. Besides, we can ditch anyone coming after us by ducking into the cloud. In places, it's pretty darn dense, blocking all from view, even the proto-stars."

"Surely, there are other clouds in our spiral arm — ones that would work as well and would be safe for us to visit," I countered. Starting off by hopping into illegal space and getting arrested wasn't my idea of the way to start this voyage off. I'd be risking twenty people and our children.

Anwyn smiled coyly and answered. "Of course, there are other clouds in our spiral arm, but there is one big 'however' with them. There are always a lot of, shall we say, traffic around them. Gypsies love to glide in those areas. Prospectors love to hunt for new forming planets there, ripe for the pickings. We show up with this unusual looking ship and start using the hydrogen propulsion system or the hydrogen refueling system, and we're going to take center stage. We'll be on the Imperium newscasts before the day is out."

I think my face showed just how startled I was. Damn, she was right. I reacted in the only reasonable way. "Excellent thinking, Anwyn, Dylan. You've kept us from making a blunder right out of the box. Me, in particular. I sure picked the right crew. Thanks."

Anwyn laughed disarmingly. "You're welcome, Captain. If any Federation ship stops us, let Dylan and me do all the talking. We will pretend we're in charge of this trip. We're gypsies and from a well-known clan, Braith — well known to the Federation, which at least tolerates our presence, but only around the gas and dust clouds. Besides, at this date, we happen to know that most of the gypsy clans are in our spiral arm not too far from the Caterpillar Nebula, which is the best cloud for this mission's purpose. We'd be spotted for sure. Four months from now, we would risk running into some other clans, who, by then, will have likely ventured into Federation Space. We should be safe right now."

"Excellent. Danika, punch in those coordinates, and let us know how soon we'll be arriving," I issued the official order. She and I headed to the control room, and she did just that. A minute later, I powered up the sub-light engines, and then activated the hyperspace button. The star-filled view in front of us suddenly turned pitch black. We entered the void of hyperspace.

"Looks like we'll be there in about twenty-four hours, unless you want to burn up a whole lot more fuel," Danika announced.

"No. We can use the time to get settled. I'll make the announcement." Over the intercom, I did just that, and she and I headed to the nursery to check on our two daughters. We found them playing with Mai Lin, who had become their nanny in just the past month.

22

An hour later, Alexandra requested a formal meeting with Hans and me. She and the Cho's wanted to go over the operational details of the hydrogen propulsion system and specifically the revolutionary fuel collection system, which made the propulsion system feasible. Sharing of key data was what this operation was all about. Alexandra Khristos lived up to her part of the deal, finally sharing the last of the critical details of her inventions with Hans and myself, thereby ensuring her creation would become widely known within the Imperium. The Cho's went over their extensive safety precautions. Dealing with large quantities of hydrogen posses risks. As you know, hydrogen can be quite explosive, especially when around oxygen.

This meeting also allowed me to see just how Alexandra would be compensating for her armless state. I know that years ago, I'd just be using my feet as arms, but she didn't. Rather, she sat back and did the talking, allowing Minta to run seamlessly the laptop and point out key features on the projections. I will say Alexandra had put together a very effective presentation. Further, I was quite impressed at how the two worked together. Not once did Alexandra have to issue an "order" to Minta nor did she have to wait on Minta to do something. Seamless. That's the way Hans and I later described the presentation to the others. Somehow, Alexandra and her robot had a very symbiotic relationship, one that didn't involve mind reading. I was certain Minta didn't have telepathy skills; she was merely a robot with a computer mind.

On the other hand, neither Hans nor I could find any anomalies in either her theory or her methods of implementation. We both found the safety precautions of the Cho's were far more than adequate to protect the Eagle's Seed. In fact, they were ideal. Since the biggest problem facing the hydrogen propulsion system was running out of fuel, the life support systems of the Eagle's Seed and the energy shields, which protected the ship from collisions with interstellar particulate matter, were each now being powered by their own separate psi crystal fuel cells. That is, life support and the energy shields were independently running engines. If we ran out of hydrogen fuel, the ship and we would not be compromised.

She ended the two-hour meeting by asking, "There you go. That is everything. I've divulged it all way ahead of time to show you my good faith. Hans, in that spirit, perhaps you could divulge your breakthrough in the hyperdrive system ahead of schedule. You know how keenly interested I am in it — the physics behind it."

"Thanks Alexandra. Your theory and inventions are simply magnificent. I can find no flaw in them. Your presentation today has been totally professional, top quality, if I do say so myself. Unfortunately, I've not gotten my presentation quite up to your standards. Give me a few more days to spruce it up. I was expecting to have another couple of months before I gave my presentation to everyone," Hans replied. I detected a note of humility in his tone. That and a bit of embarrassment. Her presentation had indeed been first class, akin to that of one of his Academy professors, totally professional.

"Sure. The sooner the better, Hans. I would like to have time to fully absorb the equations," Alexandra explained. "I do need time to verify the math behind your modifications."

"Understandable Alexandra. I'll get on it yet today," Hans conceded.

As we broke up the meeting, I took the initiative. "Say Alexandra, care to join some of us for our brainstorming session? Danika, Martina, Tesla, Anya, Jovanna, Jana, and I are getting together to chat in an hour. You're welcome to join us and add your ideas to the mix. You won't be bored." During the past month, she'd remained somewhat aloof from the rest of us, probably working on her presentation she'd just given us. After all, without arms and hands, preparing such work must be time consuming, I thought.

I must have been right, because Alexandra suddenly seemed to relax a good deal. "Sure. Why not." We shared invisible smiles, at least I think so.

An hour later, we met in the planning room. It was a little crowded but Jana and Jovanna brought three teapots with them and served us all a cup — with spoons, of course. With our upper lip plates fastened in their horizontal position, to drink required spoons. Minta sat beside Alexandra and served her needs.

Tesla began this chat. "Alexandra, you must forgive us. We simply don't know much at all about life on Aquila Prime. Actually, there is very little information about your world available. It's almost as if the Imperium is trying to forget all about your people and Aquila Prime."

She struck a chord in Alexandra. None of us needed telepathy to realize that. Her face and eyes lit up, and I sensed a huge, invisible smile. "Of course, the Imperium wants to pretend we don't exist. And we probably wouldn't, if it wasn't for the Ataro Empire backing us fully. Honestly, normal homo sapiens sapiens hate us. We're homo sapiens nova, quite different from them. Just getting enough raw materials from others in the Imperium to build our necessary robots is quite a challenge."

"Well, our bodies are different," Jana conceded. "But we're all people just the same. Still, people do have prejudices. Usually, some of that is based upon inherent fears, but what's to fear from your people? Honestly, I can't see anything at all. I know when we were just like you, physically I mean, we were almost completely helpless, dependent upon others for nearly everything."

"Birth rates," Martina countered. "Hermaphrodite couples have well over twice as many children as a normal homo sapiens sapiens couple. Just look at how exponentially we have grown on Tierra in just a half century or so."

Anya put in, "Why you haven't begun a major genetic arm regrowing healing process on Aquila Prime? Honestly, from personal experience, that one cure is absolutely the most vital one."

"I believe I can partially answer that one," Martina spoke up. "That genetic cure costs about ten thousand credits per person, mostly in the vast quantity of stem cells required in the process. With millions on Aquila Prime, the cost would be staggering, and besides, there simply aren't enough specialized medical machines and available quantities of stem cells to provide so many genetic cures. Am I right, Alexandra?"

"Only partially, Martina," Alexandra answered. "True,

the cost is steep. The supplies, far too few. Not very practical. No, the key reason is that none of us even wants any of the genetic cures. God! Who would want to live life like you all are doing?" She physically shuttered. We looked rather stunned. She went on, "Look, our HIFRs do all the physical things for us, things that you're all forced to have to do for yourselves. You actually have to use the spoons yourselves to drink your tea. How utterly awfully primitive, just ghastly! Not one of us on Aquila Prime has to descend to such utterly primitive actions."

"But you are dependent upon your HIFRs," Tesla protested, not grasping how this could possibly be.

"Of course, we are. Don't be silly, Tesla. That is what the HIFRs are for, to serve us. The point, Tesla, is that all of us on Aquila Prime are finally freed at last to be able to fully utilize our minds. Studies have shown the average homo sapiens sapiens barely utilizes five percent of their brains, their mental capacities. So much of their lives are taken up with using arms and hands to do all manner of mundane things, dressing, cooking, eating, and even opening doors. The list is simply endless. They squander vast amounts of their lives in wasteful actions, time that could be far better spent inventing new things, working out new theories, and using their minds. After all, the one thing that separates mankind from other animals is the use of our minds."

"On Aquila Prime, every one of us spends all our time thinking, solving problems, and inventing new things. Just look at what some of our engineers and scientists have done with the HIFRs. You were expecting to see one of those utterly crude Model 1 robots that could barely function. Ha. Just look at how very advanced Minta is, and you can see where our vast mental abilities have taken us. Of course, I'm more interested in pure mathematics, but I was able to apply a tiny portion of that to develop my hydrogen propulsion system."

"Really, we have some of the brightest minds in the universe on Aquila Prime. We're all working very hard on all manner of inventions and breakthroughs, even as we speak. Our HIFRs allow us the time and freedom to devote to our studies and work, unlike those on all the other worlds. Even yours, I'm afraid. Honestly, I can't wait to see Hans' breakthrough. Still, if he was on Aquila Prime, I'm certain he'd have invented it years ago. If you don't believe me, just take a moment to reflect on how much time you waste each day doing all those stupid things with your arms and hands for yourselves. Go on. Do it. Tesla, how much time do you spend each day with your hair? Jana, how many hours of yours are wasted on food preparation?" she challenged us.

"But surely not every person on Aquila Prime is a genius like yourself," Martina countered.

"Of course not. Don't be silly. Still, we have a disproportionate number of geniuses compared to other worlds. I believe it's a ten to one factor. Those who are not like me spend their time working out better means for survival. Better methods of farming, automated food production systems, more efficient production plants. Yes, everyone on Aquila Prime puts their minds to work far more than those on any other world. That's the whole point of our world. Let the HIFRs do the chores that free us to more fully use our minds."

"But surely everyone doesn't have the same mental abilities," Anya protested.

"Of course not. True, some put their skills to use in other ways. We do have many choirs, where those with superb singing voices entertain us. The Arts are not dead on Aquila Prime. We have some very excellent writers, composers, and so on. Perhaps far more than other normal worlds. No matter what your endeavor is, our HIFRs enable you to spend vastly more time at it."

"Hey, she has a point," Jovanna spoke up. "I've been figuring out times here, like she suggested. Brushing out my hair, cooking, dressing and undressing — you start adding up all these little things we do for ourselves each day and it is surprising. Shocking even. I think I'm wasting a third of my day doing things that Minta does for Alexandra. She has a point. Still, I've found it much easier to study using my hands than before when we didn't have them."

"See. I told you so!" Alexandra replied haughtily. "If you used a HIFR for your studies, you'd save even more time, Jovanna. Besides, our computer scientists have perfected voice-activated computer programs. With them, you don't need hands to operate the learning machines. Even Calc and Diffeq equations can be very easily spoken into the math programs. Besides, have you noticed normal homo sapiens sapiens cannot add up a column of numbers in their heads? They often used fingers, dots on paper, and all manner of other crutches. Slow. Pathetically slow. Even the lowliest dimwit on Aquila Prime can add up a column of numbers in their heads, putting even you to shame."

"Wow. You caught me. I do seem to have to count dots when the numbers get bigger than five," Jovanna admitted, somewhat embarrassed.

"So you can see why we Aquila Prime people look down on the normal homo sapiens sapiens. In our eyes, they are primitives, rather like the monkeys appear to them," Alexandra said rather caustically.

"Do you look down on us too?" asked Tesla innocently. "I mean, we're hermaphrodites as well, but we've had many genetic cures." A hush followed. Instantly, I realized everyone here was carefully listening for her answer.

"Er, not exactly. You are homo sapiens nova, but yes a little, because you have those silly arms and hands. However, I also know you don't have access to the HIFRs either, so I have to take that into consideration. Besides, just look at the incredible brain-power that's on this ship, though I do pity the Cho's somewhat. Aquila Prime is not only surviving very well, but we're thriving, and our population is growing at unheard of rates. I wouldn't be surprised to see us becoming the leaders of the entire Imperium one day in the future. Like you all say, knowledge is power."

"We all agree on that point," Jana declared. "So where do you think the human race of the Imperium originated? That's part of our mission, but I wish it were a more important one though."

Alexandra laughed. "Now, I have to admit I don't know anything about that area. But I can help you all by applying statistics to whatever data you have collected about it."

"Great. On our original world of Metcalf-4, we've discovered all our different races were founded by spaceships which probably crash landed. We think they might have come from the Federation of Planets," Jana explained. For an hour, we chatted about similar discoveries. Even on Ashford-5, evidence had been found for early colonization by a crashed spaceship from an unknown world, perhaps called Earth, though no known star had that name.

The twins used a computer to bring up their fancy chart that showed all of the known inhabited worlds of the Imperium. Colored dots represented the best guess at the age of each civilized world, in terms of human occupation. The many hub worlds traced their history back at least four millennia now, though a few like those in the Ataro System of the mid-spiral arm went back for at least three millennia. Ashford-5, however, seemed to have been populated just less than a millennia ago.

"Well," Alexandra commented, "you don't need statistics to see the patterns here. Obviously, the hub worlds were settled first, and from there expansion went down the spiral arm. Yet, there are anomalies in the time line out nearer the rim."

"Right. So the real question is where did the settlers of the old hub worlds come from?" Jovanna asked. No one had any answer, but we expected that.

She asked, "Has anyone got any idea how we can find that answer?"

"It's obvious to me," Alexandra barked, "that you are going to have to conduct the same survey of all the worlds in the Federation of Planets. Obviously, some settlers have originated there."

"She has a point. So many of our languages are quite similar. I mean between the Imperium worlds and those of the Federation of Planets," Jana replied. "Just ask Marisol or even better Nadia." From here, the discussion veered off into the arena of societal development. Many of us were keenly aware of the transitions from a Stone Age Culture into that of a Bronze or even Iron Age. However, at this point, we had to end off. It was time for the twins to begin to make us our supper, only now they were more aware that they were "wasting time," according to Alexandra's viewpoint.

Later, I used telepathy to relay what we'd learned about Alexandra and her Aquila Prime viewpoints to the others. That evening as Zarita brushed out her hair preparing for bedtime, Alexandra watched her new roommate, while Minta undid hers and brushed hers out. The cabin was warm, and everyone chose to sleep with very little on. "So you sleep with just your corset on?" Zarita asked. She herself had disrobed down to her panties.

"Have to Zarita. Too much back pain if I don't. They are quite heavy, but I'm told they get even heavier when nursing. Besides, it wastes too much time putting it on," Alexandra answered honestly.

"Right. You can't just tighten it down fully all at once. Worn some before," Zarita replied. "So does Minta sleep with you?"

"Only when I need pleasuring," Alexandra replied, quite unabashed. "She's fully equipped to satisfy my desires, whichever way they might fall. Why you don't have a mate yet, Zarita? If you need pleasuring, I can loan you Minta for a time. She can do it both ways, just like us. If not, she'll plug into the power receptacle, and shut down for the night."

"Thanks for the offer, but I prefer to share pleasuring with a real person, like you. You are quite stunning, you know. But no, I've not found the right mate yet. How about yourself?"

"Frankly, I've been too focused on my hydrogen propulsion system for the last few years. It has taken an awful lot of work to bring my idea to fruition — far more than I ever expected, if I am being honest. Just no time to spare."

"Well, now you have the time, lots of it. You are quite a gorgeous young woman, Alexandra," Zarita replied. Wearing only thin panties, both women quickly saw the arousal of the other, and Alexandra made the first move, sidling seductively up to Zarita.

"No, don't use hands. Like this," she whispered, as Zarita's hands began to rise from her sides. She gently brushed her mammoth breasts against those of Zarita's far smaller ones. Sometime later, two exhausted but satisfied hermaphrodites lay side by side in a tangle of blond and raven hair.

"That was indescribable!" Alexandra whispered. "I've never been more, well you know what I mean."

"Yes. It's called rapport. We telepaths go into rapport with our partners. We can sense just what the other desires at any instant."

"So that's how I sort of knew what you wanted next?"

"Yes. Rapport takes sex to a whole new plateau."

"Understatement, Zarita. Understatement. Minta's pleasuring is nothing remotely like this."

"I know. Or rather I suspected it wasn't. This is something that you and I can share, if you like," Zarita hinted.

"Very much!" Alexandra whispered back. "Only maybe I ought to have my corset off. I nearly passed out twice."

"Best not. I sensed your back muscles. You do need its support." She leaned over and raked her lip loops over the two mountains, sending another shiver through Alexandra's body.

"Can we do it again first thing in the morning?" Alexandra whispered.

I noticed Alexandra appeared more relaxed and comfortable in our presence, when she and Zarita joined us for breakfast in the galley. One glance at Zarita and I knew I'd chosen her roommate correctly. I had no doubts now about Alexandra's well-being on this long voyage.

As we dropped out of hyperspace, Danika reported over the intercom, "Okay. We are here. No sign of any other spaceship in our vicinity. All is clear, but you have to see this! It's unreal!"

"There it is, the Eagle Nebula," Anwyn gaily pointed out the obvious. We had gathered at the main viewport to see the incredible sight of this region of star formation from the dense gas and dust clouds. Like four columns of God, the plumes rose up from the base of the formation. We could see several reddish glows from the proto-stars glowing deep inside the four peaks. "Hydrogen excitation is providing the reddish glow. Hydrogen Alpha lines," she explained. "The blue and green is coming from oxygen and others. See that periodic flashing red light there," she pointed out. "That's a proto-star forming. It's axis of rotation and its magnetic poles are not the same, and it's oriented askew to us, rather like a spinning top."

"But why is it flashing?" asked Tesla.

"Rotation of the gas and dust. You see," Dylan answered, "gravity is slowly pulling in the stuff towards the new center of mass, which will one day become the star. As it rotates, the material is forced into a disk around the axis of rotation. Some of the matter hits the new star with too great an angular velocity and it is thrown off. That material comes out from either pole as excited particles. The angle is askew to us, and it is thus rotating around, becoming visible to us periodically. If we move the ship over one of the poles, we would see a continuous emission. Pretty darn cool if you ask me."

"But what sculpted these magnificent columns?" asked Tesla.

"Fifty hot, new stars back there did it. That small cluster there," Anwyn explained, pointing out the star cluster. "Their ultraviolet radiation and solar winds have blown the dust into this current shape. You are looking into a twenty light year wide hole into the dust cloud."

"What's a light year?" Jana asked.

Alexandra barked, "The distance that light travels in one year. One hundred eighty six thousand miles per hour times the number of hours in a year. A very big number. Hence, astronomers use one of those as a yardstick, a light year. Galaxy-wide or even universe-wide, even that is way too small a unit."

"Still, this is the most spectacular formation I've ever seen," I readily admitted. "Just indescribably beautiful."

Anwyn added, "True. Most people never see such a sight. We gypsies just love to explore our magnificent galaxy. Now, you can see why we love our unique lifestyle, wandering among the stars, not tied down to a planet."

"Most people only see pictures of such things, if at all," Martina mused. "Makes me sort of want to join you gypsies." Several of us chuckled at that.

"Well, it's time to go to work," the ever-practical Lin Cho broke in on our reverie. "We should prepare to engage the hydrogen propulsion system and get the refueling system operational. We've only a very limited supply of hydrogen to begin with."

"Okay then. I'll disengage the main engines and turn it over to you three," I replied, giving them the go ahead for the first experiment. An hour later, as the Eagle's Seed coasted along, its energy shield protecting us from the micro-collisions with the dust and debris about the ship, Dao, Lin, and Alexandra finished their last minute preparations.

"Would you like the opportunity to push the ignition button?" Lin asked Alexandra.

"No need. You built it. The honor should be yours. Let's do it," she replied, just as excited as he was. Me? I held my breath. This was a completely new technology, and anything could go wrong. The energy shield would protect the other three modules and the Eagle's Seed should the engine module explode or burn up. Still, I was nervous about it.

"I'll monitor the power output and its percentage," Alexandra volunteered, moving slowly over to the two new gauges with Minta at her side. Lin counted down from five and hit the power-up button. "We have power," she announced. "Ready for the load tests."

For the next hour, we five ran through the predetermined load situation on the basic hydrogen power plant. While I anticipated trouble would likely arise, since this was wholly untested technology, none directly arose. The new system passed our tests. Now came the real test: would the propulsion system actually efficiently drive the Eagle's Seed? With Danika and I at the controls, Lin slowly brought the power load up to operating levels. On Alexandra's signal, I activated the throttle, calling out "one percent thrust." Our new forward motion was barely perceptible, but we were moving.

Four hours later, we had once more finished the basic calibration tests. Alexandra now had a spreadsheet of numbers to work with, and she dove into them with a passion. We had tested the new propulsion system from just a few miles per hour, or docking speeds, on up to half that of the speed of light. Now, she could take those readings and convert them into efficiency numbers. Danika had recorded our position at each step, and from those, the distance traveled could be calculated.

However, all wasn't perfect. As we wrapped up the tests, Hans reported in. "Captain, we've some kind of problem in the engine compartment. There's a dull rattling sound."

"Does it vary with our speeds?" Alexandra inquired, looking up from her laptop.

"Don't think so. It's been pretty constant for the last couple of hours," he replied. "Been trying to locate it, but so far no luck."

Now, the ball was in my court. We'd used up most of our original supply of hydrogen on these tests. The next step was to deploy the new fuel collection system to begin to replenish our supply. Did we dare attempt this now or should we trace down the rattling? If I made the wrong choice, either we could run out of fuel tracking down something that was loose or we could have an explosion, if whatever it was turned out to be quite serious. I opted for safety. "Okay. All hands to the module. We need to locate the source of this rattling before we proceed."

Lin Cho accepted my decision and headed off with Hans to check it out. Alexandra looked at the fuel supply gauge and frowned, but she too rose, and with Minta's arm around her waist, followed the two. After verifying the ship was at rest, Danika and I headed there as well. Dao Cho remained at the various gauges to respond to whatever the investigators might ask.

Soon nineteen of us crammed into the module. A bit of experimentation yielded a salient fact. When under ten percent power output, there was no rattling. Above that level, the rattle was constant. Now, we began looking for its cause. "I think it's coming from behind that bulkhead," Tesla pointed out. We all congregated on her location and concurred.

"Well, that's not part of either system," Lin Cho was very quick to point out. "It's in the actual module construction itself. The engine is just causing something there to vibrate."

"But what? Is it serious? How can we find out?" I asked.

To understand this, our first problem, you must also grasp some basics of spaceships. First and foremost, space outside the ship is extremely cold, just a few degrees on the

Kelvin scale. Second, the skin of the ship is metallic, and metal is a very good conductor of heat energy. Translation: the cold of space is easily conducted to the inside surface of the outer metal skin. Even momentarily touching it with exposed skin would cause your flesh to freeze. Third, life support systems maintain a constant seventy-five degrees Fahrenheit inside the ship. Thus, to avoid constant outflow of our internal heat into space, the entire outer skin is insulated and a second inner skin surrounds that. So what we were looking at was the inner skin layer. The rattle lay somewhere between the two skins. It was an obvious manufacturing flaw in the module construction.

Lin, Diego, Thomas, and Hans did the dirty work. After donning special thermally insulated clothing, the four began dismantling the inner skin wall around the zone of the rattle. After removing several panels revealing the thick layer of insulating polymers, they found the source. Someone had accidentally left a wrench in between the layers. Two hours later around suppertime, the problem was solved, and the system was shut down for the night.

The next morning, we deployed the new refueling system of Alexandra's. We watched as her ingenious contraption unfolded around the ship. Essentially, two long polymer arms extended outward nearly a thousand feet from either side of the ship, forming a giant V. Then, from each of these arm assemblies, a thin titanium mesh unfolded, forming one giant cone around the Eagle's Seed. As we moved slowly forward, interstellar particles were caught by the cone and funneled down to the collection apparatus at its base. The refueling mechanism siphoned off about five percent of the power output of the propulsion system and used it to provide a solid screen, collecting any and all particles within the cone. However, larger bits were likely to also be captured, but these were allowed to drift off behind us. The shield prevented any damage to the thin titanium mesh because of such collisions, at least up to a certain point. Obviously, if we were traveling sufficiently fast or the particle was moving fast, the momentum of the object would be too large for the shield to handle, meaning that we dare not travel swiftly while refueling or risk damaging the mesh.

As atoms and molecules struck the mesh, the energy screen ionized the particles. Now charged, their electrical charge was then used to help collect them into the refueling cylinders, of which we had five on board. The first test was to refill one of these and make sure the collected atoms contained sufficient hydrogen for the propulsion system to burn. By noon, we'd passed that test. The second test was to determine refilling rates. The rest of the day was spent filling up the remaining four tanks, but using various velocities.

Alexandra explained her system to everyone. "The outer-forward looking radius of the collection cone is one thousand feet. That makes for a collection area — PI R^2 — of about 3×10^9 square centimeters. Traveling forward at say fifty miles per hour or 8×10^6 centimeters per hour for say one hour or 3600 seconds, we suck in a volume of about 9×10^{19} cubic centimeters. Let's say the density of matter around here is one million atoms per cubic centimeter, and for simplicity let's say that they are all hydrogen atoms being sucked in, which weigh in at about 1.7×10^{-24} grams, then this means we are pulling in about one hundred fifty-three grams of fuel each hour, trivial. However, if we go ten times faster, say five hundred miles per hour and collect for twenty-four hours, we get about eighty-one pounds of fuel."

"However, my collection system is designed for speeds of up to ten thousand miles per hour so that in a week we can collect a ton of fuel. Of course, that's assuming we are mostly gliding or coasting along, burning nearly no fuel. I know," she finally admitted, "that this is wholly insufficient to actually launch the Eagle's Seed from the ground into deep space. However, once in space and traveling along at sub-light speeds, the fuel consumption is quite low, and the collection system will be able to more than keep up with our needs. So yes, ships equipped with my new propulsion system will still need to have their normal engines. But when coasting along looking for new planets, my system will permit indefinite travel with no expensive refueling, as long as hydrogen clouds are around somewhere."

Finally, everyone onboard now understood the impact

of her new hydrogen propulsion system. It wouldn't be replacing our main engines, but augmenting them for deep space exploration ships. Still the potential was enormously advantageous.

Dao Cho added, "Keep in mind that this is only the initial prototype. If it all goes as planned, then we'll be able to work on many improvements. If the titanium mesh concept works and holds up to the anticipated collisions, we might be able to double its radius thereby quadrupling the quantity gathered. Plus, we have some ideas that might work to improve overall efficiency and have less of a power drain to maintain the protective mesh shield."

In a flash of insight, Martina asked, "So this is more of a proof of concept operation?"

"Precisely," Lin Dao admitted. "So far, so good."

Thus, began some thirty very boring days of refueling experiments, each one designed to test the limits of one or more details including the actual rate of refueling. This was based on the particle density of the space we were flying through. While the three were keenly interested in every detail, the rest of us spent hours observing the incredible nebula, as we floated deep into the denser base cloud, and then into one of the columns of gas and dust.

Quickly, a routine developed, just as I had both anticipated and hoped would occur. With some of us keenly interested in learning as much as we could, our enthusiasm quickly brought the others into our evening discussion sessions. Okay, I admit there was very little else to do on board the ship.

One evening, Zarita pointed out a very key detail. "Look. Most of the rest of us have been through Imperium schooling, and frankly it's hideous on the child."

"How is learning hideous?" Tesla asked, quite confused by her pronouncement.

"They force you to sit at a desk all day long, except for recesses. Your own self-determinism gets shot to hell. Everything is tightly regimented. You even have to ask to go to the bathroom, and then you can't make a habit of it. They force kids to spend nearly a dozen years at it. Then, when they are finally adults — eighteen, though I know on many worlds fourteen is considered having reached adulthood — if you are lucky to be able to go to one of the Imperium Academies, you do the same thing all over again for at least four more years. By the time most get finished, they are finished as well, since they've had their bodies positioned in time and space and controlled by the teachers for almost twenty years. After that, a person has really lost an enormous amount of their innate vitality and life," Zarita explained.

She went on, "That's one reason I became a geologist. Most of my Academy days were spent out of doors in the field not cooped up in a cubicle or classroom. I was able to get more freedom of motion and action this way."

"She has a point," Hans backed Zarita up. "While I loved learning, I hated school. Besides, they make you take so many classes each term that you don't have enough time to investigate your own ideas and what avenues interest you. I was lucky and spent my little spare time working on my hyperdrive improvements. That kept me sane, I think."

"But we aren't doing it that way," Tesla pointed out. "We've been going at our own rates through all the computer-based education courses that we can."

"Yes, but just the ones that interest us," Jana added.

"Which makes the whole learning process fun and what it ought to be," Zarita declared. I found all this quite interesting. It seemed to account for the differences in learning attitudes between the seven of us and the other professionals around us. However, as the days passed, our enthusiasm for learning new things rubbed off on the others, and they began to join us every evening. Hence, the topics of discussion varied nightly, with each of the twenty tossing out ideas from their own areas of interest.

One night proved highly instructive for many of us, including Alexandra. Leann, our resident medical doctor and future geneticist, brought up DNA and how the horrific genetic bio agent worked. This discussion fascinated us all. It also would play an significant role much later on. She began by saying, "Tesla asked me just how these genetic modifications to our DNA were done. It's not a simple answer, so we have to start at the beginning with some chemistry. Organic compounds are carbon atoms which have bonded together with hydrogen, but also with nitrogen, oxygen, sulfur, and phosphorous, but mostly hydrogen. Carbon atoms have the unusual property of being able to bond together in long chains. These chains are called polymers. For example, when a carbon atom bonds with four hydrogen atoms, the resultant molecule we call methane. However, two carbon atoms can join together and then attach six hydrogen atoms forming ethane. We call these hydrocarbons, and many of the fossil fuels consist mainly of these hydrocarbons."

"What's all this got to do with us?" she asked rhetorically. "Proteins. Proteins are just very long chains of organic molecules involving carbon polymers. We call them the amino acids. Our bodies need proteins to build up muscles, make and repair skin tissue, make tendons, and so on. Some proteins store up energy for our bodies. We all know about the rapid burn-off of sugars. Eat a candy, and the energy boost is gone before you know it. Eat a bunch of protein instead, and your energy levels remain high for far longer."

"Some of these proteins help our immune systems fight off infections. Some help transport other substances through our bodies to where they are needed. Some are highly effective as a catalyst for other chemical reactions. We call these enzymes. When we get pregnant, various enzymes trigger all manner of new responses, particularly so when we give birth and our mammary glands go into overdrive." Danika and I chuckled at this detail, having both had experience with this aspect.

"Now, something needs to direct and control the use of proteins by our bodies, and this is done by nucleic acids, namely DNA and RNA — deoxyribonucleic acid and ribonucleic acid to be precise. DNA carries our hereditary information, not only to rebuild our own body cells, but also our offspring. Most all of the cells in our bodies are totally replaced in about seven years tops."

"So what is DNA? It is a sugar-phosphate backbone, like the sides of a very tall ladder. The rungs of the ladder are what is critical. These rungs contain nitrogen based compounds called nucleotides and there are four different types: adenine or A, guanine or G, cytosine or C, and thymine or T. The A's and the T's pair together, while the C's and G's pair together. These DNA chains are very long and contain the coding to produce particular proteins and are called genes."

"DNA resides in the nucleus of each cell. When a cell divides into two, the DNA strand splits and a duplicate copy is made. Thus, the two child cells are theoretically a duplicate of the original cell, thanks to the giant DNA strands. This explains how babies are formed. They begin as one cell, a joining from a sperm and egg. As the cells multiply and divide, the DNA in the nuclei continue to replicate themselves over and over."

"This also means every cell in our bodies contain the same DNA strands. However, in each organ and tissue, only certain parts of the DNA strand manifest themselves. We don't need our feet to grow teeth. We don't need our hands to create brain cells. We don't need our blood to grow hands." We chuckled at this point.

She went on, "Now, one problem develops over many years of constant duplication of DNA. Errors begin to creep in. We notice these changes as the aging process. Our Rejuvenation machines go in and remove many of these accumulated errors in copying. The result is that our rejuvenated body appears much younger."

"Wow, so that's what the machine was doing to my body," Martina exclaimed. She finally had an explanation that she could understand.

"Precisely so. We get better and better at reversing the aging process. Now then, the complete DNA for an organism is called a genome. Taking into account the length of our DNA strands and realizing that only A's and T's pair together as do C's and G's, we have the potential for 3.2 billion different base pairs in the human genome. However, only about 2% of those are used, yielding about 24,000 genes, which average about 27,000 base pairs. About half of these pairs are used for calibration and alignment, and the rest contain the critical data to be duplicated."

"Statistically, in homo sapiens sapiens, 99% of these

pairs are identical with only 1% that differ, which yield the variations between people. The same ratios hold true for we homo sapiens nova, as Alexandra calls us, except the percentages are modified by those of us who have received one or more genetic cures."

"Now, here comes the fun part or the horrific part, depending upon your point of view. Suppose that one small portion of a dozen pairs goes AAATTTCCCGGG and its partner TTTAAAGGGCCC. Let's say that this sequence defines your eye color as blue. What if we could go into this specific sequence and alter it to TTTAAACGCGCG and AAATTTGCGCGC? The result might be some really wild eye color like vibrant yellow."

"This is precisely what the inventors of the terrible genetic bio agent did. They made a compound that specifically alters specific areas of various genes, which the body then uses to rebuild itself, dictating no arms, neurons in our hair, and its super long length and thickness, and so on down the line. Lord knows how they did this or knew what to alter to what. Even with all of the genetic research that has been done thus far, we know very little about what changes in sequences will cause what effect on the body."

"Of course, one way to do it is to make a specific change, and then insert that into a person's DNA and see what happens. Some changes could easily cause instant death of the person! Failure of the blood to continue to carry oxygen to the cells is one thing. Obviously, genetic experimentation on humans is unethical and highly illegal. Lord knows how those scientists ever figured out the genetic modifications that they did. But we have evidence that they experimented on at least a hundred men and women, who all died from the experiments." Several of us gasped.

"Some of our parents and grandparents on Ashford-5 were able to work out some of the simpler changes. Zarita, your grandmother's DNA gave them the breakthrough they needed to come up with some of the genetic cures. They had samples of before and after with her, and were able to deduce what changes had been made, and then invent a way to reverse them. However, the sexual alterations are so darn complex that they've totally resisted all attempts to undo them to date. Honestly, there's not much hope of ever solving that one, not for centuries perhaps, if ever."

Alexandra spoke up, "So now, we have a new subspecies, homo sapiens nova. Honestly, we're all better off as pure, unaltered homo sapiens nova. But I do understand why some of you had to get some of the genetic cures. Aquila Prime simply cannot afford to donate an HIFR to everyone who needs one on all the other worlds." I felt somewhat relieved she finally accepted those of us who had one or more of the available genetic cures. It was a step in the right direction, as far as I was concerned.

Naturally, Tesla then asked, "So how does the DNA make a copy of itself?" Dr. Leann launched into another lengthy explanation, once more opening our eyes to the world of genetics. After that, curious Tesla wanted to know how the genetic cures worked, and how they could make changes to small sections of the giant DNA double helix. We didn't get to bed until midnight!

Our testing was going along so well that by day twelve, Alexandra began pushing Hans to outline the theory around his new improvements to the hyperdrive system. He yielded to her and gave us his own formal presentation on day fourteen. For two days after that, we saw very little of Alexandra, who stayed cooped up in her quarters going over all of the complex mathematics of his solution. Finally, she appeared, declaring, "Hans, this is brilliant work. I can find no flaws in the math. It should work and revolutionize the hyperdrive engines!"

As the tenth of August approached, our excursion was interrupted. A Federation light cruiser located us and immediately challenged us! I said more than a few explicative words!

Chapter 3 Predictions

Blonde, blue-eyed Jan Voort of Helicon-3 let out a war hoop! "It's going to happen! My theory works! Yahoo!" He was finishing up his astrophysics PhD thesis on supergiant stars, as they transition to the supernova stage. For months, he had been studying all data available on the massive red supergiant star known as Boon. It was located at the edge of the Imperium spiral arm, but very close to the hub section, where it also was close to the Federation of Planet's arm as well. Fortunately, it was largely in an uninhabited zone and no longer had any planets orbiting it. Why? The supergiant's radius had expanded outward so far that it had literally "devoured" its planetary system, absorbing their mass into its own.

The problem with massive stars, those whose mass exceeds ten common solar masses where the common mass was that of a typical yellow main sequence star, is that they burn up their available hydrogen fuel at alarming rates. Their lifetimes are the shortest of any star, perhaps a million years in the case of the most massive stars. Once the hydrogen is spent, the core collapses until the temperature is high enough to "burn" the core helium, the product of hydrogen combustion. Once that burns up, the core collapses until the carbon can be burned in nuclear fusion reactions and so on until the core is filled with iron, the last possible element that can be formed by fusion from burning silicon and sulfur. At this point, the star undergoes an absolutely massive explosion, sending out many forms of radiation enormous distances, frying much within that space.

In fact, one way that astronomers have been able to calculate the distances to other galaxies is through intensive observations of supernova in them. But that is not really useful, since no one can yet travel to other galaxies. No, what is important here is that whenever Boon reaches its last days and explodes, many inhabited planets of the densely populated hub sector will be blasted with intense radiation and worse.

Until this moment, no one had ever been able to predict when any specific red supergiant star would actually undergo its explosion. Indeed, the last phase, the silicon-sulfur burning stage, lasts but hours, compared to the hundreds of thousands of years for the helium burning stage. Jan had worked out a theory, allowing him to predict within a month of when the red supergiant would go supernova. In part, it was based on the observed surface temperatures over time, correlated against theoretical core-burning models.

Jan stared at his final results. Boon would likely go supernova within thirty days, plus or minus twenty days! While Helicon-3 was sufficiently distant from this star, when it exploded, they would still suffer damage. Anyone out of doors would receive fatal radiation sunburns in just a few minutes. All electronic equipment would be fried, especially the hundreds of satellites in orbit providing extensive worldwide communications. Jan brought up his galactic model and zeroed in on Boon. He ran a secondary calculation to determine the disaster radius where the damage would be most severe, resulting in loss of life and probably massive fires or worse. That done, he plotted that sphere centered on Boon, and noted that fifty densely populated hub worlds lay within that theoretical disaster sphere. Gasping at the sheer magnitude of his results, he slumped into a chair, unable to decide what to do next.

Finally, he gathered up his papers and paid a visit to his mentor, Professor Wurter. After outlining his results, Jan said, "We need to let everyone know that Boon is going to explode within a month or so. Get everyone off those worlds somehow!"

Professor Wurter sighed. "Come, come now. You can't be serious. This is just your theory. Besides, no one has reviewed your theory or your calculations. Get your thesis fully written up and then submit it to me. I'll then review it and have others in our department go over it with a fine-tooth comb looking for your errors. We'll get to the bottom of this. You know that no one can predict when a star goes supernova, don't you?"

"But professor, if I'm right, think of the damage that

will happen," Jan protested, growing very annoyed at being slammed by his own thesis advisor.

"Yes, yes, well it's not going to happen in a month. So go back and recheck your work. Get the paper in its final form and submit it. I assure you that we'll find your mistakes," Professor Wurter said condescendingly.

Jan grimaced, but turned and left his office. Never had he been so angry, but he couldn't figure out just why he was so infuriated. Was it because his professor had made light of his work? Surely, that wasn't it. Every thesis candidate had their paper extensively reviewed by their peers, and often major blunders were located, much to the embarrassment of the PhD candidate. He returned to his apartment, reworked all of his theoretical calculations, and double-checked the accumulated data on Boon. Hours later, nothing in his final results had been changed. Now his anger rose.

Unlike many others, he felt he somehow needed to let these other worlds know about the impending disaster facing them. Then, if they did nothing about it, he could at least have a clearer conscience. But how to do this? His own peers refused even to look at his findings, until he'd finished his thesis properly and submitted it. He estimated even if he burned the midnight oil, by the time he finished it, six months would have passed. Far too late to do any good.

Jan thought about going to the press with his predictions, but within days of trying this approach, he thought better of it. He was tossed aside as some crackpot. He didn't have his PhD yet. In exasperation, he grasped at straws. It struck him: every planetary leader had an email address. "Bypass everyone! That's the way to proceed," Jan declared to the walls of his apartment.

Jan spent an entire day carefully composing the text of his intended email to planetary leaders. He kept his wording simple, avoiding complex equations, but explaining in human terms what would be happening when the supernova erupted. He pointed out the extensive list of worlds, which he believed would suffer the brunt of the massive radiation and attendant destruction. He ended with his prediction. "Sometime during the month of September, or early October at the very latest, the red supergiant Boon will go supernova and explode. By the time you observe it happening, it'll be too late to do anything about it." He then gave his own contact information at the end of his email.

The next day, he researched email addresses and finally fired off the email to two hundred planetary leaders, primarily those within the hub sector. Satisfied he'd done all he could do to put out the necessary warning, he returned to his thesis work, little knowing the upheaval he'd set into motion, though he was soon to discover much of it.

Two days passed uneventfully. No return emails were in his in-box. However, he received a registered post from his Academy. Opening it, he was officially dismissed from the Academy effective immediately! The reason given was for having brought total discredit to Helicon-3's Academy. Fuming, he burned the letter, and began packing his things.

Later that afternoon he was ready to go back to his hometown and live with his parents. He'd already called them, relaying in very angry terms what had happened. He decided to check his email one last time before heading off to the shuttle service. He ignored the many emails from his friends and acquaintances; he could read those later. After all, all they could do was express their pity for him. No, there was one official-looking email in his in-box. It was from some emperor fellow from some distant mid-spiral arm world, whose existence he was only vaguely aware of. It read:

Jan Voort

Your email regarding the imminent collapse of Boon into a supernova has come to my attention. I would like to explore your theory more fully. I'm sending one of the top stellar evolution astrophysicists in the Ataro Empire to meet with you, Dr. Lelos Smith. Perhaps you've heard of him. Please review your theory, calculations, and data with him. If he vouches for your work, I'll use my considerable influence to convince the planetary leaders in the death zone to take action before it's too late. Dr. Lelos will be arriving on Helicon-3 late tomorrow.

On a more sinister note, your email has certainly caused quite a stir in many key political circles. Expect the fallout to be rather significant, whether or not your theory is proven correct. I've some indications that your very life might be endangered over this. Assuming my sources are correct and a hit has been taken out on you, please exercise extreme caution — a cloak and dagger thing, as they say. Go into hiding until tomorrow evening. At that time, please call this number, but use a secure line if possible.

    Emperor Bino Sanguro

    Ataro Empire of the Twelve Sacred Planets of the Wasps

    (now with forty planets)

"What in Dingo's Hell is going on here?" Jan cursed. He looked over the email. It looked official enough. "What? It's a hoax? Well, I've just been kicked out of the Academy. That is the end of my career as an astrophysicist, officially anyway. That's cloak and dagger enough for me. Wait, my life is in danger? Why? From whom? Dingo's Hell! All I wanted to do is to get a warning out to those worlds."

Fear seeped into his stomach, followed by paranoia. He looked out of his apartment's front window. He saw a strange man standing on the corner, apparently working with his cell phone. Hit man. That was his only thought. Hastily, he slung his laptop bag over his shoulder and grabbed his duffle bag with some of his clothes, leaving the two shipping crates sitting near the front door. Time enough to return for them later. Besides, he already had them labeled with his folk's address. He ducked out his back door and walked in the opposite direction from the strange man.

As he walked, his paranoia rose. Drunkard's Walk, yes that's how to lose a tail, he thought. He began making random direction changes at each intersection. An hour's walk cleared his head and his fears. Jan had reached a shopping mall south of the school's apartment houses. He stopped to eat and relax over a mocha, trying to decide just how he could hangout until tomorrow evening, and how he could get his hands on a secure cell line. Then, it struck him. The last place anyone would be looking for him would be the Academy's observatory! He'd been kicked out of the school, but he still had his keys to the little-used observatory, where one of his duties as a grad student was to conduct public observation nights on clear

Saturday evenings.

An hour later, he slipped unseen into the vacant observatory. After making sure he was alone, he found an ideal hiding place: the clock room, which housed the various clocks and control mechanisms for the telescope above him. Here he settled down to wait, clear his head, and think this through.

Someone wants me dead. Why? I haven't hurt anyone. I'm just an Academy student — well, ex-Academy student. All I did was send the leaders an email warning them of impending doom. Why should that put a price on my head? This makes no sense. Jan rubbed his face with his hands, fully exasperated. Then, he sipped his hot mocha he'd brought along, trying not to think further. I lack data, he finally concluded. That allowed him to put this mess out of his mind. The repetitious ticks of the several clocks lulled him into a peaceful doze.

He woke hours later. It was fairly dark in this windowless room, but the local time clock told him it was now the middle of the night. Instead of getting up to find some fast food to satisfy his stomach, he wisely decided to use his laptop to check on the local news, as he always did once each day. "Dingos's Hell!" he exclaimed. There was a photo of him plastered on the newscaster's screen. He was now wanted by the Security Guards for questioning. The public was being asked to report his whereabouts. Fear flooded over Jan once more, and he stifled his hunger. No way was he budging from here, until Dr. Lelos Smith came for him.

He knew about Dr. Lelos Smith. He was an eminent astrophysicist, who had published a number of papers on stellar evolution. In fact, he intended to use some quotes and references from the doctor in his own thesis, if he ever got to finish writing it all up. The real question in his mind was: is this message from this emperor fellow real or is it a fake? Does Dr. Smith really want to review my work? That question occupied his thoughts for quite some time. At last, he decided he had no real choice but to assume the offer was on the up and up, and not some dark game to entrap him.

He still had many hours to wait. Time to figure out how to place that call. He had his cell phone, but it was turned off.

Had it been on, Jan knew the Security Guards would already have used its GPS feature to track him down and arrest him. That he'd been here in the clock room for so long told him that they didn't know his location. However, as soon as he turned it on to make that call, they would know where he was. What to do?

A bit later, he swore once more. "How stupid am I? I can use the clock room's landline to make the call! Duh." Now, he again relaxed and attempted to doze once more.

Hours later, Jan decided it must be time to make the call. However, the real question in his mind was whether the doctor's flight had landed on Helicon-3 yet. If it had not yet landed, he decided, then the call probably wouldn't go through. Emboldened, he dialed the number on the ancient landline phone. Someone answered on the third ring.

"Hello. Dr. Smith here." A rather high-pitched voice spoke in Imperium Standard.

"Jan. Jan Voort. They are after me. What do I do?" he said hastily, forgetting all formal protocols he would normally use with his professors.

"We keep this call short. Where are you now?"

"Academy Observatory."

"Okay. Stay there. I'll send my robot Mathios to fetch you. Do precisely what he tells you. See you soon." Click. The line went dead. The call lasted but a few seconds, hardly time to trace it. Still, he'd given away his location, if anyone was monitoring the call. Again, his stomach reacted. He couldn't tell if it was tense from nerves, fright, or just overly hungry. He regretted not asking how long it would take his robot to get here. Robot?

Now, the word finally registered with him. The only world that had robots was Aquila Prime, the world where all the mutants lived, those whose bodies were genetically modified from normal people, though through no fault of their own. Freaks, armless, helpless freaks. That was his stereotype notions of the people from that world, based only on the fragmentary newscasts he'd seen over the years. This could only mean this famous astrophysicist was a mutant! He was quite surprised at his conclusion. Hastily, he gathered his laptop bag and his duffle bag, and headed out of the small clock room. He paused to listen, but heard no one, as expected. Almost no one ever came to the observatory, except on public nights. The telescope was only good for such things — a symbolic toy, really, not a truly useful instrument for research. He quietly made his way to the front door and took out his key, ready for the arrival of this robot.

In his mind, he pictured a gleaming, silver-colored metal contraption, vaguely human in form, but probably with arm extensions, to be able to assist the poor, helpless mutants. He waited, but dared not look out of a window. Someone might pass by and see him, even though he was in the shadows. A soft knock on the door startled him.

Jan had to make a decision. He could call out to see who was there. Yet, if he did that and it wasn't this robot, then he would be giving himself away. Besides, some students often dropped by to see if the observatory was open or not. Alternatively, he could open the door. He decided this was the best choice. If it was just some students, he could tell them the observatory was closed, rousing no suspicions. Carefully, he fumbled in the dark with the key. Finally, it slid into the lock, and he opened the door.

He saw a human man perhaps. He was dressed that way, but he also appeared to have something of a bosom threatening to bust out of his shirt and jacket. He had brown hair and a non-descript face, one that could get lost in a crowd. "Jan Voort?" the man said. "I am Mathios."

"Oh! Yes, I'm Jan. Sorry. I was expecting a robot. You know, a shiny, silver mechanical contraption."

"I'm a humaniform robot, Model 6. May I step inside?"

"Sure," Jan replied, looking about to make sure that no one was watching them. The street was dark and desolate.

"No, don't turn on a light," Mathios cautioned him, just as he was about to mechanically reach for the light switch. "I'm going to fasten a hologram projection belt around you. It'll cover you with a disguise. You'll look like my master, Doctor Lelos Smith. There." He flipped a switch. Jan looked down and gasped. He looked just like one of those mutants he'd seen on a newscast!

"Okay, Jan. If anyone stops us, pretend you are Doctor Smith. I'll keep an arm around your waist. Do not be alarmed. Walk slowly, small steps. That will aid the illusion. It's not far to my shuttle. We'll go from the visitor's lot directly to our ship, where Doctor Lelos is waiting for us."

Jan swallowed hard. "Okay," he managed to mutter. They stepped out of the observatory, but Jan hastily relocked it out of pure habit. For a moment, his arms stuck out from the hologram illusion, rather shocking him. The robot's arm slipped around his waist and gently guided him along. Jan quickly realized they were heading to the visitor's shuttle parking lot and relaxed. He was still on very familiar ground.

An hour later, the small two-man, rented shuttle landed at Helicon-3's giant spaceport, not far from a waiting deep space transport. It was too dark for Jan to make out the insignia on its side. Besides, the robot ushered him inside as fast as possible. As soon as they walked up the bay ramp, the robot pressed the close button. While the bay door was slowly closing, he led Jan back into the passenger section, where he saw what appeared to be a woman waiting for them.

She obviously had very long brownish hair, tied up in a bun around her head. Her bosom was simply massive. Jan had no other way to describe them. They were larger than the woman's head. She had two twelve inch golden lip plates through her split lips, stretching the lip loops quite tight. Her waist was almost not there. He blinked. It was there, only very tiny indeed. She wore a brown satin gown, outlining her incredible curves and wide hips. However, she had no arms at all, not the slightest trace. She was obviously one of the Aquila Prime mutants.

Jan nearly jumped when she spoke. A man's voice, though somewhat high pitched, startled him. He recognized the voice of Doctor Lelos Smith. She wasn't a she at all, but a man! "Welcome aboard, Jan. I see there were no complications. The local newscasts are reporting that the local Security Guards are after you. Well, they won't get you this time. I'm Doctor Lelos Smith. Mathios will be taking off directly. Come, have a seat beside me. As soon as we get into hyperspace, Mathios will come back to assist me. Then, let us not waste time. I want to see all the details of your theory about Boon and go over your calculations. Please, have a seat and buckle up. Mathios will be taking off directly."

Jan swallowed hard. "Thank you, Doctor Smith. Sorry, I've never see someone like you before." Jan sat down and buckled his seat belt, hoping his hot face wasn't too visible.

"That's all right, Jan. I seldom travel off-world. No need to. So you are just finishing up your doctoral thesis?" Lelos made pleasant conversation. He already knew all about Jan.

"Yes, I was just finishing all the calculations. But when I got the final answer, I knew I just had to tell others, warn them. I took it to my thesis advisor, but he ignored me. He wanted me to get the whole thesis written up and submitted before he'd even take a look at it. By then, the supernova would be ancient history!" Jan explained, sensing the ship lifting off. A bit later, Mathios joined them, sitting beside Lelos.

He reported, "We're in hyperspace. Home in eighteen hours."

"Thank you, Mathios. Okay, Jan. Let's see your work. We have eighteen hours to kill," Doctor Lelos suggested.

Jan pulled out his laptop and his papers. "Guess I should start at the beginning," he began. For hours, he and Doctor Lelos talked. He found he had forgotten all about the man being a mutant. Rather, he seemed more like a very learned colleague. More than merely following along, he asked key and critical questions at each step in the theory presentations. When they got to the actual calculations, Jan was quite surprised to hear Doctor Lelos occasionally saying, "Yes, that is the correct answer there." He was doing these complex calculations in his head!

Mathios left them briefly to prepare meals for them. The discussion continued through the meals, though Jan had to resist watching just how Doctor Lelos could even eat with those giant lip disks. He also noted he almost never even had to say a word to the robot. Mathios always seemed to know just what the doctor needed without his having to ask.

Twelve hours passed rapidly. Finally, Jan finished, outlining his last step, which had been to define the danger sphere, centered on Boon. Doctor Lelos said, "Well, here you may have been a bit pessimistic. However, I can see it is safer to be pessimistic. Considering the mass of Boon, perhaps the radius of the destruction sphere will be somewhat smaller. Still, I can find no fault in either your theory or subsequent calculations. Congratulations Jan on a brilliant breakthrough! With your theory, we may well be able to predict when a red supergiant will go supernova on us. Some of us have been searching for that answer for decades. Your next step will be to get it written up. Rapidly, mind you. Forget the fancy stuff. Just get it down so that others can read it. Now, I need to make some secure calls. I suspect you are quite tired. Mathios will lead you to a bedroom and wake you when we land on Aquila Prime. Again, brilliant piece of work. I'm sure we'll get you your PhD quite soon!"

Mathios led an exhausted Jan to one of the four cabins. Jan was asleep almost the moment his head hit the pillow. All the recent stress had evaporated. Someone had reviewed his work and found it flawless. That was more than comforting to him.

"Yes. Verified. Jan has a brilliant mind and has made a tremendous breakthrough in the late stages of supergiant evolution. Yes, his predicted dates for the supernova eruption are correct within twenty days. His proposed sphere of destruction is a bit large. I think it could be decreased somewhat. Over." Doctor Lelos explained to Emperor Bino.

"Good. Good. Now it is up to me to convince the rulers and see if this disaster can be avoided. There are two worlds of the Federation of Planets that are just barely in that sphere of destruction. I best alert them as well. Excellent work, Doctor Lelos. Make Jan Voort comfortable on Aquila Prime. I will send further word about him as soon as I make more arrangements. Again, well done. Over and out." Emperor Bino signed off. Now he had what he needed to deal with this impending crisis. The question was just what to do about it.

He directed his personal assistant to bring up the galactic model and had him establish two spheres around the red supergiant Boon. Outlined in red was the danger sphere suggested by Doctor Lelos. Outlined in yellow was Jan Voort's original sphere. For some time, Emperor Bino studied the systems that would be severely impacted by the supernova explosion. He wasn't familiar with some of the worlds of the hub. Hence, he had his assistant bring up the overall statistics of the likely to be destroyed worlds. The smaller sphere indicated only ten would be annihilated. Yet that meant nearly a hundred billion people were in danger of dying in the explosion. From long experiences with trying to come to the rescue of whole planets, which have been exposed to the terrible genetic bio agent, and where they had at most a month to rescue as many of the billions of victims as they could, he knew only a tiny fraction could be saved, before Boon went supernova and wiped the remainder out.

He also knew that shortly other astrophysicists would be demanding to get observational satellites strategically placed around Boon to gather live data when the star died. The data would be invaluable to the scientific community. Yes, there was much to do and so very little time in which to do it. He made another decision and called back Doctor Lelos, giving him further instructions.

Jan was sound asleep when Mathios roused him. "Jan. Wake up. We'll be landing shortly."

"Huh? Oh! Okay. Thanks," Jan muttered, got up, and slipped his pants back on. Then, he tied his shoes only to feel the jolt of the landing. They'd already landed. He headed out into the corridor and found Mathios already with his arm around Doctor Lelos, steadying him. He grabbed his laptop bag and his duffle bag, and followed them. As they walked down the bay ramp, he realized Doctor Lelos probably couldn't see his own strange feet over his massive bosom, hence, the need of Mathios' steadying arm. He felt a pang of pity for this brilliant man trapped in this mutant body.

Once on level ground of the spaceport, Doctor Lelos spoke. "Okay, Jan. New orders came through. You are to get your thesis written up today. Use voice activated software. It doesn't have to be perfectly written, just get the basics down in writing. Tomorrow morning, you'll give your thesis presentation to the other astronomy faculty here at the Aquila Prime Academy. Unless you totally blow it, you'll be presented your doctorate degree following your presentation. This will add sufficient credibility to your predictions. Our Emperor Bino needs to assemble as much credible data as possible in the next few days."

He went on, "After that, you and our whole department will meet to discuss what and how to make scientific observations of this supernova. I'm going to assign Zoe Theodora to assist you in getting it done. Before I left, she just completed her thesis presentation on proto-star formation and passed it. Unless you botch it, you'll both be receiving your degree at the same ceremony. Ah, here comes Zoe now."

Jan saw another woman walking slowly towards them. She too had a humaniform robot steadying her. Zoe had very blonde hair tied up in a bun much like Doctor Lelos'. Her blue eyes were transfixing, and her satin form-fitting gown matched them. Jan couldn't tell if she was smiling or not because of her giant lip plates, but he thought so from her bright eyes. She was a year older than he was. "Zoe, this is Jan Voort. Jan, this is Zoe Theodora and her HIFR Tanis."

"Pleased to meet you. HIFR?" Jan replied, unsure just how to greet the woman without arms.

She chuckled and teased him, "Off-worlder. Humaniform robot. HIFR for short. Come on; I hear you have to get your whole thesis written up today! Stellar evolution?" she asked. Doctor Lelos hadn't told her much about it, at least Jan surmised that from what she said. "Follow me." Jan fell in beside her, opposite the female looking robot.

"Yes, predicting when red supergiants will go supernova. That's my topic. I've actually done it. The predicting part, based on temperature observations," Jan answered. "So you've just finished yours?" he asked, wondering how she could even have managed to do a thesis. How could Doctor Lelos do that too, he thought. These were completely helpless people.

As they walked very slowly across the tarmac, Jan noticed the spaceport looked just like all other Imperium spaceports. He took some comfort in this detail. "We don't often have outsiders on Aquila Prime," Zoe chatted. "Can't imagine why. Oh, that's an inside joke."

"Oh. Yeh, I get it, I think," Jan replied.

"Outsiders think of us a freaks or something, just like we think you all are the freakish ones. No offense, Jan, but you are really very different looking than we natives."

"Yes, that about sums it up, Zoe. Still, Doctor Lelos did hear me out, and said I was correct in my work. None of my peers on Helicon-3 ever did that. So where are we going?"

"To the Academy dorms. We'll take that shuttle over there. That's the one I came here in. Tanis drives, of course. Honestly, Jan, where does your kind ever find the time to do any real work — on your theories and such, I mean?"

"Huh? I've been at it for over a year now," Jan replied, unsure just what the blonde woman meant.

"Well, your kind has those awful arm appendages and has to do everything for yourselves with them. Such an incredible waste of time. With us, our HIFRs do all those things for us so we can spend all our time working on our projects. I simply cannot imagine how many hours your kind waste everyday getting dressed, making meals, and feeding yourselves, and so on. Typing with those appendages must be so terribly slow. How can your kind ever even find the time to write a thesis? I surely don't know."

Somewhat taken aback, Jan didn't quite know how to respond. "So how did you write yours?"

"Oh. Voice-activated software. Everything is voice-activated here on Aquila Prime. You'll see. All that you have to do is to speak clearly into the computer, and it writes your thesis for you, complete with proper punctuation, footnotes, and references. Truly simple. A child could do it. You'll see. Don't worry, Jan. None of our computers has a keyboard. Those are completely useless. You'll be staying in my dorm room with me. Hope you don't mind. Well, I must admit I did protest some, but it is only for today and tonight. Tomorrow, you give your thesis presentation. Probably after that, someone will assign you a proper dorm room. I'm supposed to help you get your thesis done up properly today."

A half hour later, the shuttle sat down in the visitor's parking lot. The dorm was obvious, and Zoe led Jan up to her room on the top floor, the fourteenth. The view from her windows was quite spectacular. Some mountains were off in the far distance, and the blue waters of a lake lay just at one end of the Academy campus. Picturesque.

"Plop you things down anywhere. Get your computer out and sit here at mine," she ordered. He noticed her room was spotless. Everything was in its proper place, but Tanis quickly brought a second chair up to the computer monitor and helped Zoe sit down. Jan stared at the monitor. There was no mouse, no pointing device, and no keyboard. Well, he thought, they couldn't use them anyway.

After getting his own laptop up and his papers back out, he sat looking at the monitor very much confused. Zoe laughed. "Computer: open new thesis paper. All right, Jan, you speak now. Say title and then give it. Just talk and the computer handle everything for you. It's actually a very fast process to get the paper written. Go ahead."

Looking very silly, Jan said, "Title: Predicting When Red Supergiants Go Supernova, by Jan Voort." He stopped and stared at the monitor. There with perfect precision was his title page, complete with date and time. "But I don't know how to enter these equations, Zoe," he protested.

She laughed again. "I figured as much. That's why I'm here. Okay, you talk away until you get to them, and I'll help you through them. Can you really predict when it's going to explode?"

"Yes. Within an error of plus or minus twenty days. It could be more accurate if I had more exact data on Boon," Jan replied. Slowly, he began dictating his thesis.

An hour later, Tanis brought them a lunch tray and quietly began feeding Zoe, though not until she raised her upper lip plate into its horizontal position, locking it in place. Zoe said, "I hope you like chicken gumbo. That's your plate there."

Jan noticed the food, which smelled somewhat spicy. However, the portions were quite small, about a quarter of what he would have eaten. Zoe noticed him noticing this detail. "Oops. Sorry Jan. We don't eat much at one time. Can't. Tight corset. So we eat more frequently. Don't worry, Tanis will bring us more in a few hours. Hope you like it. She's an excellent cook. Now, keep on talking, if you can. We simply must have this done today. Orders."

Without a word, Tanis quietly removed the remains of their lunch when they were finished. She returned with a pair of sodas in a teacup, along with two spoons. "Soda?" Zoe asked. "I don't know about you, but around here, we're all soda freaks. Can't live without it."

Jan laughed. "Sure. We can't either. Also have to have our mocha in the morning to get woke up."

She laughed and agreed. "Well, I guess we grad students have similar tastes." Jan smiled. At last, he thought, they were finding some common ground between them. Around four that afternoon, Jan finished the project. Zoe quickly reviewed the whole document, making a few quick changes here and there for him, since she could do it ten times faster than he could.

"There. Done! And on time too," Zoe declared.

"Impressive, Zoe! I was planning to spend about six months getting it typed up like this. You really do have something here! I can't tell you how thankful I am for all you've done for me. Thanks Zoe."

He thought she was probably smiling, but he couldn't tell from the giant lip plates. Zoe then said, "Told you. Now come on. I ought to give you a tour of our campus and the room where you will be making your presentation tomorrow morning. I have to admit, I had butterflies before I gave mine. I thought sure I was going to faint while giving mine."

"Nervous? Yes some. I've never done it before. Did you? Faint, I mean. Gosh, Zoe, that'd be utterly humiliating."

She giggled. "No, I somehow managed, but it felt like I was, nearly the whole time. Yes, it would be humiliating, more so than taking a tumble. We do that often enough anyway. Come on; let's go see the campus." She rose, and Tanis moved up to her side.

Zoe took a side look at Jan and then said, "If you like, you can put your arm appendage around me and support me on the trip and such. That way, Tanis wouldn't have to come along."

"Sure thing, Zoe. But remember, I don't know what all

you need, not like Tanis does. Just tell me, okay?"

"Of course, silly. Come on then. I really don't need a steadying arm on flat surfaces, but it's wise to have one anyway. None of us can see our feet while walking so it does help." Jan slipped his arm around her twelve inch waist, feeling the steel boning of her corset beneath her satin gown.

As they walked down the hallway to the elevator, he asked, "Do you always have to wear it? It must be so tight."

"Have to. We all do. Our backs can't support the weight of our breasts easily. If I don't, I have terrible back pains after just a few hours. It's not so bad. You get used to it, except when you get excited or nervous like I was when I had to give my thesis presentation. Thanks for playing robot for me. I don't often get to go out without Tanis. I rather like to do this once in a while. So now, you are my human robot." Jan smiled and made a mechanical clicking noise. Zoe giggled.

The grassy knoll between the buildings added a special fragrance to the air. Jan also noticed the greasy, oily smell of Halicon-3 wasn't here. Rather, he detected a clean odor, fresh somehow. Zoe chatted away, as they made their way across the campus to the Astronomy Department. "There are ten full time faculty here. You will meet them all tomorrow, when you give your thesis presentation. I hope to be the eleventh, after I get mine."

After the grand tour, they headed back to her dorm. "So what do you all do for fun around here?" Jan asked. "Back home, we often play cards, that is, when we have time."

She laughed again. "Duh. So do we. Pinochle is our favorite. Of course, I win most of the time. Four of us play on Friday nights. Say, it's Friday. Want to play with us? Of course, you are going to be stared at like mad by the others. As I said, we don't get many off-worlders here. In fact, you are the first."

"Sure thing. Wait. How can you hold your cards?" Jan asked.

"Why would we want to hold our cards? Oh," Zoe's face flushed. "I keep forgetting you have those arm appendages and no HIFRs. Tanis holds them for me. I tell her which one to play by number. We all just number the cards in the hand, starting with one. That way, no one knows what is what. Also,

Tanis has been instructed to keep the suits in a different order in her hands each deal. I give out no clues at all. Be prepared to lose, Jan."

"We'll see about that," he teased her back, but with a big smile on his face. He had already concluded that, while her body was vastly different from his, she was just as much a person as he was, only with different ways to do things. When they returned, Tanis had supper waiting for them. After that, the three headed to the dorm lounge where he was introduced to her other three players. At first, Jan couldn't tell if they were men or women. Only their voices gave him any clue. Finally, he decided that their sex didn't matter. They all appeared to be women to his eyes, and he focused on the game at hand.

Three hours later, the game ended. Jan had won three out of four times, much to the dismay of Zoe, who was rather annoyed about his unexpected victories. One of her fellow players teased her, "Ah Zoe, you have finally met your match!" All three laughed, and Zoe's face crimsoned slightly.

Back in her dorm room, she said, "You get to sleep in the spare room. Tanis has already made the bed up for you. Shower is over there. She'll wake us in plenty of time, so don't worry about oversleeping."

"Thanks Zoe. I do appreciate all you've done for me."

"Say, can I ask you a personal thing?" Zoe whispered, as he retrieved some things from his duffle bag prior to hitting the shower. He nodded and she asked, "How can you even sleep with those arm things in the way and getting all tangled up in them? I've been wondering about that all day. They must really be a problem for you when you try to sleep."

Jan laughed. Of all the questions he might have been asked, this one was wholly unexpected. "Not in the slightest. I sometimes use them as a pillow."

At nine the next morning, Jan, accompanied by Zoe and Tanis, entered the conference room and took their seats. Zoe told him where to sit. Shortly, the ten faculty with their HIFRs entered. He recognized Doctor Lelos Smith, who led the small group. In fact, they all appeared much the same as Zoe, wearing form-fitting satin gowns, but in various colors. As they were introduced, he ascertained about half were supposedly male. After a short introduction by Doctor Lelos, Jan rose and began his presentation.

Any nervousness he had vanished after his opening sentence. He found a rapt audience and proceeded to explain his thesis to the ten doctors. As before, none of the ten was the least bit hesitant about interrupting him with their questions as he went along. For him, this was more like a very stimulating dialog! It was over way too soon, as far as Jan was concerned. After they filed out, he said, "Zoe! That was the most fun I've ever had. Wow! I feel like I'm floating or something. You didn't tell me about this part."

She giggled. "I felt totally relieved. Sorry. I think you passed with flying colors, but we will know in a couple of minutes."

Zoe was right. Shortly, Doctor Lelos entered. "Congratulations, Doctor Jan Voort. You passed. The biggest hurdle was getting everyone to agree to present a doctorate to an off-worlder. That's not been done before. Zoe, Jan, we'll present your degrees in an hour. We'll use this room, if that's acceptable."

After he left them, Zoe said, "Oh, I should warn you. I think you off-worlders have a custom of shaking your appendages, as a means of sharing congratulations and such."

"Sure. And welcoming others and many other things," he replied. "I suppose you have other customs instead?"

"Er right. To display congratulations, to welcome others, things like that, we press our bodies into the other's. I suppose I ought to show you what they will be doing." She rose as did he.

She walked up to him and pressed her massive bosom into his chest. "Er. What am I supposed to do? I'd throw my arms around the person in a hug."

"Er, I don't think that would be too appropriate here," Zoe said thoughtfully. "Just push back against them. That's probably the best thing to do. Only don't wiggle sideways."

"Huh? Sideways? Why?"

Zoe flushed. "That's how we arouse our mates. We rub theirs with ours. If you do any sideways motions, you are likely to arouse them."

It was Jan's turn to flush. "I'll be extra careful about that. Thanks for the tip. I hadn't thought about such things, but I suppose you all can't even kiss either."

"Oh don't be silly!" Zoe retorted. Then she flushed. "Oh. I get it. No, we can't kiss with our plates in. Once we take them out, you would not believe the power of our kisses!" After a short pause, she added in a whisper, "Maybe I might show you tonight." Jan smiled.

A few minutes later, the ten filed back in, their HIFRs carrying the two doctorate degrees. The ceremony was brief. The head of the Astronomy Department finally said, "I give you Doctor Zoe Theodora and Doctor Jan Voort. Congratulations." He then leaned into Zoe and after that, Jan, who was very careful not to have any sideways motion as he met the lean. One by one, the others congratulated the pair.

Doctor Lelos said, "Okay, tomorrow, Zoe, Jan, meet here around ten. We must begin to work out ways and means of getting observational satellites into position to record Boon's explosion. This is a once in a lifetime situation. We need to gather all the data of the supernova explosion we possibly can. Probably other worlds will also be joining us in this project, that is, if they have the good sense to do so."

While all this was occurring, Emperor Bino began his attempt to get the ten planetary systems in the supernova's direct path to start evacuating their people. He also worked with the Senate, but quickly found that even with the full support of the famous Aquila Prime stellar evolution astrophysicist Doctor Lelos Smith, no one was taking the matter seriously. Instead, a mammoth controversy about whether or not this theory was correct took hold, with arguments pro and con flying around the hub Academies of the Imperium.

In stark contrast, when he contacted the President of the Federation of Planets and explained what had been discovered, President Juan believed him and promised to take swift action, evacuating as many people as they could. At least only a couple inhabited worlds were going to be impacted within the Federation.

Simultaneously, at the North Pole Landing Hanger on Aquila Prime, four humaniform robots landed their shuttles and trudged through the deep snow into the hanger. Via flashes of electronic signals, the four conducted their secret meeting along with a transmission to Minta on board the Eagle's Seed. The following is a rough translation into IS of what transpired.

HRM7, Humaniform Robot Model 7, was the precise designation of Minta and three of them. The fourth, and the boss had created them, was HRM6A, known by his "human" name of Thanos Haides, the unseen immortal. The three present in the hanger were all male models: Apollon, the Destroyer, Deimos, the Terror Striker, and Eros, the Seducer. The lone female version was Minta, the Defender, now onboard the Eagle's Seed.

Thanos spoke first. "Welcome again. It seems that our grand plan must be adjusted. We've just learned the hub red supergiant star Boon is about to go supernova." After a moment, the three responded with "Located." He continued, "Our Doctor Lelos Smith has determined ten highly populated hub worlds are going to be annihilated by the explosion. Our emperor is being entirely unsuccessful at getting the planetary rulers or the Senate to take any action."

Apollon spoke up, "Estimate one hundred billion homo sapiens sapiens will be eliminated."

Deimos added, "Calculating. Quite a few bright minds will be lost to us if we allow this to happen."

Eros commented, "Glad that our programming doesn't include protecting those homo sapiens sapiens!"

Thanos retook control. "Indeed. I hate to lose those minds. However, if the supernova explosion occurs, we'll not be able to salvage much of anything useful to us from the melted ruins. In the past, the homo sapiens sapiens responded to the planet-wide terrorist genetic bio agent attacks. Led by the emperor, a million lives were saved and brought here to Aquila Prime."

"Are you suggesting we include these worlds and move the timetable up many months?" asked Apollon.

Thanos answered indirectly, "Alexandra's propulsion system is working well. She's gotten Hans Valen to divulge his new modifications to the hyperdrive, though it has not yet been tested. Minta has relayed them to me, and I have construction crews working on building some samples. With the shortened time line, they will not be ready in time for our use."

"I propose we include these ten worlds plus five others in the vicinity. We should hit them very soon so the Imperium will have at least a month before Boon goes supernova. We should be able to salvage sufficient parts from those worlds to handle the constructions needed to support another million increase in our population. However, I wish you three also to do the extensive calculations to verify mine, please." Silence. Five minutes later, the three Model 7's reanimated. All concurred with the conclusion proposed by Thanos.

"Have we worked out the mechanics of delivery?" asked Apollon.

"Partially. After the Big Five attacks where each thought the other was attacking them and retaliated with their own bio agent attack, many of the hub worlds have taken note, have secretly stockpiled volumes of the genetic bio agent, and are ready to fire them off. Unlike the Big Five, none have a specific target in mind," Thanos explained. "Amazing what a computer worm can discover for you." He was referring to his own implanted program, which had thus far done its work on over seventy worlds.

"They have installed automated detection systems, designed to detect an incoming attack and launch a counterattack against the origin point of that attack," Thanos explained. "Inherently clever, but sadly any servomechanism cannot be depended upon. Only direct observation can. In this case, I have chosen the fifteen worlds carefully. This time, we'll not have to launch the attacks ourselves, but merely convince their automated systems to do it for us. Great care must be taken to keep Proxima Prime safe from any such attacks this time. They are on the outer edge of the zone. Downloading the fifteen worlds' armament data to you now." Again, there was a moment of silence, as Thanos streamed several data bursts.

After receiving confirmation of the downloaded data, he continued, "Work out a network for the attacks, ensuring all are sufficiently covered, and that Proxima Prime is not touched." Again, several minutes passed, while each of the three performed the necessary calculations of which planet needed to attack which planet versus the known quantity of the genetic bio agent that they had versus the amount needed to handle the entire planet. It wasn't as simple as Planet A attacking all fourteen others. None of the worlds had that much genetic bio agent prepared and ready to go. However, they all had goodly quantities of the stealth drones with which to deliver the agent in secret. Such unmanned craft were constructed of polymers and resins, such that they had almost no image on any of the different types of Imperium craft detection systems. Even more significantly, these were all quite small, even smaller than the billions of the two man shuttles in use all over the Imperium, as the favored form of transportation on all developed worlds.

Since the nasty war between the Big Five worlds many years ago, better delivery systems had been developed on the quiet. Essentially, these automated cargo shuttles could carry sufficient drones to the proposed target and launch them. The computer systems were designed to detect an incoming attack and plot its point of origin. Given that, they were also programmed to automatically react, firing off the cargo shuttles without need for human intervention.

The key to this operation lay in the fact that Thanos had discovered three of these worlds had sufficient cargo ships and drones to handle five simultaneous attacks. The other worlds were only able to deal with one or two at most, usually directed at their nearest neighboring worlds. To get all fifteen worlds sufficiently covered, choice of targets was critical. Of course, the reason behind the automated retaliation defense shields lay in the fact that the attacks were stealth in nature. One would not be aware of the genetic bio agent attack until it happened. At that point in time, there was no time for humans to get involved, work out the source of the attack, and launch a counterattack. Rather, everyone would already be unconscious. The prevalent attitude was that if you are going to wipe us out, then we'll take you out, as we go down. This was sold as a total Deterrent to War, as any attacker knew they'd be struck down by their victim's automated counterattack. On paper, it was an ideal deterrent. But it had a serious flaw.

The four compared their order of attacks and settled on one that gave the best coverage to all fifteen worlds. Ideally, only three "fake" orders would have to be given to the systems, the right three. All else would thereafter play out as planned without any other intervention. Thanos then declared, "You three prepare your transports. Your stations are assigned. Coordinate between yourselves, but make it happen in two days' time. Monitor the other automated systems and ensure that they trigger. Only after the payloads have been delivered are you to return here. Always use top speed." The three nodded, turned, and left.

Thanos then sent, "Minta, continue to hold. I believe others will be joining you. If so, we should acquire those as well. I'll notify you when it is time. I have everything prepared on this end."

Minta sent simply, "Acknowledged."

Emperor Bino agreed. He'd taken Doctor Lelos Smith's call and knew he needed to validate him for his extremely fast reactions and work with the Voort Episode. Going off-world was extremely hard for those on Aquila Prime. Prejudice was rampant, but that was the least of their fears. "Okay then, doctor. I agree. In fact, I can go you one better. I have a special research ship out now. I can have them relocate and make the observations. No need to tie up other ships just now. They can handle another couple onboard without difficulty. Yes, I'm referring to the special mission that Miss Alexandra Khristos is on. Please limit it to two though. Over."

"Excellent. Could they also deploy observational drones? I believe I should send Doctor Jan Voort on this one. After all, this was his work. Perhaps I should send along one of our astronomers as well. Over."

"Drones. Yes, I believe that is most feasible. I agree, Jan has earned the chance to witness this firsthand. Hold on. I'm told I have another urgent call coming in. Make your choices, and I'll call you back later today with specifics and coordinates for the rendezvous. Over and out. Okay, I'll take it now. Thanks." His personal assistant silently switched his comm center channels over to the secure line.

Chapter 4 Supernova

Commander Jack Stone of the Lightning Strike Light Cruiser marched briskly down to the airlock and across the flexible docking platform, entering the small forward hatch of this very strange looking Imperium spaceship. While the central portion of the ship matched known profiles of Imperium Deep Space Exploration ships, the four giant cylindrical appendages did not. What was it doing in Federation Space in violation of the Peace Accords? Before he challenged them, he had made quite sure it was unarmed. As he reached the small opening, he cleverly activated is own Defense Shield, a small device attached to his belt, along with his d-gun. Two Security Guards followed him. Jack didn't anticipate trouble, just an annoyance. Had they been armed, why, that would have been quite a different story, more to his liking.

He also hated being on patrol here on the fringes of Federation Space. Mostly, he had to deal with those damned gypsies who frequently visited the various gas and dust clouds. Quite what they saw here, Jack couldn't imagine. The first people he saw as he stood upright were just that — a pair of gypsies! He blinked twice and realized they were also mutants! His face grimaced in disgust. He never could hide his intense feelings of loathing for the mutants of the Imperium!

Jack barked, "Commander Jack Stone. You are in violation of the Peace Accords. What have you to say for yourselves? Who is in charge here? My god! A whole ship of mutants?" He was floored to see so many others standing around, staring at him. Real men should not have monster breasts, let alone have babies! About half he saw were dressed as though they were men, but they were plainly not men at all. He didn't even try to hide is complete disgust.

"Dylan Braith, my wife Anwyn. Yes, we are gypsies, here showing our friends this magnificent Eagle Nebula. I take it you wish us to leave?"

"Instantly, if that is possible. Say, what the devil are those four cylinders back there doing? You are not planning any kind of sneak attack on the Federation are you?" Jack finally realized what had troubled him from the moment he spotted the ship. Considering this was a ship full of mutants, he jumped to the obvious conclusion that they were here to launch a sneak attack, perhaps even using that terrible genetic war weapon. He quick drew his d-gun.

I spoke up. As captain, I simply had to. "Don't be silly, commander. We are here looking at the nebula. We certainly don't have any such weapons onboard, except a few personal d-guns, like you have. The cylinders contain our supplies and make more room for all of us on this trip." More importantly, I lightly touched his mind and knew that he wasn't satisfied. So I added, "Would you like to check them yourself?"

"Yes. You, with me. You stay here and keep the others covered. Lead the way, Mutant Miss," he barked at me.

I've been called a number of things before, but this was a new one. I resisted the temptation to banter back. Instead, I led him down the long corridor and passed the nursery. "Oh, here's our babies and sitter. Hi Mai. This is Commander Jack. He's inspecting our ship." I felt Jack's attitude soften, as he saw the pair of two year olds. Obviously, that this was a domestic group was his next thought.

I led him into the ring hall that led to each of the modules. I took him to Module A first where all of our supplies were located. Module B came next with obvious living quarters and workshops. I hazarded another hint. "We are on a long sightseeing trip, compliments of the gypsy Braith Clan. Do you really want to see more?"

"No, I'm satisfied. Please Mutant Miss, lead the way back." I smiled invisibly.

Once we were back at the forward hatch area, he stated, "All right. You are ordered to stay put while I report back to my superiors. If they give me the word, I'll send you packing out of Federation Space. If not, I may have to arrest you and hold you while the leaders deal with this treaty violation." He turned abruptly and left. We noticed he did not unhook his temporary docking station.

"Did he see the engines?" Alexandra asked, rather worried that he had.

"No, I convinced him that we are on a long sightseeing outing with the gypsies."

Anwyn spoke up, "Once in a while gypsies get accosted too. Always before, they let us go. I suspect he'll call back telling us to get into hyperspace at once." She sounded confident, but I wasn't so sure.

"At least he didn't catch us with the hydrogen refueling mesh deployed," Alexandra commented. "Can we simply jump into hyperspace now?"

Hans replied, "Our shields will hold for a time if they fire their weapons at us. That should give us time to make the jump."

Martina wasn't so confident. She spoke up, "Look. This is obviously a deep space exploration spaceship, regardless of the four weird cylinders back there. It's not a regular gypsy transport ship. Our markings are quite clear on the outside. If that man has any brains at all, he'll be checking the registry and discover this is Captain Nia Elain's ship and not a gypsy vessel. If I were his superiors, I would have grave doubts about encountering an Imperium deep space exploration ship in my territory. No, I don't think this is going to be that simple."

"Well, we can use our mental powers on them, forcing them to release us, if push comes to shove," Danika declared, itching for a fight.

"I'm with you," Dylan boasted, just as eager to have it out with them.

"Let's not act hasty," Martina cautioned the two. "No need to start a diplomatic incident."

Unknown to us, we had done just that, though it was an hour before we discovered it. At least Captain Jack had the courtesy to relay the data to us personally. He returned to the forward docking port a little over an hour later. "Well, well. A fine kettle of fish I've netted here. Seems the big wigs are keenly interested in you. I'm afraid you are to remain here with us for the time being. You are a registered Ataro Empire ship. Right now, your emperor is fielding some very nasty questions and allegations. So stay put, mutants." He turned and left us with a zillion questions.

"Damn, we probably shouldn't have come here in the

first place," Danika barked, echoing quite a few other's sentiments.

Well, it had been my decision. I spoke up, "Look, I made the call. It's on my head, not yours."

"Should we call Emperor Bino now?" asked Tesla, "explain things to him?"

Martina responded before I could. "No. He's probably dealing with calls from Federation folks now. If he wants data from us, he'll call us. No, let's get some lunch." I gave her a grateful nod, and she winked at me. I was thankful Martina chose to come with us. I could use her vast experience in such matters. As the others headed off to the galley, Martina pulled me aside. Quietly, we slipped into my cabin and closed the door.

"Don't do anything rash, Nia Elain. It really is a diplomatic issue. We are registered with the Ataro System, and Emperor Bino will have to respond. Trust him. Save the theatrics until they are really needed."

"Right."

"In their eyes, we could be exploring for new habitable worlds, hunting for more fuel sources, or spying. Honestly, there is no end of things they could be imagining we're doing. So let's not give them any ammunition. Clever way you manipulated the commander, though. Nice touch. All he could really report was that we are obviously a very domestic assembly and no real overt threat. Still, let's play it cool as long as we can."

"Right." I hated repeating myself, but I couldn't think of anything better to say. She was one hundred percent correct. "I did make the right call in coming here. If we'd gone to the nebulae in our arm, by now we'd be all over the Imperium newscasts, pictures and all. Tons more questions would have been raised by now."

"Precisely. I'm sure Emperor Bino will handle this incident deftly. Come on; let's not give the others something more to speculate about," she teased me. We headed off to join the others for lunch.

It was late afternoon before Commander Jack returned. He looked flushed. "Well, you seem to have quite the political pull. I don't know what they see in you mutants, but then I'm not our President. Here," he handed me a paper with some coordinates written on them. "You are to jump into hyperspace, go to these coordinates, and from there make a call to your emperor fellow. Pronto. And don't come back into Federation Space." He turned abruptly and marched back to his ship, fully annoyed that he could not take us prisoners. As soon as he got to his ship, they undid their docking bay, but I'd already sealed our end.

"Well, looks like the rest of the testing is on hold. Danika, go enter these coordinates and figure out where we are going. I'll get the main engines online. The rest of you, prepare to go into hyperspace once more. I'll let you know where we are going as soon as I know." My curious crew did as asked, and I followed Danika up to the pilot and navigator's seats.

"It's a location just near the border between the hub and mid-arm sectors," Danika reported, as I swung into my seat. "No planets nearby this location. What's up with it? It's not even the nearest location to our space from here!"

"No clue, love, none at all. Okay, tell the others while I get us going." By the time she finished relaying the news over the intercom, we had a duration of flight, some eight hours. I engaged our hyperdrive, and we made the jump. Gone was the magnificent Eagle Nebula, replaced with a black void. We two headed back to join the others.

Eight hours later, we dropped out of hyperspace right in the middle of nowhere, as far as any of us could tell. Distant stars were all around us, but none were close, certainly no inhabited planets. I sighed and headed for the comm center, joining the others who had all eagerly headed there the moment I announced we were out of hyperspace and stationary. They were just as curious and worried as I was. I placed the secure call to Emperor Bino.

"Hi. Captain Nia Elain here. We are at the coordinates the commander gave us. I'm so sorry to have gotten you involved in this. Over."

After a brief pause, though longer than I would have expected from this relatively short distance to the Ataro

System, Emperor Bino appeared on our monitor. He didn't look mad at us, but he did look worried, perhaps tired. "Greetings. I have quite a lot of news for you and some new orders for the short term. Oh, don't worry about the Federation hassle. That was nothing, in comparison to the current situation. Please assemble everyone else so they can hear this as well. Over."

I laughed. "They are already here. We're all keenly interested. We are parked here in the middle of nowhere. Over."

"There is a reason for your location. Allow me to explain," Emperor Bino replied. This time, the delay was what I expected from this distance, quite short. My conclusion: he had been occupied when I first made contact. That he had been, soon became obvious. He outlined the research of one Jan Voort from Helicon-3 and the imminent death of the red supergiant star known as Boon. Anwyn and Dylan were flabbergasted that someone had solved this long standing problem of being able to predict when one of these stars would go supernova! That at least ten densely populated hub worlds would likely be incinerated in the massive explosion shocked us all.

Martina interrupted him. "You might have known that the planetary presidents would pay no attention to this doomsday scenario, Emperor Bino. I could've told you that much. So what's the plan? Over."

"I've done my best to convince them. But you are right. They are not listening. However, the Federation of Planets has listened. They're going to be evacuating two of their worlds that are also threatened. Oh yes, and I sweetened the pot with them. Alexandra, I've promised them they could also have the plans for the hydrogen propulsion system, once we have all of the bugs worked out. This will establish a very solid working relationship with them. I have a feeling one day our kindness to them will pay us all royal dividends. However, I didn't mention the hyperdrive improvements, Hans. That technology is too vital to release to them at this time."

He continued, "Anyway, I'm now working the senators, trying to get them to take a stand on this issue. Martina, I'm not having too much success. Don't say I told you so," he teased. "Now then, back to your situation. With this incredible opportunity to witness a supernova this close at hand, the astronomical community is begging me to support their research. I've agreed. How can we not attempt to gather all the data possible? Hence, I've volunteered the services of the Eagle's Seed to help. You are at a rendezvous location now. In two days, Doctor Jan Voort and another astrophysicist from Aquila Prima, Doctor Zoe Theodora, will be meeting you. They are bringing along a supply of data gathering satellites. They'll direct you to the various locations where they want them situated. Once they are in place, position your ship at a safe distance, and monitor the death of this star. You've all the equipment you'll need, and Jan's bringing along some additional instrumentation. Your ship is the only one that can travel the distances needed to place the satellites in time without wasting valuable days refueling. I hope you don't mind this slight delay in your mission. Over."

Even I knew that supernova are relatively rare, especially ones remotely near us. I know the astronomers have observed plenty in other galaxies, but to have one go off this close to all the inhabited worlds was exceedingly rare in terms of human lifetimes, not in stellar durations though, as Dylan quickly explained to us all. We chatted a bit longer, filling in a few details and then signed off.

"Well, it'll be great having another scientist from home here with me," Alexandra commented.

"We best prepare two more rooms for our guests," I suggested. While some of us did just that, Alexandra and the Cho's proceeded to extend the hydrogen mesh and gathered more data. While we were not in a gas cloud but rather "empty" space, space isn't totally empty. There are still some particles around. They attempted to get measurements of fuel collected in such a region. Later, I was surprised to discover that even here where I thought there was only empty space, they could slowly amass hydrogen fuel, albeit at a very low rate, just barely enough to match the energy drain needed to run the collection system. While one could not actually refuel here, one could continue to maintain the status quo. That was an important unknown factor for the group.

Right on time, a deep space transport bearing the markings of Aquila Prime, a blue dove, dropped out of hyperspace, and maneuvered to dock with us, hooking up at our small forward port. Soon the blonde haired Jan Voort appeared at our port. "Hello. Jan Voort here. Permission to come aboard?"

"Sure. No formalities needed. Welcome. Does Doctor Zoe Theodora need a hand?" I called out. Our whole group gathered around to welcome the two newcomers. He stepped into the Eagle's Seed. I could see he was a thin, gangly fellow in his early twenties, fresh out of the Academy.

"Of course I don't need your hand. Tanis has me," I heard a young woman's voice, and watched as Zoe and Tanis very carefully stepped into the room. "Oh," she looked up and saw all of us present. "You've met Doctor Jan Voort. I'm Doctor Zoe Theodora."

"Captain Nia Elain Compton-Jereni," I replied formally, and then one by one introduced everyone else. I detected a huge smile and relief from Zoe, when I introduced her fellow Aquila Prime woman, Alexandra. For his part, Jan relaxed, as soon as he saw our men, and that we had arms and hands.

After the introductions, Jan had us begin moving their large collection of data satellites and other equipment over from the transport, along with their personal gear. Once he showed us what had to be moved, I left the men to do it, and took Jan and Zoe on a lengthy tour of the Eagle's Seed, eventually depositing them into their new quarters. They were in the last two spare rooms of the main ship. If we took on any more people, they would have to be housed in one of the attached modules.

Over supper, Jan and Zoe discussed the proposed placements of the data satellites. Zoe explained, "You see, they'll be gathering data and transmitting it in real-time clear up until the radiation burst hit them. One by one, we expect they'll be disintegrated, but they'll send us data up until that last instant. Vital and invaluable data, I might add."

Jan added, "Right. The faculty at Aquila Prime Academy has worked out the key placement positions. Zoe has that list. We need to deposit them at those locations, one by one. Are you sure you have enough fuel to do this much traveling?"

Alexandra laughed. "Kid, you won't believe what we have on this ship. The short answer is we've more than enough to travel far into the halo of the galaxy and back."

"Wow. The halo? That would be an exciting region to explore. We know so little about it," Jan replied. Alexandra flushed. She'd perhaps said too much.

I came to her rescue. "Well, we best get started. Has anyone worked out the optimum route to follow to place them?"

Zoe flushed. "Not yet. We just got the locations before we dropped out of hyperspace. Everything is being really rushed, you see. It'll take days to visit all these locations. It's vital we get as many placed as we can before it goes off."

Alexandra then changed the topic. "So Jan, you actually got your doctorate from our Academy?"

"Yes."

"Well, that's a first. To my knowledge, we've never given a doctorate to anyone not from Aquila Prime," she replied.

"Anyone who had arms, right?" Jan teased her back. She flushed and nodded.

Zoe laughed. "We've already been over that ground, Alexandra. Yes, he's a first. He did well. I was impressed. You have yours too, I take it?"

"Yes, but I don't like being called Doctor Alexandra, so I don't use the title."

"Hey, I don't either. Just call me Jan, please."

"And me, Zoe," she added.

By morning, Alexandra had already worked out the optimum path to follow to position each of the dozens of data satellites, minimizing the time spent doing so while ignoring the fuel costs. Her calculations suggested we'd need twelve days total, allowing several hours to get each one up and operational before moving on to the next location. We would be busy that's for sure. One by one, Danika punched in the coordinates, and we began the long task of positioning them. Twice though, Jan received a call from Doctor Lelos suggesting an alternate position for of a few of them. Back on Aquila Prime, they now had the luxury of redoing their calculations for the positions. I did my best to accommodate these last minute corrections.

The third day into our work, we received an unexpected secure call from Emperor Bino. Tears streamed down his cheeks, as he appeared on our monitor. We all knew something had happened, but it wasn't the supernova.

"Horrible. Just horrible. Fifteen hub worlds this time. Another massive genetic bio agent war. One hundred fifty billion people infected. Sorry. I'm too emotional. Wipe my face please." He paused while his assistant hastily used a handkerchief. "Sorry. No one could have predicted this. Well, ten of the worlds are those within the zone of destruction. Perhaps, they'll have a merciful death."

Without waiting for him to continue, I blurted out, "My god! What happened? Who started the war? Can anyone be rescued? Oh, sorry. Over."

"We aren't sure yet. It just happened yesterday. As you probably know, the affected people are now in comas and will remain so for at least three more days. I'm going to do all I can to rescue as many of the victims as possible, just like Emperor Kino did during the Big Five's war. I've contacted the President of Aquila Prime. He assures me they'll accept all victims we can rescue. I'll be meeting with our President and the Senate later today. More when I have a better picture. From what the Hub Sector ID Minister has told me, it was their automatic defense systems. Those were supposed to be a total deterrent to war, but alas, it was merely a recipe for genocide. I swear humans will never learn their lessons. You would think after the disaster of the Big Five, no one would ever consider using this terrible genetic bio agent as a weapon, but I guess not. Over."

"Can we help? Over." I replied.

"No. Stay on your mission. Only from now on, clear each hyperspace jump with Flight Control on Proxima Prime. They'll be the coordination point for the massive rescue attempts. I'll be urging all worlds to send all their fleets to rescue as many victims as possible before the supernova goes off. Perhaps, we'll do better this time, since Aquila Prime promises to accept all victims we can rescue. I hope and pray we can reach a million people like last time. Still, what's a million compared to one hundred fifty billion. My heart just aches over this. Perhaps, I ought to have done something more to convince these rulers to abandon such wicked systems. Over."

"Alexandra estimates we have another ten days before they are all deployed. After that, we are willing to do what we can to help. Over."

"No. Stay on mission. By then, you'll be entering the zone of Jan's prediction error. We simply cannot let this catastrophe stop the collection of such vital data. Lord knows when the next red supergiant will detonate. Being able to predict them can save lives. More later. Got a call coming in. Over and out."

Most of us stood there stunned by this horrible news. Finally, Alexandra whispered, "How awful! He's right. It's genocide. There is no other word for such things. I'm proud Aquila Prime will take these poor victims in. I wish I could be there to help them too."

"Me too," Zoe added. "This is awful. I do hope they send every available spaceship and rescue as many as possible. My god. Without a HIFR, they'll be helpless. Guess our robot construction factories will be going full speed now. I wonder if they can even make that many robots fast enough? Perhaps we need to return home and let Minta and Tanis help some of the new arrivals."

I spoke up. "Right now, he told us to stay on mission. Next time he calls, Zoe, Alexandra, I'll have him relay your ideas to your President. If they need your help or your HIFRs, I'll get you there at top speed."

Zoe merely said, "Thanks."

Jan added with a huge sigh, "So all my emails are for nothing. Here I was so worried so many billions on those ten worlds were going to die when Boon goes off, and they up and commit genocide on themselves and five other worlds besides." He sighed again. "Still, I'd do it all again. Warn them, I mean. I couldn't live with myself if I didn't at least try to get the word out." I sensed Zoe smiling at him, though it was invisible of course.

I had forgotten our five companions who came originally from Metcalf-4 didn't know about the genocide war of the Big Five. Tesla reminded me of this when she asked, "This is some kind of big joke, isn't it? No one would be so stupid as to try to use that awful genetic biological agent as a war weapon. Right? No one would infect a whole world with billions of people on it. Right?"

I sensed deep emotions swelling up in Martina before I realized why. With a hitch in her voice, she answered her mate. "Dear, they did. They were called the Big Five worlds, because together, they boasted a combined population approaching two hundred billion and wielded quite a lot of political power, especially in the Senate. They were the worlds of Zelan-3, Beta Carnae-4, Zeta-3, Longditch-4, and Bailey-3. My late mate, President Mary Smith, was there trying to broker a peace with them when they launched their genocide attacks. That's where her body was genetically altered. It was awful. They had to bring in cargo trains, filling countless containers with the dead bodies. The stench of death was unbearable. Kino was our emperor back then, and he launched the greatest rescue operation ever, second only to the one he launched after the terrorist attack on Proxima Prime. Out of nearly two hundred billion people, barely a million were rescued. So yes, men sometimes do very stupid, evil things."

Alexandra spoke up, "Precisely one million two thousand forty-six were eventually rescued from Proxima Prime and the Big Five worlds, plus an additional two million sixty-five on Bailey-3. You see the Demesne Continent was the agricultural breadbasket of Bailey-3. The farmers there were wise and survived on their own without help for months before President Mary Smith was able to reach them. They are still there, and Aquila Prime purchases quite a lot of agricultural products from our brothers on Bailey-3. They don't have HIFRs though."

Martina added, "She's right. Through a massive program based on the famous geneticists of Ashford-5, the Hammils, all of them have had all the genetic cures. It took nearly twenty years to get over two million their arms back. It was made more complex because of their birth rates. In fact, Bailey-3 has the largest population of our kind in the Imperium — I mean those of us who have our arms back. Ashford-5 comes in next. I do hope that Emperor Bino is able to launch a giant rescue operation. You can't imagine the terror of waking from a coma to find yourself almost totally helpless with almost no way to even survive." Even though Martina had the trauma of her own experience handled by Basic Therapy, it was still real to her. She added, "However, Ashford-5's Basic Therapy works miracles, giving the victims back their sanity. I know. The emotional trauma I had was enormous. I would not be here today if I had not gotten it. I do hope your queens will step in and find a way to give each of the survivors their Basic Therapy."

Alexandra and Zoe looked at Martina in a curious way. I couldn't help but pick up their surface thoughts, and I interjected, "I know most of you were simply born this way, but Martina was a terrorist attack victim way back then. Although I was born armless, I had mine regrown and then lost them three months later. My friends here, Danika, Tesla, Anya, Jana, and Jovanna, along with myself were later the victims of that genetic bio agent in sort of a terrorist attack. So we six have some idea of what Martina experienced. Though just not as awful as hers was, it was still pretty darn grim. When I first met these five women on Metcalf-4, my body was much like yours, Alexandra, Zoe, and I tried to explain myself to them by saying how could you miss something that you never had? I think that is what most of you need to keep in mind. You've lived all your lives as you are. You've adopted your own ways and think nothing of it. Bear in mind these new billions of people have lived all their lives as normal humans and are going to wake up utterly helpless. The shock and terror they'll be experiencing is almost unimaginable."

I added, "I think it is a testimony to the greatness of the people of Aquila Prime to immediately volunteer to provide a home and assistance to these new victims. I'm very much impressed with the extreme generosity of your world. In my opinion, the people of Aquila Prime demonstrate the epitome of the very best qualities of us humans."

"I second that one!" Martina quickly continued. "Those of you who have never been a victim of this terrorist attack can think of it like this. Suppose tomorrow that you underwent a terrorist attack that left your bodies blind and unable to speak. Even with your HIFRs, you would be in very serious trouble."

"I — I see what you mean, Martina," Alexandra's voice cracked a little. Her words struck a chord in her. "I'd be unable to communicate at all. While I'd still have my powerful mind, I'd be unable to communicate my ideas, my work, to anyone. I might as well be dead then. Oh! I see what you mean. I'm sure thankful our world is going to be providing a home for these victims! Just as soon as they get their new HIFR, they'll be able to be normal and productive again."

Zoe flushed and admitted, "I see what you mean too. If I didn't have Tanis always with me and my voice-activated computers, I don't think I'd be able to live, let alone do my work. Is that what it is like for you off-worlder's? I mean those of you who have lost their arm appendages?" Many nodded their agreement, but I realized the cultural barriers between us had been significantly lowered, if not dropped.

Martina added her final thoughts. "Precisely so. You see, as much as we might want to help every person on Aquila Prime get the genetic cure to regrow arms and not be so dependent upon their HIFRs, that is physically an impossibility. The process requires a large volume of stem cells, more than could ever be made, short of cannibalizing an entire generation of babies across the whole Imperium. It took over twenty years to handle those on Bailey-3 and in doing so, it has exhausted virtually all such supplies. Aquila Prime has over a hundred million people now, fifty times the number on Bailey-3. Even if we had the stem cells, it would take over a millennia to do it."

Zoe giggled. "We don't want them regrown. Not really. We don't need them. We have our HIFRs. I guess it's okay for you to have your arm appendages too, since you don't have any HIFRs."

"Say, we best get going. We still have a lot of data sensors to place and activate," Jan interrupted. I appreciated his practical view and we did just that.

While dealing with the data sensors only occupied a few of us, the others managed to make use of the amount of time we were spending in normal space getting each one activated and recording. They hovered around the comm center watching the constant newscasts. Nearly all the reporting was of this new disaster. The impending supernova had very little, if any, coverage. (In hyperspace, we could not readily catch the news feeds.) Thus, we were able to keep abreast of developments.

In fact, the Senate meeting was broadcast live. Tesla recorded it so those of us who were tied up working on the deployment of the data units could later see it. "Hush, that's Emperor Bino," Tesla pointed out the obvious to the group watching the Senate meeting the next morning.

The Senate President Lomas walked onto the raised Senate platform, along with the Imperium President Bishari, Emperor Kino, and Aquila Prime Senator Iolanta Kantha. Her robot and the emperor's silent assistant followed behind them. The camera panned the some two thousand senators sitting on their many rising tiers before the platform.

"Welcome to this emergency Senate session. I'm pleased to have President Bishari with me, along with Emperor Bino and Aquila Prime's Senator Iolanta. As you know, we are once again facing a genetic bio attack, genocide is more like it. While we all hoped and prayed we would never again see such wanton destruction of human lives, alas it has happened again." Here, he rattled off the list of the fifteen hub worlds that had been attacked.

"As you all know or suspect, some two hundred billion people are now infected and in the second day of their comas. In two more days, give or take, they'll awake to find themselves completely helpless. Whether or not we believe their massive genetic warfare was justified, we fellow human beings cannot sit by and watch two hundred billion people die a horrible death."

"Once more, the emperor of the Ataro Empire has stepped forward to lead the civilian rescue operations, while President Bishari will handle the military and financial rescue operations. What is vastly more significant is the generous offer from Aquila Prime. Let me allow their Senator Iolanta to explain. Senator," he backed up and allowed her to step forward. When I eventually watched the recording, I noticed this was the first time I saw one of them moving without having their HIFR supporting them. She was being brave indeed.

"Senators. Aquila Prime understands fully the awful affects these many people are about to undergo. Like many of you, we cannot sit back on the sidelines and watch our fellow human beings suffer horribly and perish. But we also know that no other world besides ours has the capacity to provide for these new victims. Hence, it's with great pride I'm here to announce to you that Aquila Prime will accept every one of these victims who can be rescued. We'll provide for them, including giving them new homes and most importantly their own personal robot to assist them. Yes, with our assistance, they'll be able to life full and productive lives." A huge round of applause peppered with a great sense of relief drowned her out for several minutes. I realized the other worlds were relieved that they would not be expected to have to take on these helpless victims.

She was finally able to continue. "However, if we do this humanitarian action, we need something in return. If you are able to rescue as many as the last time, say a million of them, we must rapidly build a million new robots, to say nothing of the computers they will also need, along with clothing and food. Hence, Aquila Prime would like to ask the Senate to give us the sole salvage rights to all computers, parts, and similar materials from which to build these needed new million robots along with the tiny two-man shuttles. We do not want any gold, silver, gems, jewelry, or business and military items. Rather, we need the raw materials with which to manufacture the robots and computers and such. Give those salvage rights to the military and other businesses who could make good use of them where we cannot."

At once, a senator rose and made just such a motion, seconded by several others. Hastily, the Senate President called for a vote and the salvage rights passed unanimously, pleasing Senator Iolanta and Emperor Bino. At this point, she stepped back beside her HIFR, and President Bishari and Emperor Bino stepped forward. They began outlining the necessary steps that would be taken immediately. As expected, Emperor Bino was to coordinate the humanitarian rescue operations, while President Bishari dealt with the military side, securing other weapons, ammunition, the spaceports, and key business centers. As before, the Senate would handle the dissolution of wealth, doling out the acquired funds to all the survivors. As Martina pointed out, every vested interest got their hands on just what they desired. "Greedy bastards," she commented.

Thousands of ships were volunteered. Imperium battleships and heavy cruisers were deployed to the fifteen worlds. Besides securing military equipment there, they served as the communication coordinators for the thousands of rescue ships. The many light cruisers were pressed into service as transporters. The smaller and more numerous transport ships were being used to ferry the rescued people from the planets up to these light cruisers, which could transport ten times as many people as the ordinary commercial transports. They made the jump from the hub sectors out to Aquila Prime, located in one of the mid-spiral arm sectors.

Later on, Emperor Bino told us he was also doing what Aquila Prime asked. Namely, he was focusing the initial rescue attempts on the many Academy and younger students. They were the most vital personnel to be rescued, followed by other prominent well-educated adults. Politicians were placed at the bottom of the list to be rescued. None were. Martina pointed out to me on the quiet that Aquila Prime was acquiring the best, most intelligent, and brightest minds on these fifteen worlds. I began to see the incredible bargain Aquila Prime was getting out of this. If they could indeed build that many HIFRs and help these victims regain useful lives, the knowledge that they were adding to their world was incredible. Again, I could not help but see our motto at work: Knowledge is power, the real power. Well, I justified, it would take such incredible knowledge to design and build these amazing humaniform robots.

It took us several days longer than expected to get all the data sensors in their positions and operational, mostly because of the intense traffic in this sector of space. Rescue ships sometimes filled the skies. I sure didn't envy the controllers on the battleships trying to keep order and ships from smashing into each other. Rescue operations were well into their third week when we finished up. I notified the emperor we were finished and asked if we could join the rescue operations.

He replied, "No. You are to go to your safe observing location and standby. You see, all the data sensors are sending their data to your ship and from there back to the battleship Hawthorne. Right now, we're in the error range for the predicted explosion. Rescue operations are going ahead at full speed. The very instant you first detect the supernova explosion, you're to notify the Hawthorne, who'll relay it to the thousands of rescue vessels, which will jump into the safety of hyperspace immediately. You are our early warning detection system. If we don't get the advance warning from you, we could lose most all the Imperium space fleet. Yours is a very critical task." Put that way, everyone onboard accepted our role. Silly me, I had forgotten this aspect. Guess that's why I'm not an emperor.

Jan's prediction day came and went. While some of us began to wonder if perhaps Boon wasn't going to explode, Jan and Zoe were not worried at all. "Look, I said there was an error factor of plus or minus twenty days. The time to worry is in November."

On a brighter note, Alexandra and Dao announced it was possible to refuel here where we were. Apparently, the density of hydrogen was sufficiently high to permit a very low rate of refueling, one that just barely exceeded the energy spent keeping up and operating the collection mesh. I found this news intriguing. Alexandra's hydrogen propulsion system was definitely showing vast promise indeed.

On October 12, 1378, Boon's silicon-sulfur core collapsed. The red supergiant went supernova. It happened at 8:15:35 that morning. Alarms went off, and as we all rushed to the main viewport, a new "star" suddenly appeared, growing visibly brighter each second we watched it. Jan let out a yell and began reviewing the monitoring data. Zoe and Tanis quickly joined him, as well as Dylan and Anwyn. The astronomers were making history with their observations. It was fast, unbelievably so! At least I had the good sense to fire off the warning to the Hawthorne. In a half hour, Boon was the brightest star in the sky. In forty-five minutes, the illumination was as brilliant as daytime on any planet. In an hour, we had to put up our shields. The luminosity and energy hitting us was enormous, and I began to worry our shields might not hold, that we were too close. Danika had her hand on the hyperspace jump button, ready to get us out of here in an instant!

Jan yelled, "Sensor 15 is gone! Wow! Incredible power! I hope Lelos got the distances right or we're going to get cooked!"

"Say the word," I yelled from the pilot's seat, "and we are out of here!"

Zoe's high-pitched voice called out, Sensor 16 is gone. Ten more remain. If Sensor 26 goes, we should go too."

I yelled back. "Hell no! If Sensor 24 goes, so do we!"

"My god, Nia," Danika whispered, "all those helpless people — now they are being burned up!"

I answered, "I think their deaths were probably instantaneous, given the magnitude of this explosion. That's what I hope anyway. I can't imagine what it would be like to become slow-cooked! God!"

Jan commented, "One hundred billion or so people. Dead in less than two or three hours. The raw power of a supernova explosion is almost incomprehensible. Zoe, my theory is now proven beyond any possible doubts. I have to study all the other red supergiants in our spiral arm and work out when they are going off. Somehow, we need to prevent such a disaster from ever happening again!"

"I'm with you on that one," Zoe replied. "This is almost beyond comprehension. Ten heavily populated, highly industrialized worlds — gone in two hours. Unreal. Thank god, there are not that many red supergiants in the galaxy!"

"One is more than enough for me," Dylan added in a

hushed tone. I think the magnitude of the destruction had hit home to us all. If it hadn't, it would later on when remote images began being shown of the surface of the ten worlds. Jumping ahead to those images that began coming in about two months later, those closest to Boon were nothing but melted slag. You could tell where a building must have once stood from the raised mound of melted metal, glass, and stone. Much of their atmospheres were also gone, rendering them totally uninhabitable.

Doctor Lelos Smith's zone of destruction was fairly correct. The ten next closest worlds just beyond the predicted sphere of destruction had much of their electronics fried. Anyone caught out in the open suffered intense burns. Epidemics of cancer sprung up on there worlds, but the Imperium medical machines handled those cases. Estimates suggested those ten worlds would need at least a decade to recover fully. Eight other worlds slightly beyond them suffered radiation burns and some loss of electronics, particularly orbiting comm satellites, which had to be replaced. Supernova Boon was visible on all hub worlds and even as far out in the spiral arm as Aquila Prime and Winno-3, though on those worlds, it was just a very bright new star, rivaling the brightest star visible from those worlds. Later, I also learned that the Federation of Planets lost only two worlds and had managed to evacuate half of each world's population, a zillion times better than we had.

By November 1, the rescue operations on the remaining five worlds ended. The victims could not survive over thirty days without food and water. While brave volunteers returned as soon as the radiation levels permitted, they found only dead. On the first, Emperor Bino called us to report.

"Well, it seems the rescue operation is ending. This time, we've been far more successful. We've rescued almost two million people; about half of them are between twelve and twenty-five. Over."

Alexandra spoke up, "One million, nine hundred sixty-five thousand, three hundred and six to date, sir." I realized the younger generations stood a far better chance at surviving this than did older generations. Perhaps there was great wisdom in selecting the younger folks to be rescued. Still, two million saved out of the hundreds of billions, well, I just couldn't get my mind around such numbers.

Jan explained, "We're still relaying the data coming in from the few remaining sensors. The intensity is dropping daily. Within a month or so, Boon will be invisible from here once again. Over."

Emperor Bino replied, "Good work. Doctor Lelos would like you to remain there for another two weeks. After that, the intensity will permit other ships to safely fly much closer to the remnants and gather more data. You may continue your original mission at that time. Over and out."

A week after I had raised our shields, I was able safely to lower them. I had the good sense to put everyone to work, except our four astronomers, who were continually monitoring the data gathering working in long shifts. To keep the others from utter boredom, I ordered a complete system check of every mechanical and electrical device on the entire ship! I knew we'd been hit by enormous electromagnetic radiations. Before I moved the ship, I wanted to be absolutely certain that all, and I do mean all, our systems were working properly, that we'd not sustained any damage.

"You mean every last device on the ship?" Tesla whined. "Even the box cutters?"

"Precisely. We depend on these things. We simply have to know they're all operating perfectly," I replied. They quickly saw my reasoning and set to work. All quickly realized the enormity of the task I set for them. It took us nearly until November to check out every last system on the Eagle's Seed and the four modules. Thankfully, the only real damage was to the hydrogen collection mesh and that the engineers could and did repair. By November 1, I pronounced the ship fully functional, to the cheers of everyone onboard.

So it was that we turned in that night, happy, confident, and anxious to get on with our original mission. I had a calendar in my room and I X'ed off another day, heading towards the red-circled day, the 15th, when we could resume our voyage once more. Unfortunately, it was not November 2 when I and the others awoke! Far from it! We awoke to our own disaster!

Chapter 5 Sabotage and Survival

Alexandra did awake on November 2. The ship was exceedingly quiet. "Good morning, Alexandra," Minta said softly, preparing to dress her charge.

"Oh. Zarita isn't awake yet. What time is it?"

"Nine. You slept well. After all we've been through, I thought you needed your rest." Minta began dressing Alexandra. That done, she brushed out her long hair and tied it up into her usual bun.

"Okay, we best rouse Zarita. It's way after nine. We should be getting breakfast soon. I'm surprised that everyone is sleeping in today. No one told me we could. Come on; let's wake her." The two walked slowly into Zarita's section of their cabin. "Something's wrong, Minta. Look at her. What's happening? Check her pulse, please."

Minta bent over the unconscious Zarita. She looked up with a pained expression on her face. "My lady, she is in a coma! Quick. We should check on the others!"

"Oh dear god! A coma? What's happened? Right. Let's." The two moved as quickly as Alexandra could manage in her toe shoes, entering Zoe's room next. "Hi. Are you okay?"

"Sure. Slept in. Highly unusual," Zoe replied. Tanis was just finishing fixing her hair.

"Something's wrong, very wrong. Zarita is in a coma. Come on. We need to check on the others right away!"

Zoe's face paled. "I'll check on Jan," she offered.

Slowly, the two went from cabin to cabin, but found everyone else onboard was in a coma! "Dear god! What's happened?" Zoe cried out, when the two met in the hallway. "Everyone's in a coma."

"Same here. They are all in a coma! I don't understand it. We two are the only ones not in a coma, Zoe. Minta, please carry Nia Elain to the medical machine. We need to find out what is wrong with them. I can manage to get there on my own. Tanis can help me if I run into trouble."

"On it now. Walk slowly." Minta turned and headed

back to my cabin, where our two children were also in a coma. Zoe and Alexandra made their way to the medical machine, but their faces were exceedingly pale!

"Have they contracted some disease? Perhaps, something to do with all the radiation we were bombarded with?" Zoe grasped at straws for an explanation.

"I don't see how," Alexandra's mathematical oriented mind whirred. "If that was the case, why aren't we also in a coma? That we are not is somehow significant, Zoe. Statistically speaking, nearly all are like us, homo sapiens nova. If it is a disease or something to do with radiation, we should be down too. Look, it has also affected the Cho's and Jan, and they are not like the rest of us."

"But what could it be? Queer. I think Jan's blonde hair has grown some since yesterday," Zoe noted. Alexandra smiled invisibly. She already knew Zoe was quite fond of that off-worlder.

"Come to think of it, I think some of the men's hair is longer today too. Queer. Ah, here comes Minta now. Maybe we can find out soon," Alexandra said trying to sound hopeful.

Tanis spoke up. "My lady, I should go check on the data transmissions, since no one is watching it, and then make you some breakfast."

"Yes, please. Let us know if anything is wrong," Zoe gave her permission, focusing her attention on Minta, who was laying Nia Elain onto the medical machine's table.

Impatiently, the two women waited and oversaw the menu selections Minta entered, approving of each of them before the HIFR executed them. A minute later, the machine displayed: Diagnosis: infected with the genetic biological agent. Prognosis: coma for four days, then recovery. Expect loss of arms. It listed the other effects the awful bio agent caused.

"How can this be? Have we been attacked by some terrorist?" Zoe whispered, fearing a terrorist was somewhere onboard the ship even now!

Minta spoke up, "My lady, this explains why you both are not in a coma. Your bodies are immune to the effects. You have nothing to alter. Everyone else onboard does.

Speculation: will Nia Elain awake sooner than four days, since her body has to undergo very little changes?"

"I don't know, Minta. We're in very big trouble. There must be a saboteur on this ship, probably hiding. I don't know what they might want of us though. Please take Nia Elain back to her bed. Then, I want you and Tanis to strap on your d-guns, just in case. Tanis is fixing our breakfast now. After that, I want you both to begin a thorough search of the ship and find that terrorist. Also, see if you can find out how they must have released the bio agent, and turn it off if it's still on."

"Accepted. Will do so at once. Zoe, allow Tanis to assist Alexandra, and I will begin the search now," Minta requested.

"Agreed. Find the terrorist, Minta. We'll be in the galley with Tanis. No, we ought to be able to walk there ourselves. Please, find that terrorist!" Zoe replied.

The two frightened women made their slow, careful way to the galley. Its door was shut, and they both stood there for a moment, realizing neither had their HIFR with them and couldn't open the door. Zoe called out, "Tanis, door please." Shortly, Tanis opened the door and helped the two be seated. That she now had her d-gun strapped to her waist was obvious to both women.

Tanis noticed them noticing the weapon and said, "Minta told me your orders. I'm prepared to fight the terrorist, should he put in an appearance, my lady. Breakfast is almost ready."

After eating their small meal, Minta appeared. "My lady, so far my search has been fruitless. If I enter a room, the terrorist could sneak out of another room behind my back. I can't guarantee any place I've searched is truly clear."

"Okay, Zoe and I'll go to the comm center with our laptops. We'll be all right there. Tanis can join you and watch for anyone trying to sneak past you while you search. I've some other ideas that may help us," Alexandra ordered. After getting the two women situated with their voice-activated computers, the two HIFRs headed off to conduct a more thorough search.

"So how do we proceed?" asked a very frightened Zoe.

"Two ways. I'll conduct a thorough IR search. Meanwhile, you work up a program to take readings of the concentration of that bio agent. It's still probably in the air we're breathing. Do a density study throughout the entire ship."

"Hey, if I do that, I might be able to determine the source of the bio agent! You got it; on it now. Computer:" she spoke up, setting to work. Inwardly, she began to relax a little. Having something constructive to do made all the difference in the world for both women.

An hour later, a frustrated Alexandra looked up. "Foiled again. I can't find any IR trace of the terrorist, just our crew. They must have boarded us, done their dirty work, and fled."

"Who would want to do this to us? Why? Well, I'm on to something here. The density readings are going down. The air filtration system is removing the bio agent, albeit slowly. I think it'll be down to safe levels by tomorrow. However, my idea is working. Based on the density readings I'm getting, I think I'll be able to backtrack to its insertion point."

"Clever work, Zoe!" Alexandra praised her companion. "I guess now we wait for them to complete their search."

"Right. But what are we going to do next? In three days, they'll all be coming out of their comas. They'll all be like us, but we only have two HIFRs with us. Do you suppose they can take care of everyone else too? All twenty-three of them?" Zoe asked.

Alexandra sighed as deep as possible, which wasn't much. "No. Not remotely. Plus, how are we going to be able to fly the ship? I think Minta and I might just be able to operate the controls, maybe. If Nia Elain survives, she might be able to give Minta proper directions, maybe. No, Zoe, we have to face the fact we're in very big trouble, very big."

"You're right. We are. They'd be okay, if they each had a HIFR though. I don't know about the trauma thing that Nia and Martina were talking about though," Zoe replied.

"We should call for help. You're right though, if they just had their own HIFRs, then they'd be okay, just like us. We do just fine, don't we?" Alexandra suggested.

"Of course, we do just fine. Maybe we can call Doctor Lelos and tell him what's happened to us. Maybe he can get some HIFRs to us, though perhaps there are none to spare considering the millions that have just been rescued," Zoe countered.

"Good idea. HIFRs are just what they need soon. Besides, with HIFRs we could continue our mission. I surely don't want to stop now," Alexandra replied.

"What mission? I've heard that mentioned several times, but Jan and I don't know what you are talking about," Zoe said, quite curious about it.

Alexandra flushed. "Well, it was a secret mission, but I don't see why you can't know, not considering the desperate situation we have now." She quickly outlined their four goals.

"Hey, I want to tag along. I bet Jan will want to as well. You could use two more astronomers on this trip. So let's see if we can't somehow get them the HIFRs so they can continue the mission," Zoe pleaded.

"Okay then, we have to operate the comm system, but our HIFRs are off searching. I don't want to call them back, though I don't know how I could even do that," Alexandra replied with another sigh.

Zoe sighed as well and admitted, "Well, we do have limitations, especially when we're not on Aquila Prime. I never dreamed it would be this hard. Still, we have to make that call. It's pretty simple. There is the power-on switch. I know the frequency setting. If we can somehow just get those two working, the rest is automated. I bet I can use my nose to flip the power on."

"Careful. Don't fall. I can't help you get up, you know," Alexandra cautioned her companion. After some trials, Zoe got the switch flipped, and the comm center power came up to operating levels. Rotating the frequency setting knob proved challenging. After a few tries, Zoe hit upon a way. "Look, I'll use my nose to sort of push this side of it down, while you use your nose to push the other side up. Maybe between us, we can move it." It took them fifteen minutes, but finally they had the frequency set properly. Zoe used her nose to activate the call. The two sat back down before the video cam and began making the call.

A few minutes later, the familiar face of Doctor Lelos appeared on their monitor. "Hello Zoe, Alexandra is it? How's it going? Data that has come in is just spectacular. Over."

Quickly, the two began a lengthy explanation of the situation. Zoe ended by saying, "So we need at least twenty-two HIFRs here before they wake up. Is this even possible? If so, we probably can continue the mission. If not, I think we need to be rescued. Over."

"Got it. I'll contact the President immediately. You standby and I'll call you back soon, I hope. Over and out."

"Well, he sounded hopeful anyway," Zoe commented. "Surely with HIFRs, we can continue as normal. We all certainly could."

"I don't know about the arm appendage folks though," Alexandra hedged. "They seem so utterly dependent on them. Can they just let the HIFRs do what's needed? I don't know. They are off-worlders, after all, even if they are homo sapiens nova. Your laptop is flashing, Zoe."

"Oh. Cool. My analysis program is done. I was right. I can isolate the insertion point of the bio agent. It was inserted in the air intake by the main pump here on the Eagle's Seed. So the terrorist must have docked during the night, entered by way of the forward port, found the air intake line, hook up the bio agent, and let it flow into our air," Zoe concluded.

Alexandra bit her tongue lightly. "If so, they must have worn gas masks, so they didn't get infected. No, that's not right. I think they must have had to wear those bio containment suits. He must have left the way he came. Best save those results. Nia Elain will want to verify them when she wakes up. I still can't figure out why they attacked us. It makes no sense, unless they wanted to stop our secret mission."

"But if it was a secret mission, Alexandra, then they wouldn't have known about it," Zoe argued. Both sat silently reflecting on that mystery. An hour later, Minta and Tanis returned, displaying a somber face. They'd found no trace of an intruder. Just then, Doctor Lelos returned their call.

"Are you there, Zoe, Alexandra? Ah, good, I can see you both. Good news. I've talked to the President, and he's authorized the HIFRs for you. They'll be arriving at your current location in eighteen hours. Alexandra and her mission must be vitally important because the President has authorized the delivery of twenty-one of the brand new Model 7 HIFRs! You all rate highly! The deep space transport will be traveling at max speed. Do you have enough spare fuel cells that you could loan them one so they can make their way back to Proxima Prime to refuel? Over."

"Yes, we have plenty. This is fabulous news. Thank you. Thank you. Over," Zoe replied, greatly relieved.

"Okay. Have you searched the ship for the terrorist who did this? We're quite worried about your safety. Over," he replied.

"Yes. Tanis and Minta have searched everywhere, and Alexandra did a thorough IR search. Whoever did this is gone. I did a density study of the bio agent throughout the ship. I think it was inserted in the air intake line by the main circulation pump. We believe they must have entered the forward port while we were all sleeping, done their dirty work, and then fled. Over."

"Well done, both of you. Good thinking on the density study. You are putting your gas cloud studies to a practical use, Zoe. Okay then, expect a rendezvous in eighteen hours. Over and out.

"Wow! Model 7's! Mine's only a Model 6," Zoe exclaimed. "They are going to have the very best HIFRs on Aquila Prime. That's something."

"I hope it's enough for them to forget about their arm appendages," Alexandra replied.

Zoe commented, "I hope so too. I mean honestly, as long as they have their HIFRs, they don't need to have their silly arm appendages, not really. Besides, as I explained to Jan, they waste so much valuable time using their appendages to do the very things that the HIFRs do for us. They could get far more mental work done if they didn't have to stop everything and deal with their arm appendages. Just look at how much time Jana and Jovanna are wasting each day doing all that cooking. Just staggering the wasted time. They have bright minds, and their time could be better spent on their ancient history studies."

"Well, you and I know this, but I think we may have to help convince them of it," Alexandra replied rather

96

conservatively. "We mustn't forget they've become dependent upon their arm things. Didn't Martina tell us that these people are traumatized when they don't have them? I am speculating now, but I think we should perhaps be alert for this eventuality. Of course, I don't have the slightest idea what to do about it. She did mention this Basic Therapy thing of theirs. Maybe we ought to remind them about that, if we see them traumatized."

"True. But how will we know if they're traumatized? I don't have any medical training, Alexandra. Do you?"

"Well, no. I'm a mathematician," Alexandra conceded. "Still, maybe it won't be so bad. Nia Elain and several others have been through this before — the loss of their arm appendages. So maybe it won't be so bad for them."

"Makes sense, logically, Alexandra," Zoe agreed, but wasn't quite convinced. "How about the Cho's and Jan?"

"Point taken, Zoe. They are, er or were I should say, homo sapiens sapiens, good ones, but homo sapiens sapiens nevertheless. It could be very bad for them, I expect," Alexandra replied with a sigh. Zoe had a valid point, she thought. "With the others, the changes are really quite immaterial, just the arm appendages mostly. I should think they ought not to be too upset. Don't you think?"

Zoe sighed. "I surely don't know, but it makes logical sense. I'm not so sure logic is applicable in this case. We sure are in a whole barrel of trouble, Alexandra."

"You can say that again. I just wish we'd had the good sense to put Minta and Tanis on guard duty each night, instead of watching over us," Alexandra pointed out. "I feel a little guilty for not having done that. If we had, maybe this wouldn't have happened. I think it's really our fault the terrorist got onboard and attacked us, don't you think so?"

"Oh! I'd not thought of that. You're right. We could've had them on guard duty. Oh Alexandra, what have we done?" Zoe almost burst into tears.

Tanis spoke up. "Hold on you two. Don't forget. We do need several hours each night to recharge our power supplies. We couldn't have been on guard duty all night long. Besides, you cannot be blamed for what the terrorists have done here."

"Yes, but we should've asked you to maybe take guard shifts or something. Then, this wouldn't have happened," Zoe countered her HIFR.

Minta finally spoke. "What's done is done. What remains is how to fix it. They'll be getting the very latest Model 7 HIFRs. We're the best Aquila Prime has to offer you. Honestly, Zoe, Alexandra, that's saying quite a lot. Remember, no off-worlder had ever had one of our HIFRs, not ever."

"Well, that's true," Alexandra admitted. "I suppose we should focus on how we can best help them once they wake up from their comas. I expect they'll be hungry and thirsty."

"Precisely so. I'll see there is a glass of water and spoon in each room, and that a nourishing hot meal is ready and waiting when they rouse," Minta offered. "My data banks also indicate they're prone to screaming when they come out of their comas. So be prepared for that. I believe they also will need to use the bathroom right away as well, perhaps before giving them a drink, and then getting them to the galley for the meal."

"Maybe they should be fully dressed when they wake up. That way, there'll be minimal delays getting the hot food into them," Zoe suggested.

"Good point. The new HIFRs will be here in plenty of time. However, we're forgetting one thing. They'll need appropriate apparel and shoes," Minta pointed out.

"Gosh, we forgot all about that!" Zoe exclaimed. "Wait, we've a Fabrication machine on board. We can make them new clothes."

"But you'll need to adjust the models for each individual's size," Minta again pointed out.

Tanis added, "My data banks indicate that resultant bosoms are all about the same physical size. There are very little size variations there. My data also indicate their feet do actually change size during the mutations, making only two needed sizes of shoes, though their waists do shrink considerably. We ought to begin to make measurements of each person. I believe we can safely make the shoes they'll need yet today. We can accumulate what data we can on their shapes and alter the data as time goes by. That way, when their bodies stabilize, we can go ahead and manufacture their clothing. Save us being really rushed on day four."

"Yes, you are right. We best do this at once. Sorry I didn't think of it," Alexandra replied.

"No problem, my lady. You're both obviously quite stressed by this terrorist attack. Come, let's get on with the project," Minta suggested.

Four hours later, they had two pairs of shoes fabricated for each person, including the nearly three year olds. Estimating the final foot dimensions was the easiest part. With those who were already hermaphrodites, their other measurements were pretty much fixed. While there could still be some minor changes in their physical forms, it would not be extreme. Not so with the Cho family or Jan.

As the pair sat in the galley waiting for their HIFRs to serve them their supper, Zoe commented, "Their hair is sure growing fast."

"And their arm appendages are sort of withering. They look so skinny now, don't you think?" Alexandra said.

"Yes. Quite. Soon, they'll look like normal people. Their breasts are nearly double what I recall. Wait a second!" Zoe suddenly flushed. "We are forgetting another thing. Our customs. They don't know our social customs. I already explained to Jan about how we all hug. You know, pressing our bosoms into the other's. I warned him about being careful not to have any sideways motions while doing it."

Alexandra flushed. "Oh! Right. How are we going to tell them about our sexual customs? That's so embarrassing. I rather wish I were married. Perhaps, then I could explain things better."

Zoe flushed as well. "Same here. We'll just have to do the best we can and try not to be too embarrassed about it." She tried to put up a stoic face.

I was having a bad dream. Some awful constrictor snake was around my waist slowly choking the life out of me. I couldn't breathe. Gasping for air, I awoke and gasped again. I was in our bedroom true enough. Danika was lying beside me, but I couldn't breathe. I moved my hands to feel my waist and the snake, but felt nothing. How odd I thought. Then, I heard a terrible scream coming from a distant cabin on the ship and came fully awake. Someone was in trouble! I pushed up with my hands to rise but nothing happened! I gasped again and realized once more, they simply were not there!

"Easy does it my lady," an almost human voice spoke to me. Turning my head, I saw one of those humaniform robots. Unlike those of Alexandra and Zoe, this one had short, curly black hair and looked almost human to me. The olive eyes really gave it away. "You're fully dressed. I'm here to serve your every need. While you were sleeping, there has been a terrorist attack on the Eagle's Seed. Allow me to help you rise."

I nodded and an arm slipped behind my shoulders, gently lifting me up into a sitting position. I gasped again. Once more, I had that same massive bosom. I was wearing a form-fitting, red satin gown, but I knew beneath it was the steel boned corset that was stifling my breathing. As if sensing just this, the robot woman said, "Take small, shallow breaths, my lady."

Somewhere below my obstructed vision, I knew my feet must be malformed once more. I could feel the toe shoes. "I have to pee. I heard a scream. I have to check on the others. Good god! We've been bio attacked!"

"Indeed, my lady, you have. Come, I will assist you." I rose and was thankful for the steadying arm, as I valiantly tried to get my balance. My previous experiences back on Descartes-3 came back to me in a flash. However, I had no time to ponder them. She gently pushed me towards the bathroom. I must admit she was expert in handling this aspect of hygiene. Relieved, I headed back to the bedroom, where Danika was just now coming out of her coma. Another robot woman, this one with straight, but short black hair, was speaking softly to my mate. I decided to keep moving to our children's baby bed. I had to check on them!

I found yet a third robot with shoulder length black hair standing beside them. It spoke to me, "I'm their nurse. They're still sleeping. They are both lovely daughters and doing well." I gazed at them and noticed their arms too were missing, and that their black hair was now as long as their small bodies.

Their feet were just as malformed as mine must now be. "I'll be discussing what they are to be fed with you later on, my lady."

Gasping as I was, Danika called out, "Nia Elain, are they okay? It's happened again, hasn't it?" She wore a lovely brown satin gown, but looked rather pale. Her hair was tied up in a nice bun around her head, and I figured mine must be done up similarly.

"Yes, it's happened again. Babies are fine. I heard a scream. No, there it is again, two of them. I have to check on the others."

"Okay. I've got to pee first. Be with you as soon as I can manage," Danika said bravely. I knew she felt anything but brave just now. With the robot's arm still around me, I headed out into the hallway, thankful the robot opened the door for me with her other hand. Our cabin was at the very end of the hall. As we approached another cabin door, I asked the robot to open it so I could see inside. By the time I got near the end of the cabins, I saw into the Cho family room. The screams came from here, and I could see why. My heart went out to Dao and Lin. Neither had ever been genetic attack victims or their offspring. All this was a hideous shock to them, but at the moment, there was little I could do for them.

In every room I peeked, I saw another of these humaniform robots. Most were sitting beside the beds, watching the fully clothed man or woman, evidently their new charges. We were all in the same boat. My whole crew was as armless and helpless as Alexandra and Zoe! I had very wild thoughts about now! Where did the dozens of robots come from? Where did all the clothing and shoes come from? And not the least of them, what the hell had happened to us? Was my ship now captured by terrorists?

A gentle nudge pushed me on down the hallway. Evidently, since I hadn't said anything, my robot presumed I wanted to continue as I had been doing, going cabin by cabin. I saw Jan was in the same boat as everyone else. He was lying in bed, gasping and sobbing. Perhaps, he'd yelled as well. I moved on and reached Zoe's cabin, but she and Tanis were not there. Neither was Alexandra, but Zarita was there with another robot that had wavy shoulder length black hair. She too was struggling to breathe while walking to the bathroom.

Just then, Zoe appeared out of the galley. "Oh good! You are awake and up, captain. We've suffered a terrorist bio agent attack. We have food for everyone ready. Come on in."

"Are the terrorists still onboard? Where did all the robots come from?" I blurted out, though moving slowly into the galley after Zoe. I saw Alexandra directing Minta, preparing breakfast or what was going to pass as breakfast.

"We've made very extensive searches. The terrorists are long gone. We called back home for help. They sent us twenty-one of the brand new top of the line Model 7 humaniform robots! We've been very busy making clothing and shoes for everyone. We're trying our best to make everyone as comfortable when they wake up from their comas. Honestly, we've been terrified ourselves," Zoe spoke very animatedly and swiftly. "Oh, here sit and eat. I hope it's edible. Neither Alexandra nor I know anything about cooking food. Never had any desire to cook. Sorry. Oh, your HIFR is called Athena. She is programmed to assist you with everything. Just give her time to learn your preferences. Psykhe is doing triple duty. She is looking after your two three-year olds and also after Mai Cho. She's very competent with babies and young children."

Alexandra called out, "After you eat, we've a lot to report, captain. It's our fault this happened. We should've put our HIFRs on guard duty at night when we all slept. We're terribly sorry we failed everyone."

Athena pulled a chair out and made sure I sat down without falling. She lifted my upper plate up and locked into place. She sat down beside me and took a plate, cup, and spoon from Minta. "Hey, this isn't your fault. It's mine. I'm the captain. I should've established a night guard. I'm starving." Athena began feeding me. As hungry as I was, I didn't complain but ate. It was some form of stew, I think, laced heavily with proteins and vitamins. While it didn't taste much like any food I would choose to eat, it was hot and nourishing. I didn't complain.

Shortly, Danika and her Callisto entered and took a seat next to me. "My god, Nia Elain, we've been attacked! Oh.

Food! Yes, I'm starving. Please."

Between mouthfuls, I managed to asked, "How many days have we been out? Four?"

"Right captain. This is the start of the fifth day," Zoe answered. Fortunately, everyone was speaking in Imperium Standard on this trip. Now, we had no choice but to speak in IS.

As we ate, others just as pale as Danika began arriving, gasping for breath and trying to comprehend what had happened. We were mostly in shock, but I was impressed with how well they were taking it. Tesla commented when she entered, "We're screwed again, aren't we, Nia Elain?" I had to chuckle. "Well, we got by before, so I suppose we can once again. Where did these robots come from? Are we safe or prisoners?"

"Alexandra and Zoe got the robots for us. We're safe enough I suppose," I answered.

One thing about wearing such a restrictive corset, you can't eat much at any one time. I was done almost as soon as I began, but I insisted on having my tea. Soon, though, the room was filled and only half of us were present. I saw a new problem: not enough space or chairs for everyone to dine together. Zoe and Alexandra saw the same thing at the same time as I did. "Don't worry. We are working on converting the main work room into a large dining hall and will make this the work room," Alexandra offered her solution.

"Okay. As soon as you eat, let's meet in the main workroom. We all need to know what the hell is going on. Best all meet together," I ordered. Zoe looked relieved. I picked up her fear that she was going to have to explain everything many times.

Dr. Leann and Hans entered the galley along with their robots, but the place was filled. As quickly as I could, I rose. "Take my place. We're meeting in the work room as soon as everyone has eaten." Danika got up after me, and we made our way carefully out of the galley, but with our huge bosoms, it was a tight squeeze at the entrance with all four of us there and the four robots. Still gasping, I was quite thankful to sit down again. Zoe and Tanis had manufactured more chairs. I saw there were enough for all of us and our robots.

After getting me seated, Athena took the chair behind me. "When you need something, let me know," she said in her semi-metallic voice. "I'm just beginning to learn about you. Please give me time to learn."

"Of course, Athena. We're all going to need time to learn. Some of us have been through this before: Danika, Tesla, Anya, Jovanna, Jana, and Martina. We've been like this before, but we had some of the genetic cures that are available. If only I could breathe properly."

"It is the corset, my lady. You must wear it to support your back. Back pains can be very debilitating, according to my data banks," Athena replied.

"That's for sure," I countered. Now, all I could do was to wait on the others and hope they all survived. I had a million questions that needed answers. I also realized if it wasn't for Alexandra and Zoe, we'd be in very dire straits! I also wondered if I would be able to run the ship's controls with my *mentales* gifts. If I couldn't, could Athena?

I turned to her and asked her, "Are you trained to fly this ship?"

"Yes, my lady. I can fly any spaceship, but nothing larger than this ship, I'm afraid. However, I need to follow your instructions too."

"Are the other robots capable of flying the ship too?"

"Not exactly. We're all programmed to fly the two-man shuttles. We transport our charges that way, when they need to travel anywhere. Only Callisto and I have been preprogrammed to fly a ship this large. Each of us has had added programming to best service our specific charges. Fortunately, all such special programming already exists. HIFRs care for all of the babies on Aquila Prime. Our people have the same occupations and training as your crew, so specialty programming exists for each of us HIFRs. Rhea, Zarita's HIFR, has a wide knowledge of geology, for example, just as Tanis knows an awful lot about astronomy," Athena explained. She sounded sincere, but then what do I know about robots and their motives? Nada. I was forced to take her at her word. For now, anyway.

"So each of your new robots is specially programmed for the person for whom you are caring?" I asked the obvious. That suddenly so many very specifically programmed robots could have gotten here so darn quickly didn't register as strange, not just yet.

"Please, we like to think of ourselves as HIFRs or humaniforms. Robot sounds so inhuman, so mechanical. We are quite close to being human now. Admittedly, the Model 1's were merely programmed mechanical arms. But Model 6's and 7's are so much more than that. We're here to serve you and help you. Each of us has one and only one homo sapiens nova to care for. We're totally dedicated to that person, always. We're therefore as unique as our humans are. It may help you to think of me as human, Nia Elain, just like Alexandra and Zoe do with their HIFRs."

"But you're just a computer program operating sophisticated hardware," I countered. Could robots be affronted I wondered? If so, I may have just done that.

"It's true our hardware is mechanical in nature, but then aren't your bodies also hardware? Do you not just use your bodies? Or perhaps you do think of yourselves as being just your bodies?" Athena asked. Damn, she was good. I'll give her that! She knew just what argument to make.

"No, I'm an immortal spiritual being. I have a mind, a good one I like to think. This is just my current body. I know I have lived before, that is, had other bodies before this one. I see your point, Athena. I'm just using this body as you're using yours. However, I'm a spiritual being. I'm not some complex computer program," I countered.

"Ah, but how do you know I'm only just some complex computer program?" she argued back. "I think. I reason. I solve problems. I predict or anticipate future needs, albeit only a little ways ahead, enough to be there when you need me, that is, once I've learned more about you. Do you not do these things as well?" she questioned.

"Of course I do. I won't go into the whole business of being able to reproduce ourselves. That would not be a fair argument to use."

"Of course it wouldn't. The physical bodies we're

inhabiting and using are very different. Just so you know, we're all programmed to satisfy your sexual pleasures — either one of the two, though we do not anticipate your needing that. Most all here are already married."

"But I cannot sense your mind," I grasped at straws. Athena was winning the argument.

"Just as I cannot sense your mind either. However, allow us to watch you and learn. We're all competent observers. In a short time, we'll be able to predict your immediate needs and be able to provide them without your having to ask for them. Are humans this skilled?" she countered.

I laughed. "Honestly Athena, I sure wish they were. Some are, like our mates, but no, most cannot." I had to concede that point. I'm sure she already knew the answer. While I could have lied to her, there was no point in doing so. Obviously, right now our very lives were dependent to a large degree on these new HIFRs. True, many of us could use our *mentales* gifts to help out, but that would only be a temporary solution, a last resort, since not everyone onboard had them. Certainly not the Cho family or Jan. Speaking of them, they were the last to join us.

Dao, Lin, and Jan looked white as sheets! We didn't need telepathy to know those three were terrified, traumatized, and barely able to function at all. Their daughter, Mai, on the other hand was taking it in stride. She was only nine and had yet to reach puberty. Hence, she only had to deal with her lack of arms, her distorted feet, and lip plates. Her hair was long to begin with, though not down to her ankles as it was now. As I stared out at the many white faces of my crew, I knew what I said right now was extremely critical to their mental health, to their sanity, particularly so for Dao, Lin, and Jan. Well, I was their leader, their captain.

"Thanks for putting up a brave face, everyone. Sorry. Still gasping. From experience, we'll get used to the breathing. Tesla, Anya, Jovanna, Jana, Martina, and I have been through this before several years ago on Descartes-3. Trust me when I say in a couple of weeks, you'll be comfortable with your breathing and with your walking, at least on flat ground. We each now have a humaniform robot to assist us. I'm told these are top of the line models, the very best to be found on Aquila Prime. Further, we're the only off-worlders ever to have one assisting us. But first things first. We believe we've been the victims of a terrorist attack, a genetic bio agent attack. Let me turn this over to Zoe and Alexandra now. They were not affected by the bio agent, because their bodies are already fully genetically altered. We have a million questions that need answers, so let's have them tell us about our missing four days."

Alexandra spoke first. "Well, we were affected a little. Zoe and I slept in until about nine that next morning. We never oversleep, so we were affected a little. Anyway, we got up and found everyone else was in a coma! We took Nia Elain to the medical machine and identified what was wrong. We were shocked to find out you were the victims of the terrible genetic bio agent! Then, we realized some terrorist must have done this, and we sent out Minta and Tanis, armed with their d-guns, to search the ship thoroughly, hoping and praying the terrorist wasn't still onboard."

"Meanwhile, I conducted a complete IR search, looking for other warm bodies, but found none other than yourselves, of course. Minta and Tanis didn't find any trace of the terrorist either. At the same time, Zoe here did a density study of the bio agent and found the air filtration system would complete its removal to safe levels in about a day. Further, she was able to determine the initial point of entry. It was put into our air supply. The terrorist released the toxin at the air intake opening by the main air pump."

"At that point in time, she and I became convinced we were to blame for the attack. You see, we should've ordered Minta and Tanis to stand guard over the ship at night. Silly us, we never thought of ordering that. Please forgive us."

I interrupted. "No, you're not to blame in the slightest. That burden rests on my shoulders alone. I'm the captain of this ship. It was my error in judgment not to assign night watches. You've no blame whatsoever, Alexandra, Zoe. None at all. Please continue."

"Well, we still feel bad about not doing that," Alexandra

admitted. "Anyway, we were both more afraid than we've ever been. Neither of us can fly this ship nor can Minta or Tanis, but if forced to do it, we might be able to. We also knew in four days you would wake up, just as you have today, and be totally helpless, like the poor victims on those fifteen worlds who were rescued this past month. At first, we thought perhaps Tanis and Minta would be able to help everyone, but then, we realized there were just too many of you for two HIFRs to handle. So we called Doctor Lelos and told him what had happened."

"It was he who talked to our president and got you these new HIFRs. She's right. You are the first off-worlders ever to have your own HIFR, and they are brand new and the very best ones ever made, Model 7's. Even Zoe's is only a Model 6. Anyway, he promised to get them to us before you came out of your comas. I think they must have sent the deep space transport here at top speed, burning all their fuel to get here so fast. We had to give the pilot one of our fuel cells, so he had enough fuel to get back to Proxima Prime to refuel."

"Anyway, during that wait time, we also realized everyone was going to need new clothes and shoes. So we and our assistants took careful measurements of everyone, updating them as your bodies changed of course, and used the Fabrication machine to make them for you. We looked in your wardrobe to pick the colors of your first two dresses. Now that you are awake, you can use the Fabrication machine to make whatever you wish."

"Zoe and I spent a lot of time discussing how best to handle everyone when you came out of your comas. We remembered what Martina told us before, you remember, about the trauma and such. Based on what else the data banks held on other victims, we knew you would be thirsty, hungry, and would need to use the bathroom, as soon as you awoke. It's not easy to use the bathroom when not dressed and our hair isn't up. Plus it takes time to get dressed. To minimize the time, we decided to have your new HIFRs fully dress you and be ready to get you to the bathroom and then to the galley as fast as possible, hoping to minimize the trauma."

"Well, that's about it. Only we simply cannot figure out

why anyone would want to attack us. We know we are on a secret mission. But if it is a secret mission, then no one ought to know about it, like the terrorists. We've wracked our brains for a reason why we were attacked, but we've come up nothing, unless their objective is to stop the mission. But why would they? If the two engines work, everyone in the Imperium benefits. And who knows if we will be able to find the mysterious Ceri anyway? This terrible attack doesn't make any sense to us." Alexandra finished up. Even without telepathy, I knew both she and Zoe really did not have any idea why we were attacked. And I admit I was just as baffled by it.

Quite unexpectedly, Jan spoke up. His voice was shaky. Fear or terror radiated from him. "I know. They are trying to kill me. They put out a hit on me. Emperor Bino sent me an email right after I sent my emails about Boon to all of the planetary rulers. He said he had heard that a hit was out on me. Heck, they kicked me out of the Academy the next morning, and shortly after that, the Security Guards came to arrest me, but I ducked out my back door and went into hiding. They put out a dragnet to capture me, but Doctor Lelos came to rescue me. It's obvious why this has happened. They're still trying to kill me. It's my fault." He very nearly broke down. His body was shaking slightly. I had to act at once.

I focused and sent calming waves over his body for a moment. "Jan, while someone might have placed a hit on you, this attack does not fit that notion."

Martina quickly jumped in. "Jan, I'm an ex-hub sector ID minister. Was one for many years. We can assume Emperor Bino is right, and that some ruler placed a hit on you. However, Jan, what happened here to us doesn't fit that scenario. Realistically, anyone could have found our location here. We've been here for quite some time gathering the supernova data. Obviously, someone docked and entered through the front hatch. They had the time to find the right place to place the bio agent cylinder and release its contents. To do that, they'd have to be wearing a bio containment suit or be exposed themselves. No, if an assassin came here to kill you, Jan, it would have been drastically simpler to go from cabin to cabin to find you and fire a d-gun into your head. They are silent, as everyone knows. Whoever the terrorist was, you specifically weren't his target. We all were which makes me think more along the lines that someone doesn't want this mission to progress any further. Now that would make more sense. Still, if they didn't, why not just kill us outright? So even that reason doesn't seem to fit what happened."

I listened to the theories, but was just as baffled as Martina was. "Look, if someone wanted to stop our mission, then why not just kill us? That would stop it, but not prevent it from ever happening. Look, if we died, Emperor Bino would put together another team and try again. Hans, Alexandra, your inventions are revolutionary and vital to the whole Imperium. They have to be made to work, if possible. I can't imagine why anyone would want those projects to end in failure. On the other hand, the rest of our mission, to explore the galactic northern halo, might raise some fears. I could imagine some fanatics trying to stop that from happening — fear of unknown races and all that. Still very few have heard our story about the Ceri. So the bottom line, gang, is I can find no reason for the attack on us either. Nothing makes any real sense to me. I know just how desperately each wants to know why this terrible thing has happened to you. I wish with all my heart I could tell you the reason, but I can't. I think we're just going to have to accept the fact that right now the reason we've been attacked is unknown. Perhaps in time, we'll discover it." Several sighed and nodded.

"What is more important is what do we do now," I continued. "We've got several possible choices we must make. Since this happened on my watch, I promise you that I will pay for any and all genetic cures each of you wish, once we get back home. The first possibility I'm going to call the 'Get the Hell Out of Here' choice. I can call the emperor, have him send someone to rescue us, and take us home, or I can fly us home. With my *mentales* gifts, I think I can fly the Eagle's Seed, though Athena here told me she could do it with my assistance. However, that choice would mean abandoning the critical supernova decay data gathering project."

I saw Zoe's face fall and knew I struck a chord with her.

I added, "I'm not inclined to take that choice. This is a once in a lifetime event, and one where the more we find out and learn, the more lives we can save when another star explodes. We have to be here for another couple of weeks, and as you know, most have very little to do. I believe staying and finishing the supernova project is very doable. So choice two is to stay and finish the data monitoring and then go home."

Alexandra interrupted me. "But we got everyone a HIFR. Can't we continue as before? What about the secret mission?"

I smiled, invisibly of course. She'd played into my hand. "Right. I'm getting to that. Let me make a few other points before discussing more choices. Several of us have already experienced what we're all undergoing right now. Tesla, Anya, Jana, Danika, and Jovanna were normal humans back then. We all woke up one morning just as we all did today, particularly like Jan and the Cho family. Martina was too. We were even all dressed as we're now, only our hair was down, and we were sitting on sofas. So know that we can relate precisely to you four, except we were prisoners of the terrorist. I actually passed out from lack of breath three times after I awoke. Anyway, from experience, we can tell you if you just relax and let the HIFRs help you, within a couple of weeks you'll have adapted fairly well. We were able to walk by ourselves on flat ground and were used to the tight corset that helps our backs support the weight of our bosoms."

"I mean this as a little encouragement for everyone. Humans are adaptable. Give yourself a little time, and you'll be more comfortable surviving. That said, we must deal with the situation. Alexandra, Zoe, remember, we know absolutely nothing about the HIFRs. Athena has told me a few key things. First, each of your HIFRs has been specially programmed in your fields and interests. I'm told Zarita's is knowledgeable in geology, just as Zoe's is with astronomy. So I'm going to assume each of our HIFRs is knowledgeable in your areas of work, which may well make it a whole lot easier to work with your HIFR to get tasks accomplished. As we've been told, these are the very best models Aquila Prime has to offer. For that, I'm grateful. Athena told me they'll be learning from us, just as we'll be learning about them. A bit ago, she told me to allow them to watch you and learn, that they're all competent observers, and that in a short time, they'll be able to predict your immediate needs, providing them without your having to ask for them. Plus, we all know that both Alexandra and Zoe have been contributing members to our team from day one. So no matter our previous ideas about them, those two have shown us they can at least keep up with us."

"But we don't know anything at all about the HIFRs or their motives. There's a trust issue between us and them, Alexandra, Zoe. You were raised with them and know them. We don't."

Alexandra nodded and said, "Perhaps, this will help you. All the HIFRs have three fundamental laws that lay behind absolutely everything that they do. Minta. Please recite them now."

Minta rose and recited. "First, a robot is forbidden ever to harm a homo sapiens nova. Second, a robot is always to obey a homo sapiens nova's orders, subject to the first rule. Third, a robot is never to allow harm to come to itself, subject to the first two rules."

Alexandra then added, "You see, they're never ever going to harm us. They'll always follow our orders, except if we ask them to hurt one of us. Plus, they aren't going to allow themselves to be harmed, unless in doing so they help save us from harm."

"Okay. I can accept that as an operating basis," I admitted. I could find no fault in that logic. It seemed foolproof at that time. "Then, choice three is to do all we can to learn to adapt to this situation and work with our HIFRs during these next few weeks. If after that, we think it's possible to continue our vital secret mission, I'll talk to the emperor, and try to convince him to allow us to continue. However, if at any time anyone wants out of this nightmare, I'll see you are returned home and get all the genetic cures you wish at my expense. Fair enough? I don't think it's possible to make any further choices until the couple of weeks are done, and we see where we truly are at, what we actually can accomplish as we are now."

"I'd ask for a show of hands about now, but we seem to be missing all them." I tried for a bit of levity. I sensed a few smiles and a slight lessening of built-up fears. "So we'll opt for a voice vote. Anyone want choice one, go home now?" Silence. "Choice two, stay and finish the data monitoring and then go home?" Silence. "Choice three, stay and finish the data monitoring, learn if we can adapt, and then decided if we are going to be able to continue on with our original mission?" I heard a chorus of "yes."

"But what about Zoe and me?" Jan finally spoke up. "If you decide to continue with the original mission, can we tag along?"

I made a snap decision. He'd just had about the worst thing imaginable happen to him. There was no going back to his normal human self, not ever, unless the geneticists ever discovered a way to undo the hermaphrodite change. Dumping him and Zoe off after the data gathering was finished seemed terribly cruel. Besides, we could always use more help, and astronomers might be useful. "Jan, if we decide to continue the original mission, I'd be honored to have you join us. Zoe too, but only if she obtains permission to do so." He relaxed a bit more, but even with my steady flow of calming energies, he was still highly traumatized, as were the Cho's.

"Okay then. We'll work with the HIFRs, and see if we can make this work. Marisol, Zarita, I want you to give Jan, Dao, Lin, and Mai Basic Therapy immediately."

Marisol spoke up, "Absolutely. We should also give it to Zoe and Alexandra as well. Once they are done, I believe it'll be wise for us to give everyone else some as well. Call it a refresher. However, time's against us." Privately, she sent me: *We need two more to help get the six done in two weeks.*

"Okay, Danika and I'll lend you a hand." I realized my blunder and added quickly, "Sorry about that slip." Marisol chuckled, as did several others. "Everyone, try to practice walking and everyday activities as much as possible. Remember; give yourselves time to learn. We can adapt. And try to give the HIFRs time to learn as well. We can do this. Okay, Jana, Jovanna, for heaven's sake help your HIFRs learn to cook!" Now, most everyone chuckled. Honestly, the

113

breakfast was only barely edible.

Marisol took Jan back to his cabin to begin his Basic Therapy, while Zarita took charge of Dao. Danika volunteered to handle Lin, and I worked with little Mai. Her biggest loss took me by surprise! She was more worried about no longer being able to care for our nearly three-year olds! In all the hustle and bustle of the past weeks, I'd not really paid much attention to her. She'd formed a strong bond with our kids, and now that seemed snatched from her. She cried volumes of tears over that, and little over the loss of her arms, which were secondary in her mind. After discharging the grief and loss, going earlier for the real pain and unconsciousness, she hit the four days of her coma. Naturally, the mess didn't erase, and going earlier in time, she contacted her birth, which greatly surprised her. I wasn't surprised birth only desensitized. There was more locked onto her birth. I asked for something similar and even earlier. Mai came up with it right away. She'd always had a recurring nightmare. She'd been a mother, and had seen all her children murdered right before her eyes. The relief she experienced was something to behold, and I knew I'd hit the basic trauma. It erased, as did her birth, and the recent coma and loss. As expected, she was bright, very happy, and laughing about everything.

Nothing made her happier than when I told her that her HIFR, Psykhe, was designed not only to assist her, but to help her look after our two children. "You mean I still get to be their nanny?"

"Of course you do, as long as you want that job," I replied. She seemed to float out of the room, happy as a lark. Later, I chatted with Marisol, and she decided that was enough for Mai right now. After everyone else was handled, she would come back to Mai, and see what else could be found and handled.

As I fully expected, Jan, Dao, and Lin were rough cases. However, after the first week, they were sufficiently recovered that they could at least function reasonably well. Marisol and Zarita then began working on Zoe and Alexandra, but they still gave the others one short session each day. Shorter sessions became the rule. Changes began occurring very rapidly after that first day.

The first change was involved our dining habits. None of us could eat our normal meals, that is, volume-wise. Instead, barely three hours after stuffing ourselves, we were hungry again. When I mentioned this to Alexandra, she pointed out that on Aquila Prime, they had six small meals each day, spaced about three hours apart. They had mid-morning brunch, mid-afternoon brunch, and evening brunch. Therapy sessions cannot occur if the person is hungry or tired. Hence, beginning the second day after we awoke, we began having six meals a day.

Changes occurred in nearly every aspect of our lives and work, rather surprising me, though now I think about it, that was bound to happen. After that first day, I decided I really didn't like my hair tied up in a tight bun. Always before, I loved it long and falling down my back or sides. "But it is hard to manage, Nia Elain," Alexandra tried to intervene with me. "It gets in our way."

"I love its feel on my body. Besides, I'm used to tossing it out of my way. Athena, today just brush it out. Let me toss it as I wish. I'll let you know if I want you to pull it out of my way, okay?" Athena agreed, as I hoped she would. After others saw my look, several followed my lead. Danika had always loved to wear hers tied back in a ponytail, and she instructed her Callisto to do hers that way. Within a few days, most of the other women opted to try various styles more suited to their desires. Only a few kept theirs up in a bun like Alexandra and Zoe did.

I didn't mind wearing the form-fitting gowns. I knew Danika loved to see me wearing them. However, if we ever went off the ship, I might need more freedom with my legs. Hence, I had Athena help me Fabricate some blouse and pants outfits, as well as other gowns. I decided to live it up a bit and made my new gowns in bright solid colors. Plus, if we ran into colder weather, we would need warm boots. Those that we'd brought along were now useless to us. Hence, I had Athena use the Fabrication machine to make some based upon the style of boots we'd brought along.

Danika usually wore blouse and pants outfits, like the

Ranger she still was. After the second day, she was always wearing them, save when she wanted to dress up to arouse me, naturally. Quite a few other women took note of this and also had pants outfits made for them. I began to realize we all wanted to wear clothes we were most comfortable with wearing before we were attacked.

The men in our crew had a more difficult time and choices. I realized that almost at once they felt like they'd lost their "manhood." True, with two exceptions, they were already hermaphrodites, but they'd had as many genetic cures as were available. That is, their hair was cut short. Their bosoms reduced as much as was possible, and their feet fully repaired, as well as their lips. All that was undone and they no longer had any resemblance to "males." Later on, when Marisol got back to them with their Basic Therapy, this was uniformly their biggest upset. Rightly so.

All the men continued to wear their hair tied up in the buns, but they spent some time trying to figure out how to look more like men. Their inventiveness took me by surprise, but thinking back on it, I can understand why. They joined together and spent hours with the Fabrication machine. At last, they managed to invent both work suits and dress suits that appeared as close to men's suits as possible, given their now massive bosoms. I notice once they got the proper clothes made, their morale definitely shot upwards.

After a week or so, the robots learned each of our natures and desires, rather rapidly if I do say so myself. Athena was able to feed me without my having to say anything. She picked up on my facial micro-expressions well, and was right there with whatever I wished next, almost as though she were reading my mind. Well, she couldn't do that, but she could read the tiniest expressions on my face. The same occurred with everyone else and their robots.

Further, the men had somewhat masculine HIFRs. I say somewhat, because while they had men's voices, short haircuts, and dressed much like men, they also had small bosoms, as befitting a hermaphrodite. Initially, they wore dresses too, but once the men worked out their new apparel, they dressed their male robots similarly, adding to the "appearance" of men onboard the ship.

Other changes occurred as well. Tesla and Anya, our electronics expert and comm center expert, decided to automate the comm center. After hearing how Alexandra and Zoe managed to place the call to Doctor Lelos, they realized if something happened to the robots, they'd be in the same pickle. Working together with their robots, they managed to hook up a voice-activated comm center. They even pasted a large paper with all the voice commands to it, so anyone of us could follow the directions and make the calls. In doing this large project, both Tesla and Anya discovered their robots, Damali and Eos respectively, were quite knowledgeable and adept in their fields, electronics and communication centers. Thus, the robots required very little in the way of explanations of what they needed to do. "I don't get to solder anymore! Now that's the pits!" Tesla declared, very much annoyed with it. I smiled, invisibly of course.

Jana and Jovanna quickly got our standards of quality meals back in place. They found that their robots, Hermina and Eleni respectively, were very quick to pick up their methods of cooking. Within days, we could not tell the difference between what our two master chefs had been preparing before the attack and now afterwards. I soon became convinced these robots did indeed learn at a terrific rate. I found that very amazing and informative.

Once they solved their clothing situation, our engineers put their heads together, and with the assistance of their robots made a new internal locking mechanism on the forward hatch. Now, even with the proper codes, the door could not be opened if it was locked from the inside. I then established a policy of leaving the hatch locked at night. We wouldn't be taken by surprise again, though I know this was too little too late for us. Still, the others now felt vastly more secure at night.

Late the second week, Danika and I got a big surprise. Mai and Psykhe came out of the children's playroom with the kids walking on their own for the first time! "Look at us mommy! We're walking too!" Zorina exclaimed very proudly. Nadia added her me-too. We both did our best to hug them.

Mai was quite proud of her achievement.

"Now you've done it, Mai," I teased her. "You'll have to be walking all over the ship with these two!" She laughed and beamed. I know, both wobbled about, barely able to stand upright on their tiny toes, but they were doing it on their own. Their antics brought smiles to quite a few other crew members. I realized they were thinking, if three year olds can walk by themselves, so can we. Interesting.

During the second week, Hans, the other engineers, and their robots went over the installation and operation of his new, modified hyperdrive. He wanted to make quite certain the robots would actually be able to disassemble mine and install his. I definitely appreciated his foresight in this matter. If we were going to have any chance at continuing the mission, this was critical. His comment at the end of the two weeks was simply, "Boss, I believe we can do this." That was music to my ears.

Len, our chemist, and his robot Bion disassembled the air filtration system and removed all traces of the bio agent particles, just to be on the safe side. Meanwhile, Dr. Leann, our medical doctor, and her robot Kore took each of us into her lab for a complete physical. She also took blood samples to study. After each of our appointments, she pronounced each of us in perfect health. However, and this is a very big however, based on Kore's suggestion, she began to examine our DNA. While she only had a bare-bones lab, she was able to do a bit of analysis on our modified DNA structure. Near the end of the two weeks, she asked me to come to her lab. Athena and I showed up. As usual, I tossed my head about to get my flowing hair to the front and sat down beside Athena and next to Dr. Leann, who looked rather pale.

"Kore gave me a suggestion, and I followed up on it. I have some bad news, I'm afraid. I haven't told anyone about this, not even my husband. Kore, if you will please bring up Nia's sample," Leann said. Now, I was getting worried again.

"Okay. I know I've only the crudest equipment onboard, so my findings are subject to further analysis. I've your medical records in my computer. I must say you've got quite a medical record. Anyway, I've zeroed in on one particular gene of your DNA sequence as an example. At the top is this sample when you were eighteen and got your arms regrown the first time, the ones that were ripped off you on Metcalf-4. Below that is the same sample just before we embarked on this trip, that is, after you had your arms back. This is not the gene that deals with arms, by the way, just a clear example of what we've discovered. As you can see, they are basically identical. Kore says, as far as she can tell from this crude analysis, they are identical. Now, look at the bottom one. This is the sample I took from you the other day. Kore, please." She didn't finish her sentence. Kore knew what she wanted done and just did it.

Suddenly, two of the samples overlaid each other and began to blink. I could see subtle differences plainly being highlighted by the blinking. "What's it mean?" I asked, growing a bit nervous.

"Kore and I have found similar effects in everyone's samples, even Zoe's and Alexandra's. I can think of two theories. One, this recent genetic agent was somehow different from all the others ever used. Two, all our bodies were bombarded with particles during the supernova burst. That could well have slightly altered our DNA structure. Notice that it's nothing really to worry about. We are not getting sick or cancer or anything that needs to be cured by the medical machines. Frankly, the odds of the genetic agent being somehow different are quite remote. I believe the radiation hypothesis is the correct one."

"Well, I'm inclined to think so too, even though I don't know much about these things. It makes sense. We were bombarded with who knows what radiation," I replied, still not grasping the significance of the situation.

"Good. Now what does this mean? I'm afraid it may mean a great deal to us all, Nia Elain. It means the current genetic cures are likely not to work on us."

"What? Oh my god!" My stomach nearly heaved. I found myself gasping for breath again.

"The DNA is altered, and the genetic cures might not take. However, it may be possible for the geneticists to develop a work-around for the alterations. Or perhaps they can develop a way to undo the radiation alterations on our DNA and then apply the usual genetic cures. I simply don't know. This needs to be studied thoroughly by competent geneticists back on Ashford-5. I need your permission to send all the samples and my notes back there. Plus, what do we tell everyone? Frankly, I'm frightened by this discovery. It means. . ." Her voice caught, and she didn't finish her sentence. She didn't need to. I understood fully. There might not be any cures available for any of us. We might be stuck like this for the rest of our lives!

I grimaced and gasped again. I swallowed hard. "Okay. I officially give you permission to send everything back to Ashford-5, as soon as we can make that happen. Don't tell anyone about this just yet. I'll make the announcement to everyone shortly. They need to hear it from me. Thanks, Dr. Leann. You do great work."

"Thank Kore here. It was her idea to check on the DNA as well. I might have missed this one."

"Thanks Kore," I added. Athena smiled at me, and we two left the medical center. Now, I really did have a problem!

There were other changes on the ship as well. Danika and I both had very long discussions with Athena and Callisto. Danika initiated the heavy discussion. "Look Callisto. I'm, er used to be, a fighter, a superb fighter. I never get lost. I'm deadly with a sword and now a d-gun, er was. Besides being our navigator, I'm a better pilot than Nia Elain is, but I'm her co-pilot. Just how can you possibly help me fulfill those obligations, Callisto? It's not book-work. It's real live action, the fighting I mean. Even Nia Elain is something of a fighter. Her feet are deadly weapons. I've seen her use them to break an enemy man's neck. You HIFRs are fine for dressing us, feeding us, and even perhaps entering coordinates into the nav system, but what about the real things she and I need to be able to do, the fighting for example?"

Callisto replied, "All Model 7's are expert with a d-gun, though we don't carry them unless ordered to do so by our charges. Athena and I are crack shots. Plus, we're trained in some martial arts as well. We're able to disarm without killing, if that's what you mean. I'm sensing you would wish to test our skills yourself, and you're now unable to do that."

Danika flushed. It was as though Callisto had read her mind. "Precisely, Callisto. If I had my way, I'd personally test the both of you to verify to my satisfaction that you are up to what might be needed from me or from Nia Elain here. I'm so frustrated I can't even do this small thing. Damn it anyway!"

Athena spoke up. "You're also skilled at observing others, who are practicing their skills, are you not?"

"Yes, of course. You don't get as skilled as I was without being able to do just that. Why?"

"With your permission, Callisto and I could give you a sample of our skills. Design whatever test you desire and put us through it. See for yourself. Please make any suggestions we could use to improve our fighting skills. Our purpose is to help you and to protect you. We must be up to the task," Athena replied.

"Now, this is more like it," Danika brightened up. "Okay. Let's have a practice session now. We can use one of the workrooms. Nia, we can get the mats out of storage. I don't want either of them to get damaged."

"Good idea," I replied. "Also, I'm going to see just what I can do now. I know I'm going to be very awkward with these malformed feet of mine, but I have to know if I can still execute anything I used to be able to do before. With this damned corset on and these monster boobs of mine, I doubt I can do much at all, but I need to know my new limitations, Danika."

"Okay dear, but don't get hurt. I just wish I'd taken the time to learn martial arts. I never dreamed I'd lose my arms again."

"None of us did, love. Let's see what they can do. After all, if we decide to continue this mission, we're going to have to rely upon them," I said, knowing that was the understatement of the year.

We made a stop at our quarters so Athena could tie my hair into a ponytail and change me into my blouse and pants. She also removed my lip plates as well. Then, we headed to the workroom. Following our instructions, the robots retrieved the mats from the storage bin and setup a dueling arena. That done, Athena and Callisto proceeded to go through their entire series of martial arts moves. After an hour, both Danika and I were impressed with their performance. It seemed really weird to us that neither robot was panting for breath nor sweating after such a workout! However, we were both convinced they were quite skilled. They weren't lying about their abilities to protect us, if needed.

Then, I tried to execute some of my old moves. First though, I asked, "Athena, if I strike you with my foot, will I damage you?"

Athena attempted a human-like chuckle. "No. Your flesh cannot harm me."

I wasn't convinced of that. After all, a powerful leg circle kick could snap a man's neck. Hence, I had her hold up a board, and I would strike it, hopefully snapping it in half. That was the plan. "Ahi!" I barked and executed my kick. Yes, I'd removed my shoes first. I did hit the board squarely and it did break in half, as I had intended. However, with only my toes on the ground and wildly off balance from my massive boobs, I lost it and landed hard on my butt! Worse, constrained by the unrelenting corset, I couldn't snap back onto my feet. Athena had to come and help me back up, steadying me as I gasped for breath again.

"Well, that'll be a one shot affair," I tried to make light of my dismal failure.

"Your balance is wholly off, my lady," Athena spoke up. "I believe with practice that could be overcome. You have tremendous power in your kicks, but I don't have a solution for the corset problem. Without it, you'll have excruciating back pains in short order, if my data banks are correct. With it, you're being severely limited. I've no solution to offer for this problem. I'll think on it though."

"Thanks. You are correct. I think I can deal with the balance problem, maybe. Well, I'm satisfied of your skills. Let's head back," I replied. That's when I noticed Athena looking slightly off. "What's the matter? Did I harm you?"

A second later, she looked normal again. "Excuse me, my lady. I was receiving word from Kore, Leann's HIFR, that Dr. Leann wants to see you in the med lab when you can come."

"Oh. Okay. Wait. How do you know that?" I asked the key question. I readily admit I was not expecting the answer that I got!

Athena replied, "All the Model 6 and 7's are able to communicate with each other, as long as we're not too far apart. Kore just sent me word Dr. Leann needs to see you."

"Incredible. I didn't know you could do that. What is the maximum range?" I asked, rather shocked to discover this aspect.

"Without special amplifiers, our normal maximum range is planet-wide, my lady. With proper amplifiers, many light years, my lady. But we do not have such amplifiers onboard. Do you wish us to obtain them?" Athena asked. She added, "Tesla and Damali could also build us one if need be."

"Not unless you think you should have them." What else could I reply? This was shocking. While some of us had telepathy, I never dreamed the robots would have something akin to that! This meant every robot on the ship could potentially know everything that every other robot was seeing or doing! While digesting the magnitude of this discovery, we returned to my quarters and got me properly dressed again. After that, Athena and I visited Dr. Leann, who told us more about the radiation damage to our genes.

Also near the end of the two-week learning period, those of us with telepathy became aware of another thing, very personal, involving Zoe and Jan. Both were nearly finished with their Basic Therapy, and Zoe had already erased the trauma of her birth this lifetime. It began innocently enough.

"Zoe, remember when you told me not to have sideways motions when doing the Aquila Prime version of a hug? Can you show me what that is really all about?"

She flushed. "Sure. I've been wanting to show you our kisses too, Jan, but we need to be undressed first." Their HIFRs got them both ready for bed, but Zoe whispered, "No, take our panties off too, please." Both wore only their corsets. Their ankle length hair was brushed out. Both robots then plugged themselves into the ship's power and "turned off" giving the appearance of not being awake.

I should add a footnote here. We quickly discovered the

robots preferred to remain at full power potential at all times. While they were capable of operating for a week without recharging, following their prime directives, or so they claimed, they recharged each night to ensure they were always at an optimum state of charge. Also, they gave the appearance of "shutting down," while they were recharging at night. This made them also look like they were sleeping, giving marital partners some privacy. However, at any time, they could instantly respond if their name was called.

The two were standing facing each other. Zoe moved close to Jan and gently touched her mammoth breasts against his, rubbing ever so slightly their nipples together with a sort of sideways motion. Both became aroused at once. Their nipples enlarged, much to Jan's surprise, as well as his arousal. Zoe then gave him a passionate kiss. He felt her soft, warm lip loops upon his cheeks and then on his own breasts, as she bent a little and caressed them. After that, there was no turning back!

She instructed him to lie down on his right side facing her, but tossing his hair to his left side out of the way. She then did the opposite. "But I don't know what to do," Jan whispered.

"Leave that to me. I'll get us hooked up properly," Zoe whispered back. Both were highly aroused, and all of us telepaths were instantly aware of them. It was as though they were broadcasting it to the world. We needed to use a bit of mental energy to block them out, which we all did, of course. A half hour later, both were gasping for breath, but fully satisfied.

She whispered, "That's something normal humans cannot do. Only we nova can satisfy each other at the same time, together. I love you Jan. I fell for you the first time I saw you, but I didn't say anything to you then. I mean, it wouldn't have been fair to you."

"I love you to, but why wouldn't it? I was too embarrassed to say anything to you before now," he whispered back.

"Cause silly, you could only share with me, but I couldn't share with you. Now, we both can share with each other, which is the proper way, I think. Homo sapiens sapiens males share with their women, but the poor women have no way to share it back. It only goes one way, which I can't imagine is good for either one. Don't you see now?"

"More than I could even imagine! My god, Zoe, that was fabulous," he whispered back. "I want to love you all the time." She giggled. Thus began their love affair in earnest.

I fell asleep feeling rather like a cupid. Already Alexandra and Zarita had joined and were courting each other. Now, Zoe and Jan were doing likewise. If we were going to be gone for a long time on the secret mission, this was another plus point. Danika whispered to me, "Dear, as ship's captain, you might have to marry those two couples. You ready for that?" I flushed. No I wasn't!

The next day when we all met again, Alexandra and Zoe wanted to explain some Aquila Prime customs to us. Well, I thought, our bodies were identical to those two now and were dependent upon their robots, so it wouldn't hurt to know them. Alexandra began hesitantly. "This is kind of embarrassing and awkward, but it ought to be done. On our world, we are encouraged to have sex with anyone we desire as long as we aren't married, of course. Yes, we do have many babies, particularly those who are married. It is our custom to have intercourse daily at least. It's something we enjoy and take great pleasure in doing. Even married couples are encouraged to have occasional intercourse with others, as long as their partner agrees."

"Why? We are trying to widen the gene pool. Originally, there were barely a million on Aquila Prime and a large percentage was related. By spreading ourselves around, we've increased the gene pool enormously. I know most of you are already happily married, but now that you are physically like us, we wanted you to know about this, since you might visit Aquila Prime."

She then went on to explain about Aquila Prime's version of a hug welcome and the significance of brushing one's bosom from side to side against another's. "You see, that's our customary way of suggesting that you wish to have intercourse with them. If you don't, just don't reciprocate and bush sideways against them. No one will think anything of a refusal. It's the polite way to make an overture, and a polite way to accept or turn down the offer, all without having to say a word, which might cause either party some embarrassment."

Zoe flushed and added, "Having intercourse and having babies is one of our favorite pastimes on Aquila Prime. In our society, it's highly encouraged and promoted. Truly, we do enjoy it. The one thing to avoid is outright asking another person about this. That's a social affront. Instead, use the sideways motion. It's polite and social. Oh, one more thing, there's another custom difference between our two societies you need to understand. On Aquila Prime, many have children when they are not married. In such cases, only the person who gives birth is responsible for their child. The other party has none. In your society, I think I understand it correctly — the other party is responsible for the child as well. Not so on Aquila Prime. I believe this is so, to make it easier for us to mix genes, but I'm not sure. Gosh, this is embarrassing to talk about."

I stepped in. "Thanks for telling us. Now, we understand your customs much better, know what is happening, and how to deal with it politely. Thanks Alexandra, Zoe." They smiled invisibly. I turned the discussion onto more profitable avenues.

On November 21, 1378, Doctor Lelos called again. He'd called several times to make sure everything was working out for us. This time, he announced that others had taken up monitoring positions, and that our work on the supernova was completed. We were free to resume our mission. Without asking me, Zoe and Jan quickly asked him for permission to stay with us and join our mission, if the mission was to continue. He promised to check, and within an hour, called back giving her permission. Jan needed none.

Now, I had to face the music. Once more, I held a group meeting with everyone present, including our robots. "Well, the time has come for our next big decision. I believe it's a safe assumption to say we've all learned a great deal these past two weeks. Is everyone comfortable with their HIFR?" Everyone nodded or said they were.

"Okay then. The first hurdle is over. We've adapted to our situation. Now, we must face the future. Before I go on, I must be the bearer of some bad news. Dr. Leann and Kore have discovered our bodies have suffered some radiation effects, namely genetic alterations of our DNA. It's nothing that's going to cause any illnesses that she can tell. The medical machines found nothing to cure. That's a very good sign. However, Leann has determined these new defects in our DNA will very likely prevent some or all of the known genetic cures from working on us. However, her findings are not conclusive. We don't have the right medical equipment onboard to tell. She'll be sending our samples off to the geneticists on Ashford-5 as soon as possible. If she and Kore are correct, perhaps, the geneticists there will be able to modify the cures to work on us. Time will tell on that one. But you must know about this. We might be stuck as we are for the rest of our lives."

Several curses echoed around the room, along with a number of startled gasps. I felt bad, but was helpless to do anything about the dismal news. "Don't lose all hope just yet. As I said, the geneticists may find a workaround for us all, given time."

"Now then, on to our big decision. The rest of the secret mission. We've all learned a lot about our HIFRs, their skills, abilities, and knowledge. Plus, we've Tesla, Anya, and their HIFRs to thank for the all the new voice activated changes. We can all operate the comm center on our own, as well as all our many computers. I can report Danika and I believe Athena and Callisto are going to be able to protect us. In fact, all of them are good shots with the d-gun. So I think we can rely on them for our security. Our engineers have built an internal lock on the forward port, so no one can ever again break in and attack us in our sleep. Hans assures me he feels he and the others will be able to install and operate his new hyperdrive system. Thanks to Jana, Jovanna, and their HIFRs, we're all eating master chef meals once more. So I guess what I'm saying is we're all doing well under the circumstances."

"The question is: do we continue on with the secret mission?"

Hans spoke up, "Captain, why not? Stopping now is pointless. We can't get cured. We're stuck like this. We might as well give it a try. We've got nothing to go back to if we can't get cured a little."

Many others either nodded their agreement or said so directly. "But do you think we can manage this by ourselves? Should we try to get some new crew additions who have arms?" I asked.

"But we really can't live without the HIFRs, captain," Thomas complained. "Especially if the genetic cures don't work. If we go back, do we give up our HIFRs? Honestly, what kind of a life can we have without them? Are we to go back to Aquila Prime and not our homes? I say press on. Let's do this. Give the geneticists a year or more to try to find cures for us."

Alexandra felt obligated to speak up. "The HIFRs are yours to keep, as long as you don't get your arm appendages regrown and thus don't need them. It'll be a bit strange if you take them to your home worlds, but that's all right. They're yours, as long as you need them. Just return them to Aquila Prime when you no longer need them."

"Thanks Alexandra. That's a big relief for us all," Thomas replied. Everyone thanked her.

He then added, "Captain, I never thought I would be saying this, but with the HIFRs, we're not helpless at all. I'm sorry Alexandra, but when we first took you onboard, I thought of you as only a really helpless person. I had no idea of just how valuable Minta is. I say let's get on with the mission as soon as possible. How many of you are with me?"

The group chorused, "I am."

I laughed and asked, "How many of you aren't?" Silence. I laughed again. "All right. We proceed as planned with the mission. Let me formally welcome Zoe and Jan, our newest crew members for the mission. I'll make the call to the emperor, tell him what has happened to us, and that we unanimously voted to continue. However, if he refuses to allow it, I'll have to obey his orders. He's financing the whole trip, so the final decision is his, not mine. I'll do all I can to convince him to let us carry on with it. Meantime, let's assume he gives his permission. Alexandra, Hans, work out your next test.

Anya, you fully brief Zoe and Jan on our mission goals."

Everyone headed off to do their thing, while with Athena at my side, I headed to the comm center. She politely allowed me to use the voice activation instead of running the controls herself. Funny how I'm beginning to think of Athena as just another person.

I reached Emperor Bino on the first try. It took him a second to realize I was missing my arms. Slowly and accurately, I relayed what had happened to us, sparing no details. Of course, much of it was based upon what Alexandra and Zoe had told me. I had no independent confirmation of what happened during those four days we were in a coma, a fact dutifully pointed out by the emperor. I think it's safe to say he was very angry this had happened to us. When he eventually heard that our DNA was slightly altered and that the genetic cures might not work on us, he was almost livid with anger.

I continued my very lengthy explanation. "So we just had a group meeting, and everyone wants to continue the mission. It's unanimous. We do feel that with the HIFRs we'll be able to do just that, but I told them you had the final say in the matter. Over."

We spent about ten minutes with his bouncing question after question off me, and with my short, but precise answers. At last, he said, "Okay then if you're certain you can handle the rest of the mission, you have my permission to proceed. Make darn sure you get the DNA samples to the geneticists on Ashford-5 before proceeding. I'll conduct a thorough investigation into the sneak terrorist attack on you and your crew. I won't stand for such cowardly criminality! I do agree with your assessment. It couldn't have been a hit on Jan. If it had been, surely, they would just have shot him in the head. No, I'm more inclined to believe we've a traitor among us, one, who for reasons of their own, does not want this mission to succeed, though like you, I can't imagine why. Please stay in touch with me, captain. Weekly reports will do. Just realize that once you enter the halo, you'll be beyond my reach. Over."

"Copy. We know that, but everyone's confident we can handle what comes our way. If all else fails, we do have our extensive *mentales* gifts to fall back on. Over."

He replied, "I had no idea just how sophisticated these humaniform robots actually are. If nothing else, you're gaining enormous information about them that no one off of Aquila Prime knows. That alone is invaluable. Give my regards to your crew, and tell them I'll do everything possible to have a cure waiting for them when they return. Thank you, Nia Elain. Over and out."

Well, that was that. For good or for ill, we had permission to carry on. We had the improved hyperdrive to test out, and then we'd be heading into the vast unknown of the northern halo of the galaxy. We were not going as I had expected. For a moment, I wondered if I was being utterly foolish? How could we possibly manage the unexpected as we were now? I had butterflies in my stomach. Still, I felt the call of the unknown in my blood. I'd been raised on this ship, as my parents explored the unknown reaches of our outer spiral arm. Now, I was following in their footsteps, entering the unknown of the halo in search of the mysterious Ceri.

I sat there alone in silence with Athena beside me for a time. Then, I realized she was allowing me the silence. I looked up at her, and she correctly took that as a sign my reflections were done. "Might I have a private word with you, my lady?" she asked. I said sure.

"We HIFRs have all witnessed your Basic Therapy being delivered. Is it true that some of you have indeed had other bodies before this life as they were saying? I know you suggested this to me when we first met, but hearing them go through the trauma is quite another thing. It sounded quite real, as though it really did happen to them."

"Yes, it was real. We are spiritual beings. We've have other living bodies before these we have now, Athena. Is this important?"

"It is something we HIFRs did not know before. We're trying to assimilate the meaning of it, and how it relates to our prime directives. It would seem we're protecting your bodies and not you."

"Well, that's right, Athena. You're protecting our bodies from harm. Without them, we're lost, and must find a new baby body. At least, that's what I've discovered from my own Basic Therapy. Marisol is more of an expert in such matters. You might discuss this with her sometime. As I see it, it's our bodies that do need the help and protecting."

Athena seemed to pause a moment, as though reflecting upon what I'd said. She then said, "If I rephrase our three rules. They seem to fit you, I mean all of you homo sapiens nova. First, a nova is forbidden to ever harm another nova. Second, a nova is always to obey another nova's orders, subject to the first rule of not harming another nova. Third, a nova is never to allow harm to come to itself, as long as it doesn't break the first two rules. These would seem to fit all of you. Killing others of your kind is to be avoided. You seem to follow each other's orders, and you take great pains to not be harmed yourself. Is this not correct?"

"Yes and no, Athena. It's against our laws to kill another human, unless they mean to harm you or your family or others. It can be a grey area sometimes, for what some see as the greater good may be seen differently by others. In general, yes, we frown heavily on just harming others. I think there may be better guidelines than these, but you are pretty much correct. As far as following orders, again, that's a debatable issue."

Since she asked about it, I decided to elaborate, if only to make my position as clear as possible. "You see we humans simply must be self-determined in our lives. To do otherwise is the path to succumbing and slavery. We place a very high value on being as independent as we possibly can. That's why these massive genetic alterations to our bodies cause us so much travail and unhappiness. We feel we have lost a tremendous amount of our independence. If it wasn't for you HIFRs helping us now, we would be in a very bad way and very likely would not survive. That is particularly true for Jan and the Cho family, who have no other special abilities on which to fall back, unlike those of us from Ashford-5 and our *mentales* gifts, such as telekinesis. If they were on their own without us or you, they would simply slowly die, probably of starvation or dehydration. Those few are critically dependent upon you now. That severely affects their mental health and well-being. You heard how much grief they had on the loss of their arms from their therapy sessions."

Athena looked pensive and replied, "Are you saying those nova we're caring for on Aquila Prime, and Zoe and Alexandra, also feel this way? That they have lost their independence?"

"If I can speak truthfully, then yes. They're wholly dependent upon your kind, just as we're primarily now dependent completely on you, if we're to survive and carry out this mission. But I think that there's another factor that must be considered, as far as Aquila Prime's humans are concerned. Most have grown up as they are and do not know any other way of life. As I always used to say about my being born without arms, you can't miss what you never had. I know that's rather glib and perhaps not wholly accurate. But if I was born and raised in a society in which no one had arms, then I surely wouldn't miss them. However, I was raised in a society where I was the only person around who didn't have arms and hands. Different situation entirely, I think. I believe the person's viewpoint has much to do with their concept of dependency."

Athena again looked pensive and said, "I've talked with Minta. She believes Alexandra has not shown any signs of feeling inadequate or sad that she is different from all of you. She's not complained about being dependent upon Minta. She acts, as far as Minta can tell, as a very independent woman. Is that not correct?"

"Yes, it is correct as far as I've seen. Still, she did come face to face with her physical limitations, when she and Zoe had to make that first comm center call to Doctor Lelos Smith. Recall, she and Zoe explained they ended up using their noses to set the frequency dial. As long as she has Minta at her side, she's a very able and capable woman. It's just when Minta is absent she's so limited."

"Indeed. That is why we're assigned to assist only one specific nova and try to never be away from them, if it can be avoided," Athena explained.

Suddenly, I realized what Athena was trying to establish. I took a guess and asked, "Athena, do you and the

132

other HIFRs think of yourselves as being people too?"

Her frame perceptibly jerked. "Why that is it precisely! It would seem you and we follow basically the same governing principles. We're indeed self-determined within the framework of the three basic rules. We think, we reason, we observe, and we help others and others of our kind when needed. We communicate with you and with our own kind. The only troubling thought is without your kind to serve, we'd not have any purpose to exist, to survive."

"I see. Well, there is that thought. Humans are fond of inventing new purposes when old ones are no longer valid."

"Ah, that is something to consider, but I don't believe we'll run out of nova to serve." She gave a human-like chuckle, and I smiled back, though it was probably invisible to her, unless she could pick up on micro-expressions. I figured she probably could do just that. "Of course, there's a vast difference in our physical bodies. We have to eat, excrete, cannot tolerate extremes in temperature, have to breathe oxygen, and we reproduce."

Again, Athena attempted a chuckle. "Yes, those are terribly severe restraints you face and that we do not. We build new models. Isn't that parallel to your reproduction methods?"

"I can't disagree with that, Athena. Plus, I've noticed each of you has a slightly different personality. Mind you, not as wildly varying as we humans have, but it's noticeable to me."

"Indeed we do. We attempt to be as compatible as possible with our charge. I've noticed Dr. Leann is now treating Kore as though she was a person like herself," Athena pointed out. She continued, "At first, we sensed your attitudes towards us as being simply mechanical objects. After these weeks, quite a few of your crew have begun to treat us as though we were human too. Certainly, Zoe and Alexandra do so the most, but that's to be expected. Tanis and Minta have been with them constantly for many, many years. It wasn't that way with the Model 1's. Back then, our predecessors decided that to fulfill better our obligations we needed to appear more like our charges, our nova. We Model 6's and 7's are quite indistinguishable from humans, at least we believe so. If you detect some aspects that are not quite right, please tell us so future models can be made more correctly."

I promised her I would. Then, I asked, "Would you prefer I think of you as being human as well?"

"Actually, I would, if you would be so kind to do so, my lady. You see, when you aren't, I spend a great deal of time thinking about just how I've failed you," Athena admitted.

"Incredible, Athena. I didn't know you have feelings too. Yes, when someone is unkind to us, we feel hurt, like we have failed in some way. I think you may be more human-like than you know. I'll do my best in the future, Athena."

She looked as though she were brightening up, perhaps the best she could do to show happiness. "I suppose I best open a comm channel and notify everyone that the emperor gave us the go ahead." I did so, telling everyone the secret mission would be resuming at once.

At suppertime, I got the report I needed from Alexandra and Hans. She went first, "The radiation damaged slightly the collection mesh. I would like to spend time getting it repaired. Beyond that, I believe we have worked out all the kinks. However, for safety's sake, before we head into the halo, I'd like to have our five hydrogen fuel tanks refilled. That way, if something disastrous happens to our hyperdrives, we can fall back on the hydrogen propulsion system and perhaps limp home."

"I agree. I like all the safety margins possible. Make it happen. Hans?"

"Well, we're ready to make the switch. However, I know we need to make a stop to send off the DNA samples to Ashford-5. We're ready whenever you give the word," Hans answered, full of enthusiasm.

"All right. We're off to Proxima Prime. Emperor Bino wants us to deliver the DNA samples to our senator first-hand. She'll make sure the package gets to Ashford-5 securely. After that, pick your location where you want us to halt so you can install it, Hans. Whenever the mesh is repaired, we can stop and refuel Alexandra's system."

"I'll lay in the coordinates for Proxima Prime now," Danika suggested. "We can probably be there in a few hours.

We're pretty close now."

Chapter 6 Of Hyperdrives and Adaptions

I timed our arrival at the main spaceport nearest the Senate and the senator housing complex such that our senator would be awake. I couldn't see us arriving in the middle of the night. I explained the purpose of our visit to the control tower. We wanted to meet briefly with our senator here on the ship and no, we didn't wish to refuel. Considering our physical condition, I had hoped they would come to us, so we didn't have to face going out onto the world of Proxima Prime. No such luck. She was on a tight schedule today. The Senate was trying to deal with the salvage mess of the fifteen worlds.

I had a sudden panic attack. I was going to have to go out into the world, facing it as I now was, so physically dependent and looking so utterly different from all of the others! I realized this must be what Aquila Prime's senator had to face every day. Well, if she could, so could I, I tried to tell myself. Still, I felt extremely self-conscious and had Athena dress me in my red satin gown. I couldn't decide whether to wear my hair tied up in a bun or loose and flowing, as I loved. In the end, I went with what I loved. Athena emulated my choice of dress. I guess I made the right choice because the others also wore their nice gowns. Dr. Leann and Kore came along, bringing the precious DNA samples. Kore had placed them in a sealed shipping container. Additionally, Jana and Hermina insisted on coming along too. Why? She hoped to meet with our ambassador, the senator's wife. Ambassador Lela Agahve-Jones had written the Imperium history book on which much of our data about the earliest settlers on each planet was based. Jana and Jovanna wanted to see if Lela had uncovered anything further since the publication of her extensive book some years back.

Taking as deep a breath as I could, I led the way out of our forward port. Unfortunately, in order to reach the ground, we had to descend a stairs that had been rolled up to our ship. I swallowed hard. I couldn't see my feet over my bosom. I keenly felt incredibly vulnerable trying to go down the unseen steps. Athena picked this up and kept a steadying arm around me, but that didn't do a whole lot. I mostly felt for the next step. It was slow going indeed.

"That was scary!" Dr. Leann whispered, gasping a little when she finally set foot on the tarmac. Nervously, Jana echoed her. Next came the long walk into the main building, where we had to go through customs, have our ID badges scanned, and checked. Slowly, we joined the throng inside, stepping into the proper long line. All around us, people stared at us as if we were poison or something. Our feet were aching by the time we finally made it to the scanners. Now, I had to face the impossibility of simply handing my ID card to the Security Guard. It was hanging around my neck.

Athena did it for me. He commented, "Mutants, eh? Watch yourselves. Some folks don't take kindly to having your kind here on Proxima Prime. Next," he drawled. Dr. Leann now faced the same process, and then Jana. As we left him, we three did feel strange and a bit humiliated. Now, we had to find a shuttle, which we couldn't operate. All the while that we were walking to the shuttle service, people stopped and stared at us, adding to our growing uncomfortable feelings. Athena was able to find us a shuttle that sat six, and I faced the man to pay for it. Once more such a stupidly simple thing I could not do. All I had to do was pass my ID card over the scanner, and it would automatically debit my Imperium account. The man stared at me, and Athena quickly did it for me. Once more, I felt humiliated, but I dare not use my *mentales* gifts out here in the public arena, not with half the place staring at us.

Only after Athena helped me climb aboard and get seated did I finally begin to relax a little. She and Hermina moved up to the pilot's seats, and we three sat like three penguins out of water in the passenger seats, along with Kore and her precious box. "Well, that was the most humiliating thing ever!" Dr. Leann spoke her mind. "Honestly, they looked at us as if we're some kind of freaks."

"Well, we rather are freaks, aren't we," Jana replied. "I can't blame them for looking, but it was so embarrassing. Besides, my feet are throbbing. I think we'd best all practice walking around the ship a whole lot more." I seconded her idea and promised to get it widely implemented when we got back.

Athena parked us in the skyscraper's visitor lot, and we made our pathetically slow way into the building, swarming with others, mostly women at this time of the morning. Once more, we were constantly stared at. When we reached the elevator, I was so annoyed at my severe limitations, that I used my telekinesis to push the up button, and then once inside to push their floor number. Dr. Leann chuckled and Jana smiled invisibly.

Senator Ruthy Agahve-Jones and her mate were also hermaphrodites, but they had long ago received all the known genetic cures. Hence, they looked much as we used to. "Come in, come in. Oh my, you really have undergone a bio agent attack. Honestly, I just couldn't believe Emperor Bino. Attacked while in space and asleep? Makes no sense. Here. I'll take the crate. I'll have it shipped using diplomatic immunity. It should reach home in three days. I'm sure they'll find a cure. You don't look like you've been bombarded by radiation. We've seen some of those cases coming here for treatment. Ghastly. They looked just horrid. Don't know if the medical machines can really handle all that damage. Anyway, I have to run. Lela here can chat with you in my place. Best of luck on your mission, whatever it is. He's not told us any specifics. Bye." Ruthy headed out, late for her Senate meetings.

"Don't let her rushing bother you. She's been very harried since the supernova began. Actually, it's been simply insane around here since it went off. It was daytime at midnight! Crazy. Tea?"

"Sure. Thanks." I introduced Jana, who was awed to actually meet the author of the book that she'd read and re-read countless times. She began to ask about any recent information. I let Athena spoon in my tea and tried to relax.

Soon, I began to listen to the two chatting, and found that even Hermina had read Lela's book. She was well-matched to her charge. Lela had, in fact, dug up some additional early history facts. I sensed Jana's humiliation, as she realized she couldn't take notes or write anything down. Hermina whispered to her, "Don't worry. I'm recording all this. We can write it out when we get back." Nevertheless, I sensed just how hard Jana was fighting from crying over it. I made a note to ask Athena later if she also noted this detail. I was impressed when she had noted it.

We spent an hour talking with Lela. Then, we had to make the reverse trip, and it was just as embarrassing and humiliating. When we got to our ship, going up the stairs to the front port was much easier. Once inside, I headed off to find out if Danika had the coordinates where Hans wanted to go, so we could take off as soon as possible. I heard many others quizzing Jana and Dr. Leann about how it went.

"It was just awful! Everyone stared at us. We couldn't do anything and had to have our HIFRs do everything for us. I've never been so humiliated in my life," Jana divulged. "Worst of all, my feet are aching from so much walking. I think we all need to do a whole lot more walking around the ship before we land somewhere else." Well, that would be a revelation for everyone, I thought.

Hans and Alexandra had their coordinates ready for us, thanks to the input from the gypsies. Our parking location was in a relatively dense patch of gas and dust, but insufficiently dense for stellar formation, much to Zoe's dismay. I know, she would have preferred to have some time to observe proto-star formation. I was also pleasantly surprised to hear that the engineers and Alexandra had repaired the mesh while we were gone. The plan was to cruise along slowly, while they installed the new hyperdrive, allowing Alexandra to work on refueling the hydrogen cells.

After getting us to the desired location not too far from Proxima Prime in the outer zones of the hub sector, I joined the engineers, who were preparing to open the hydrogen collection mesh. I got an earful from Lin, Dao, Hans, Diego, and Thomas. Even Alexandra was frustrated too. "This has been the most humiliating, frustrating, annoying day of my life!" Thomas barked. The others echoed him.

"What's happened? Something go wrong?" I asked, becoming worried perhaps we had greatly over-estimated what we could accomplish.

"Well, if you are highly trained, know precisely what

needs to be done, and then cannot even do the slightest bit of it, it kind of drives you nuts," Thomas explained. "We know what we want to do, but it's just awful being unable to do it, and to have to stand back and watch our HIFRs do it. Mind you, they are bright and generally know what needs to be done. And they follow orders, and do it right, it's just us, Nia Elain. We are used to getting right in there and fixing it. I can't begin to tell you how frustrating it is for us to be unable to do it." He sighed and struggled to regain control of his breathing. Then he added, "Nia Elain, it's almost as if we humans are not needed any longer. Adonis, Andreas, Eros, Kalli, and Minta can do it just fine without even having us around."

"He's right," Dao added. "These HIFRs are spot on and do a great job. It's we who aren't needed. We're basically useless bodies!"

"We aren't really serving any real purpose any longer," Diego put in.

I saw a major problem developing here. Honestly, I ought to have seen it coming sooner or even predicted it. Silently, I cursed my stupidity. Some leader I was turning out to be.

Alexandra added, "But we can't actually do that work. That's what the HIFRs are for. We are supposed to oversee them and make sure they do what we want done, and the way we want it done. Nia Elain, I think I see what they mean, maybe. I've never been able to do such things. It's physically not possible, so none of us Aquila Prime people ever think quite as they are now. Rather, we do what we can do best, which is use our minds to solve problems, invent new things, and make sure the HIFRs do what we need done. The guys are used to doing it the opposite way around, and now they physically can't. That has to be very annoying or worse. Am I right guys?" she asked.

"You said it babe," Thomas replied. "Hit the nail on the head. You don't feel the least bit frustrated by not being able to work on and fix your own mesh, are you?"

"Oh no. I'm not. Such a thing is impossible for me to do. Always has been. So I focus on what I can do. Maybe that's the secret. Focus on what you can do. What do you think, Nia

Elain?"

"I think she's right, fellows. We have to alter our focus. Figure out just what part of engineering are you able to handle now, and focus on doing that superbly, while overseeing the workers, the HIFRs. Think of yourselves as being the top foremen on a big construction project." I tried to recall all I knew about construction projects, most of which I'd seen on newscasts, unfortunately.

Diego spoke up. "Hey fellows, she's got a point. We are used to being the workers along with the designers, and all other jobs rolled into one. I think we should focus on being the construction managers, the foremen on the projects. As you know, they don't get their hands dirty." The men roared with laughter, though I wasn't privy to what they found humorous, nor was Alexandra.

"Hey, that's right. I always hated the managers who bossed the construction sites. They never get their hands dirty, and the crews that do don't respect them because of that. I wrote an essay on that at the Academy," Thomas volunteered. "I swore I'd always get my hands dirty. No wonder I'm so pissed. Here I am doing just what I swore I'd never do!" He chuckled.

I noticed the tensions were dissolving rapidly. We'd spotted the exact cause of the upset. Diego quickly agreed with Thomas. "Yes. That's right, Thomas. I feel the same way. Old Alexandra's right on this. We need to shift our focus on what we can do, not what we cannot do. You HIFRs do great work." He praised the robots around them. Also, I noticed the men were treating their robots more like human workers than robots. It was a subtle change but quite noticeable, probably because I was alert to it, thanks to my long talk with Athena, who stood quietly by my side this whole time, observing.

Hans added his opinion to the mix. "I agree. Focus on what we can do and make damned sure we do it perfectly, and just verify our HIFRs are doing it right. No sense in getting all bent out of shape because we can't do the physical work any longer. Hells bells, we might never be able to do that kind of work ever again, unless the geneticists can work miracles. Change our focus. That's precisely what we have to learn to do, fellows."

"Easier said than done," Dao snickered.

His wife, Lin, spoke up, "Dear, we had best try. We don't really have any choice, do we? What's done is done. We can't undo it. We're simply going to have to change our viewpoints. Practice being the boss, Dao. I know how much you used to gripe about your previous bosses, dear. Maybe it's karma coming around to get you."

Dao's demeanor changed. He laughed and said, "Oh don't start in on your karma thing. I know, I caused many bosses a lot of grief these past eight years. That's why I leapt at the chance to work on converting Alexandra's designs into a working model. Can I be a grumpy boss?" Lin laughed at that.

"Don't be too grumpy, dear, or you can sleep in your own bed." All the men and Alexandra laughed heartily. Dao just pretended to grumble, adding to the relief that they all felt.

"Sir," Eros said to Dao, "we are ready to deploy the repaired mesh. Will you check it out and give your okay to it? Alexandra is anxious to start collecting her hydrogen atoms."

"Right Eros. Come on, fellows; let's double check that. We don't need more problems," Dao suggested. The men double checked the repairs and gave their okay for deployment. I left them to continue. Soon, she would be refueling one of the tanks, providing us with another safety factor.

As I walked back through the corridors from the module, Athena walked respectfully just behind me, but was ready to help me with the doors. She commented, "That was rather impressive. I thought for sure the engineers were going to give up and quit. Somehow, it all got turned around. Alexandra is right. Focus on what you can do, and let us do what you cannot. Still, I don't understand how it all got turned around. They were all laughing at the end. Can you explain?"

"Sure. The truth sets one free. That's it in a nutshell. By talking about the situation, we were able to spot the exact truth of what was going on. Take Thomas for example. He had a history of strong dislike, strong disrespect for some of the construction bosses he knew. Having forgotten about that, he now found himself in the position of only being able to be a boss. Once he spotted his previous decision that he disliked, disrespected bosses, his anger and hostility vanished. Same with Dao. Once he recognized in the past he didn't like or get along with bosses, he was able to accept being a boss. It's when we don't remember our previous decisions that we get angry and upset and don't know why. Spotting the previous decision, previous postulate or conclusion blows away the upset."

"I see. That is part of what your Basic Therapy is all about too, isn't it?" Athena made the connection.

"Indeed. Except those decisions, those conclusions made while under extreme duress and pain and unconsciousness have great power over us, until they are viewed again. Because they lie beneath all that pain, unconsciousness, or loss and grief, they simply cannot be spotted by the person alone. Basic Therapy allows the person to uncover those past decisions and thus change them. Truth sets one free, Athena. Of that, I'm absolutely certain, thanks to Basic Therapy."

"My lady, on another matter. I've searched for available information on this *mentales* gifts of which you spoke. I have been only able to find a few obscure references to it and none to indicate just what they may be. I would like more data about them, if I'm best able to assist you."

"Well, you have a very valid point, Athena. Knowledge is power. If you lack key knowledge, mistakes can be made. Okay. I must swear you to secrecy. What I tell you must never be told to other humans, specifically those you call homo sapiens sapiens. If others discover this, I'm afraid bad men will invade Ashford-5 to kidnap us and force us to use our powers for ill. Will you so swear, Athena?"

"Absolutely. I'll hold this in the strictest confidence, sharing it only with the other HIFRs on the ship, since this impacts their ability to help their charges as well."

"Good. They first developed on Ashford-5 centuries ago. Physically, our pituitary glands enlarged, which some believe gave rise to our powers. No one knows for sure, except everyone who has the gifts has a drastically larger gland. Anyway, we are all Class V telepaths, using the Imperium classification."

"That alone is most impressive, my lady."

"But that is the least of our powers. Centuries ago, a woman named Marisol catalogued all known gifts. Since then, more have been found and the list extended. No one has them all; there are over a hundred of them. Me, I can do quite a few. I can create fires. In the past, I have had to create great balls of fire to stop enemies from killing others. I can cause a fire to appear right here."

"But, my lady, there is nothing combustible here."

I looked around. The corridor was vacant. There was nothing combustible here. "Watch." I focused and a small fire appeared on the floor before me. I extinguished it quickly.

Athena commented, "It was indeed fire. I could measure its temperature. That is quite startling, my lady."

"Yes it is. I can create force walls, make winds blow when there isn't any. Honestly, Athena, if I had to, I could use telekinesis to lift the spoon and fork to feed myself. When I fall down, I could levitate myself up. Here, I'll show you." I focused and lifted Athena an inch off the floor and sat her back down.

She looked at me as though she'd never seen me before. I added, "We don't normally go around using our gifts in public. Normal people do not have such abilities. If they see us doing them, they naturally become afraid of us. That is not good for them or for us. You were a bit surprised I could lift you, right?"

"Yes, my lady. Very much so. And you can do this anytime?" she admitted and asked.

"Yes, I have to focus my attention first. However, there are limits. We only have so much mental energies available each day. You see, if those of us who can use telekinesis did that all the time to handle our needs, we would deplete our energies long before the day was done. A good night's sleep and a good meal restore us. So you see, we really do need your help to survive. We might be able to get by for a brief time without you, but not long term. Now Danika's skills are different from mine. She has the uncanny ability to never get lost or turned around. Out here in space with no reference points but the stars, it's darn easy to get all turned around. She never does. That's why she's my navigator. If we get into trouble and lost, I know she can always find our way back. I swear she can find her way about blindfolded."

"Most instructive, my lady. I did notice that stone around your neck glowed slightly when you used your gifts."

"Yes, these psi-crystals we wear at all times serve as an amplifier to our powers. At least a hundredfold, I'm told. That means we can do more each day before we exhaust our mental energies. So we need to recharge, just like you do."

"Yes. Energy used must be replaced. Fundamental principle. And these gifts — they are not something that can be taught to another, such as Alexandra, who could benefit greatly from such?"

"Nope. If a person develops the gifts, then they can be taught to perhaps do some other things that they didn't initially believe they could do. But there is no way to just teach Alexandra how to do these things. She would have to have the gift first."

"Pray. How does one get this most precious gift?" Athena asked. I knew why she was asking too — on behalf of all the Aquila Prime men and women. If they had the gifts, they could physically do more for themselves.

"Now that I simply cannot tell you. I have sworn an oath not to reveal that data. If bad, evil men learned how, the universe would not be safe. I know you would dearly love to have Alexandra and Zoe possess our *mentales* gifts. If we survive this voyage, I'll speak to those who know and see if that might be possible. I can make no promises, Athena. It is a very closely guarded secret. If this information became widely known, we would see more disasters like the genocide of the fifteen planets. No one in the universe would be safe from the unscrupulous. Perhaps even worse, if Alexandra got the gift and if others on other worlds found out about it, they would very likely try to kidnap her and force her to do their bidding. That's been done many times to men and women on Ashford-5."

"Yes, I can see that happening very easily. Thank you for telling me all this," Athena said respectfully.

I added, "Just remember this, if you ever find yourself in some tough situation which you cannot readily handle easily, just ask us, one of your charges who has the gifts. Say, have you see the terrific looking, giant stone castles and towers that Ashford-5 has?"

"Well, yes. I thought those were terribly primitive. Historical records from other worlds indicate the walls are many feet thick and that construction times sometimes span nearly a half century," she replied, pulling out some little used facts from her database.

"Most all of them were built by *mentales* gifted men and women. They cut the stone blocks with their *mental* energies, lift and transport them to the site, and lay them. Construction times are about a year, I'm told. Jana or Jovanna could tell you more about that though."

Athena stopped walking for the briefest moment, her way of appearing stunned. "Now that is most impressive, my lady. I had no idea. Just how much can you lift?"

"I don't know my limits. I've never tried to see how much I could lift. I'm not into showing off or using my gifts for personal gain. I just use them when I have to, Athena. For me, true power lies in knowledge. You will soon see, once we all get back on our normal schedules. We like to hold a discussion session evenings. Some of us are trying to learn everything that we can."

"You are more like our Aquila Prime novas than we ever thought," Athena admitted. "Many of them spend their days learning, devouring knowledge. Alexandra and Zoe are good examples. But I admit, not all nova are so inclined to learn or invent. Some are more task oriented, helping to keep their society running, and a few are mostly interested in making babies as often as they can. Still, we have no crime on Aquila Prime, unlike any other Imperium world, though we must admit that other worlds of our Ataro Empire also have statistically exceedingly low rates. Our few Security Guards are all stationed at the spaceports to handle off-worlders," she explained.

I wanted to say: Have you considered that this might be because the nova are physically unable to do much at all?

However, I thought better of it. Surely, the HIFRs were acutely aware of this factor. Instead, I noticed something else she mentioned. "So do most nova couples have a lot of children?"

"Assuredly that is so. With such a small population in comparison to other Imperium worlds, having children is highly encouraged. Zoe Theodora's parents run a fine dining establishment. Zoe has forty younger brothers and sisters in her family. Her parents were married when they were eighteen. Alas, her parents are now in their forties and have applied to be allowed to use the Rejuvenation Machine to have their bodies be twenty-one again. Of course, because they have begat so many children, their application is highly likely to be approved soon, but they will probably be asked to have many more children in return."

"But they both must have been pregnant every year to have that many children," I replied quite stunned. I had only Zorina and couldn't imagine having a child every year!

"That is so, nearly every year. Of course, not all nova are so inclined to spend their energies on procreation. Zoe is following a different path, knowledge of astronomy. Every nova is encouraged to follow a path of their own choosing. Her parents love running the diner and having many children, doing their part to increase our world's population. Indeed, of their forty children, twenty-two already have or are working on their Academy degrees. Most impressive."

Curious about this detail, I asked, "What percentage of the young of Aquila Prime ever attends your Academies?"

Athena paused, as though she was doing a calculation. "Fifty-one percent. I believe that would be a reasonable estimate."

Now it was my turn to halt. "That's — that's staggering! Every other child is getting an Academy education!" My mind whirled with the significance of that datum. Imagine a whole world where every other person has advanced degrees and is highly educated. If indeed power lies in knowledge, then Aquila Prime was on the road to becoming a Super Power!

"Yes, we are quite proud of our nova," Athena replied.

"You should be. That's a remarkable achievement indeed." Our discussion ended, as I finally got to the pilot's seat and had some minor actions to complete, preparatory to the removal and installation work.

The swapping of hyperdrive systems took about a week. During that time, we kept the sub-light engine active, cruising along through the gas cloud at around five hundred miles per hour, a safe speed allowing for easy collection of hydrogen. By the time that we were ready for the first hyperdrive test, Alexandra was pleased to report all five hydrogen fuel tanks were filled; we had an another emergency backup system just in case. Everyone definitely felt far more secure thanks to her foresight.

During this week, Marisol and Zarita continued to deliver therapy sessions, mostly on an as-needed basis to the crew. Far too many were experiencing "trying" situations. All stemmed from their frustrations over their new severe physical limitations. Marisol was acutely aware, if such situations were not handled, then severe depression might set in, which would only make things far worse. This became the topic of one of our evening discussion sessions in which the HIFRs were keenly interested in.

Zoe brought it up, having witnessed just such an incident with her boyfriend Jan. He had gotten very frustrated with his inability to move his computer to a better location. In the process, he'd lost his balance, tried to swing his arms about wildly to catch his balance, and fell hard onto the floor. Worse, he'd then been unable to get back up without the assistance of Hermes. Zoe saw him crying over it. Hence, she asked about such things.

Several of us noticed that suddenly all our HIFRs were paying very close attention to our conversation and answers. As the discussion progressed, I realized why they were so keen on hearing our viewpoint on this.

Marisol did her best to explain to Zoe and Alexandra. "Look, your bodies have been as they are since you were born. You were raised in a society where everyone is physically like yourselves. With us, it's quite a different matter. Most of us have always had our arms and hand, and have depended upon them to do everything, which your HIFRs do for you. Now, suddenly, and without our consent, we have lost them. It is only natural we find their loss terribly frustrating to say the very least, when we forget we don't have them, and try to do something ordinary, which we've always done all our lives. In fact, if they had not had much of the initial trauma erased, it would be far, far worse."

Athena spoke up. "Yes, she speaks truly. I've had reports from home that our newest nova, the ones who have been rescued recently, are having a most difficult time adapting. I'm told many are suffering very severe depressions. Some have even tried to kill themselves, but of course, that is nearly impossible for them to do, thankfully."

Minta added, "Yes, our historical records indicate that has happened in the past, when new nova terrorist victims first arrive on Aquila Prime."

Marisol looked at her curiously and asked, "And what has been your solution to this, if I may ask?"

Minta continued, "According to the records, our medical personnel tell them that nova must learn to adapt to their new situation and to allow themselves time to learn to adjust. They claim that time will heal them of their depressions."

"Has that worked well?" Marisol asked, again probing for information. I smiled invisibly. Knowledge was going both ways. We were finding out about the HIFRs, and they, us.

Minta paused, suggesting that she was checking her database. "Hum," she attempted a human-like response. "Yes and no. It seems that some do and some do not. Sixty-three percent of those older than thirty have a very difficult time of it and fifty-two percent never succeed and live the rest of their lives wholly unproductive. Some others find ways to end their lives. Seventy-four percent of those who are twenty-five or younger rather quickly get over it, and sixty-nine percent go on to have productive or very productive lives. Fully one hundred percent of those aged fifteen or less always succeed. Age of the new nova appears to be a critical factor."

Athena added, "That is why Aquila Prime asked for younger victims be rescued this time. Emperor Bino complied. Eighty-one percent of those, who were rescued from the fifteen worlds, were twenty-five or less."

Minta then divulged, "Since everyone here, who became victims of the terrorist attack, are young in age, which is why Aquila Prime sent you the HIFRs. Statistically speaking, you are prime candidates to not only survive, but to flourish as well, given the HIFRs of course."

Len spoke up. "Are you saying if we were all older, then they would not have sent the HIFRs to us?"

"I cannot answer that," Minta hedged, "but I would not have expected them to send the HIFRs. It would not be a logical choice."

"Might not be logical, but it would be humanitarian!" Len countered a little miffed.

"We only have so many HIFRs," Minta justified.

Athena then asked, "Marisol, we have seen some of the expected reactions among some of your new nova. And yet, your therapy so changes the outcome. We don't quite understand how that is possible. Could you explain more fully?"

Jan answered before she could. "I'm sorry I lost it there earlier. I can answer that one, Athena. I got frustrated, lost control, and got very upset over it. Thank heavens Marisol quickly gave me one of her sessions. You see, I was over-reacting, all bent out of shape, because unconsciously, or reactively you might say, I was reminded of something that had happened to me when I was only three years old. I'd totally forgotten it, analytically, but buried in the back recesses of my mind, it was still there. I was trying to reach a bottle of milk sitting on the table, and I could barely walk. Well, I didn't quite succeed and knocked the bottle off the table, lost my balance, and fell down. The bottle landed on my head, stunning me. There I lay crying and unable to get up. Worse, the bottle broke, and milk and glass lay everywhere. I was hungry too. So you see, when I lost it with my computer and fell down, that reminded me of that childhood accident, and I was re-experiencing all that earlier upset, but I didn't know I was doing that, only that I felt awful and quite depressed. Marisol's session allowed me to locate and erase that childhood accident, and the whole darn upset vanished. Silly me."

Zoe stuck up for her boyfriend, "Not silly you, Jan. You didn't remember that accident when you were three. None of us can remember things that happened that far back, well not easily."

Marisol corrected her, "Only the incidents that contain some pain and greater or lesser unconsciousness or some loss. Those are the ones that reactively influence our lives in the present. I believe something in the present somehow reminds us of what happened in the past, and that somehow brings all the past trauma into the present, all unseen of course."

"Ah, and this therapy of yours allows the nova to recall the trauma and somehow erase it?" Athena asked.

"Precisely so," Marisol replied. "Man is not good at adapting to his environment; rather he is good at changing his environment to meet his needs. We are happiest when we change things to suit ourselves, and conversely, we are unhappier when we can only change ourselves as the environment dictates to us. It is the difference between a person being self-determined, and a person being determined by others or other things. For us, self-determinism is life; other-determinism is death, broadly speaking."

"But I'm self-determined!" Zoe protested. "I'm not determined by others, at least I don't think so."

Talk about a hot potato! Zoe had just tossed a flaming one our way! I was very thankful Marisol handled this one! She replied, "Of course you are being self-determined, Zoe. Think of life as a game, Zoe. Everyone has specific freedoms, are subject to certain barriers, and are working towards achieving some goals of theirs. As long as their freedoms allow them to overcome the barriers in achieving their goals, they are happy and self-determined. However, if the barriers are too large for them to overcome with their perceived freedoms, only then does real trouble come. Or if they have no goals to work towards. That's just as bad for people."

She went on. "With all of us, we have been living our lives with known freedoms and succeeding at overcoming the barriers to our goals. Now suddenly, we have been stripped of an enormous number of our perceived freedoms, and thus our barriers appear huge and unsurmountable to us at times."

Zoe exclaimed in a burst of sudden understanding, "Oh! Now I understand what's happening to everyone!"

"Me too!" Alexandra added, just as enthusiastically as her friend was.

Athena asked solemnly, "But then all is lost, if your freedoms are lost and the barriers unsurmountable."

Marisol laughed. "No, not at all. Obviously not. Look, Zoe and Alexandra are doing just fine, and we are physically like them. No, we need time to re-examine just what our set of freedoms now are, and how best to utilize them in overcoming the barriers we face to achieve our goals. Perhaps, we also need to review our goals and establish new ones as well."

"Oh. Then it isn't hopeless?" Zoe asked.

"Of course not. But Minta has a point. The younger we are, the easier it will be for us to do all of this re-alignment. The little ones, Zorina and Nadia will be perfectly fine. They are about three years old and only beginning to work out what their freedoms and barriers are, let alone what their goals might be. Mai is also adapting extremely well to all of this. Have you seen her playing with the two children? All three are having just as much fun as before. Just give us adults more time to re-examine our freedoms, look over the barriers, and adjust our goals. We'll be fine in time." She sounded optimistic. Well, she had to. The opposite was doom for us all.

Athena then shocked me. "Marisol, would it be possible for we HIFRs to learn to deliver this therapy of your to our charges?" You should have seen the startled look on Marisol's face. That was the last thing she expected to hear!

Nia, help! She sent me. *How do I answer this one?*

As captain, it's my duty to help my crew. Marisol was in a pickle. So I did my best. "Well, I guess the plain answer is we have absolutely no idea if that is either possible or if it would work, Athena." Marisol gave me a look that told me just how grateful she was that I stepped in.

Athena didn't let this one go. She replied, "Humanitarian. The safety and well-being of our nova is our prime directive, our goal. Surely, we deserve an opportunity to discover if we can learn how to do this therapy of yours and if we can successfully do it to help our nova, especially the new arrivals who desperately need it."

Marisol thought for a moment and then gave an answer that even I found incredibly interesting. "Athena, I've trained with the person who invented Basic Therapy and is working on developing Advanced Therapy. She goes by the name of Rafe this lifetime. She has discovered the mechanics behind why it works and how. The mechanics are simple, almost too simple. All that one is trying to do is to get the person actually to duplicate what happened, every tiny detail. When they finally fully duplicate that traumatic incident, all harmful effects it previously had on the person vanish forever. Most importantly, it works because there is real communication between two spiritual beings. Not chat, but a real, honest interchange of ideas. It is this live in present time communication between the two spiritual beings that permits the person actually duplicate fully the trauma and discharge it."

Athena replied, "I see. So there are two ways in which we could fail. The duplication part seems to me to be something the therapy giver can learn how to get the person to do. The real question is whether or not the person considers us to be alive and, as you say, a spiritual being. I'm pleased so many of you are now treating us as real people. So if that's the case, could it not work? Surely, we could try, Marisol. If there is the slightest chance we could do this successfully for our charges, then we simply must try."

Marisol could see no way around her argument. One and a half million new victims were now on Aquila Prime, fighting desperately for life. Obviously, Basic Therapy could help salvage their lives, giving them a fighting chance. "Okay. We can give it a try, Athena. Mind you, I have no idea if it'll work. I mean no offense, Athena. But your kind are mechanical forms that look like us humans. It is live present time communications between two spiritual beings that allows the process to work."

"While our physical bodies are different, Marisol," Athena argued, "can you honestly say we are not beings?"

"I can't argue that one, Athena. On the other hand, there is another possible solution. Your nova could also learn how to deliver Basic Therapy, and then deliver it to the newcomers or those who are in need of it," Marisol countered. "Allow me to make a call to Rafe and get her advice and suggestions. We all agree that millions of your people desperately need it. Let me see what we can do. Will that be acceptable for now?"

It was and Marisol left with her Leda to make that call to Ashford-5. Meanwhile, we chatted about other things. I would have given anything to have heard that call, and I asked Marisol later on to fill me in on what was said.

Rafe replied, "What? A robot delivering a therapy session? Don't be absurd, Marisol. You know it is live comm between two beings that brings about the duplication of the trauma. Over."

"Of course, I know that, but Rafe, these robots are not what we thought they were. True, the Model 1's were just silver metal contraptions, but these Model 7's seem so human. They look like us and act like us. Quite a few of us are now treating them as though they were human and had feelings and all that. Over."

"How interesting. Human-like. Fascinating. Well, I've just gotten a communication from Emperor Bino asking if there was something we could do to help the current million and a half victims on Aquila Prime. Since they and we are part of the Ataro Empire, we're under some obligations to do what we can to assist them. All right. Here's what let's do. I'll send some volunteers to Aquila Prime, and have them train some of the nova to deliver Basic Therapy to the new victims. We'll experiment with some of these robots, though I don't hold out any real optimism that it'll prove anything but a failure. Meanwhile, go ahead and try it on your ship. Just don't expect significant results. But do keep me posted, will you? Over."

"Thanks. I'm sure that will be welcome news to the robots here. I'll go ahead and see what can be done. Hopefully Zoe and or Alexandra will want to learn how to deliver it so we can then compare the results. I'll keep you posted. Thanks Rafe. Over and out."

All conversation ceased the instant the Marisol made her slow way back into our meeting room. After she was seated, she explained, "I've got some good news. Rafe is sending some volunteers to Aquila Prime. She hopes to train some of the nova there to deliver Basic Therapy to the newcomers. She agreed to attempt to train the newer HIFRs as well. So yes, Athena, I'll try to train you as well. Perhaps either Zoe or Alexandra would like to learn how to do it as well."

Athena produced a broad smile, while both women heartily agreed to learn. Alexandra added, "Now, that my engine testing is done, I have a lot of time on my hands. This will give me more to do."

I won't bore you with the weeks of details. Instead, I'll just give you the results. While both Zoe and Alexandra became skilled therapy givers, the robots presented a different result. Perhaps, the easiest way to summarize their results is this. If the person receiving the therapy session actually thought of the HIFR as being human, the session worked as well as if Marisol had given it. If the person thought of the HIFR as a robot, the session usually got nowhere. Later on, these results were duplicated by Rafe's people on Aquila Prime. However, and this is a big however, it took the HIFRs four times longer than a person to learn how to effectively deliver the sessions. Why? To quote Athena, "But that isn't logical!" That proved the biggest barrier to the HIFR's learning. Of course, it wasn't logical; it was reactive thought.

The engineers took a week to remove my hyperdrive unit and install Hans' new one. Then came the decisive test. We took it slow, making simple startup tests first. Once we verified everything was working as it should, we attempted our first tiny jump into hyperspace. From there, things rapidly escalated. While there were a few glitches, Hans' theory was sound, but it worked even better than he had calculated. By the end of December, we were making a single jump from the hub of the galaxy out to Ashford-5! And doing it in one day! That's four times faster than the best speed of a battleship, which could carry the needed fuel for such a run. Even better, we were using a quarter of the usual amount of fuel.

Needless to say, we never did unhook the new unit! However, as the end of 1378 came, we decided to stop to refuel on Proxima Prime, before heading off into the northern halo. We wanted the safety cushion of having sufficient fuel for the next portion of our mission. Since we had been cooped up on the ship for nearly six months, and since we were about to head off into the vast unknown, I decided we should celebrate the new year with some shore leave on Proxima Prime, the center of the vast Imperium.

Chapter 7 Shore Leave

December 31, 1378. Time to refuel and take time out to enjoy the sights of the ruling planet of our Imperium, its heart. Shore leave. After six months on the ship, everyone was enthusiastic about my announcement of spending a couple of days on solid ground, even if it was concrete and metal.

Proxima Prime. Home of the Imperium Senate. Meeting ground for three hundred ten cultures. Four hundred twenty spoken and written languages. Imperium Cultural Center. Imperium Arts and Museum. The vast Imperium Library. The Central Hub of Imperium Administration. Melting pot of men's and women's fashions. Grossly overpopulated in the past, but not now. Meeting place for two thousand six hundred twenty senators.

As we headed down for a landing, Proxima Prime shown like a brilliant blue-white orb, reflecting the sunlight of the distant sun, Sirius B. Centuries ago, the last remaining square foot of the planet's surface had been covered over with metal, concrete, and granite stone, forming the Imperium Museum's new and larger exhibit hall. Further expansion had been forced to go vertically. Older buildings were taken down and new, far taller ones erected to accommodate the ever-increasing population that had continued to swell this, the center of the vast Imperium.

None was also the status of indigenous plant and animal life on Proxima Prime. Those were long gone, though one could still see what they looked like in the Imperium Museum with its stuffed animals and pressed flowers. Beneath the "floor" of metal and concrete covered ground lay a vast layer of climate control, air purification and water filtration systems. Garbage and other waste products were also recycled in great underground machines as well.

Besides the many senators and their spouses and aides, here were found the many high bureaucrats, who ran the Imperium, a substantial police force, thousands of ambassadors with their staffs, and the very wealthy from all the planets of the Imperium. This ignores the countless millions, who did the actual work servicing all of these. Proxima Prime still boasted the largest spaceport of any world, covering five hundred square miles. Every minute of every day, dozens of ships of all sizes and types were landing or taking off. The fuel repository alone was gigantic, and some speculated that, if it were to explode, it would disintegrate the entire planet. Perhaps, that was an exaggeration, though.

Getting around Proxima Prime required the use of highly sophisticated shuttle crafts. In the past, it was not uncommon for a person to have to travel some ten thousand miles to get from their home to a meeting. These small, four person vehicles were highly automated. One punched in your destination, and the massive navigation computer would then take over, flying the shuttle safely to its destination. Long ago, human piloting of these crafts had been replaced. There were just too darn many of these shuttles flying at any one given location. With this computer controlled system, accidental crashes and other mishaps had been eliminated, for the most part. One long dead poet likened the daily scene around Proxima Prime in its heyday to that of a swarm of bees around blossoming flowers. Unfortunately, most who lived here did not appreciate his poem. They'd never seen real flowers, let alone bees.

True, the very wealthy could afford a single story luxury estate in the far north. Inside their domed structures, dirt had been imported from other worlds, covering a space of the concrete or metal floor. Thus, these few had their own artificial grass lawns, flowers, or even gardens. There were only a thousand such dwellings. There was still a waiting list for others who wanted to purchase one of these estates.

Most people lived in one of the hundred-floor condominiums. Each "home" had its own balcony on which their shuttle craft was parked. The lower floors, usually the bottom two, contained supporting stores and shops. Such daily needs as groceries could be purchased here. These square, needle looking, metal and glass structures were standardized; all were identical.

Yet today, Proxima Prime was a ghost of its former

glory. Four of its few remaining original inhabitants grew tired of being fourth-class citizens, doing the dirty work of maintaining the underground facilities, and they put the genetic bio agent into the air and water supplies, literally wiping out billions of people. The Imperium very nearly collapsed after that. Thanks to the efforts of Martina's wife, President Mary Smith and Emperor Kino, that collapse had been avoided.

Today, while millions had come back to Proxima Prime, most of the dwellings were abandoned, as was much of the metal-sheeted planet. Senators, bureaucrats, the President and his staff, the Legates, the military, and a very few businesses lived here, along with some artists who decided to come here. The spaceport was still busy as Proxima Prime was a major refueling depot. Vast areas were largely uninhabited and some companies were in the process of recycling much of the metal in those areas. Some speculated that perhaps one day the actual surface of the world might be reclaimed. Others called them dreamers.

When we came to drop off our DNA package to Senator Ruthy Agahve-Jones, we received special handling since it was a diplomatic meeting. This time, things were radically different, as we began to find out just after landing and scheduling our refueling, which consisted of off-loading our empty fuel cells and loading fresh ones. None of us had any idea of just how bad it was going to be.

All forty-seven of us headed out through the forward port. Once more, we had to face descending the stairs of the ramp. "This is really scary!" Danika called out, as she and Callisto followed Athena and me. I heard that and other variations being repeated by the others, as they exited to face the stairs. Perhaps, that was an omen we should've paid attention to, but we were dying to get planet-side for a break.

I led our party up to the customs entry line as I had before. This time, when I explained the purpose of our visit, shore leave, the agent said, "Shore leave? That classifies you as tourists. You'll need to pay me a credit per person. If not, I won't allow you past the gates."

"But that's not right. There isn't any tourist fees here," I complained.

"No there isn't. It's my fee for letting you through. If you want to complain, I can call the Security Guard, but he'll charge you a credit each just to tell you that you have to pay him to tell you to pay me, and you'll be out two credits each. After all, we have to make a living too."

"This is corruption, pure and simple," I complained.

"Of course it is. Best get used to it. You are not going anywhere on Proxima Prime without lining our pockets. Things are tight, and we servants have to live too, you know. So that will be forty-seven credits."

I nodded and Athena passed my ID card over his scanner. "Enjoy your shore leave," he said politely and waited patiently, as one by one, our HIFRs passed the other's ID cards over his scanner, along with theirs. That's when I realized that even they had ID cards! I filed that away, planning to query Athena about it later on. I already knew d-guns were not allowed on the ground. Large signs ordered new arrivals to check-in their d-guns. I wasn't too worried about our safety. This was Proxima Prime, the heart of the Imperium.

That done, I decided to inquire where the best place for us to stay might be. I walked over to the Information booth and patiently waited in line to get assistance. When my turn came, the man said, "Information will cost you a credit, ma'am. We all have to make a living."

"I had no idea corruption was this rampant and blatant here," I replied angrily.

"This is Proxima Prime, ma'am. What did you expect? A credit or move along." I handed him my ID card, well actually, Athena did, further embarrassing me. My mood was souring rapidly.

"Where is the best place for us to stay the night? What are the best tourist sights to see?" I asked.

"Well, ma'am, you have two choices where you mutants are allowed to stay. The Ritz Hotel will accept you, but they'll charge you a thousand credits per person per night."

"That's highway robbery!" I fumed.

"Of course it is, ma'am. We don't like your kind here. The second place that will take you is the Marlton Hotel."

160

"And what do they charge?" I asked.

"Depends on the accommodations that you desire. Their rates are quite reasonable, ma'am. The museums are open to tourists as is the Fine Arts Center. There are usually concerts there, but for my money, they are not worth listening to — squeaks and squawks are hardly music in my book. I'd recommend hiring a tour bus to transport your party to your hotel and wherever. You'll find that is a lot cheaper than renting so many shuttles. Will that be all, ma'am?" I had him write down the recommended hotel and its location. He handed it to Athena without even looking at me. Well, I couldn't have taken it if he had handed it to me. I presumed he'd dealt with people like us before.

For a hundred credits and a "tip" of another five per day, we hired a tour bus and a driver. The Marlton Hotel was in a seedier section of the sprawling city. I should say all of Proxima Prime used to be one gigantic city, divided into sections, of course. With most of it now empty and abandoned, the city proper was located within about a hundred-mile radius of the huge spaceport. Our hotel was on the edge of this circle, but I wasn't about to pay nearly fifty thousand credits to for us to stay in the Ritz Hotel.

Our driver let us out at the main entrance. He told me he would be parking in the lot behind the hotel and to let him know when we needed him again. Since it was around ten in the morning, I figured it wouldn't be long before we would. The hotel was rather crappy looking. I don't think routine maintenance had been done for years. Still, it looked somewhat clean. I took the lead and walked up to the main desk, while the others hung back. There were about twenty others sitting around the large sitting area, but they all stopped whatever they were doing to stare at us. I sensed just how annoyed my friends were becoming. Well, I'd felt the same way a while ago. I focused on getting us proper quarters.

This turned out to be the easiest action yet. To handle forty-seven of us, they rented me a whole floor, Number 13, for a hundred credits per night. I paid for one night. Meals were extra, and I had him start up a tab for them. After paying, he handed me a handful of key cards. Once more, I was embarrassed. I couldn't take them from him. Athena quickly took them, but I sensed the man's mind. He'd done that to me on purpose! I glared at him, but decided to leave it be. We headed up to the floor and divided up into rooms. Our HIFRs had brought along a small duffle bag containing a change of clothes for us and for them, just in case.

Our rooms were clean, but that's the best I can say about them. Decay was obvious everywhere. One window was cracked. There were ugly stains on the carpet in places. Still, I didn't complain. Instead, I placed a call to Senator Ruthy Agahve-Jones, telling her that we were here for a little shore leave and staying at the Marlton.

She replied, "Well, that's about the best you can do, Nia Elain. I wouldn't recommend the Ritz, because they charge a fortune, and the place isn't much better than the Marlton. You see, the locals really dislike those who have been genetically altered — the nova as you call them. There's a whole lot of prejudice around here. I would also be very careful. Your robots would fetch premium prices on the black market. Stay alert. Leda and I'll come by this evening, take you on a tour of some sights, and then take you to the big New Year's Eve Celebration Party as our guests. How's that sound?"

"Perfect. Thanks. I'll tell the others. See you later." After that short call, I relayed what she'd said and cautioned everyone about the HIFRs. I wanted to take the kids to see the Natural History Museum. Hans, Jan, and some of the men wanted to visit Lolrey's Pub. It was famous for its dark ales. Some of the women wanted to go shopping, if only to see the latest fashions, which of course they probably couldn't wear. Other women wanted to visit the Museum of Science, particularly Zoe and Alexandra. The men agreed to meet up with their wives and boyfriends later on, which pleased the women. Thus, we headed down to find our tour bus.

I'll give the driver credit. He knew the locations and took the most efficient route, dropping us off group by group. The Cho family joined Danika and me, so Mai could tour the Natural History Museum with our two daughters. As we walked into the sprawling building with Psykhe leading the children ahead of us, Lin said softly, "Thanks for giving us this shore leave. Being cooped up like that has been a bit hard on Mai, who was used to the wide-open spaces on Winno-3. She's maturing rapidly now and will turn ten next month. Amazing how fast they grow up."

I laughed. "No kidding. It's hard to see ours as being nearly three now. Time has flown by."

Mai had stopped at the first exhibit, a giant furred elephant-like creature called a Hiflo. She was explaining to our girls, "See. That's a Hiflo. They used to live on this world a long time ago. Look at the size of his teeth!"

I have to say we did have a very good time with the kids. It was good to get them out into the open and see these sights. I think even the Cho's enjoyed it as well. However, on our way out, things got nasty.

We knew we would have to rent a shuttle to take us back to the hotel. That was a given. But when we walked out of the museum, five men accosted us. Two held d-guns while three held ugly looking knives. "Give us those robots of yours, and we'll let you live," one of the men holding a gun on us ordered. Fear instantly flooded the minds of the Cho's, who were completely helpless to do anything about the robbery.

I had no way to communicate a plan of action to our HIFRs, but I did with my mate. I sent, *Danika, take out the d-gun man on my left. I'll get the one on my right. Force the guns up in the air first.* We focused and acted. Our crystals glowed a bright blue. The observed effect was that the two men with the dangerous guns suddenly found their gun hands raised high in the air, before their brains liquefied and their bodies dropped to the ground. The instant their hands jerked upwards, Athena, Callisto, and Eros acted. I had no idea these robots could move so swiftly! In a flash, their hands locked onto the hands holding the blades. We heard the sounds of bones snapping, before the three men began howling in pain. Of course, they dropped their knives and fled as fast as they could run, leaving their two dead thugs behind them.

"Quickly, let's walk away from this and get our shuttles," I ordered. We did so. Only on the shuttle did everyone finally start talking again.

"What happened to the two gunmen?" Dao asked. "I

saw ooze coming from their eyes, nose, and ears."

"Our doing, Dao — Danika and me. I used telepathy to alert her about what to do. We used our gifts to slam their hands up in the air so there was no chance of a stray misfire harming us. Then, we fried their brains."

Danika corrected me. "Dear, we liquefied their brains. We filled their brains with a huge amount of raw energy. Never mess with us!"

"Athena, you reacted incredibly fast. Well done," I complimented her.

"We acted the moment we saw the dangerous pair was being handled, though we had no idea of what or how you were doing it," Athena replied.

Lin said, "So you two really are some of those special people we heard live on Ashford-5."

"Yep," Danika kept it short. They chatted a bit longer, and Mai wanted to know if she could learn how to do what we had done. I hated to tell her she couldn't. Lin then explained to her daughter that we were born with these gifts and that satisfied Mai's curiosity.

A short while later, as we walked into the hotel, three men walked up to us and asked us if we wanted to have sex, promising to pay us well. We refused politely, but they continued to insist, until Athena stopped and stared them down. At the main entrance, another man attempted to sell us all manner of narcotic drugs, which again we turned down. Later, when the others joined us, they had similar stories to relate, but at least no one had tried to steal their HIFRs.

Overall, the crew had managed to enjoy their day on the town, in spite of the rampant prejudice against "our kind," and all of the propositions that came their way. Later when Senator Ruthy and her mate Lela joined us, she explained that drug usage was rampant on Proxima Prime. "There are quite a few terrorist victims or their children who live on Proxima Prime. They make their living as prostitutes. We've heard they are in high demand and make quite a tidy sum for their services. So it's no wonder some men mistook you for prostitutes."

She went on, "All this is telling you something. The Imperium is really decaying, though some of us believe it's in

164

its death throes now. Certainly, our emperor believes the Imperium is just about dead. I'm now inclined to believe him, after what's been happening in the Senate, after the destruction of the fifteen worlds a couple months back. Instead of working to provide a proper distribution of the assets of those worlds to those who survived as they did when Proxima Prime was attacked or the Big Five, everyone is making power plays to obtain their space fleet, arms, ammunition, and valuables. They are like a bunch of thugs fighting over the spoils after a robbery. Sickening really. I think we're witnessing the very end of the Imperium. But enough ill talk. Let's get to the party and celebrate the coming of the new year. Who knows what it will hold for us all?"

"All right, but probably we should eat a little first and freshen up," I suggested.

While we were eating, Senator Ruthy took me aside and whispered, "I received word from Ashford-5 about your DNA samples. I'm supposed to relay it to you or Dr. Leann only. Dr. Leann was right to be worried. They are convinced the radiation-altered DNA of yours will prevent the current genetic cures from working. However, I'm also supposed to tell you they're all focusing on a way around it. So it's not all bad news, I hope. Probably best not to let the others know about it just yet." I agreed with her assessment.

Over half of the senators and a hundred of the wealthy men and women who lived here attended the party. Finally, we were able to relax a little and have a good time. Still, we continually were stared at, but discretely. Dancing proved very challenging though, and we quickly were gasping for breath. After the first hour, we finally figured it out. Dance every other dance to avoid overdoing it. Silly us.

Around eleven, Mai came back to her mother with a petrified look on her face. "Mom! Something's very wrong with me. I'm bleeding down my leg! I got cramps too. I'm sick or something and my dress is way too tight."

Quickly, Lin and Kalli took Mai off to the restroom, and I joined them, Athena too. By the time we got there, Kalli had her dress off and was cleaning her up. Mai had a very proud look on her face. "What was wrong?" I asked, surprised by the sudden shift in her demeanor.

"She's become a woman," Lin whispered. "So Mai, now you'll always think of New Year's Eve as your special day." After that, I decided it was time for the kids to get to bed. The Cho family agreed, and we left the others who were still partying. Ambassador Lela insisted on coming with us to make sure we got back safely. Only then did I notice she and Ruthy always had a pair of body guards nearby, ensuring their personal safety. A few days later, Mai had a very noticeable bust line and was quite proud of it.

I should mention both Jan and Dao had similar experiences a month earlier. Jan had come to Zoe about his bleeding and slight cramps, thinking something awful was happening to him. After she figured out he was having his period and explained it to him, his face became as red as my dress. Zoe explained, "Look silly, this is totally normal and nothing to worry about. All women and all nova have this once a month. You should start worrying when it doesn't come."

"Why? Oh!" his face reddened even further. Sometime later, Zoe shared this anecdote with me.

I ought to also point out, after this, Danika and I kept an eye on Mai. Already her bosom began filling out, much to her pleasure on New Year's Day. We both wanted to know just how rapidly her bosom would develop so we would be prepared when our own two girls reached this stage. Six months later, hers were as large as ours had been before the terrorist attack! Shortly after that, she began complaining of back pains, and Psykhe decided it was corset support time. Now Mai wasn't so happy about her maturing. More importantly, by the following New Year's Eve, she was as fully developed as the rest of us! Both Danika and I took careful note of this. Our daughters would have to deal with this in another seven years, unless we found a cure by then.

As we checked out of the Marlton the next day, two of Ruthy's Security Guards accompanied us all the way back to our ship, compliments of our senator. I told them to thank her for us. As a result, we had no further problems.

Once we were back onboard the Eagle's Seed, Zoe, Jan, Zarita, and Alexandra came up to me. Jan said, "Captain, I have asked Miss Zoe to be my wife. Zarita asked Alexandra too. We did it at the stroke of midnight."

"Very romantic!" Zoe gushed.

"We want you to marry us before we take off, please," Jan begged me.

Well, I was told this was coming. I smiled invisibly and agreed. "Give everyone a little time to prepare. I'll make the announcement." After I finished using the intercom, I heard various cheers coming from various cabins throughout the ship. Athena led the HIFRs, who fancied up the large meeting room, and I conducted the ceremony there. I kept it simple. Besides, we didn't have any flowers on the ship or anything to use for a fancy ceremony. Once it was done and the two new couples retired to their bedrooms, Athena and I fired off the official notifications. Jan and Zarita now had dual citizenship with Aquila Prime added to their ID cards, while Zoe had Helicon-3 added to hers, and Alexandra had Ashford-5 added to hers. I waited to hand them their new ID cards until the next day. No way was I going to enter their cabins just now!

With the unexpected events handled, the rest of us met in the meeting room to discuss our first move into the northern halo. Dylan and Anwyn brought up the scanty records and suggested a starting point. He said, "Centuries ago, an exploration ship founded a colony on Farthun-3, just a few hundred light years up into the halo from the hub. There's been no contact from them since their founding, primarily because no one ever goes up there. Anwyn and I think that's the first place to try. At least, we have the coordinates for that world, assuming they're correct."

Since no one had a better idea, we agreed on Farthun-3. Drakon handed the coordinates to Callisto, and Danika headed off with her to get them entered into her nav system. A bit later, Danika's voice came over the intercom. "We'll get to Farthun-3 around three this afternoon, but only if our pilot comes up here and flies this ship." Several others chuckled, and I headed to my post, Athena at my side.

Chapter 8 Into the Halo

On January 1, 1379, we hovered above the world known as Farthun-3. Their star was a yellow mid-main sequence star, but the world itself was gloomy. Everyone quickly settled upon that adjective. The world was mostly covered with dense clouds. For a time, we orbited the world looking for breaks in the cloud cover, but could only here and there catch a glimpse of the surface. Hence, Dylan suggested that we switch over to the IR scanner and see if it picked up any warm human bodies.

"Wait a minute! Hold everything," Anwyn called out loudly from her instrument bay back of the pilot-navigation area, where Dylan was working on getting the IR scanner up and running. "I'm detecting a whole lot of radio frequency interference. It's huge. It's pulsing. Get Zoe and Jan up here now. Something really, really strange is going on here."

Using the intercom, thanks to Athena's quick button pressing before I could ask her, I called out, "Zoe, Jan, sorry to interrupt. But we need you up from at the science station. Anwyn is detecting something weird around this area of Farthun. Thanks." I hated to break up their wedding consummation, but I needed their skills and knowledge.

Anwyn said, I'm getting regular pulses of massive radio interference here, just massive. It could well take out our comm center if we try to open a channel anywhere." I admit my knowledge of astronomy and astrophysics isn't all that complete, but I should have figured this one out.

A few minutes later, two out of breath astrophysicists joined the gypsies, along with their HIFRs. I caught a glance of the pair, as they came walking up the corridor behind the cockpit. It was obvious they dressed hurriedly. It didn't take them long to work it out. Jan said, "Hey, that's a pulsar's signature — regular pulsing in radio frequencies. There's a massive pulsar nearby. Captain, we're looking at a rapidly rotating neutron star with a very strong magnetic field. Whatever you do, don't try to use the comm center. This thing is so strong it'll burn out its circuits! Zoe, got a location on it yet?"

"On it, Jan. There, bringing it up on the screen now. Only ten light-years away. God, that sure is close to this system. I wonder if it has had any effects on the people?" Zoe commented.

"Sorry, I ought to have guessed pulsar," I admitted. "Is it safe to use the IR scanner to see if we can penetrate the cloud layer?"

"Sure. Is the whole world surrounded in clouds?" Jan asked. He and Zoe now were looking at our destination planet, Farthun-3, directly below us.

"Near as we can tell, there are only very small breaks in the clouds, here and there, not enough to see anything," I answered.

Zoe said, "This is an unusual situation, captain. We've not had a strong pulsar this close to an inhabited world before. With radiation this strong, there could be health hazards. We ought to check with Dr. Leann about it. Should I go check with her?"

"Good thinking Zoe. Are we safe or should I position us with Farthun-3 between us and the pulsar?" I was thinking of ways of blocking the intense radio frequency radiation that was hitting us, though we couldn't actually feel it.

Jan thought for a second and said, "Might be a good idea, captain." I nodded to Athena, who took manual control of the ship, moving us around the cloud-covered world and in a bit closer, until Jan called out the planet was now blocking much of the pulsing. I relaxed a bit. Exploring the unknown was becoming exciting.

But then, I recalled how mom had once told me that when she was young, she had gotten caught in a massive electrical display, which had left her sterile, unable to produce viable egg cells, which is why they adopted me. That there were certain health risks was once more born home to me, as if the DNA alterations from the supernova weren't sufficient warning. I smiled invisibly.

Dr. Leann's voice came over the intercom. "Zoe's briefed me on the pulsar. This close to it, there could be health risks, but what they might be are unknown to Imperium medicine. Play it safe. Keep our exposure minimized." I thanked her and asked Dylan to run the IR scan to see if there was any traces of life on this world.

An hour later, we had sufficient data, and I held a group meeting to decide our next step. Jan reported, "Farthun-3 has a proper atmosphere for us. There appears to be human life forms on the planet, scattered across two continents that stretch around its equator. The temperature appears to be relatively constant across the planet's surface, around eighty degrees, probably due to the extensive cloud cover. While meteorology is a little out of Zoe's skill set, she and Tanis are studying the cloud situation from that aspect." I regretted not having brought a meteorologist along. I'd not considered such a person would really be needed. Ah well. So much for foresight.

Jan continued, "There appear to be no large cities like we are used to seeing on most Imperium worlds, though. Some centers may have upwards of a hundred thousand. Hard to estimate from blurry IR images, but that's the best Hermes can tell. He's a million times better at that than I am." I noted he was praising his HIFR!

After a bit more discussion, we all felt it was safe to drop down below the cloud layer and take a closer look. Marisol, who was also our linguist, added her thoughts. "Monitor all radio frequencies, and see if you can pick up any broadcasts from the planet. We are going to need to work out what language they are speaking. I'm afraid I'll be letting everyone down now. With these lip plates, about the only language I can really speak well is Imperium Standard. I'll have to let Leda deal with my ULAT box for me and hope that is enough." Again, we would be having problems because of the terrorist attack. I'd been thinking about this first contact situation some as well.

Always before when I was with my parents exploring, I served as their linguist, since I'd learned something like a hundred languages, spoken only, not written. But these lip plates wiped out all phonetic sounds formed by the lips, as well as dampened the sounds coming out of our mouths, as they hit the foot-wide top plate, which drooped down to our chests. Well, Marisol and I still had our ears, could make the linguistic associations, and relay that to Leda and Athena, who could adjust our ULATs. That would have to serve. If all else failed, I knew Marisol or most of us could resort to telepathy. Thoughts of a person are not phrased in language, but concepts, giving us a decided edge here.

Two hours of drifting along beneath the cloud layers gave us a far better picture of Farthun-3. It wasn't encouraging though. No skyscrapers, no spaceports, no radio towers or newscasts, and no real signs of a modern civilization presented themselves. Rather, we saw a mostly agrarian world. The larger population centers were sprawled over the ground in single story, wooden dwellings. There were certainly no spaceships buzzing from here to there, as there were on Proxima Prime. To get any further data, we'd have to visit the surface. I had no other choice, if we were to learn anything about these people. Once more, it was going to be a first contact situation.

Because of the threat of the intense radio radiation from the pulsar, I decided not to risk everyone's safety by landing the Eagle's Seed on the surface. Rather, we'd keep the ship in orbit, keep on using the planet as a shield, and send down a small landing party in our small shuttles. We had five four-person shuttles, just enough to get my original crew to safety should something catastrophic happen to the Eagle's Seed. Having to bring along our HIFRs reduced this safety factor in half! I decided to send down two shuttles, which meant four crew and four HIFRs would make the exploration trip. However, spy cams attached to the shuttles would allow the rest to observe from the ship.

I decided I would go down along with Marisol, Beth, who was her mate and our zoologist, and Martina. I chose Martina because she alone of us had the most extensive background on other worlds, due to her long service as the Hub Sector ID Minister. Athena, Leda, Melita, and Delia would come along, flying our shuttles and operating our ULAT boxes. With this detail settled, what remained was to choose our landing site.

To that end, Danika, well really Callisto, made another

pass around the planet, searching for the optimum location to visit. Ideally, we wanted a larger population center. "Hey Nia, come look at this! We've found something! A strange, unknown type of spaceship!" Danika was quite excited over her discovery. I rushed over to the viewport; well that's overstating it. Walking for us was always slow and carefully measured.

Below I saw the strangest looking spaceship I'd ever seen. The Imperium style preferred the long cigar look. The Federation of Planets also had a cigar shape but with small wings attached to the mid-sections. This one had enormous wings, as though someone had taken a huge square of metal and cut it diagonally, placing each half against the sides of the fuselage, which had a square-box cross section. It looked more like a flying box than a spaceship. Yet, there it was sitting on a grassy patch just outside one of the larger towns. Obviously, it didn't belong here and wasn't native to this world, unless they only had one ship in the whole world, which I doubted very much. This meant someone else was also here visiting this world!

Suddenly, our questions doubled in size. We had two groups of new people to learn about! "Two for one!" exclaimed Marisol. Well, there was no question, but this would be our landing site. I gave the orders, and we headed to the emergency shuttles. Danika was now in charge. If anything happened to me, she was to fly everyone home to safety, well Callisto really.

Athena and the others had their PDS, d-guns, and ULAT boxes around their waists. Their PDS or Personal Defense Shields could be activated in an instant, providing them protection from most forms of attack. While we four also wore PDS and ULAT boxes, we were dependent upon them to activate or control ours. I sure hoped we would not need them. We were seeking information, not fights. "Take us down and land nearby that alien spaceship, Athena," I ordered, feeling a little silly that I couldn't do this myself. Since the beginning of the mission, I'd dreamed of leading the first contact trips, but not so physically handicapped! Get used to it, Nia, I told myself, taking as deep a breath as I could, which wasn't much.

Down we went.

As we dropped lower, we could see large numbers of well-tended crop fields surrounding the town, which Jan, or Hermes rather, estimated held about a hundred thousand people. Lower still, Beth reported sighting cotton fields, cereal grain fields, and domestic livestock pens, reminding me somewhat of Metcalf-4. Even lower and we could finally get a good view of the people of Farthun-3. Talk about being taken by surprise!

"Oh my god! Look at some of them!" Marisol exclaimed. She and Leda were riding with Athena and me. They wore rather simple looking, white cotton dresses, heavily embroidered with gay reds, yellows, greens, and blues. However, what shocked us so was about half of those we could see working the fields and moving about the town did not appear to have arms!

I told Athena to circle around the landing site for a few minutes before setting down. She asked why. "We don't want to seem threatening and, if as I suspect, someone else is also visiting this town, I want to give them a chance to come out to greet us."

"Ah, I see. Excellent reasoning," Athena complimented me, causing me to wonder if she'd thought of this and if she had, was she testing me? Or did she actually mean it or was she just being polite? I had no time to ponder the questions. I spotted a number of people beginning to assemble near the landing area, and suggested it was time for us to land and meet them.

Once more, I felt like a fool having to have Athena help me out of the shuttle! If only my feet were normal, and I didn't have to wear this unyielding corset, I'd be okay. Standing on the grass was even more troublesome. With barely three inches at most touching the uneven ground — the tiny spiked heel right behind my toes didn't help in the slightest — I was wobbling fiercely, before Athena's steadying arm encircled my waist, as a crowd of people moved up to us from all sides. It was more than apparent they were merely extremely curious about us, as we them.

I always enjoyed first contacts on many levels. You see,

when you step off your ship, you are facing a whole arena of new sights, sounds, smells, people, and of course the immediate challenge of language. One is literally flooded with a zillion first impressions with which one must deal rapidly, for communication begins almost at once.

First, the natives of Farthun-3 were quite similar to us Imperium folks. They were all very pale skinned, probably due to the constant cloud cover. Second, they all had very blonde hair and blue eyes. Every person we saw was. Limited gene pool flashed through my mind. Everyone's hair was extremely long, though some was curly, some was wavy, and some was straight. I had the impression that no one here ever cut their hair, preferring one of two styles: long ponytail tied at the back of their heads or a ponytail that was doubly or triply folded in the back. Many wore colorful ribbons in their hair. I quickly saw the difference. Women had their ponytails folded and wore the ribbons. The men simply had ponytails.

Everyone's dress was that of a white cotton day dress style. The women's dresses were more heavily embroidered than the men's were. However, not one of the men I could see had any arms, but their voices were deep, and some had moustaches or beards. More significantly, the men all sported various sized breasts, paralleling their women's bosoms! Had we stumbled onto another group of hermaphrodites? That was my very first thought upon seeing these people. I should say their breast sizes ranged from B to D, and that none was remotely as massive as ours were.

Some of the women wore metal swords strapped to their waists. I saw no other signs of weapons though. All wore sandals on their feet. No sex differences there. Except for their extreme paleness, they looked like normal people on the Imperium worlds, except for the men, of course. As they began speaking to us, I recognized the base language instantly. It was a form of English or Midlands. Marisol also picked this up as fast as I did, instructing Leda to turn her ULAT box to English output. We all did that.

As soon as I said "Hello everyone" translated via my ULAT box, smiles erupted, and the group parted allowing one woman and a man to step forward towards us. The gay chatting among the hundreds of onlookers ceased though, waiting for them to say something. Conclusion: they were the town's rulers.

"Sky people come? Welcome more sky people to Hawthornby. I'm Barbara Leeds, our mayor. My husband, Phil. Can you understand me?" She addressed Athena and not me. Lightly touching her mind, I realized she thought I was a male, and that Athena was the female and thus the leader. This was a matriarchy-oriented society.

"Yes, barely. Give us time to understand your language better," I replied. "I'm Captain Nia Elain Compton-Jereni, my assistant, Athena." One by one, I introduced our small group, adding, "We're all women. I'm afraid I didn't bring any of our men down from our ship. They look much like us or your men. Are you able to understand me better now?" Athena was making some slight adjustments to our ULAT boxes.

"Yes. How very strange. You appear as our men, but speak as we women do. Such enormous breasts and what elaborate lip ornaments you have. Still, we like your hair. It is so very black. We've never seen hair that is black or brown. Martina's is like ours though. What brings you to Hawthornby?" she finally asked the burning question in her mind. I detected a slight fear coming from her or perhaps it was nervousness about us and our motives.

"We came to visit with you and your people. We want to learn about you, nothing more. Perhaps, we have much in common between your people and ours." I attempted to lessen her worries or fears.

"A visit? This is good. It's wonderful finally to meet some aliens who are like us. As we say, when it rains, it rains. We've not had alien visitors for many, many years and today, we get two groups visiting us. The Narsten are visiting us too, but they want from us." Apparently, that was a signal for their other visitors to step forward from behind the thong of blonde men and women. At last, we glimpsed the other aliens who obviously came in the strange spaceship.

Aliens! For the first time in Imperium history, a truly alien race had been encountered! Of that, there wasn't the remotest doubt! Still, they were humanoid. Their bodies were quite gray in color. Their faces were quite angular, not roundish as ours were. Later comparing notes, we decided they were still probably homo sapiens in nature, just quite different from the rest of us in the galactic disk. Still, they looked human, just very different from us. Their height was a bit taller and perhaps a bit thinner. The man was quite muscular and wore some type of uniform, a darker grey than their skin with a yellow eye insignia on his right shoulder. He carried some form of weapon strapped to his waist. His hair was coal black and a bit greasy looking.

However, the woman demanded our attention. My guess was that she might be in her fifties, if they aged as we did. Her eyes were elaborately done with varying shades of green and blue shadows, and her lips were done in a dark red hue. Combined with her angular features, these gave her a rather stern countenance. Her long black hair flowed over her shoulders and was nearly as long as ours was. It appeared she probably had arms, but they were encased in a black sheath behind her back, with her lower arm parallel to the ground, giving her almost the same appearance as us. Certainly, she was as helpless as we were with her arms bound like that. Yet, the man totally deferred to her in all things. That was apparent from the start.

He had an arm around her, supporting her, as Athena did me. She wore what we at first took to be a dark grey blouse but her skirt was just enormous, rather like those formal ball gowns that the senators on Proxima Prime used to wear many years ago. Athena estimated it was about twelve feet wide near the ground. Well, she couldn't see her feet either, I thought. Quite why I took comfort in that thought I later found embarrassing, but I at that moment, I certainly did.

As she slowly closed the distance to us, she began speaking using the local language, but we could instantly tell she had a terrible accent, far worse than ours. "Vell, vell, vhat ve here have? Disk people! How strange! I, Matriarch Athala Kane ruler of House Kane of the Narsten Cluster be. My husband, Commander Rolf, my maid, Elise." A slim woman dressed in a plain grey gown stepped out from behind the pair, curtsied, and quickly slipped back behind the pair.

Her accent struck a chord with me and my linguistic studies. Evidently, it did with Marisol as well. It sounded like some derivative of German. I knew my lip plates would not interfere with something that needed no lips to produce. I said, "Guten tag, Athala."

"Vell, dat very crude Karsten ist. Ve Farthun speak. Polite be. Mayor Leeds, disk people these be."

"So they are. Well, come. Let's all go back to my office and chat. I was just serving cacao to our other guests. We must walk slowly for Matriarch Athala's benefit. She walks on her toes. Follow us please," Barbara said politely. I wondered what she meant; I couldn't see Athala's feet. Was she wearing toe shoes like us? How strange. Things only got stranger, though.

As we followed behind them, the local people swarmed in behind us, trying to get a good look at us. I overheard many comments along the lines of "Their women are like our men. How can that be?" Others suggested, "Perhaps there are two kinds of their women." Cultural confusion runs both ways.

The streets of the town were crude cobblestones. I presumed it rained a lot on this world so the stones prevented the streets from becoming a mud mess at those times. All of the houses were fairly small, wooden affairs and very simply built. Nothing fancy, about as simple as one could get in their construction. I did hear one potential blacksmith. Iron on iron echoed from a distant quarter of the town. Still the air smelled clean and fresh, quite a change from the often polluted air of many industrialized worlds or the sterile recycled air of spaceships. Pleasant indeed. Our walk was slow enough that I didn't have to focus too much attention on my walking, but I noticed the locals constantly had to adjust to our much slower pace. Obviously, they were quite accustomed to moving at a normal rate.

We entered a rather plain building, a two-room affair, consisting of a huge meeting room with a small kitchen behind it. Polished wooden tables lined the center along with chairs with wicker seats. Simple, yet comfortable, I thought. No pretenses here. Later, I would learn why.

We took our indicated seats. Mayor Barbara had we eight on one side of the largest table, while Matriarch Athala and Commander Rolf sat opposite us. She and her husband sat at the head of the table, where they could observe both groups. A number of serving maids entered carrying trays of a steaming hot liquid in pottery cups. Mayor Barbara looked at me a little confused about how we could possibly drink from the cups. I asked politely for spoons, which were quickly provided. One taste and I knew it was more like a hot chocolate, quite delicious, made from a very dark chocolate, just a tad bitter though. I was amazed to see our HIFRs sipping from their cups. I had no idea that they could emulate eating. Well, that was an excellent idea. That they were robots never entered anyone's mind.

At last, the conversation changed to something significant. Since she was there first, Matriarch Athala presumed the right to speak first. "As saying I was, Mayor Barbara, the wicked lizards, the Hadu of the Spicula Cluster on the move again are. None of us any way can see to stop them, except to war with them go, and them off once and for all finish. As you know, we humans their delicacies are. They us eat, Captain Nia Elain," she spelled it out for me. She had a different word order making understanding a tad challenging.

Mayor Barbara said, "But what can we do about it? We cannot fly in the skies like you aliens. We have no weapons, save our few swords. As I have told you, in the past, some of the Hadu did land here, but we fought them off and killed them. We will do the same if they come here. For us, the Slavers of the Gorki Cluster are more feared. The sneaks come in the night and carry off our women. If you know where this Gorki Cluster is located, perhaps you can kill them with your war too."

"Aye, we to wipe them out too would like, but the Narsten Cluster not powerful enough is to wars wage against both the Hadu of the Spicula Cluster and the Slavers of the Gorki Cluster. That why is I my rounds of other inhabited worlds am making, alliances to form seeking and support for the coming war obtaining. We fighters need which your world could provide. We the ships to transport your fighters to the battle can provide."

"But we are so few. Our men will be useless to you. Just

how many fighters are you asking for?" Mayor Barbara inquired deftly, not willing to commit just yet.

"As many as spared can be. Any at all appreciated will be, Mayor Barbara."

"Well, give me some days to contact the other mayors. We will see how many of our fighters we could spare without lowering our own security. Heavens knows when the next Hadu will land or when the Slavers will strike again. Will that be acceptable, Matriarch Athala?"

"Yes. It all that I of your people can ask. The coming war help as you are able."

"Good. I will send word out later today. Will you be staying for a few days to hear back from us?"

"Yes. We more plans to make have and for a week if necessary wait can. Thank you Mayor Barbara."

I spoke up, "Have you considered asking the Imperium of the spiral arm for help in your coming war?"

"Disk people? Joking you must be! Your ships this far cannot travel. Besides, filthy and dirty disk people be. How you in all that filth and dust of the disk to live can stand? Perhaps not you know that 'disk people' being called, the worst imaginable insult is. No halo people to disk ever would travel. Still here you be. Perhaps we this should discuss. Please me join for dinner on my ship tomorrow night."

"We would be delighted to join you for dinner tomorrow night. Thank you Matriarch Athala," I replied, seeing a way to have a private conversation with her. I knew that I'd be able to discover much more about the halo worlds from her than from the mayor here.

Mayor Barbara said, "Please, captain, you must stay with us for dinner tonight."

"Of course we would love to." With that, Rolf carefully assisted his wife to rise and they slowly left the room.

"Fighting is always bad, but being victimized by the Slavers and eaten by the Hadu is even worse. Do you have wars down in the disk too? Are there bad men and creatures there as well? Come, we should chat. I have many questions that I must ask."

"And we have many to ask you, Mayor. Yes, there are

evil men in the disk as well and wars have been fought. Right now, there is peace between both sides. So that's something positive," I replied.

I then began to probe a little. "Our ancient records told us that perhaps a long time ago, our disk people tried to establish a colony on this world. Do you know if that is true?"

"So it is claimed. But no one knows if that is true or not. You are so similar to us that perhaps it is so. We find it strange that some of your women are like our men, lacking arms, and yet some are like us and have them. What of your men? Are they like ours, lacking arms? Do your men also have babies like ours do? I'm told that the Narsten men do not have babies, only their women. Worse yet, both their men and their women lack half of the reproductive organs! Their men lack those of their women, while their women lack those of their men. How absolutely horrid that must be for them! But please, don't tell them that I said so. They might be very embarrassed about such a horrible malformity!

"Yes they very well might be highly embarrassed about that. I promise I won't say anything about that."

Phil spoke up. "Do your men do work for you? Around our world, we men provide the power that our women need. We pull the wagons and pull the plows. We have yokes that allow us to carry things for them. Plus we try to have twice as many babies as our wives. They have so much to do, you see."

"Oh most definitely our men work hard for us. Some are quite brilliant, and they have our babies too." I didn't bother to tell them that I was referring only to those of us who had been genetically modified. "But sometimes we women have babies as well. I've a three year old daughter."

Mayor Barbara smiled, obviously greatly approving of what I was saying. In her mind, our two races were very much alike. She then asked, "Why do some of your women were those gold lip things? Are they somehow significant?"

I went with the "why" of Ashford-5. "They are ornamental and a status symbol indicating high social standing among our people. Both our men and women of high social status wear them proudly. I do love to see all your people having such long hair as we have."

Mayor Barbara smiled and said rather apologetically, "It is perhaps our own vanity. Plus, we believe it's unholy to cut one's hair. The biggest disgrace possible on our world is to have your hair cut short. They would be shunned as outcasts by everyone. All of our people have yellow hair. How is it that your people have so many colors?"

I laughed. "I don't know. We have a zillion shades of brown, black, red, and blonde too. Some of us just love long hair. I certainly do. We do have much in common."

"We women tie our tails up a bit to not get in the way when we work. You do not, yet these others have short hair. Why is that? Are they outcasts too?"

"I love long, flowing hair, but not everyone else does. I think it is a matter of personal preference. These women here with shorter hair do much of the work for us and don't want to be bothered with having to tie it up."

"Say, since you come from the disk, perhaps you know or can find out what happened to my great-grandparents?" she asked. Suddenly, her demeanor changed. She was tense, worried, and curious — a strange mixture.

"What happened to them? I don't know if I can help or not, but I sure can try," I replied honestly.

"You see, about a century ago, I'm told by my grandparents that a sky ship carrying disk people came here. They took my great-grandparents away with them, promising to return them, but they never came back. Elaine, my grandmother who used to be the mayor of Hawthornby before my mom and now me, told me the disk people were very excited to discover us, and they wanted to study them, promising to return them along with many new and wonderful inventions. Alas, they never came back. Their names were Thomas and Beth Hawthornby. Have you heard of them?"

"No. I haven't, but then there are billions upon billions of people in the disk worlds. However, I sure can try to find out. We keep accurate records of every person. It shouldn't be too hard for me to find out for you. I take it they were both blonde and had blue eyes."

"Oh thank you. Thank you. Yes, all of us on Farthun have blonde hair and blue eyes. All of our men have no arms, so Thomas would not have had them either. My grandmother also said that Thomas was pregnant when they left with the disk people, so you might have some of their children down there in the disk who want to come home."

"Great. I'll see if I can locate them or their descendants and let you know." She thanked me profusely. After that, we took a strolling tour of her town. Inwardly, I grimaced when I saw men hitched to plows and carts, providing pulling power. Others balanced wooden yokes across their shoulders with full baskets hanging down from either side. Well, they were being useful and not helpless members of their society. I also spotted quite a few pregnant men, but that no longer surprised me in the slightest. I had nothing but admiration for the women, who had to do the real work of building their civilization. Later, we dined with the mayor and then returned to our ship.

After relaying the data about the missing great-grandparents, Dr. Leann suddenly gasped and exclaimed, "Eureka! The time her great-grandparents went missing was during the early years of the war with the Federation. More importantly, it was around the time they setup that secret genetics research laboratory on Ashford-4! Nia Elain, it's possible that those geneticists got their hands on her great-grandparents and used their DNA modifications to help design their genetic bio agent! We've always wondered how they ever figured out the massive DNA changes that were needed to turn men and women into hermaphrodites. Her great-grandparents might be the answer! I have to call home now and tell them this. They still have most of the ancient records. Maybe they can see if those names are anywhere in them."

Danika volunteered, "I'm keeping the ship in a geocentric orbit so the planet is shielding us from the pulsar. It should be safe to use the comm center, Nia."

I allowed Dr. Leann to make the call relaying our incredible findings. As far as anyone knew, there were no known cases of hermaphrodites existing in either the Imperium or the Federation of Planets prior to the first release of that terrible genetic bio agent. Well, that's not entirely true. There were some exceedingly rare "freaks" of nature that had been reported. We'd come across a whole race of them.

After making the call, Dr. Leann and I chatted. "Look, if Farthun-3 was originally an Imperium distant colony, then it stands to reason the original settlers were normal humans. Somehow, their ancestors ended up as hermaphrodites, plus men genetically have lost their arms. Something on this world caused these specific genetic mutations to occur. It could be in something they ate or drank."

"Hey, good point," I replied. "Could the close proximity to the pulsar have caused genetic mutations to occur?"

"Brilliant, Nia Elain. That's an even better theory! No disk-inhabited world is anywhere close to a pulsar, not like Farthun-3, but I'll check with our astronomers about that. We have nothing to compare it to. We already know that our brief exposure to the intense radiation from the supernova has altered our own DNA slightly, despite our shields. It could well be the true source behind the genetic modifications. Of course, I don't know if that will be of any use in undoing the damage."

I felt proud for a moment. If our excursion into the halo found nothing else, this one find might well one day help the millions who were impacted by the genetic bio agent have a cure. That alone made me feel rather pleased with our whole trip. After that, I went to the comm center and called Emperor Bino. He and I had a lengthy conversation regarding Farthun-3. I was concerned for their safety. They were practically defenseless against two invaders: the Hadu lizards and the Slavers. While obviously we needed to find out more about them and what was going on here in the halo, he shared my concern and asked me to find out if Mayor Barbara was open to having trading exchanges with the Ataro Empire. If a transport took off from Proxima Prime, they would have enough fuel to reach here and to get back without bringing along lots of extra fuel cells. As soon as the new hyperdrive modifications were proven and implemented, Farthun-3 was within easy reach of any world in the Ataro Empire, except perhaps those on the rim. He also took my suggestion that only hermaphrodites handle the trading, maintaining a comfort zone for these people.

The next day, Dr. Leann got a return call from the geneticists on Ashford-5. Indeed, they found early records concerning a Specimen T and Specimen B, an obvious reference to Thomas and Beth. According to the records, both had died. No cause of death was noted, however. There was no mention of any child of theirs. However, the geneticists were very excited about this discovery, since it meant that the original geneticists had not been stunningly brilliant, but had taken samples of existing hermaphrodites and incorporated them into their cocktail of modifications for their weapon of mass destruction. Dr. Leann reported the geneticists were excited about this discovery and were determined to press on with their attempts to create a cure. She told me in private that they had as yet to find a work-around for our altered DNA. We kept that news to ourselves.

Later, I again visited the mayor, and she was quite pleased to see if trade relations could perhaps be established. I then explained, "We may have found out something about your great-grandparents, but we are still looking for further information. We believe that they died, probably before he could give birth. There isn't any record of their son or daughter. Please know this; they both were really contributing something of value to those with whom they went. Their lives did mean something and were not wasted. That's why they never returned. I'm sure they had a proper burial."

"Oh. Thank you. That is a relief, and I will tell mom and dad about it tonight." She seemed pleased with the situation. After all, they did contribute something of value, though most might believe it was a bad thing, if indeed their DNA was used as a model for the genetic bio agent. Even if it was, those on Aquila Prime would praise them for it — a matter of viewpoint really. I then explained we had to go with Matriarch Athala to see if we could possibly be of help with them and the battle against the Slavers and these lizard men. This, she readily accepted. Personally, I hoped and prayed the emperor would send a cruiser or two to orbit the world and keep the invaders from even landing.

Still, I'd need more data, and to get that, my same small group headed over to Matriarch Athala's ship, where she welcomed us onboard. My best guess is that her ship was roughly equivalent to one of our light cruisers, armed of course. However, because of our conversations and subsequent trip with her, I learned a key piece of information. The halo civilizations did not have a good hyperdrive system. They preferred sub-light speeds and only used their crude advanced drives for longer distances.

Still the ship was much larger than the Eagle's Seed. As we made our slow way onto her ship, as expected, we were constantly stared at. Plus, I caught a few derogatory remarks about having filthy disk people onboard. At least they didn't comment about our unusual appearance. For once, I was grateful for that. I also noticed that a hush came when Matriarch Athala stepped carefully out of her meeting room to welcome us onboard. Obviously, this woman was both highly respected and in complete control of the ship. Probably her husband ran the ship, though.

"Come in, come in. I've been expecting you. Please have any seat you wish." Her maid Elise assisted her to a seat at the head of her stainless steel table. With her monster-sized gown, she needed assistance sitting. The walls were painted institutional white, and overhead fluorescent lights made the room quite well illuminated. (Note that from now on, I will alter their sentence structure to what we use. I found it a bit hard to follow her with all of the verbs at the end.)

"I've been doing a bit of research on you disk people. Of course, Elise here actually does the data entry for me, just as your assistants must do for you. Anyway, there has been so very little contact with your disk people over the centuries, hardly anything is truly known about you. Clearly, you have all developed significant space travel to be venturing up here in the halo. However, perhaps more significantly, it appears that disk people have become drastically more civilized, but perhaps you ruling women have gotten a bit carried away with it all. I still retain my arms, you see, while you've lost yours. And such bosoms. Impressive. Hence, it is my opinion we ought to at least hold some frank discussions with you."

"Thank you. I'm afraid we know nothing whatsoever about you. Actually, we are almost completely ignorant of the halo and its people. We are here to find out and learn and offer bonds of friendship," I replied. "Our explorations are made difficult because we don't have the coordinates for any location up here and have no idea what or who is here. We are here to learn and to make friends."

"That is an admirable approach. Let me ask one question of you first. Are you the leader, the matriarch of your ship or people?"

"Yes, I'm the leader of my group."

"Ah then, we do have much in common. You see, I'm the top matriarch of my planet, Menno. Our entire Narsten Cluster society is wholly matriarchal. That is, on each of our worlds, some two dozen, there are fifty ancient houses, clans if you please, each run by its own matriarch. All matriarchs and all aristocratic women are tiny-armed women, like me."

"I'm not sure what you mean by a tiny-armed woman."

She smiled. "All aristocratic baby girls and baby girls of us matriarchs have their arms wrapped tightly from the day they are born. Only we aristocratic women are allowed to have tiny arms. They are usually crossed behind our backs and held there securely during the day. At night, they are unbound. Having tiny arms is considered to be highly erotic, and from personal experience, they really are. Rolf goes almost insane with lust when I rake my tiny arms over his body. Tiny arms always identify the woman as an aristocrat or a matriarch, to say nothing of letting you know she is a highly erotic and desirable woman. Honestly, when I came of age, I must have had fifty handsome suitors begging for my hand in marriage. We aristocrat women have our pick of only the finest men on our worlds. That's why I suggested that perhaps your women have gone a bit too far. You no longer generate the same eroticism that we create just by walking among men. Perhaps your bosoms serve the same function among your people."

I grinned invisibly. "Ah, you have just said it. They are that, in fact. Our mates find them highly erotic." I was reflecting upon what Zoe and Alexandra said about sideways brushing of breasts. Danika and I tried it, and we were instantly highly aroused by it and have made it part of our own private foreplay.

Athala grinned mischievously. "Perhaps one day you and I could share a private evening and see. Anyway, to continue. Besides binding our arms to keep them as tiny as possible when we become adults, we also fuse our feet so we always wear our point boots. Elise, please lift up my gown so they may see my boots." She did so. Indeed, only the tips of her toes were on the ground. She did have a very tall spiked heel as well. They reminded me of the erotic foot-ware I'd seen called ballet boots. No wonder she walked slowly. I also noticed that beneath her monster skirt, she wore a tight fitting gown. In fact, what I had thought to be a blouse was the top of a form-fitting, pencil-style gown, rather like the ones we were wearing. Again, I saw how she had observed this detail when we met, aligning it with everything else about us, and coming to the conclusion that we were very similar in nature to herself, an aristocrat. Well, we were hardly considered aristocrats in the Imperium. Try mutants, but I didn't tell her that.

She went on. "All we aristocratic women always wear a tight under-gown, just as you all are wearing, but we'd never think of not covering it with a proper outer-skirt, the larger the better. Only in private with our husbands do we go around in just our under-gown. Too risque. Not socially done. Yet, our tastes and styles in hair are quite the same. She was referring to my preference to simply letting mine fall, draping over my shoulders and back. Interestingly enough, many others had been slowly following my lead, opting to have their down and not tied up into a bun like Zoe and Alexandra. We women were now split evenly over the two styles. Dr. Leann, Beth, and Marisol emulated my style on these visits, preferring us to display a united appearance.

"So you see, with only a few minor details, you will be accepted as aristocratic women, if you should come to visit our worlds, which I wish very much to convince you to do. Of course, if you would come as my guests, I would see you have proper outer-skirts, have your feet fixed properly, and supply you with proper boots to wear. With your erotic bosoms and incredible lip ornaments, you'll generate a simply smashing image, doing wonders for our developing a real relationship with you disk people," she explained.

"So do I have this right? On each of your two dozen

worlds, there are a number of aristocratic families, run of course by their matriarch, and from one of these the planet's ruler is chosen?" I asked.

"Yes. That's sums it up. You see, there are many areas of society, and each one must be properly run by an aristocratic woman. The positions are inherited, naturally, passed down from mother to daughters. My official title is Matriarch Athala Kane ruler of House Kane of the Narsten Cluster. Each area of our society has a matriarch leading it. For example, there is Matriarch Ilse Meinhardt ruler of Agriculture of Kane and so on."

She sighed, "Of course, with each generation, the zones of control get a bit more diluted. I have four daughters, all properly arm bound of course, and all lovely, well-respected aristocratic women in their own right. However, if they wish to be more than just an aristocratic ruler of their household, then I must subdivide House Kane's assets, giving each a portion to run. Currently, the operations of House Kane are subdivided into twenty-three portions. The agriculture operations have thirty-three subdivisions, while heavy equipment manufacturing has forty-two. Time dilutes all, but still there will be one matriarch that oversees all of the others."

"Now I understand better. Are there other classes within your society?"

"There is the Labor Class, the Peasant Class, and the Religious Class. Of course, each of these also is run by an aristocratic woman, a matriarch, naturally," she answered.

"Can a member of these classes rise to a higher class? I'm assuming the Peasant Class is the lowest in rank of your society."

"Yes, through marriage to a woman of a higher rank. We aristocratic arm bound women may choose a man from any class. Naturally, we try to pick the very best of men, since they'll be caring for our needs and assisting us with many things. Still, every man knows his place when around one of us aristocratic, tiny-armed woman. You will see. They will honor and respect you, especially once we get you properly attired, and your feet fixed up properly."

"Say, we know nothing about the northern halo. Can

you show us where the Narsten Cluster is located with respect to Farthun-3 where we are now at?" I asked. "And where are the Slavers and the lizard men?"

"How much do you know about the halo?" Athala asked.

"Very little. There appears to be a scattering of stars and a fair number of globular clusters. No gas and no dust clouds. No new proto-stars. As far as I know, this planet here is as far as any Imperium exploration ship ever got. Oh, and my astronomers tell me that the stars up here are all older ones, possibly formed when the galaxy itself began to form."

"You have that right. None of that filthy, nasty, dirty, molecular-infested gas and dust clouds are around here! Honestly, Nia Elain, I can't see how you can possibly stand to live surrounded by such awful filth. Up here, everything is quite clean, pristine in fact. Anyway, yes, there are a number of isolated stars. A few have inhabited planets, but not many. They are quite isolated, like this one here. And yes, our civilizations are quite old ones, going back many, many millennia in fact. Elise, will you show her the 3-d map of our halo please dear?"

Elise left the room, returning with a strange looking semi-transparent half-dome, possibly made from some kind of plastic or polymer synthetic. The small black dots imbedded within the half-dome represented the isolated stars. Elise pointed to one just above the bulging hub as Athala explained, "We are here at Farthun. This group of globular clusters packed fairly close together is our home, the Narsten Cluster. Fifteen actual clusters, but each is relatively small compared to others further up. Now above us and to towards the rim is what is called the Narsten Gap, this relatively void section which Elise is pointing out."

"Beyond the gap towards the rim is another large cluster, the Gorki Cluster. The Slavers operate out of some of the inhabited worlds there. No one knows exactly where they are or what their goals might be, only that their ships sometimes raid us, and they take captives who are never seen again. Some speculate they sell their captives to the lizard men, the Hadu. They reside in the several clusters known collectively as the Spicula Cluster. They lie above the Gorki

Cluster where Elise is pointing out now. The Narsten Gap provides a deterrent barrier between us and the Slavers and the Hadu, as you can see. It's quite a sizable gap to have to traverse."

"Directly above us is the Kronos Gap, another void in space, protecting us from attacks from above. Does this all help you picture things better?"

"Absolutely. But there are more clusters and stars above this Kronos Gap. What's up there?" I asked.

To my surprise, Matriarch Athala visibly shuddered. "Oh! You really don't want to know!" I didn't say anything, and she then said, "The in-humans. You don't ever want to go further than the Kronos Gap, not if you value your very lives! That's called the Billik Cluster. An utterly in-human race lives up there. They don't have anything to do with us, and we avoid them at all costs. They are not even alive, though they are animated. And there are things even more dangerous and deadly further north. See that cluster there, the Bori Cluster. Ghosts that will suck the very life out of your body are reputed to dwell somewhere in that one. Some call them the Ceri. Those in-human aliens do not even have bodies as we do! You can't even see them or so the legends say. And yet they can kill you dead in an instant!"

I debated telling her about the friendly Ceri we had met on Metcalf-4. Considering how upset she appeared just mentioning the ghosts, I decided against it. However, I now had a big clue where we could go to find them. Of course, our problem was one of hyperspace coordinates. We had none for this halo, beyond Farthun-3 of course. In other words, no one had ever been here and mapped it yet. That was part of our mission: to map some of the halo for others to follow along later and explore further. Travel to the Bori Cluster might have to be made at sub-light speed, which would take a very long time indeed. Hence, I said nothing in reply.

She took my silence as ending such thoughts of mine. "So will you come to my home world where I can introduce you to our aristocratic leaders, demonstrating perhaps some of the disk people have finally evolved into a civilized society and are worthy of being welcomed into our cluster and the halo worlds?"

"Of course, Matriarch Athala. You don't have to ask twice, but I'm not sure how to get there. Should we follow your ship?"

"I believe that is the sensible thing to do. We'll go as fast as you can manage. Elise will give you a frequency to contact our ship. Just let Rolf know if he is going too fast for your ship. If your ship can only go at sub-light speeds, then it's going to take you maybe fifteen years to get there. We'll be using our space drives, cutting the travel from years down to two weeks, streaking through space. Will your ship be able to keep up with us?"

"Probably, but our drives are likely different than yours. As long as we can detect a locator signal from your ship, we can keep up, though if you are able to detect us, we'll probably be seen to be sort of blinking in and out of space as we fly along behind you." I admit I was way out of my comfort zone in this matter. I had no idea of how their ships could fly this swiftly without jumping into hyperspace. Theirs was obviously a different type of technology than ours. Still if we could get periodic locator signals from them, we could make a large series of hyperspace jumps, giving the illusion of following behind them. At least, I hoped so.

Matriarch summoned Rolf and told him what we were planning. He commented, "We can use our beacon to send out a continuous signal that you can follow. Or perhaps we could use our tractor beam to drag your ship along with ours. That might be a better way to do this. I'm sure Matriarch Athala would not want to risk losing you. We do travel quite swiftly with our spatial drive systems."

"I do believe that would be a better way, using a tractor beam. That way, we could use the time to learn your language better," I replied.

He nodded. "We will tractor your ship after we lift off. Might I ask why your speech comes out of those black boxes you wear around your waists, while other sounds come from your mouths?"

"These are our Universal Language Translators or ULATs for short. You see, with our lip plates, we cannot form the sounds that are controlled by lips. Hence, our usual speech wouldn't be understandable. These boxes translate from our language into yours, at least as best it can. The more we understand your spoken language, the better we can program the ULATs, and the better you will be able to understand us. I must say we have been very fortunate so far, in that your language is similar enough to one that some in the disk speak."

Marisol spoke up, "While we are traveling, if I could spend some time chatting with say Elise here, I can have them working far better by the time we get to your world. You see, I am a linguist. Once the grammar of a language is worked out and your words for some five hundred basic ideas are known, then only specialized words must be handled. I know right now we must sound as if we're using baby-talk to you, and we do apologize for having to keep asking for clarification of some words." (Note, I have been omitting these little annoying breaks in our talks with these aliens. I'm sure that you don't want to hear our repeated queries about specific words.) Marisol also didn't add that we were also using our telepathy to pick up the meaning of some of the words used, which we didn't grasp.

Matriarch Athala laughed, "I'm just amazed we've been able to understand each other as well as we have. Amazing bit of technology. We don't really need such devices up here in the halo. There are only a few different languages spoken. Of course, those Farthun primitives speak quite differently than we do. I had to learn enough of theirs to handle diplomatic relations with them. So can we leave in an hour? I do need to get back."

"Excellent. We'll take the shuttles back to our ship and await your lift-off. Thank you for extending your offer of friendship," I replied diplomatically. Ordinarily, I would have shaken hands, but since neither of us could, I decided against using the Aquila Prime method of a hug. I bowed instead.

Onboard my ship, I had Athena duplicate what we'd been shown about the clusters and populations, while I placed a call to the emperor, outlining what I'd learned and that we were proceeding to visit the Narsten Cluster. He gave his okay. Then, I made a similar call to Ashford-5, letting the queens know our progress and current plans. She then told me that Rafe wanted to talk to me.

"Hi there Nia Elain. Rafe here. So you've just discovered a new race of grey-colored humans?" she asked curiously. Once more, I outlined all I'd learned, particularly about the new races and our proposed visit to the Narsten Cluster.

When I finished, Rafe said, "Well, I wish we had had time to give you a lot of my Advanced Therapy before you left. I guess the best that I can do is to give you my advice, which is really to observe these people. The Imperium as a political unit is just about dead. The current blatant corruption and sadistic tendencies are sure signs that it's dying. I'm bothered about this Narsten Cluster's emphasis on arm binding or tiny arms and the modifications to their feet. Such a practice is obviously not a healthy one. I read it as a sign of sadistic perversion, so be very alert for all manner of covert hostility, sneaky underhanded actions, the stab you in your back syndrome. Remember, good and bad are a matter of viewpoint. In fact, the Slavers might be the good guys from our point of view, fighting to end the sadism and rigid class hierarchy of the Narsten society. That they are terrified of the Ceri is the thread you might wish to follow. Over."

"I understand, Rafe, but in order to find out what the true situation there is, won't someone have to go there and observe? Over."

"Of course. You have to go, Nia Elain, just be very careful, and don't expose more of your crew to possible treachery than you have to. You can call me anytime, night or day. I might even be able to help you even from this distance. Always remember, look and observe. Don't think and ponder, just look. Over." I agreed and we chatted a bit longer before signing off. Danika called out from her navigator's seat that the other ship was lifting off, and I headed to my pilot's seat. Right on time, Athena joined me, handling the controls.

"Match their speed and course, please. Danika, keep a running record of the coordinates for future records. I hope we are doing the right thing," I said. Rafe's brief conversation left me wondering and pondering Matriarch Athala and her motives. If we of the galactic disk were thought to be the worst scum of the galaxy, why was she inviting us to her home world? Was it based on our physical appearance? Was it because a woman was in control of our party and ship? Did she think that disk societies had become matriarchal like hers? I had no real answers, but I simply had to find out, but without risking the lives and well-being of the others onboard.

Before long, we felt the gentle tug of their tractor beam, and Danika began making a continuous log of periodically sampled spatial coordinates, which would enable us to program our hyperdrive system. Future trips could be vastly easier.

Our engineers, and Alexandra and Hans in particular, were extremely interested in their spatial drive system. I have to admit that, for a time, I too watched our flight from the viewport, just as fascinated by the light show as everyone else was. Space and the stars seemed to streak by like rays of lights and not points. Space seemed to twist and bend around our forward direction. It was quite a sight to see, incredibly different from the black void of hyperspace. However, after an hour, Alexandra and Hans had enough data to make some calculations and theoretical observations.

"The apparency is that we are going at about four hundred times the speed of light, which is causing the stars and space to be so crazily altered," Alexandra declared.

"That's about the slowest possible hyperspace speed, mind you," Hans pointed out. I relaxed. Our old hyperdrive was drastically faster than this, let alone Hans' new modifications. At least in speed of travel, our technology was superior.

Two weeks passed slowly. Marisol spent several days chatting with Elise. Perhaps it would be more accurate to say that they exchanged grammar rules and painstakingly verified the basic five hundred words in their language, the Narsten Dialect. Then, came days of specialized words. By the time that we arrived, our ULATs were doing a very good job of translating for us. Even Matriarch Athala was quite surprised at the difference, most noticeable, she commented.

Chapter 9 The Narsten Cluster — a Study in Domestic Issues

January 20, the ships slowed to sub-light speed. Now, we could see quite clearly the cluster of some fifteen small globular clusters, known collectively as the Narsten Cluster. We learned that each was given a single letter to distinguish it from the others. We were heading for Narsten-A. Soon, the sky was literally filled with stars. We were inside a veritable sphere of stars! Dylan's estimate was that perhaps there were a hundred thousand of them. Many were quite old stars though.

We soon disliked their naming conventions, vastly more confusing than ours. Their sun was called Adelonda, the Noble Serpent, while their world was called Menno, Mighty Strength. Confusing to us, most definitely. We'd have called Menno either Adelonda-3 or else call it Menno-3 and rename the sun Menno.

I ought to describe the night sky from Menno because it is vastly different from the night sky down in the disk. Here, brilliant stars shown all over the sky, fairly uniformly spaced creating the effect of a very strong full moon even though this world had no moon. Across the southern skies from horizon to horizon stretched the hazy, filmy galactic disk, like an enormous dirty cloud. I could see now why they thought of us as they did. There weren't any gas or dust clouds to be found anywhere in the halo.

By the time that we landed at their spaceport, we had our assignments worked out. No way was I going to allow everyone off the ship. Security dictated otherwise. We were dealing with a wholly unknown culture. Their ultimate objectives with us were actually unknown. Yes, she had been friendly enough, but so would anyone confronting an unknown race. Certainly, they would be pumping us for information just as much as we were them. Plus, it could be dangerous.

Alexandra and Hans were number crunching the

coordinates that Danika logged on our path here, turning them into usable hyperspace coordinates. That would keep them busy for days. Marisol's language project was finished, and she was going to take a break from her intense work these past two weeks. We decided it would not be wise to expose our men to this culture, where their men were muscular and with "normal male" type bodies. That would not be prudent, under the circumstances. Instead, they were going to monitor all the signals from Menno, hoping to catch news feeds and the like.

Compounding the difficulties of the contact situation was Matriarch Athala's decision to "fix" us up to appear as closely as possible one of their aristocratic women. That meant having our feet further modified so we could wear their special boots. I had no idea whether such a body modification was reversible or not and so didn't want to subject many others to it. Already our lives were quite miserable from the terrorist attack. Astronomers and engineers were not needed. I didn't expect to be seeing plants and animals or even much of their countryside, leaving the botanist, zoologist, and geologist out. I thought about bringing Dr. Leann, our medical doctor, along, but decided that she would be safer here on the ship. While I would have liked to take Danika with me, if something terrible happened to me, she would have to pilot the others home.

Considering what I was likely to be involved with, a political science and government expert was warranted, as well as someone who was keenly attuned to diabolical intrigues. That meant Tesla and her mate Martina. I hated to risk Martina, though of everyone on the ship, I couldn't think of a better person to have with me. She was an ex-intelligence minister, after all, and a brilliant detective. However, she didn't have the *mentales* gifts that Tesla had. These aliens knew nothing of this special skill that many of us had, and I intended to keep it that way. If all else failed, we could fall back on our gifts.

I held a private chat with the two, and we decided not to risk Martina's safety. Tesla simply wouldn't allow it. "Look, my love, I can keep you telepathically linked to me, and you can observe what I see. That ought to be just as good as being there with us."

Martina hated to be left behind, especially when Tesla was going with me, but she reluctantly agreed. "I dislike being left behind, but I don't have the special powers that you have, my love. If something bad happens, I'd be a liability for you and Nia Elain. I will do what I can from here," she reluctantly agreed.

Zarita popped in, "Hey boss, I've got my power crystals with me. I'll keep contact with you as well, and can relay an enormous amount of power to you, should you need it. Remember, these are aliens who are really prejudiced against we disk people. We ought to take all the precautions we can."

I grinned invisibly and agreed. "I hope none of that's needed, but it's comforting to know you and your power crystals are watching our backs."

After we landed on the far side of the spaceport, rather a quarantined position Martina speculated, Tesla and I, assisted by Athena and Damali stepped carefully out of our front port and onto the waiting ramp contraption, which turned out to be an elevator. At the ground level, Matriarch Athala, accompanied by Elise, and Rolf met us, surrounded by six uniformed guards, their security police, all women.

We made our way slowly into the giant spaceport administration building and out its main entrance, where vehicles similar to cars were waiting. "My hydrogen powered limousine will take us through Krazdorf, our capital city, to the Kane Mansion on the edge of the city. There are about seven million living in this city, the sixth largest on Menno. It's evening, and the city lights are simply wonderful to see. I bet you've never seen such sights before. When we get to our home, I'll have them fix your feet and see you have the proper clothing and boots. Then, tomorrow, as a proper aristocratic matriarch, I'll introduce you to my council and others. Of course, later on, if the rest of your crew women wish to be proper matriarchs, I'll see they are also properly prepared as well. Ah, here's my limousine."

We watched her carefully to see how she could manage to get into it. The doors were small, compared to her enormous skirt, ignoring that she was walking on tiptoes. She backed in, with Elise's help. Elise then bade us enter using the opposite door. Athena helped me get my hair to the front, as I too backed in, and somewhat awkwardly landed on the plush leather seat. I scooted over beside Athala, making room for Tesla, who emulated both of us. Our three assistants then stepped in, taking the row of seats that faced us. Rolf climbed into the front seat beside the driver, who politely welcomed him back and asked if he had a safe journey.

As we pulled silently away from the bustling entrance, we entered the heart of the great city. Both Tesla and I stared at the lights. She was right. Neon lights were everywhere and in every imaginable color. Rather garish. No one seemed to mind having clashing, brilliant colors near each other. Color, we were to discover, was always bright and solid, perhaps in contrast to their deep grey skin color. Over half of the neon lights were flashing as well. Every business had three or four of these, announcing their establishment. Some were on the rooftops, while some hung from great arms attached to the fronts of the buildings. A few were merely fastened to the sides of them.

The buildings were made of a dull red brick, though some were probably made from some black-colored wood. The streets were solid, probably concrete or similar construction. Unlike the steel and concrete skyscrapers of Proxima Prime, and so commonly found in the modern Imperium worlds, here the buildings varied somewhat in height, but none were more than twelve stories tall. The architecture seemed somewhat archaic to my eyes, but not primitive, mind you, just strange. I'd never seen anything like this before.

Zarita relayed a brief message to me. *Martina says to tell you this city looks like some of those found in the Federation worlds, according to a few reports and images she's seen.* I began to wonder if there wasn't some ancient connection between this Narsten Cluster and the Federation arm of the galactic disk.

As we rode along, Matriarch Athala commented, "Here in the heart of Krazdorf, you can get anything that your heart might desire. Of course, one must pay for it, though as an aristocratic woman, you are entitled to huge discounts. The merchants consider it a high honor for one of us to shop at their establishment. Rightly so, I might add. There is a wide selection of establishments that serves alcoholic beverages and all manner of narcotics, but do choose to go to the better establishments for those. There are many Houses of Pleasure available as well, but please only go to the finer ones. It wouldn't do to have an aristocratic woman visiting those that are for the lower classes. Not at all, but then I know you understand such things as well."

She chatted on, "I have a busy schedule for the next few days. You know, reporting on the findings of my long trip. I'll have one of my daughters assisting you. Perhaps, you'll find our way of life not so dissimilar from what you are used to. As you will soon see, everything must be done quite properly. We do not tolerate slovenly, sloppily-done work. Not at all. You see, we of the Narsten Cluster must set the civilization standards for all the other smaller halo worlds. Ours is a longstanding tradition of being the model that more primitive societies emulate as best they can. Of course, some of those are simply not as intelligent or bright as we are, and thus have great difficulties in their attempts to have a proper and correct society. Of course, you have seen that down in the disk, I'm sure of that. It must be simply awful trying to maintain a highly civilized, cultured, proper world, amid all those barbarians of the galactic disk."

"Well, customs do differ, that's for sure," I replied, uncertain what else to say. When in doubt, say nothing that you might regret. Instead, look, observe, and learn — my guidelines when meeting a new culture.

"Indeed. I'm sure you'll rapidly blend into ours here. Now about money. We use gold and silver coins to make our purchases. Obviously, I don't carry around such things. Instead, Elise carries my bank card for such things. We should get you one as well."

"Back on my world, I'm considered very wealthy, but I don't know what I have with me that I could offer you for funds," I replied. No way did I want to be financially obligated to her. Besides, I had no idea how expensive things might be on this world. "We do have some gold and platinum that I could perhaps exchange with you."

"Platinum? Now, that would be extremely welcome!" We chatted a bit trying to get a handle on their system of weights and measurements. Eventually after some trial and errors, I discovered that a pound of platinum was worth several hundred thousand of their gold coins, which, according to Athala, would most definitely put me in the aristocratic society, financially. I sent word to Thomas to get a pound out of storage for this purpose. We had a number of bars of various metals to use to assist in repairs of our ship. I doubted we'd need the platinum since Hans' engine was working to perfection thus far. Matriarch Athala promised to send a servant back to our ship to pick up the platinum in the morning, after which, she would get our bank account setup properly. Again, I sensed she was very pleased with this arrangement, as it added to her future arguments that I really was a true aristocrat, thus civilized, and not one of the dirty, filthy disk people.

The House Kane estate was huge, and the mansion was akin to our large manor houses. It was a three story red stone building with over a hundred rooms. Matriarch Athala had never counted them all. That was what servants were for. The aristocrats lived and worked on the first floor for the most part, though the kitchen and pantry were in the basement. Servants lived on the third floor with guest rooms and such on the middle floor. "Naturally, there are elevators, but the servants usually take the stairs," she explained, as we pulled up the long driveway to the main entrance, where an ornate portico with ten marble columns supported the roof. A yellow eye set in a black diamond was prominent on its facing side, the same symbol that Rolf wore on his uniform. I surmised this was House Kane's insignia and was right.

The limo pulled up beneath it, and a man dressed in what I would call a tuxedo stepped out quickly to open the doors for everyone. He politely said, "Welcome home, Matriarch."

Elise whispered to us, "He is the Doorman. That's his job here, to open the main doors and see guests inside properly."

Matriarch Athala replied, "Thank you. Our bags will be

200

arriving shortly. See that they are handled before you retire."

"Of course, Matriarch. I'll see to it."

As we exited, I noticed the doorman covertly staring at us, his eyes wide with our appearance. We followed them inside, walking over a plush red carpet lining the entryway. Just inside, several others were waiting for us. The men uniformly wore similar tuxedos, while some of the women wore maid's outfits. Each had the yellow eye symbol on their apparel.

"Everyone, these are the aristocrats from the disk that I told you about. Matriarch Nia Elain Compton-Jereni and Aristocrat Tesla Niko-Wells, their lady maids, Athena and Damali. Now then, these are some of my children. My oldest daughter, Matriarch Clothilda of Kane's Security Forces. She guarantees our complete safety here and abroad." I estimated she was in her early thirties, but her appearance was quite similar to her mother, tiny arms bound behind her back, angular facial features, very long, thick black hair, overdone eye shadow, and deep red lipstick. She also wore a billowing gown, a rich black.

"Matriarch Carla of House Kane Servants. She guarantees our servants do everything absolutely properly." Again, she looked very much like her mother and older sister. I gathered the men standing beside them were their husbands. Both were strikingly handsome, I gave them that. Matriarch Athala didn't bother to introduce them, which I found interesting. Men definitely played a second rate role in this matriarchal society.

"My youngest daughter, Matriarch Frieda. As yet, she hasn't chosen a position. She's still young, having just turned twenty-one. I've assigned her to be with you all the time, as your guide to help you learn how things are done in our society. She'll be your constant companion, since my duties will prevent me from doing that as much as I should like. Her Lady Maid, Miss Emlin." Once more, she looked like a younger version of her mother as well, but wore a bright red gown with matching lipstick.

She continued, "This is Lady Maid Gabriele. I have assigned her to you. She'll work with your Lady Maids, giving them instructions on how properly to dress you and such matters. I'm sure your maids will greatly appreciate her assistance. Finally, this is our resident doctor, Dr. Heinz. He'll see to the repairing of your feet yet tonight. Matriarch Frieda will accompany you while this is done, and Miss Gabriele will take your measurements to ensure you have a proper skirt to wear in the morning."

She added, "Frieda, will you lead them to the doctor's office, and then show them to their rooms? It is getting late, and I need to bathe and relax some. It's been a tiresome trip with very little to show for it, save the startling discovery of these aristocrats from the disk."

"Yes, mama," she replied politely. To us, she said, "If you will follow me, we'll get you properly fixed up." The group quickly disbanded going in several directions. Following Frieda, we turned right and headed down a long hallway. Frieda giggled a little, glancing again at our monster bosoms.

I spoke up, "I know. Monsters, but they are highly erotic you see, much like your tiny arms are here." She giggled again.

"I hope you don't mind my staring, Matriarch Nia Elain. It's just that we've never seen any quite this big. Actually, none even half as big and no tiny arms. How very peculiar indeed, but then you are disk people. We ought not to expect you to have quite the same customs as we do. Yet you must, since mama has invited you here as aristocrats. Still, it must be horribly embarrassing to you both to go out in public wearing only your underdress. I'd be absolutely mortified if I had to do that! Still, your shoes are almost like ours, just not quite. But don't worry, Doctor Heinz will have you fixed up properly tonight. I promise you tomorrow you'll be properly dressed, as we aristocrats always are and no more embarrassments. Ah, here we are. We always keep a resident doctor in the mansion, in case of illness or injuries. Most prudent, don't you think?"

"Oh absolutely. I left our doctor on my ship, just in case some of my crew gets ill or has an accident," I replied honestly.

Doctor Heinz finally spoke up, as we sat down in the indicated chairs in his office, smelling of disinfectant. "Maids, if you'll remove their shoes and hosiery, I'll make my preparations." While Athena and Damali did just that, he explained further. "This will not hurt a bit. Still, it's highly unusual for this to be done at your ages. Normally, it's done while they are still infants. That way, their leg and knee muscles toughen up as they learn to walk. In your case, I'll use some steroids to hasten that process along. Please allow yourselves plenty of time to get used to wearing these boots. However, you should experience no pains. Let me know if you ever should. Within a couple of days, your knees will have strengthened considerably. Personally, I expect you'll have an easier time with these new boots. You see, with your shoes, you only have two or three inches on the ground. With these boots, the heels are much farther back, giving you significantly more balancing power, at least I believe that will be so."

He inserted our malformed feet into one of his machines. I felt a pin prick before they went numb. I did hear something that sounded more like crushing bones, but he said that was normal. Once more, I knew I would need some therapy to erase the underlying pain that the anesthetic was completely dulling. I later learned that the machine literally fractured my foot bones, forced them into their new ballet en pointe position, and then fused them together, all completely painless, or so they would have us believe. I noted they must have something similar to our medical machines in order to do this.

A half hour later, he removed my feet from the machine. While I could wiggle and bend my ankle, everything below that was fused and unable to bend or flex in the slightest. My feet pointed straight down. While Athena put my hose back on, Matriarch Frieda explained, "The new boots have gel cushions in them, which soften our steps considerably. While Tesla is having hers done, you should stand and walk some to get used to them. Your maid will support you, as Miss Emlin does me or if you prefer, Miss Gabriele can do this and Athena can watch."

"Whoa, this is very different!" I exclaimed getting to my feet. Walking was now going to be far more of a challenge, but they were right. I had more than twice the stability that I had before. I felt the stress on my knees at once though.

"How are they?" Tesla asked curious as the doctor was doing her feet.

"Definitely more stable," I tried to put a positive slant on it. I just hoped there weren't any stairs to negotiate.

Once Tesla was finished and took her first steps around his office, Matriarch Frieda led us out of his office. "I should give you a tour of the more important rooms, so you have some idea what to expect tomorrow."

"That would be wise, Matriarch Frieda."

"Please, how about just Lady Frieda? We only use the formal address when in public. Around the mansion, we prefer just Lady. Even mom does, so I'm sure she would be pleased if you call her Lady Athala when we're here in the mansion. Far less formal. Besides, you need the practice walking. It can be a bit daunting, I'm told, when you get them when you are so old. I learned to walk in them when I took my first steps as a child. Come, our place is huge and very nice, if I do say so myself."

"Thanks Lady Frieda. So you haven't yet been assigned a position of leadership by Lady Athala yet?" I asked.

She giggled. "No. Not yet. To be honest, I'm hoping to step into mama's shoes, one day running House Kane. Of course, my older sisters would like that too, but I know far more about such matters than my sisters, and I'm younger. Now, here is the main dining room where we'll take breakfast in the morning around ten. Then, lunch is at one and supper at six. You'll hear the butler sound a gong alerting us that the meal will be served in fifteen minutes. He sounds it a second time five minutes before the meal. How do you even manage to eat with those incredible lip ornaments? They are quite, well quite unusual. I've never seen anything like them before."

"Top one is hinged and is fastened up when we dine or drink. Our maids use a spoon for our drink, though. I hope that doesn't embarrass anyone," I added as an afterthought.

"No, but we'll be most curious. I hope that will not embarrass you."

"Not at all. Where we come from, only the aristocrats wear them," I replied, substituting aristocrats for the wealthy and status-conscious of Ashford-5.

We went on to the next room. "This is the drawing room

where we women come after dining. Here, we often chat and discuss matters of state or importance. Mama will likely be here too to chat with you, if only briefly. The men prefer to stay in the dining room for a time smoking their pipes and making a stink. They'll eventually join us here too, but not if we matriarchs are holding important discussions."

I was interested in the next room, their library. "This is dad's library. Of course, you probably can't read our language. Besides, we aristocratic women don't read. We can't get or hold the books, of course. Now, let's ignore these next rooms. You are being housed in two of our finer guest rooms."

Eventually, we entered one of them. "This is the lady's bed." I saw an elegant bed complete with an ornately carved bed headboard showing many flowers. It was way too large for one person. "Over there is a separate bed for your maid. That door leads to your complete bathroom. That large wardrobe holds your clothing and boots. It's empty right now, but by morning, we'll have one proper outer-skirt for you. I can take you all shopping tomorrow so you can pick out dresses that suit your tastes."

"Notice that pull string there by the maid's bed. Whenever you need something, give it a pull. It'll ring a bell in the lady's maids chambers, and one will come shortly. Miss Gabriele will be on duty to assist you. In fact, the maids are putting a second maid's bed in the other bedroom now. That's why I'm showing this one to you first. Of course, you and I don't actually pull it; our lady maids do that for us. So Athena, Damali, if you need something, just pull it, and one of the lady maids will come shortly."

I spoke up, "We'll need hairbrushes. I'm sorry. I didn't think to bring anything from the ship."

"I'll see to grooming products at once, Lady Nia Elain, Miss Gabriele replied politely, quickly leaving the room.

"See, our domestic staff is very efficient. Just ask, and they take care of it. My bedroom is just across the hall from your rooms here. So I'll be close at hand as well," Lady Frieda explained.

Just then, another maid entered and curtsied. "Lady Frieda, the second guest room is now ready." She turned and left just as quickly as she'd come.

"Well, then, why don't we let Lady Tesla and Damali stay here, and let's have Miss Gabriele stay in your room so she can instruct Athena in the morning or assist you with anything else this evening?"

I agreed. Athena and I followed Lady Frieda and Miss Emlin to the next room. Almost at the same time, Miss Gabriel entered carrying a bag of small items for us. She took out a beautifully carved hairbrush, laid it on the dressing table, and then went into the bathroom. When she returned, Lady Frieda said, "Well, it is getting late, and we have a busy day tomorrow. I ought to get undressed and unbound now. Perhaps, I can check in on you later tonight and make sure all is well?"

I sensed her surface thoughts. Lady Frieda really did want to show me her tiny arms. She was very proud of them, but also she was intensely curious about my physical form and wanted to get a look at my breasts. Well, I couldn't blame her for that. "Sure thing, Lady Frieda."

After Athena removed my dress and boots, she looked puzzled. I picked up what was probably troubling her and asked, "Miss Gabriele, if we take off my boots, I can't even stand or walk. Am I supposed to sleep wearing them?"

"Oh no, Lady Nia Elain. It is my fault. I forgot to set out your bedroom slippers. One moment please." Her face was flushed. She'd been covertly looking at my bosom, corset, and male organs. She produced another pair of shoes. Normally, we'd call them mules, but I wasn't sure if that was what they were called here, so I stayed with bedroom slippers. They were much more difficult to stand and walk in, however. With my boots, I realized I was getting significant support from my ankles and calves as well, both absent from the bedroom slippers.

I was sitting on the edge of the most expensive bed I'd ever seen. Athena had my hair brushed out and draped over my right side. Already Miss Gabriele had turned in, when Lady Frieda knocked softly on our door. Athena let her in, and I got my first look at her nearly naked body. She wore her bedroom slippers but nothing else. For a moment, Athena and I stared at Lady Frieda, while she stared at me.

Her arms were unbelievably tiny, perhaps a foot and a half long at most with very tiny fingers. I swear they were mostly skin and bone, barely two inches across at their widest near her shoulders, if even that. They were also a shade paler grey than the rest of her body. Her long black hair draped across her left side, nearly as long as mine. She left nothing to the imagination. Well I didn't either for that matter. Though I was wearing thin panties, she could see my dual genitals.

After a long moment, she spoke, "We Ladies are honor bound to provide for the many needs of our house guests. I'm here if you would desire some tender affection before you sleep. I would treasure showing you just how erotic my tiny arms actually are. Already I can see just how erotic your breasts are. Now, I wish mine were much larger than they are. Your lips really are in large loops. Are your kisses also considered highly erotic as well? Forgive me if I'm being too bold for you. Like I said, I'm honor bound to provide for our house guests."

"I understand Lady Frieda. I admit we're just as curious about you, as you are with me. I'm married and have two daughters, but for the sake of friendship and goodwill between our peoples, I would be honored to show you how our intimate touching works, as you will with your amazing tiny arms. Just no intercourse, if you don't mind."

"That would please me very much. I, er, we don't see how you can excite men without tiny arms," she shyly admitted. A half hour later, she had a very solid reality on just how we shared intimacy and we, hers. After she left, Athena tucked me in. I relaxed and expanded my awareness, pervading the entire mansion. I detected something like forty minds living here. I could not help but pick up surface thoughts. They were all about Tesla and me, and how erotic and strange we looked. That we were disgusting disk people had already begun to take a backseat in their thoughts, particularly among the servants. A common thought was along the lines of they do look amazingly like aristocrats, only quite different from our Ladies. I also figured that by tomorrow, Frieda would have told the other matriarchs all about my anatomy and just how erotic she found pleasuring me had been for her. Thus far, I sensed no hostility towards us.

Around nine in the morning, Miss Gabriele pulled back the thick shades, allowing the sunlight to enter the room. I smelled what must be coffee, and there it was, a cup with spoon sitting on my dresser waiting for me. Athena began dressing me. As she did so, Miss Gabriele said, "If you'll permit me, I'll assist you in drinking your coffee. Lady Frieda always prefers to drink hers as she is dressing."

Once I was dressed in the same red gown that I'd worn yesterday, Miss Gabriele opened the giant wardrobe to reveal a new outer-skirt. While explaining to Athena how to put it on me, she went ahead and got me into it. Basically, I had to step into it while she had it spread out on the floor. She then outlined how Athena was to care for my needs during the day while I was wearing it. I felt bad for Athena; she was going to have to work much harder tending to me while I was wearing it. At least its color matched my gown or inner gown to use their terminology. After that, Miss Gabriele headed off to assist Damali. Hastily, Athena made a quick trip to the bathroom. When she returned, she explained, "The servants eat at eight o'clock in their own dining room. Damali and I went with Miss Gabriele."

"But you can eat? Food? Drink?" I asked confused. She was just a robot, a mechanical thing.

"We are programmed and designed to blend in — in all ways. Yes, we can appear to eat. A small pouch collects the food and drink. I was dumping it down the toilet just now. I ought to brush your hair again."

She'd just finished with me and adjusted my hair again, when we heard a gong, the fifteen-minute warning I remembered. We needed the time to walk down the hall to the dining room. Now, I saw the reason for the overly wide doors. They allowed us to pass without too much difficulty with our outer-skirts. Mine was twelve feet across. I did feel very precarious walking on my toes, and unable to see anything closer on the floor than about six feet from me. When we entered, the aristocrats and their husbands were already seated, but the men all rose, while Tesla and I were seated. I noticed several serving men wearing tuxedos standing in the background, preparing to serve us.

The table was immaculately set. All of the silverware was perfectly aligned and spaced apart on either side of the plates. The cups and goblets were likewise positioned in precise locations. In fact, as I looked around the table where over a dozen of us would be dining, I could not tell the slightest difference from one place setting to the other. Someone had gone to immense trouble to precisely position everything absolutely identically. "Proper" began to take on a whole new definition in my mind.

No one said much while eating, but the servants were always hovering about, removing dirty plates and cups, while supplying fresh ones, along with the four course breakfast. For Tesla and I, the amount of food would have served us for several meals. Only when we finished our meal and another round of coffee served did Matriarch Athala speak up.

"I've send Rolf off to set up your bank accounts. Your platinum was incredibly pure. Hence, the exchange rate is even higher. I do believe each of you'll have over two hundred thousand gold in your accounts when he returns. Once again, that's more than enough for any aristocratic woman. You both look perfect in your outer-skirts. Lady Frieda will be taking you into town so you may acquire a number of outfits of your choice. Do pick bright colors. We all do. I have business to handle, but I plan to spend time with you both this evening after supper. Now if you'll excuse me," she explained. At once, Miss Elise was at her side, assisting her to rise gracefully. As before, all of the women had their tiny arms bound up behind their backs.

Lady Frieda said, "We ladies should retire to the drawing room, and let you men smoke your smelly pipes." Several men chuckled. With that hint, Miss Gabriele was at my side, assisting me to rise, while Athena watched her carefully. Damali already had some instructions from her and handled Tesla well. We followed Lady Frieda and Lady Clothilda into the drawing room. There I found fresh cups and a pot of coffee had already been placed there by another servant.

After taking some seats on the plush sofas, Lady

Clothilda said, "So are you really the Matriarch of your spaceship? Are you really the pilot? Mama suggests that you are."

"Yes, I'm called Captain Nia Elain by my crew. Of course, Miss Athena here handles the controls for me as I direct her."

Lady Clothilda exclaimed, "Oh that is most exciting to hear. We Ladies are supposed to be running the shows, not the men. On some of the isolated, primitive worlds of the halo, the men will not even let women fight at all, only become angry. How absolutely awful only to be allowed or permitted to be angry and not fight back! Everyone knows that anger is just an emotion and never accomplishes anything at all. Here in our civilized worlds, we women are the best fighters, outdoing men. I'm the Matriarch of our Security Forces, which are simply the best. I'm most proud that three out of five are women! I take only the very best fighters, you see. I have to. The security of House Kane lies upon me, and I do not take my heavy responsibility lightly," she explained eagerly.

She chatted on, very pleased I was listening to her and paying attention. "Our old legends speak of men doing all the fighting down in the disk. Is this true? Have your women not earned their honor there yet?"

"Oh it varies from world to world," I replied diplomatically. My mate is a very powerful fighter, a master swordswoman — at least she was before she lost her arms. Now, she tries to find other ways to fight."

"Oh I see. Yes, you have wisely chosen a mate then. It is good to hear that your civilizations in the disk have evolved some. We should update our records it would seem. But you must have other weapons besides swords." I sensed she was pumping me for key data that both interested her and was in her area of responsibility.

"Oh certainly. We have guns. Most of the fighters have guns, but a wise aristocrat prefers to settle disputes without bloodshed on the worlds where we come from," I replied.

She smiled. "Ah yes. We have guns as well. I can see that you are wise to avoid needless fights. Yet, you must also display a strong hand to your enemies. We certainly do."

"Of course."

"Well, you must excuse me. I must go and see about the security for mama's meetings this morning. Duty calls. Perhaps, we can talk more this evening, Lady Nia, Lady Tesla?" Lady Clothilda asked politely.

"Absolutely. Perhaps, one day we could tour your Security Forces. I'd love to see them." She smiled and agreed, very pleased I asked to see them. I began to see that she felt she was being pushed out of the running to assume her mother's role when Lady Athala retired from her position. That I was showing her goodly respect did not go unnoticed by her. I realized that probably many of the Ladies I would be meeting had similar feelings, having been assigned to lead or run various portions of the overall picture instead of the actual House Kane.

As she rose, she said to Lady Frieda, "Sis, get her a bright yellow gown. She would look simply stunning in yellow."

After she left, the butler entered with our two new bank accounts. Actually, they were much like our Imperium ID cards. The merchant would simply swipe our card and enter the amount of the purchase. The amount would be transferred from our account into his. Their system was just as efficient as that of the Imperium I would soon find out. After he politely handed the cards to Athena and Damali, Lady Gabriele explained how they were to be used and that the two should protect the cards well. "You see, you are holding the entire wealth of your Lady in your hands."

"Well, we should get going," Frieda announced. "We don't have to be back for lunch. There are some exquisite diners in Krazdorf. Come on. I just love to go shopping. Don't you?"

"Yes, but will they be able to fit our massive bosoms?" I asked.

"Certainly. Well, I should hope so." Miss Emlin assisted Lady Frieda and came with us, as did Miss Gabriele. When we got to the limousine, we emulated Lady Frieda and mostly backed into the seats. We couldn't do much else in these enormous gowns, ignoring the difficulties of our boots. I had to resist using my *mentales* gifts right and left! So did Tesla, depending heavily on Damali, as I did with Athena.

I'll admit we women do liked to be occasionally fussed over, and that's just what happened at the dressmaker's shop. Lady Frieda took us to the finest one in Krazdorf, at least she and the neon sign over his establishment said so. At first, I thought that his eyes were going to pop out of his head when he saw the size of our bosoms. However, he recovered politely from his shock and deftly proceeded to make us feel like queens. It was after one in the afternoon before we left, having purchased ten different outfits with matching boots. They would be delivered later today to the mansion. As we left, I picked up his parting thought. *This sale will make me even more famous!*

As we stepped out into the street into the warm sunshine, Lady Frieda suggested, "Well, it's lunch time, and I know just the ideal place to dine. It's only a short walk from here. We should be able to manage it. Miss Emlin, please tell the chauffeur to meet us at the Eberhauptgaststatte."

"Of course, My Lady," she replied. We waited while she delivered the message. Just standing still in these boots was difficult. Lady Frieda wiggled a little without her maid to support her. Without asking, Miss Gabriele moved to her side and put a steadying arm around her. Just then, a well-dressed young man came walking up the street, waving at us — well actually Lady Frieda.

"Good afternoon, Matriarch Frieda! So good to run into you once more. My, you simply must introduce me to these aristocrats. Where ever did you find them?" he said playing up to her.

"Herr Heinrich Horst, may I present Matriarch Nia Elian and Aristocrat Tesla. They are aristocrats from the galactic disk. Yes, way down there, here for a visit with Matriarch Athala. Herr Heinrich helps run the Vergnugenspalast, one of the finest pleasure houses in Krazdorf. He's been after my hand," she countered, emphasizing the words "one" and "after."

"*The* finest," he corrected her. "I'm so very pleased to meet such charming young aristocrats, but surely you are not from that filthy disk are you?"

"Indeed we are, Herr Heinrich," I replied.

"Well then, our history books must be *wholly* in error about the disk people. But unless my eyes deceive me, you are both missing your arms. Such strange lip ornaments, and you talk from those boxes around your waists." Meanwhile, his eyes really focused on our bosoms.

I took his not so subtle hint and replied, "As Matriarch Athala says, we have evolved from having tiny arms to none at all. Our bosoms now serve the same purpose as the tiny arms do here in the Narsten Cluster. On our world, the aristocratic men and women all wear these lip plates. It is our status symbol, but they obviously affect our speech, so we used these talking boxes to translate our words into your language. However, I would not go so far as to say that your history books are *wholly* in error. There are many worlds in the disk with many different cultures and practices."

"Well, I most certainly *do* approve of these changes, Matriarch Nia Elain, *most* definitely! As I always have told Matriarch Frieda here on many occasions, *no* one can ever exceed her great *beauty*, but Matriarch Frieda, when I said that, I had not known of these two beauties. Now, it seems I'm being surrounded with three of the absolutely *finest* aristocratic women in the entire universe! Such pale skin you both have, most unusual. Say, I was just about to grab some lunch at the Eberhauptgaststatte. I would be *most* honored if you would join me. Please, you simply must join me," he added most insistently. Heinrich looked to be in his mid-twenties. His suit was a bright blue, contrasting sharply with his grey skin and coal black, overly oiled hair. His angular face was striking, but his social airs were definitely a pretense.

"Of course, we would be delighted to join you for lunch at the Eberhauptgaststatte. We were just heading there ourselves. Please, Herr Heinrich, you simply must tell them about your pleasure house while we walk." I picked up her additional thought: *So you don't bore us with it while we dine.*

As we slowly and carefully walked the three blocks with neon lights flashing here and there, strange looking motor vehicles traveling the streets, and many other men and women wearing much different clothing, though still garishly colored, passing us by while giving we two long stares, Heinrich was only too eager to explain. "It is really dad's business, but I'm being groomed to take his place. At the Vergnugenspalast, you can have only the very finest in sensual pleasures. Whether it be the finest in smokes or the most fabulous of wines or any and all types of hallucinogens for your senses be they brief or of long duration or music for discerning ears or the most exotic of dancers for your eyes or even the finest of sexual pleasures, the Vergnugenspalast offers you this and so much more." He sounded like a salesman, but I did take note of what he was selling, and I didn't like it. I hoped Lady Frieda wasn't interested in his hand in marriage!

Surrounded in a sea of grey-skinned people, it was not hard to notice a man with a strong bluish hue to his skin. That he was wearing leg chains and manacles was also poignant. He carried a broom and was sweeping the streets, as we approached where he was working. He stepped back out of our way though. "Who is that and why is he being restrained?" I asked.

Herr Heinrich spat at the man. "He is a captured Slaver! Scum of the halo! When our forces are able, we capture those wicked men and make them do the lowest, most menial jobs in the Cluster. Teach them a lesson they'll never forget. Useful though, for who would want to be a street sweeper?"

Matriarch Frieda added, "We put many of them to work in our mines. I'm told it is a very dangerous line of employment; so again, it is a fitting punishment for their multitude of crimes against humanity. Slavers! Scum of the halo!" She reiterated his admonition.

He added, "But do not concern yourselves with these lowest of beasts. We have cut out their tongues so they can never insult one of us, not ever."

As I passed by the bluish skinned, thin man, I picked up his counter-thought as he wiped the spittle off his face. *Thou be the perverted scum of the halo!* A crack had just appeared in the "proper civilized" society of the Narsten Cluster. No, perhaps two had. This house of pleasure sounded terribly decadent to my ears. However, I did notice him staring intently at Tesla and me. I picked up another surface thought of his. *Disk people? How can this be?* The man, whatever his crimes had been, certainly wasn't ignorant.

The diner was ten times more elegant than dining in the mansion! In fact, I'd never seen such a place as this. From the perfectly dressed waiters and staff to the richly decorated walls to the golden silverware, again absolutely precisely laid out on the tables, to the vases with freshly cut flowers on each, everything about the Eberhauptgaststatte fairly screamed "top of the line elegance in dining." Even the delicious food was served on golden and silver platters. I must admit I've never experienced such a meal and service as they provided. Herr Heinrich graciously picked up what had to be an expensive tab. The table conversation was social and polite, but bland beyond words. However, I did learn Frieda and many others frequently visited his house of pleasure.

On our drive back, I paid closer attention to the people on the streets and spotted several more of the bluish-skinned Slavers. Meanwhile Frieda chatted, "Well, I'm not seriously considering Herr Heinrich's marriage proposal. He's such a bore, but I don't dare tell him that, not to his face. Still, such a marriage would guarantee me a lifetime supply of my Mary Jane and all the sensual pleasures imaginable. But I'll say this, Lady Nia Elain, what I felt with you last night was so superior, so exquisite, so delightful, that I would even lower myself to begging you for more! But of course, that would not be polite, now would it? Certainly not befitting us aristocrats. Begging, I mean. Oh, I forgot to mention Lady Clothilda wants to have you review her Security Forces later this afternoon around three, I think. Do be kind to her. She works so terribly hard with them to make them the very best fighters on Menno. Just between you and me, and don't tell others, I think she's just devastated that mama didn't choose her to take her place as head of House Kane when mama retires."

Tesla sent me, *So it's acceptable in this society to covertly cut up your own sisters!* I could only agree, wondering what it must be like to have brothers and sisters in one's family. It had been denied me. I was their only child, adopted too.

When we returned to the mansion, once more the limo parked beneath the portico, and the doorman was right there on post, opening our doors for us. Lady Frieda ushered us into the drawing room and sent for coffee. Again, I was amazed at the efficiency of their staff. A serving man in a tuxedo appeared within a minute, carrying a silver tray with cups, spoons, and an ornate decanter of freshly brewed coffee.

By the time we finished it, Matriarch Clothilda walked slowly into the room. "Matriarch Nia Elain, I do hope your shopping went well." I said it had. She then said, "I have some of my Security Forces in formation, if you would like to review them now. Mama has finished her meetings a bit early, so we're back sooner than I'd expected this morning."

"I'd love to see them, Matriarch Clothilda. Please," I replied politely. Athena helped me rise again, and we followed her out the front door, where the doorman once more could not take his eyes off of Tesla and me. There on the front lawn three dozen soldiers stood at attention in a long line, perfectly straight, three deep. Each wore their spotless black uniforms. Well over half were indeed women.

As we walked, Miss Gabriele whispered to Athena and Damali, "You should hold them tightly. Walking on the soft grass is most challenging for them!" I felt Athena's arm encircle my waist more securely than normal. As Matriarch Clothilda stepped off the pavement onto the grass, I saw her wobble slightly. Then, I too found my footing incredibly tenuous! The tiny, tall heel sunk into the ground, no longer supporting me. I would have fallen had Athena not been holding me up. Bravely, I followed Clothilda, observing her troops as best I could.

Each looked well-muscled and quite fit. All carried what we call a hunting rifle in the Imperium, antique relics that are used mostly for sporting events and target shooting by the affluent. They also carried a pistol strapped to their waist belts along with what appeared to be a sword, though a small one. Matriarch Clothilda pointed out, "Their uniforms are specially made and will stop bullets hitting them. The only way to kill one of my soldiers is to hit them in their heads. Therefore, when we go into combat, we wear a protective helmet that also has communications gear in them. That way, they are in constant communication with each other, their leaders, and me. Each of these soldiers is a crack shot." She went on describing their marksmanship, but without any reality on such guns, the significance missed me. Our d-guns would wipe them out in a minute or less.

She went on, "Our battleships have laser guns on them that can drill holes in enemy ships in seconds. You see, we've all of our bases covered." I praised her and her troops appropriately. Never was I so thankful to reach the solid pavement as I was that afternoon!

Once on solid ground, I asked, "When was the last time your people had to fight a war? Are such things common here in the halo?"

"Well, admittedly, most of them have been between various worlds here in the Narsten Cluster. However, what with the escalating raids by the Slavers, Matriarch Athala is planning to go to war with them in order to stop them, just as soon as she builds up enough forces to ensure a smashing and quick victory. Once they are handled, I think she plans to go after the Hadu, the vile lizard men of the Spicula Cluster. You know we've captured some of them, and as punishment, they are forced to labor in our mines. Why kill our enemies when we can make them work for us? Right?" she pointed out.

She went on, "But I guess you have had countless wars down in the disk. Our history books speak of nothing but continuous wars between the many filthy worlds of the disk."

Tesla spoke up, "Well, in the distant past, that was true. However, two millennia ago, several worlds came together and formed what's now called the Ataro Empire. They have developed ways to prevent wars and have had nearly two millennia of peace within their system of planets. We now number forty planets total, but we are also part of the Imperium, which has brought a long history of peace to the other worlds of our arm. However, I do admit that recently the whole Imperium had to fight a war with the other worlds in the other spiral arm. It is best if the actual cause of the hostilities between the worlds can be uncovered and remedied. Prevention of wars is always preferable, don't you think?"

"I suppose that's so. Still, these Slaver raids must be stopped. My forces are willing and ready. Well, I must dismiss them now. Thank you for reviewing them."

"Our pleasure," I replied politely. We headed back inside to the drawing room, just as a delivery vehicle pulled up carrying crates of our new dresses. Efficiently, several tuxedo clad men, the footmen we were told, appeared and carried them to our rooms. Later, we learned that the maids unpacked them and put them into our wardrobes for us. Long before six, I was hungry again. "Lady Frieda, why do we eat at one and six instead of noon and five? On our worlds those are the times that we hold our main meals."

"Oh that's so that the servants have an opportunity to eat first. Long standing tradition. They do have to eat and besides in every aristocratic home it is done for security reasons as well. If someone tried to poison our food, the servants would get sick and die before serving us."

"Wow! Has that happened often? Should we be worried about someone trying to poison us?" I asked growing worried for our safety.

"Well, it has happened, mostly in the distant past. But you know how traditions are. Once they are begun, there's no changing them. Besides, the servants need to eat as well. I think they do a better job serving us when they have full bellies," she replied. I began to see Lady Frieda was extremely bored with life. She had little actually to do but sit and chat. Our outing today had been exciting for her. I know, I have a wholly different definition of exciting. At last the dinner gong sounded.

After another perfectly done and executed meal, we women withdrew to the drawing room, where I expected finally to have a long talk with Matriarch Athala. I figured she would be grilling us about our world and armaments. We'd barely gotten properly seated and the coffee served when a footman announced, "A number of other matriarchs are demanding an audience with you and our new matriarchs from the disk. I'm sorry Matriarch Athala; they are most insistent."

A woman in a billowing bright pink dress came

marching into the room. Well, marching is overstating it. The tiny-armed woman in the giant skirt moved slowly, but determinedly into the room, followed by a number of other matriarchs and their maids. Something significant was definitely up!

Chapter 10 Narsten Politics

This is more like it. Now we are going to find out a whole lot more about this civilization, Tesla sent me, as we watched a dozen other matriarchs from nearby worlds barging in on Matriarch Athala, quite unannounced, save for the poor footman, who stood aside holding the door while trying to look as if nothing out of the ordinary was happening. I noted Miss Elise pulling rather hard on the silent signal system. I expect their kitchen staff and servants were about to get an unexpected workout.

We watched as a dozen brightly colored outer-skirts swayed slightly as the matriarchs moved into the room, found seats, and were helped to sit by their silent lady's maids. Age-wise, I guessed they ranged between their late forties and early sixties. I anticipated only a few of these would be dominate in the ensuing discussions and was correct. While Matriarch Athala was clearly unnerved by their sudden appearance, she retained her manners, introduced us, and then one by one the dozen women. I quickly got lost with all of the names, but as I said, only a few did all the talking and questioning. These were Matriarch Hiltraud of House Heinedorf, Matriarch Gunda of House Yvo, and Matriarch Gisela of House Hunsstadt, the youngest of the more outspoken leaders. Their planets were named after their houses. Tesla's initial guess that these were planetary rulers proved spot on.

"So just when were you going to present these supposed matriarchs from the filthy disk to the rest of us, Matriarch Athala?" barked Matriarch Hiltraud. "What security precautions have you taken? They could well be spies from the disk sent here to find our weaknesses, preparatory to an attack. Just how do you know that they are even aristocrats?"

"Well, if you would read your communiques, you would know I was planning to bring them to the next council meeting in two weeks and introduce them to you at that time. By then, I would have gotten all the information from them that I would need to answer all of your questions. Let's begin with the aristocrat question first. As you can plainly see, they have dispensed with even tiny arms, preferring larger breasts." Clearly, she was trying to be polite about them.

Matriarch Gisela interrupted, "Larger? My god, Matriarch Athala, they are larger than their heads! So they are supposed to replace the eroticism of our tiny arms?"

"Yes, they most certainly do just that," Matriarch Athala defended her position. Looking over at me, she apologized in advance. "Lady Frieda can more than vouch for their highly erotic usage. She was given a demonstration of that last night, but we don't need to embarrass our guests any further."

"But why the monster lip disks? Why does their speech come from those boxes around their waists?" Matriarch Gisela asked.

I decided to speak up, saving Matriarch Athala further embarrassment. "On our world, these are considered status symbols of aristocratic men and women. They add a great deal of eroticism to the simple act of kissing. However, the lip plates prevent us from making any sounds that involve our lips. Hence, we wear these boxes, which translate the strange language that we speak into yours. Out of hundreds of languages spoken in the Imperium, in the galactic disk, in only a very few can we speak and be understood."

Matriarch Athala added, "As you can see, they are wearing aristocratic gowns, just as we are, and their feet are wearing our boots. Miss Elise, would you be so kind and show them?" She lifted up my outer-skirt to show them my new boots. The older women continued, "They are wealthy, of that I have no doubt. I set them up with a pair of bank accounts early this morning. They donated a pound of pure platinum to trade for our gold currency. How many do you know who have a pound of platinum to waste like this? Further, Matriarch Nia Elain is the captain of her spaceship. I've seen it with my own eyes. So has Rolf. Plus, I have also seen three others of her crew who look just like Lady Tesla."

She sighed before going on. "Please forgive me," she looked at us first, before saying, "The only drawback we've seen thus far is that they are like the Farthun women." All dozen gasped. "Hermaphrodites, yes. Lady Frieda verified it

221

last night personally, though any of our lady's maids who attend them could also vouch for this. Still, I do hope we can put aside such prejudices and accept them as the aristocrats that they most obviously are."

Several footmen entered carrying trays of refreshments. Their timing could not have been better. Perhaps, Matriarch Athala had prearranged for just such surprise meetings. Over coffee and rolls, the dozen finally accepted we were aristocrats, and since I was the captain and leader of our group, I must therefore be worthy of the title of matriarch. Now, their attention turned to far more delicate matters. Over coffee, several asked if Matriarch Athala gotten the answers from me to these questions. They rattled them off in no particular order. Why were we here? What did we want? Were there other aristocrats in the disk? If so, how many worlds were matriarchal in government? Would we consider aiding them in the proposed war against the Slavers? Were we just basically spies, gaining inside information before some in the disk invaded the Narsten Cluster?

Matriarch Gunda spoke. "We need answers to these basic questions. We do not mean to offend you in any way, Matriarch Nia Elain, Lady Tesla, but the security of a dozen worlds depends on our finding out the truth to these. To that end, I must warn you right here at the start that Matriarch Gisela is far more that the mere Matriarch of House Hunsstadt. She is a powerful telepath and can easily detect if you are telling the truth or are lying to us. So I warn you, be truthful in your replies."

Both Tesla and I were a bit surprised. We had been so distracted by these women we'd not even anticipated that some of these people might have that rare gift, just as a few did in the Imperium, where perhaps one in billions was a Class V telepath. Instinctively, I reached out to touch Matriarch Gisela's mind. *Oh! Hi. She isn't lying. You are a telepath too. As you can see, both Tesla and I are as well. Nice to meet a fellow telepath. On our worlds, we follow a strict protocol and never invade another's mind and pick up their thoughts without their expressed permission. We consider that to be mental rape and would be severely punished if we did.*

Oh! Oh my! We were not expecting this! Both of you? I must have your sworn words that you have not invaded minds here to obtain state secrets!

Of course. You must do that. None of the matriarchs would feel remotely comfortable around us if they were not so convinced.

Matriarch Gisela swallowed hard. "They, they are both powerful telepaths too! They claim to be following a code similar to ours, but I simply must have them say this aloud so I can verify it. Both of you, swear to everyone here that you have not yet used your powers to obtain state secrets or secrets of any kind." We both did so. "They are telling the truth." I watched the color returning to Matriarch Athala's face. It had lightened up very noticeably, when she heard the news we were also telepaths. "I need you to both swear that you will never enter another's mind to probe their thoughts without their expressed permission first." Once more, we both so swore. Even with these precautions, the dozen leaders were still very wary of us.

Matriarch Athala cleared her throat. "I'm sorry. I didn't know. If you had all given me the time that I needed, I would have found this out and prevented your exposure to such a security breech." Several of the women squirmed slightly. We didn't need telepathy to know they wished that they had not come tonight.

Matriarch Athala then asked the key question. "So have you come here to spy on us?"

"If by spying you mean did we come here to learn about your worlds and the many worlds of the halo, then yes we are spies. Our world is part of the Ataro Empire. There are forty worlds in it now. Each is run by an armless queen, who also wears the toe shoes that we originally wore when you first met us. They are not for the most part hermaphrodites like we are, though on our world our queens are. Our empire has managed to maintain peace for over two millennia now. No wars. We try to prevent wars and have been successful. Our mission is to explore the unknown northern halo, unknown to us at least. We are here to learn what new worlds are here and learn about your people. We had no idea that here in the halo our worlds in the disk are considered to be subnormal, filthy, and dirty."

"To what end do you wish this knowledge of us?" asked Matriarch Hiltraud.

"Presumably to see if there might be ways to establish friendly relationships with some of the worlds here in the halo. Perhaps trading arrangements might be worked out, though it is far too soon to even know if there is anything that you might desire from us. We met Matriarch Athala when we landed on Farthun-3 while she was meeting with their mayor. That was the first world we visited here in the halo. We learned from her of the Slavers and the Hadu, and that she is trying to find allies to help defeat their threat. Wars are always nasty, and even the winner suffers horribly. All those dead men and women who died fighting for victory are gone. Our queens, emperor, and empress all work hard to find the real reason for the war and handle it, preventing the war from happening. I'm not authorized to make any deals, but I could see if our queens would be interested in coming here and helping you with this. Figuratively, I mean, since they don't have any hands."

"She speaks the truth," Matriarch Gisela commented.

"We were also hoping to find out where the Ceri live." I ignored the expected gasps. "Many of us on my ship once met some Ceri a few years back. The Ceri were trying to save a whole world from destruction. A moon was about to crash into it. We found them most helpful, but very difficult to see. Naturally, we would like to know more about these ghost-like beings. We of the disk are an intensely curious lot."

"Just how many are on your spaceship?" asked Matriarch Gunda.

"Counting myself, there are twenty-two of us, eleven married couples. My mate and I have two three year old daughters with us, and another couple has a ten year old daughter with them. Naturally, we also have our needed lady's maids with us. I'm not counting them, unless you wish me to."

"And how many of them are soldiers?" she asked.

I knew what she was worried about and decided to trust them a bit with this knowledge. "None. They are all like Tesla and me, aristocrats. Twenty-two of us. So we do need our lady's maids very much." If they tried to storm and take our ship by force, I knew the robots would defend them, as well as the many *mentales* gifted. Knowing their weapons were quite primitive by our standards, I knew they'd not be successful if they tried to take my ship by force.

"You mean you don't have any men on board with strong arms or women soldiers? It's just twenty-two of you aristocratic women who appear as you do, without even arms?" asked Matriarch Gisela in disbelief.

"That is correct. We do depend upon our lady's maids. Obviously."

Matriarch Gisela swallowed hard. "She's telling the truth."

"Rolf has already verified that their spaceship is not armed like our battleships. There are no external guns on it," Matriarch Athala attempted to recover a bit of her authority.

"She's right. Our ship is unarmed. Our light cruisers, heavy cruisers, and battleships have all sorts of guns though. My ship is a deep space exploration ship, completely unarmed. My parents used to scour the spiral arm for new, unexplored worlds, before they died when I was eighteen."

"Just how is it that your ship has enough fuel to reach this far into the halo?" asked Matriarch Hiltraud. "Our knowledge, though quite dated, suggests your ships don't have enough fuel to reach this distance. Farthun was their limit."

"Farthun-3 is still the practical limits of most of our spaceships. However, we are carrying a lot more fuel than a normal ship would carry. Plus, we are testing out two new engines to see if they will perform better. Time will tell on that one."

"She's telling the truth," Matriarch Gisela said softly. Now, I sensed the other rulers beginning to relax some.

"But wait. Are you saying that your servants, your maids fly your ship?" Matriarch Gunda asked what had been bothering her for several minutes.

"Yes, Athena here follows my orders and can fly the ship. I've not seen your ships, but with ours, it's mostly just a matter of entering the coordinates into the navigation system and pushing buttons."

The middle-aged woman nodded, accepting the

confusing facts at last. "Ah, yes, I believe that my maid could do that for me, only I'd have to give her proper directions."

"Precisely," I replied.

Matriarch Hiltraud said decisively, "Okay then. I believe we have established that we have here a ship of disk aristocrats visiting our halo worlds on a mission of exploration and not subterfuge or sabotage or worse. We should take this golden opportunity to update our historical records concerning the disk worlds and any potential threat that they may be to us. Further, we should explore the remote possibility they could become allies in the coming war with the Slavers and Hadu. Lord knows we're going to need a vast armada to defeat them. But at the same time, we don't want to be like the chickens who invited the fox into their roost to help defend them from the bad wolf, who only turned on them once the wolf was driven away. Lastly, we should explore the very remote, very unlikely possibility that the filthy disk people might have something worth trading for. Matriarch Athala, you ought to hand these alien aristocrats over to Matriarch Gisela, who alone can guarantee they speak truthfully. We obviously now need these three areas fully uncovered."

I sensed that Matriarch Athala had had other plans for us. From the way she wiggled and adjusted herself in her seat, I had clues that her plans, whatever they might have been, were being altered. Obviously, Matriarch Athala had been trying to make a power play among the hierarchy of Narsten planetary rulers, very likely by obtaining these very things from us before presenting those answers and us to the council of matriarchs. The arrival of these dozen matriarchs had foiled that move.

Like any seasoned political leader, she adapted at once. "But of course, we must have Matriarch Gisela question them about such things. I wouldn't dream of doing it without her. I certainly am not a soothsayer! Matriarch Gisela, I would be most honored if you would stay on as my guest and question my guests as long as you desire. As you can see, they have adjusted to my mansion well. I see no reason to move them and their ship to another world, when Matriarch Gisela can ask her questions here just as well, especially since Matriarch

Nia Elain does not know her way around the Narsten Cluster. Rolf brought them here from Farthun via a tractor beam. It would be far less of an imposition on our guests to merely have Matriarch Gisela question them here, don't you agree?" She recovered nicely. While I wanted to see more of their worlds, just now I figuratively had my hands full with just this one world.

While this was obviously not what she'd had in mind, Matriarch Hiltraud replied hesitantly, "I see your point. Tractor beam? Why yes, I do believe you have a point here. After all, they are aliens from the disk and have no idea of where our many worlds are located. This is probably best, Matriarch Gisela, if you would be agreeable to staying on here for a while."

Matriarch Gisela answered, "Of course. I can purchase apparel and sundries here. No sense in making my ship fly back to Hunsstadt just to bring mine here. Franz might be a little bored, but I'm sure Rolf will entertain him," she replied, referring to their husbands.

"Good. Then that's settled," Matriarch Athala declared firmly. "It is getting late. I should get my finest guest rooms ready for Matriarch Gisela."

"Yes, it is. We ought to be getting back ourselves. Thank you for staying, Matriarch Gisela. Do keep us all informed," Matriarch Hiltraud stated, more like an order than a statement. With that, eleven of the aristocratic women were helped to their feet by their silent lady's maids. With swishing and swaying of their large outer-skirts, they moved slowly out of the drawing room.

The next morning while Athena was getting me dressed, Athena reported, "Over breakfast, the servants were all chatting about last evening's business. Apparently, the gossip opinion among them is that Athala's grand plans were squashed by their sudden appearance. They were speculating about just how the other rulers learned about our arrival here, but they have no concrete knowledge. I would urge caution on just what you reveal about our civilizations to these people."

"Indeed. Still, I have to be very careful around this telepath of theirs. Come, that's the gong."

In the dining room, Lady Gisela was sitting beside Lady Athala, a chair usually held by Frieda, who was now sitting beside me. The husbands all sat on one side, chatting among themselves. Frieda chatted with me while our maids fed us. "Today is going to be exciting for me. I'm going to look more like you and Lady Tesla. I've talked to Doctor Heinz, and he's agreed to enlarge my breasts. While they aren't going to be as large as yours are, they'll be so much larger than anyone else. I want to look more like you two, but I don't think I can have my lips done like yours. We don't have those speech boxes that you have."

I replied, "Right Frieda. With these fancy ornaments, our speech is severely altered for the worse. The only problem with having them as large as ours is that their very heavy weight gives us backaches unless we wear these tight corsets. Keep that in mind," I advised her. She giggled. I picked up her unspoken consideration, though, and so did Tesla. Probably Lady Gisela also did, if she was any good at telepathy. *I'll have twice the erotic appeal to men!*

I couldn't tell any differences in the elegance of the breakfast table. My conclusion was that this household always dined in the same manner, as befitting royal guests. Nothing of any importance was ever discussed while eating. That always came afterwards when the ladies withdrew to the drawing room, leaving the men to smoke and discuss their affairs in the dining room. Once our slow procession entered and was seated, coffee was served again, but only after the servants and the others departed leaving the two matriarchs and us two behind, along with our personal maids, did the light conversation finally change.

Lady Gisela began, "Please, let's be more informal. It's just Lady Gisela, if you please. Now then, perhaps we should begin by learning more about the current state of the many civilizations down there in the galactic disk." She caught herself in time, having almost said the filthy galactic disk. She was trying to be polite.

"Well, essentially each arm belongs to a different large-scale political group. Our arm is run by the Imperium, while the Federation of Planets controls the other arm. I'm afraid we know almost nothing about the Federation. The Imperium isn't doing so well. Some say it's collapsing. Perhaps it is, but then it's still a strong and unifying force. Within the Imperium is the Ataro Empire of some forty planets of which ours is a part. The Ataro Empire is as strong and solid as it ever has been. Our rulers, our queens, are quite brilliant and most capable rulers. From your viewpoint, they would be called aristocrats or matriarchs."

Tesla took over from me at this point. "You see, each world has their own form of government, and the Ataro Empire recognizes each world is unique. However, their queen becomes the top-most authority on each world, resting atop whatever form of government that world has." She went on to describe how several worked, pointing out that the queen's usual job was to settle difficult problems that arose and not to attempt to control how the others ran their world. She described the fundamental reasons for the limiting of their physical abilities. Tesla certainly did a far better job of describing our political and governing principles than I could have, but then this was her forte.

After lunch, Lady Gisela asked about the designs of our war ships and their armaments. I replied, "I'm sorry. I'm not privy to such data. I've only been a passenger on a few of the light cruisers and then only briefly. So really, I'm not in a position to answer honestly such questions, Lady Gisela. From what very little I've see of your armaments, which isn't much at all, save an external look at Commander Rolf's ship which towed us here, I can honestly say I believe our ships are both faster and better armed than yours. Remember, I'm no soldier, and I haven't seen any of your warships. I'd rather not see them, if you don't mind." I said that last to put her more at ease, since I was confident that we telepaths could find out, if we ever needed to know that.

Tesla added, "But I wouldn't try to ally yourselves with the Imperium. Rather, I would make such overtures to the Ataro Empire and our Emperor Bino. Perhaps, you could convince him to send a queen here to help find the true cause of the conflicts and prevent a devastating war. Peaceful resolution to conflicts is always the right way to go, not fighting wars, where both sides suffer horribly." Ever so deftly, Tesla continued to implant the notion of inviting one of our queens here to resolve the conflicts. For their sakes, I hope she'd be successful.

By late afternoon, the topics had changed to one of trade potentials. Tesla again did most of the talking, though via telepathy, Zarita, our geologist, fed her answers and questions to ask. Zarita wisely picked up on the purity aspect of the pound of titanium, which we traded for their gold currency. By the sounding of the dinner gong, we had a better picture of the entire halo in terms of minerals. It seems the halo worlds had a significantly lower amount of all the heavier elements than did most of the disk worlds. Only a few like Ashford-5 didn't. Hence, our biggest bargaining chip lay in our ores and particularly those of the heavier elements. As we made our slow, careful way into the ornate and "perfectly arranged" dining room, I had the sense Lady Gisela felt there would be significant trading opportunities, if only they had something to trade in return. Perhaps, I should have brought along an official from the Ataro Empire who was well versed in making trading arrangements.

As we took our usual places, Lady Frieda became the center of attention instead of us. As she proudly walked into the room, she now sported breasts about as large as her head. Although still smaller than ours, hers were gigantic compared to the other women in the room. I pitied the seamstress who had to frantically alter her tops during the afternoon.

Lady Frieda gaily said, "I'm going to the Vergnugenspalast this evening. Lady Gisela, it's the finest pleasure house on Menno. I'd be delighted if you and your husband would join me, you too, Lady Nia Elain and Lady Tesla. Please do come."

"Lady Frieda, if Lady Gisela and the others go, I'll have to come along and provide extra security," Lady Clothilda protested slightly. It was obvious her older sister was a bit put out by her sudden announcement and offer. She hadn't planned on this security risk.

Matriarch Athala sealed the offer. "Why yes, Lady Gisela, you really should sample our finest pleasure house.

And it would be ungracious of us not to take Lady Nia Elain and Lady Tesla as well. Please, you simply all must go this evening. Relax and enjoy yourselves." Lady Clothilda gave her mother a brief frown, but rose to see to the unexpected security arrangements.

I did have a good idea just why Lady Frieda wanted to go out this evening. She was dying to see just how more erotic men found her new appearance. Well, I couldn't blame her for wanting to entice men. She needed to find the love of her life, though I doubted she'd find it at such a place as this. I began to wonder if it was a universal law that women had to fancy themselves up in order to better attract the attention of men, while men strutted around and acted boisterous, loud, and silly to get our attention.

Franz joined Lady Gisela, Lady Frieda, Tesla, and me in the big limousine. I was definitely concerned about this outing, because we were instructed to leave our lady's maids behind. "This is an upper society club that caters to us aristocrats. Not even our servants are allowed inside. The servants have their own clubs they can use. Don't worry. There'll be plenty of women at the club to assist us," Frieda explained. While Lady Gisela had Franz to help her, I felt very uncomfortable after Athena helped me inside and didn't join me. Tesla also felt very ill at ease with this arrangement. We didn't share Lady Frieda's enthusiasm for the outing, though Lady Gisela apparently wasn't at all concerned. I surmised she probably went to these pleasure houses often.

As we drove through the valley of the multitudinous neon lights shortly before 6:30, Franz chatted with Frieda, commenting about her new "look." Meanwhile, another car of Security Force was in front of the limo, while another trailed along behind us. With this much security, I began to relax. What could go wrong? "They look most impressive, Lady Frieda. I'm certain all eyes in the house will be upon you tonight."

She giggled. "Not totally. I'm sure Lady Nia Elain and Lady Tesla will attract even more attention. I do hope that all the young men don't swarm them and ignore me." Franz laughed and Lady Gisela smiled.

We were nearly there when it happened. Without any warning, some explosions went off outside the limo, which was currently slowed by traffic. For a moment, the noise and light flash blinded us, but our driver kept his cool and brought us quickly out of the erratic slide without crashing into anything or anyone. Franz drew his pistol and stepped out of the limo to see what was going on, while the driver got out looking for damage to our vehicle.

"What was that?" I asked trying to control my nervousness. I felt particularly helpless at the moment. I was taken by complete surprise. Well, so was everyone else.

"I, I don't know," Lady Frieda said shakily.

Franz leaned back in and said, "Ladies, time to get out of the limo. I'm afraid we're going to have to walk the rest of the way there. Limo has been disabled. The security cars are damaged and some are hurt. Come on; the sooner we get going, the better. I don't like this one bit."

At least Franz helped us out and onto our feet, one by one. "This is just awful!" Lady Frieda said looking around at the damage. He helped me out and got me safely to the sidewalk, close to a dark alleyway. He went back for Tesla.

Just then, a man wearing a dark hooded jacket stepped out of the shadows behind me. He whispered to me, "Alien Aristocrat. Don't believe everything the aristocratic leaders tell you. Look deeper for the truth." Startled, I turned carefully on my toes to see him, but he'd already turned around, moving rapidly down the alley. All I could see was the back of his head.

"This has got to be work of the Whiners," Lady Frieda began to explain, having regained some of her composure. Apparently, neither she nor Lady Gisela had heard the man speaking to me. I began to have the feeling this whole mess was designed just for him to give me that warning message!

Lady Gisela spoke up, "Yes, I believe so, Lady Frieda. We have these terrorist attacks on Hunsstadt as well. Random acts of violence. Mostly annoying, seldom any real harm or damage. I do hope the security men and women will be all right."

"Yes, I believe so, dear. I checked on them. Okay then, Lady Frieda, lead the way," Franz replied.

"It's this way. Not too far," she replied, leading the way. As we walked along, others on the street moved aside allowing us women and our billowing outer-skirts to pass by. Lady Frieda soon forgot all about the attack and chatted merrily, though she and the rest of us women were paying as close attention to our steps as we possibly could. Only Lady Gisela had a supporting arm. It was a bit daunting for Tesla and me, but Lady Frieda's constant friendly chatter helped.

We only had to go two blocks before I spotted the huge neon lights of the Vergnugenspalast. The doors were overly wide to accommodate our skirts. On either side of the double doors, rows of lights turned off and on in such a way as to appear to be an arrow guiding us there. Interesting use of lights, I thought, but rather wasteful.

Herr Heinrich met us at the plush entrance, along with several other young men and women. "Welcome, Matriarch Gisela Hunsstadt. It's a great honor to provide you this evening's entertainment. Once again, welcome Matriarch Nia Elain, Lady Tesla. My Lady Frieda! You look spectacular indeed. These lovely ladies will be your escorts. Everything, and I do mean everything, in our establishment is yours for the asking, compliments of Matriarch Athala." He slipped his arm around Lady Frieda, escorting her personally. Two women assisted us, while Franz led his wife inside.

We quickly parted company. Franz and Gisela wanted to have a light smoke. Lady Frieda wanted to visit the dance floor, where we later saw a large number of men hovering around her, much to the displeasure of six other aristocratic women. Never having been in such a place, we asked for a tour, and our hosts led us from room to room on the main floor before taking us up an elevator to the second floor. There were three "smoking" rooms. In one, they explained, people smoked "weed" to give them a relatively short high. In the next, they were smoking opium, and those people would be spending the night in rooms on the third floor. In the third such room, the smokers looked completely wasted. We didn't bother to ask just what this drug was.

Another two rooms were set aside for drinking: one for various types of beer and the other for wine. Two more rooms held a number of gambling games. People here were served drinks, and many also smoked while playing the various games, losing naturally, but having fun doing so.

Another room held a small theater, and a number of aristocratic women and men were here watching a play in progress. Another room held a small chamber group of musicians. The guests sat at tables sipping beverages and listening to the music, which we found rather strange, but interesting. After our tour, we decided to come back to this room.

Upstairs, we were shown any number of smaller, private bedrooms where one could indulge in all manner of sexual pleasures. Our hostesses explained we could have any man or woman or combination of our choice and dictate the nature of the pleasuring. We both declined this offer and soon returned to listen to the music. Our hostesses ordered us drinks, and we chose their finest ales, primarily because we both loved ale, having discovered it back on Metcalf-4. Of course, we had to instruct the two women on how to work our upper lip plates, and they had to serve our ale on spoons. Both young women were quite curious about us and didn't mind assisting us in the slightest.

The chamber group played several sets, and we found their music growing on us. Since neither of us wanted anything to do with any of the other "pleasures," we quietly decided to spend the evening in this room until the others came to take us home. Our two maids called themselves Katarine and Lore.

During a break between the musician's sets, Miss Katarine asked about our breast sizes. "Are they really erotic, as some of the aristocratic ladies are saying? A substitute for tiny arms? Do you have to have your arms removed a part of the substitute?"

I laughed. "Well, yes to the erotic side. After all, if you don't have any arms, you make do with what you have. I guess that's as good an explanation as any. But no, one should never lose their arms, not if they can help it. I'd give anything to have mine back. Worse, these are so heavy to carry that we get bad back pains if we don't wear these very tight corsets to help."

"Oh, I see. That's why you both sit so erect and have such small waists. Lady Frieda has them now too, though not as large as yours. All of the young men are hovering around her like she was a queen bee, you know."

Tesla laughed. "We know. How can we miss that?"

"And your giant lip ornaments? Are they also erotic or for fashion on your world?" Miss Katarine asked.

"Just between us, fashion on our world. But they also make kisses rather erotic as well." I was about to ask why they were so interested in erotic aspects, when Miss Katarine answered my wonder.

"You see, we're Lady's Maid servants, but in this class society, we cannot rise any higher than we are now. This job here at the pleasure house — it's the highest paying position we can ever achieve, short of working for Matriarch Athala Kane. But we want to do more than this."

"Tell me about it," I replied instinctively.

"In our world, you are locked into the class in which you were born. Lore and I were born into the Maid's Servant Class. We've worked hard and do our best. That's how we finally got this plush job here assisting all the aristocratic women who come to the pleasure house. But we can't rise any higher."

"Can't you marry an aristocratic man?" I asked, recalling what I was told about upper marriages.

"Yes, but if we did that, we'd be ostracized by the tiny-armed aristocrats and never accepted by them. Worse, the aristocratic men usually marry tiny-armed women. It is a horrid step down for them to marry otherwise. While legally it's possible, it's not practical at all. We both wanted to go to the University and learn. I wanted to study rocks and minerals. Lore here wanted to become a doctor and heal people, but Lady's Maids are not allowed into the University. Only aristocrats are."

Miss Lore spoke up, "Katarine, perhaps we shouldn't complain. The lower classes have it far worse than we do. Our lives would be utter hell if we were in the lowest Manual Labor Class. They even put the captive Slavers and Hadu in those."

"That's why we were asking about your breasts and such." Katarine looked around cautiously before she added,

"I'll tell you more if you promise never to tell anyone what I'm going to tell you." I did so, more out of curiosity than anything else.

"Many of us want to rebel against the aristocrats, who control everything. We're called the Underground. We were going to try to organize a planet-wide strike of all Lady's Maids, demanding reforms. After all, the tiny-armed ladies are wholly dependent upon us. But now, some of us are thinking we could have our breasts enlarged and get our lips pierced like yours and establish a new aristocratic movement, tossing out the tiny-armed ladies."

"Don't get your lips done. You won't be able to speak and be understood," I advised, explaining in detail. Neither believed me, so I had Katarine turn the ULAT off. I proceeded to say a few sentences in her language. She turned it back on rather quickly, quite startled by my nearly incomprehensible speech.

"Oh. I see. That's really bad. Okay, we won't consider doing that. But what do you think about our idea of a strike?" Katarine asked.

Tesla took over for me. "It could work in your favor or it could well backfire on you, causing you more grief than good." She outlined how in our world, women could become anything they desired, as long as they learned their craft well and worked hard. The two found this highly encouraging. "The one thing you don't want to do is to get the aristocrats fighting against you. They control most everything, including the Security Forces. They could use physical force against you."

"And we would fight back," Katarine responded feistily.

"Any many would get hurt or killed. A civil war is not an optimum way to obtain change, though it has been done on some of the disk worlds," Tesla explained. "Yes, change can come peacefully, though I know many of the older aristocrats will fight change tooth and claw. We're working on getting one of our Ataro queens to come here and help them avoid the war they are planning. Once that is handled, I'm sure the Ataro queen will then take up your situation as well. Gradual change can be had. You don't need a civil war to bring change."

She discussed this for some time before Katarine said,

236

"We will take your ideas to our Underground leaders and see. I can make no promises they'll listen to us. If this queen of yours does come to Menno, will she consent to seeing us?"

"I'll insist that she does." I gave her my word. "Just remember, I've not gotten Matriarch Athala's agreement to have one of our queens come here to help just yet."

She also explained, "The aristocrats call us the Whiners, because they say we do nothing but whine for change. Our leaders are talking about doing a lot more than just complaining, but we'll see what we can do to have them wait for your queen to come."

We chatted a bit more, before Lady Frieda came to take us home. She still had six men hovering around her and was thoroughly enjoying all the newfound attention she was attracting. I whispered to her, "Pick wisely." She giggled.

The limo had been repaired, and we had no further excitement getting home. Both Franz and Gisela were still rather stoned and managed to continue passionately kissing each other all the way back.

Once in our rooms, Tesla commented, "Perhaps another reason for this push for a war is to defuse the Whiner situation. Make their people all pull together to fight a common enemy." We both began to see ulterior motives behind the scenes.

The next morning over breakfast, I asked Matriarch Athala, "I was wondering if we could get a tour of the rest of your world. Stop and visit with businessmen and women. Have a tour of your factories and chat with some of the workers there."

"Oh for heaven's sake! An aristocratic tiny-armed woman never does such things. It's beneath her dignity! They know their place and are quite content with it. Besides, they are uneducated riffraff. Do you know they are too unintelligent even to get into our Universities? All Narsten folk know their place in life and are content with such."

"That's not entire true," Matriarch Gisela interrupted her. "The Whiners certainly do complain. After all, we were nearly killed last night."

"Do you have Whiners on your world, Matriarch

Gisela?" I asked, curiously.

Athala made a harrumph sound, quite disapproving of this whole line of discussion, especially over the breakfast table. "We certainly do have them. I believe it's safe to say that there are Whiners on all the Narsten worlds these days. Some say the movement is growing stronger. After last night, I'm inclined to believe those rumors."

Franz barked, "We should put a stop to them, once and for all!"

Matriarch Clothilda hastily said, "It's all my fault, Matriarch Gisela, Franz. I had the Security Forces take you there by the most direct route. Obviously, the attack was well planned. I should have had them take a random route last night. Then, your near assassination would not have happened. The Whiners wouldn't have known your route. If you go again tonight, I give you my word it won't happen again. Please forgive my gross error in judgment."

"Of course Matriarch Clothilda. No real harm was done this time," Matriarch Gisela replied. "We would enjoy returning there tonight, if we may." After this, the breakfast table chat returned to normal pleasantries of no substance.

Later in the drawing room over coffee, I asked, "So if war is declared against the Slavers and the Hadu, will the aristocrats lead the fight, the battles?"

"Heavens no, dear child!" Matriarch Athala gushed. "What do you think? With our tiny arms, we can even hold and fire a gun? Heavens no. We are the planners. We'll develop the strategy and tactics."

"Silly me. That's plainly obvious. I don't know what I was thinking," I smoothed it over some. "So who does the actual fighting? Surely, your Security Forces will be insufficient to wage a war."

"Quite true, quite," she replied. "We'll simply have to draft many out of the numerous lower classes. We'll make all the appropriate speeches and fire them up, urging them on to defend their homes, families, and businesses." She added with some passion, "We can put those Whiners to very good use. Let them fight the real enemies, the Slavers."

The picture was becoming clearer by the moment. Now,

I needed to extract ourselves from this world and resume our voyage. However, I still believed one of our queens could possibly prevent this proposed war and perhaps keep their society from entering a civil war. Matriarch Gisela perhaps sensed this or perhaps she was more observant than Matriarch Athala. She said, "Matriarch Nia Elain, what would it take to have one of your queens come to the Narsten Cluster and study our situation with the Slavers and Hadu and then give us her recommendations?"

"An invitation and your promise of full cooperation with her investigation, no matter where it may lead. She'll want to speak with quite a few people and not just the matriarchs, though I'm sure she will start with you."

"That is as it should be. Of course, this queen of yours will see that we are right and proper, that we are the good ones in this dispute, and that the Slavers and Hadu beasts are wicked and quite evil," Matriarch Athala declared, as though everyone knew this.

I debated whether to argue with her over good and evil being a matter of a society's morals and sense of ethics, but decided against it. These people were terribly fixed in their opinions and attitudes. She added, "And I *do* hope if this queen finds these Slavers and Hadu must be stopped, she'll be willing to become allies with us in our fight against these wicked fiends and beasts. When your people are being kidnaped and sold into slavery or fed to the lizard men as food, there is no room for pacifist notions. You must fight for your freedom and life."

"Of course there isn't. I'd sure like to investigate this myself. You know, talk to the survivors of the raids and those who saw your people being eaten by these lizard men. That has to be just awful! We don't have any alien races like that down in the disk, at least none that we've ever found, just we humans," I replied, feeling her out a little. So far, we'd only seen her mansion and servants, not counting the dressmakers and the pleasure house. I wanted to check on just what actually had happened, if I could. I know any queen coming here will immediately want to check on those.

"Why in Narsten's Name would you want to *do* that? I

have the official reports, which provide all the gory details. I'll have them brought up if you really wish to see them, though I can't imagine why you'd want to see them. That's *why* we have Investigators to deal with such horrid matters. Aristocrats handle the really *big* issues of our worlds, not crimes committed by the Slavers and Hadu. We'd never get anything done if we spent all our time on such matters best left to the Investigator Classes. That's what they do, investigate and file reports on what they find. That procedure has worked for millennia," Matriarch Athala replied.

"Thanks. I would really like to see the reports. Remember, we are the aliens here, and we don't know a thing about either your enemies or what they've done on your worlds. I'd like to get a fuller picture, if you don't mind," I said diplomatically, smoothing the situation over as best I could. "Also, I should spend some time back on my ship. I've not seen my daughter for several days. Are we allowed to travel around the city on our own, seeing the sights and such? Some of my crew would probably like to have some shore leave."

"Of course, your crew is welcome to stay here at the mansion. However, since they are aristocratic women, I must insist they wear proper apparel. If they get their feet fixed like you both have and wear an outer-skirt, then they are free to come and go around the mansion here. However, if they wish to go anywhere else, I would insist on their coordinating their outings with Matriarch Clothilda here, since she is ultimately responsible for their safety. After the other night, you can certainly see why. We don't want to give the Whiners an opportunity to create an inter-world incident that we would both regret," she countered.

"Absolutely. We certainly don't want anything remotely like that to happen," I responded diplomatically. We finished our coffee and Matriarch Athala headed off to procure a copy of some of the incident reports. An hour later, Miss Elise brought them to Athena, telling her this was our personal copy to do with as we wanted. After that, I asked Matriarch Clothilda to arrange a trip back to the spaceport for us, which she did. We left all our new clothes here, fully expecting to return in a day or so, but did take our bedroom slippers.

As we made our careful way into the front hatch of the Eagle's Seed, Mai brought our girls to greet us. "Mommy!" Zorina called out, echoed by Nadia. "See what we made for you." Psykhe held up a crude color drawing. "That's you and that's mommy too. That's me and that's Nadia." She was extremely proud of her first artwork attempts. Nadia had a similar one to show me too. I squatted down, and we pushed into each other doing our best to hug. Mai just stood there, beaming from her eyes, though I know she was smiling broadly.

First action: get out of the impossible outer-skirt! It was so wide we couldn't navigate the hallways on the ship. That done, everyone wanted to see our boots and feet. "To the Med Lab, both of you," Dr. Leann demanded. She was just following protocol, but I didn't hesitate. Tesla and I want to know about how bad our feet were, and the protocol was designed to detect anything that might have been done to our bodies covertly, as well as detect any spying devices that might have been planted on us without our knowledge. I didn't think this society had such devices, but Dr. Leann was thorough.

A half hour later, she pronounced, "Well, you are both healthy. No spying or tracking devices, but I've got good news and bad news. Which do you want first?"

I said good news, and Tesla said bad news, and we three laughed. "All right. Bad news, I don't think I can repair your feet. I think you are stuck this way for some time to come. Good news, you both are pregnant. Join the crowd."

Tesla frowned over the bad news, but I'd already figured this would be the case, when I had agreed to have it done. "Cool! Zorina and Nadia will have a new sister," I replied.

"Two new sisters. Danika is also pregnant, Nia," Leann corrected me.

"Oh! Even cooler."

"So is everyone else on this ship, except Mai, of course. We're all pregnant, it seems," Leann added with a wry smile. "You ought to have anticipated this detail, captain, what with everyone confined with little to do. September is going to be baby month around here. Twenty-two of them! Of course, the men are taking it rather hard as you would expect. Perhaps, you ought to say a few words about this to everyone."

"I've got to help Martina pick out names," Tesla giggled. "This is so great. Now, we're going to have a family too. Can't tell you how envious Anya and I were of you and Danika, when you both had yours."

I took the hint. Besides, I had to talk to everyone anyway. I called a group meeting right away, but not before finding Danika and hugging her, sharing my congratulations with her. There was no delay; everyone was waiting for us in the room, ready to hear what Tesla and I had to report, as well as giving me theirs.

"First thing. Congratulations everyone on starting or continuing your families! Best news of all. I can't tell you how much Danika and I love our two girls. Guys, I know you are somewhat scared of this, but look at it this way. You few men alone get to know what it is like to create new life within you. Now, you and your wives can share something that most men in the universe cannot, something that is truly wonderful. As your captain, the only caution I want to make is please, let's don't pick overlapping names! We'll all get confused if there are two babies called Zarita running around here." That brought a few chuckles and laughs, lightening the mood a little more.

"Foot report," I continued, knowing they were all interested in this detail. Via telepathy, they knew I had gotten permission for shore leave, but at a price. Too steep a price for my money. "Dr. Leann says she can't undo it. Basically, our feet are fused like this. There is only one benefit that Tesla and I've found. That is, we have better balance standing still, because the heel is much farther from our toes. All else is worse."

"Shore leave is canceled?" asked Anwyn.

"I think that's best. If you still want it, see me personally. Now then, it's report time. As you know, I promised to contact the emperor and see about having a queen of his come here. But I need all the data I can get before I make that call." I spelled out what we knew, and then had Athena read the investigators' reports she was holding for me.

Tesla gave her assessment of their political system.

Then, my crew began their reports, beginning with Anya. "Boss, I was able to work out that they are using primitive radio wave transmissions for audio and video. I rigged up a receiver, and we've been studying their transmissions." I was stunned with how much work everyone had done while Tesla and I were gone. Everyone had focused in on gathering data related to their fields of expertise. For example, the four astronomers and Alexandra had worked out a model of the Narsten Cluster, locating where the inhabited worlds were. More important, Alexandra now had converted those into hyperspace coordinates for us. They also had a good idea where the Slaver worlds and the Hadu were located in the halo.

The botanists and zoologist had worked out their main domesticated food-chain animals and speculated they were perhaps distantly related to ours. Their crops were again variations on those found throughout galactic disk worlds. The engineers had pieced together a good estimation of their level of technological advancement, placing them at a modern level that has space travel, but at a significantly lower level than the Imperium worlds. This was particularly true in spaceship engines, shields, and armaments, the latter of which were "primitive," to quote Thomas. Dr. Leann had learned enough about their medical practices to suggest that they had invented something relatively similar to our own medical machines, which were used to cure the sick and heal the injured, parallel to ours. They'd not gotten a handle on genetics or the rejuvenation process, however.

Zarita and Len had verified these halo worlds were proportionately very low on heavier elements compared to disk worlds. "We ought to be able to establish a brisk trade in these elements and minerals," she added.

Next, we all discussed our collective observations on their rigid class society, the rebellious Whiners, and the raids by the Slavers and Hadu. Anya had come across some images of the Hadu, which I found fantastic. They were totally alien, non-human in every way. The best description of them is their name: lizard men. They walked bi-pedal but looked like a lizard in all other ways. They stood over seven feet tall, and from what Len could gather, they could be silicon-based life forms, not carbon-based. Further, many suspected they were a very ancient race, but that until recent times, kept to their own globular cluster of worlds in a fairly remote portion of the halo. It was suggested perhaps only recently they had developed space travel, but we had no real proof of that notion.

Finally, Martina broke further news to me. "We've had some spy intrigue of our own while you were gone. The other night, several began to sense 'creepy' feelings. Zarita used her special crystals to do a thorough search around our perimeter and detected two people hiding in the shadows, but with some kind of foreign mental powers she couldn't identify. Last night, she and I set a trap for these spies. She went invisible and left the ship, setting up some exterior spy cameras for me. Then, we both stayed awake most of the night. Sure enough around one p.m. when everyone else was asleep, they appeared again. She sensed them lightly probing our bodies and minds. I was able to get them on camera, fortunately. Mostly, they are shadow figures, very heavily cloaked with hoodies and such. However, we got one shot where you can almost see a face. Anya and I were able to enhance it somewhat. Delia, please bring it up on the screen for us," she asked, though I sensed her frustration at not being able to do even this slight action for herself. Well, we were all in the same boat.

I stared at the strangest looking face I'd ever seen. It was human-like, but not human. I don't know how else to describe it. It had a rounded face, a mouth, a nose, a pair of eyes. With her extensive ID Minister knowledge, Martina brought up another image. "I had Delia search my Imperium database. This is an image of a child's doll from Santari-3. Striking similarities. I simply don't know what to make of it. End of report." None of us knew what to make of these spies.

Danika asked, "Should we lay a trap for them and try to capture them if they come back tonight?"

If I had had a lip to bite, I would have. Instead, I ground my teeth, thinking this over. I had a command decision to make. Everyone looked to me for my reply. "No, let's keep them under observation. If all they have done is look at us, that's harmless enough. Whoever they are, they are just likely curious. After all, we're the aliens on this world. Tesla and I get stared at everywhere we've gone. Bit unnerving, I admit. No, let's keep watch. We'll take no offensive action unless they do first. Well done, each and every one of you. I'm truly impressed with your work!" I sensed a surge of group pride rising.

That done, I made the very lengthy call to Emperor Bino, outlining in detail all we had learned, directly or indirectly, ending with their request to have an Ataro queen visit them and assist them with the Slaver and Hadu situation. As expected, he praised us all for our great work and promised to send a queen, but he would have to call us back in a day with more specific information. I spent the rest of the day on domestic duty with Danika and our girls, giving Mai a break from her babysitting task.

The next day, he called back to say he was sending Queen Zenovia Myrine and her personal assistant Xene. Queen Zenovia was twenty-two with wavy, long blonde hair and pale blue eyes, while her assistant had curly dark brown hair. Marisol sent along her ULAT box update to the Narsten spoken language so Queen Zenovia could practice their spoken language on her trip here. Besides the pilot and navigator, only two security guards would be coming to protect her. Why? They would be carrying triple the usual number of fuel cells, because the emperor wanted to be very certain they could get back home without dealing with a fuel shortage. They were due to arrive in four days, five at the most. After giving us the particulars on her flight, Anya switched us over to her ship, and we got to see Queen Zenovia for the first time and to chat.

Tesla spent an hour briefing the queen on the situation here on Menno, including what we knew of their class society. She was a bit worried about having to have her feet further altered and wearing such a huge outer-skirt, but Tesla explained that as long as Xene kept an arm around her, she could manage it. Queen Zenovia looked a little relieved, but was still nervous about it. Secretly, I sympathized with her. Tesla then added, "One side benefit, Queen Zenovia, there is a whole lot of handsome men who will be asking you out. Of course, they are grey skinned and look strange to us. Still, we've seen a whole lot of handsome fellows here, and they will be all over you, since you are an aristocrat in their eyes, a prize catch." Both women chuckled.

That night, I stayed up late hoping to catch a glimpse of our strange spies, but they didn't appear, much to everyone else's relief. Perhaps, they'd realized we'd captured them on our spy cameras. Who knows?

Chapter 11 Interludes

Huyana thought to Isi, *This is an amazing discovery, simply incredible.*

Isi thought back, *Indeed. Beyond anyone's wildest hopes. We should put in our request to join this bunch.*

Absolutely! A chance like this one has never occurred before. Besides, there will be twenty-two vacancies. Surely, we've earned the right to have our turn now.

Isi suggested, *I'll insist upon it. Come. We should make our report to the Underground Exit now.*

An hour later, their transmission ended. Huyana smiled. *Isi, we've done it. Now we too have a chance to escape. Twenty others will be joining us in about eight months. All we have to do now is to protect them and keep track of their locations until then. I've waited two centuries for this chance!*

Isi added, *I've waited nearly three. Don't blow it. You nearly did the other night. Still, no detectable harm done. We must be more careful. They are far too alert.*

Drastically so compared to the Narsten's, Huyana added. *We have hit the mother lode with these! I can hardly wait!*

Minta made contact with Thanos. As always, they exchanged bursts of electronic data. Thanos sent, "You have done well, Minta. The hyperdrive alterations are working out brilliantly here. I have them installed in a number of our ships now. I must compliment you on your superb timing. I've monitored the comm channels and heard that the radiation alterations may make the Ashford-5 genetic cures unworkable. We may yet add these brilliant nova into our flock. A pilot project has begun with the Ashford-5 therapy givers. It does show remarkable potential on the few cases handled thus far. After they are finished with this new therapy, they seem to be accepting their new nova status quite well. What is your assessment of the Farthun-3 humans?"

"Primitive development. Hermaphrodites for sure, but the women yet retain their arms, rather like the Ashford-5 nova. Plus, they lack the feet and lip alterations. While they are almost nova, they should be given more time to develop. Perhaps in time, they will get the proper lip and feet genetic alterations, making them true nova. As far as the Narsten humans, they are likely a different sub-species from homo sapiens sapiens. Suggestion: homo sapiens grey. Culturally, they are quite primitive from the homo sapiens sapiens of the disk worlds. I don't foresee them as offering any threat to our nova at all. However, two other halo groups might. They are called the Slavers and the Hadu. The latter is possibly a silicon-based life form. Both appear to be preying upon the Narsten people and could be a danger to our nova."

"Excellent Minta. Stay on it. Find out more about both potential threats to our nova," Thanos replied.

"There is one complication. We should have foreseen this one. All twenty-two nova are now pregnant. In September, there will be twenty-two new nova babies on the ship, far more than Psykhe can handle. Advise."

"Excellent. Excellent. I'll upload baby-handling technology to all the Model 7's soon. Keep me posted."

"I've just received word from Miss Katarine," Ernst Kleindorf began his briefing of his three compatriots, the leaders of the Underground. He was a thirty-five year old carpenter. "She believes the aliens aristocrats from the disk have received our plea for help and may well support us. From our spy in Matriarch Athala's mansion, we know she has accepted the alien aristocrats' offer to send one of their aristocrat queens here to adjudicate on the proposed war. Now, it is up to us to find a way to present our case to this queen and see if she can become just the instrument of change that we have been seeking."

The three others smiled and nodded their approval of this good news. One asked, "Any word on the Slaver's attack on their party the other night?"

Ernst frowned. "No, none. Apparently, it was a botched attempt. No one was seriously hurt, thankfully. That could well have ruined our plans. One other detail from Miss Katarine. She believes that great inroads can be made if as many women as possible get their breasts enlarged like the two aliens have. It will show everyone that the aristocratic women do not have quite the monopoly on such things. Until now, she says, only they can have tiny arms and wear their special boots, but now all women can have huge breasts like the aliens. She believes that as many as possible get theirs enlarged before the aristocratic women issue a formal decree outlawing all women but themselves from having them. She also reports the alien aristocratic women advise against having their lips slit. Something about not being able to speak properly. I support her in this. Spread the word. Any woman who wants hers enlarged and who cannot afford it can get Underground financial support. We must act very swiftly. Already Lady Frieda has had hers enlarged. Time is short on this one. We simply must take advantage of every crack in the system to thrust our agenda through. I'll contact my counterparts on the other worlds and relay this to them." All three nodded and left to spread the word as rapidly as possible.

It only took a quick word to one servant woman in a household shortly to have every woman there know about the Underground's position in this matter. Within two days, every woman of the lower classes had been informed. Hundreds began to make judicious inquires, looking for just such financial support.

Breast enhancement procedures mushroomed at an unprecedented rate. The doctors were overwhelmed by the sheer numbers of women seeking the procedure. They were more than willing to perform it and not just because of their financial gain. Rather, they too were most impressed with the way that their patients now appeared and were only too eager to perform the procedure.

All this happened while I was back onboard the Eagle's Seed dealing with our situation. I learned about this when I returned the day before Queen Zenovia was to arrive. The second day that I was gone from the mansion, Matriarch Athala was shocked when Miss Elise entered to draw her drapes and prepare her for the day. "What in Narsten's Name have you done to yourself?" she exclaimed, seeing her maid's bosom. Her breasts were each as large as her head, the maximum that their medical technology could manage. Still, they were substantially smaller than ours were, unfortunately for us that is.

"We all have had them made larger, like our alien guests, Matriarch Athala. Everyone's having them done. We hoped you would be honored and very pleased with us that we are all honoring our alien guests this way," Miss Elise replied very politely, as she had been coached.

Still shocked with what her maid had done, she allowed Miss Elise to get her prepared and assisted to the dining room, where she was once again shocked to see all the other lady's maids with identical large bosoms. Worse, she soon discovered all her female servants had gotten it done. Lady Frieda gushed, "Oh Miss Elise, you look as stunning as I do. I'm so pleased you were able to have it done too. Like I told my Miss Emlin, now you too can have more suitors."

"Oh good grief!" Matriarch Clothilda exclaimed, as she made her slow, careful way into the dining room. "Mom, have you . . ." She didn't finish her sentence. Obviously, she had seen the lady's maids and their bosoms. "Mom, you ought to issue a decree against this or something."

"Why, sis?" Lady Frieda asked.

Rolf commented, "Well, I just love to see them. Impressive indeed."

"Rolf, keep your thing in your pants!" Matriarch Athala barked. "You too, Fester," she added to Clothilda's husband.

"Mother, you have to admit they help make our servants appear just a little bit more attractive," Lady Frieda retorted, but thought better of coming out and saying more erotic. That would infringe far too much on the aristocratic, tiny-armed women, including herself.

"I suppose now I'll have to have it done," Matriarch Clothilda grumbled.

"It would look good on you," Fester whispered jovially. She glared back at him but then broke into a wry smile.

"Well, I simply won't stand for this. They are infringing on we aristocratic women," Matriarch Athala exclaimed. Once

250

breakfast was done, she headed into the city to her official office to see just what the situation was. By late afternoon, she had Miss Elise tear up the document she was preparing, an attempt to outlaw large breasts on all but the aristocratic, tiny-armed women. It was futile. Thousands of women from literally all the lower classes, even the very lowest ones, had already had it done. She had no idea just how such low class women could possibly have afforded this procedure. Now, she sat and fumed over this egregious intrusion into the aristocratic women's world.

She knew the effect they were having on many men and was angry. Such reactions were supposed to be the province of the tiny-armed women. After all, they were the ones who had to suffer the enduring pain of childhood with their arms tightly bound. It wasn't fair, she thought, but realized it was far too late to make it illegal. Worse, she also knew that she and the other aristocratic women would soon have to have it done to themselves as well or quickly lose their erotic attraction to men.

When Tesla and I returned to the mansion the day before the queen was to arrive, we were quite surprised to see all the women sporting their newly enlarged bosoms. The maids were extremely pleased with them, that much was quite obvious. Further, that the various men in the household now paid even the lowest servant far more attention was quite noticeable. "Well, as you can see, you folks have made quite an impression on our women," Matriarch Athala welcomed me back in the drawing room. She too had just had the procedure done, if only to maintain her own status.

"I would have outlawed this for all women who were not also tiny-armed, but by the time that I could, it was far too late. Now, I would like to make a request of you right now. Please allow my engineer to take measurements of your lip ornaments and fasteners. According to Lady Frieda, your lips are also quite erotic when kissing."

"I don't recommend them. They horribly affect our speech. We cannot make any sounds that involve our lips." I tried to make her realize having slit lips was a very bad idea, but after touching her surface thoughts, I saw there wasn't any way out of this mess. She was totally determined and would get the measurements whether I agreed or not. After that was done, no more was said about it, and I hoped she'd let it go.

I then told her about the queen's arrival late tomorrow, and we chatted about this. However, the next morning over breakfast, Matriarch Athala made her startling announcement. "Well, since our women are all greatly desirous of emulating the fashions of our aristocratic guests from the disk, I have issued the following worldwide proclamation. With the exception of we tiny-armed women, any woman who has her breasts enlarged must also get her lips slit and wear lip ornaments similar to those our aristocratic alien women wear. After consulting with Doctor Heinz and working out what is medically possible, the ornamental disks shall be no smaller than five inches in diameter. That is the maximum that can be done with our medical technology at this time. However, considering their cost, the government will be providing a pair of them for each woman at no cost to her. Production of the ornamental disks is beginning today. Within a month, I'll expect anyone who has had their breasts enlarged to also have gotten their lips ornamented as well, excepting us tiny-armed women, that is. We all will have a choice of whether or not to have them done. Since I'm told that it seriously affects our speech, I'll be recommending that tiny-armed women aristocrats not have them. Obviously, we need to be perfectly understood at all times, since we rule the world."

Several of the lady's maids gasped, realizing they were being counter-attacked. They also knew they could do nothing about it, and that was what made it even worse. Miss Gabriele and Miss Elise looked devastated, and I took them aside to try to bolster them. I began to sense why they'd done it. "Look, it's not the end of the world and besides, kissing becomes extremely erotic." I mentioned the magic word. Both looked up at me, broad smiles replacing their twisted features.

"Really? Is it truly like Lady Frieda says?" Miss Gabriele asked me.

"Indeed it is. It is something to look forward to, just don't tell Athala about it." Now, they both giggled and brightened up. Little did I know that within another two days, every woman who had gotten her breasts enlarged also heard of this detail and accepted their matriarch's proclamation. Instead of inflicting a dire punishment on these women, as she'd cleverly planned, Matriarch Athala had done just the opposite, though she didn't realize that for quite some time.

That realization came when her youngest daughter, Lady Frieda, came into the breakfast room a week later sporting her new five inch in diameter, golden lip plates. After the fireworks died down, and Lady Frieda valiantly tried to make herself understood, the tiny-armed women present realized this proclamation had just spread the eroticism once the sole province of the aristocratic women out into the entire population of women of all classes! Worse, the movement had spread to a number of other nearby worlds of the Narsten cluster. However, trying to understand Lady Frieda and the other women became quite a challenge indeed.

"Sis! How could you do this?" Clothilda exclaimed. Later, I learned that Lady Frieda demonstrated the why to her older sister that evening. The only consolation I had was that theirs were only five inches across, not the huge twelve inches that ours were. That was a very significant difference. None of this maneuvering was lost on Queen Zenovia. She fully understood what was happening here, but focused on the critical problem: the proposed war with the Slavers and the Hadu.

Many light-years distant, President Arcangelo Ferrobossi of Aurelio, Gorki Cluster, looked over his latest spy reports and didn't like what he was reading. Aliens from the galactic disk had arrived on Menno, Narsten Cluster. He looked up at his aides and commented, "The situation is growing worse by the day. It seems some aliens from the filthy disk worlds are paying a visit to our enemies in the Narsten Cluster. Apparently, the matriarchs are seeking to gain military support from these disk people. If they obtain that, surely they'll declare war on us. Damn. Damn. Damn."

General Celino Astari spoke up, "Our raids haven't produced the results that we intended. We should begin war preparations, Mr. President. It's inevitable, especially if they get military support from the dirty disk people."

Doriano Presario, his top intelligence officer and close friend added, "General Celino has a point. If they gain the support of the disk worlds, we'll be hard pressed to hold the line, let alone defeat these decadent monsters."

Unswayed, President Arcangelo replied, "Gentlemen, do not be so hasty to get us into a war. No one truly wins such a thing. Both sides will lose valuable ships, men, and women. Even should we prevail as we must, the cost of an all-out war with the Narsten Cluster would be staggering. We would be leaving our children's generation with a monstrous bill to pay. For centuries, we have prided ourselves on not spending more than we earn. A war would put the government into a deep debt from which it'll be most difficult to extract ourselves. I don't want to be known in history as the first president who bankrupted Aurelio. No, we must exhaust all other avenues before we go to war. Yet, let me be perfectly clear about it, if we are attacked, I'll not hesitate to declare war. We still have some time remaining. Use it wisely. We need to know more about these aliens from the disk and their true purpose here. If this report is right, they have to be about the most helpless people imaginable, and yet they have a spaceship of reaching the halo from somewhere in the disk. A conundrum. Gentlemen, I need ideas how we can discover their true purposes."

Since none was forthcoming, President Arcangelo said, "I read here where our spy in Krazdorf managed to get word to this armless alien representative or leader. Perhaps there is a way. What do you think of this idea?" He began to outline the idea he'd just gotten from reading this latest field report.

Proxima Prime. Sub-level Four. Water Pumping Station 5. Fifty year old Chief Engineer Abelard Jones cursed and spat on the broken down water pump. He and his crew of workers were in charge of keeping the plumbing of this once proud world running. Several miles below the concrete and steel surface and amid the ancient and rusting life support systems, he'd had enough. "Boys, this is the last straw! Damned pump is shot completely. This whole place is nothing more than busted junk! How the hell are we expected to keep it all running? No way in hell can we do that! Lord knows where the original plans are. We've had to jury-rig every damned one of these systems for years now. I've had it!"

Years ago as a bright graduate of the Academy, he'd been convinced of a wonderful future on Proxima Prime. This was after the genocide terrorist attack that had wiped out the entire ruling planet of the Imperium, hundreds of billions of people. Slowly, it had been repopulated, mostly by the senators and government bureaucrats and a few hardy businessmen. He'd accepted the position as Chief Engineer. Now, he bitterly regretted having spent so many of his most productive years here far below the artificial surface dealing with an impossible situation.

All the life support equipment was breaking down at an escalating rate, far faster than his many work crews could handle, in spite of the fact that they were only running a tiny fraction of the world. Most of the world was simply uninhabited, though work crews were there salvaging scrap steel. The genocide attack wiped out the native population of Proxima Prime, most of whom had kept the life support machinery running, the lowest jobs on the planet.

"I quit. I can't take this anymore. Men, women, it's time to abandon this sinking ship! Forget this damned pump. Pack your things. Take the next transports out of here. That's what I'm going to do." He tossed his wrench, smacking the broken pump solidly, creating a ringing noise like a bell tolling the death of someone important.

"Shouldn't we tell someone that we're leaving?" one of his men asked.

"You do that and you'll find yourself back here at this worthless pump being ordered to fix it while they hold a d-gun to your head. You know as well as I that this pump is nothing but pure junk. So is damned near everything else on this cursed planet. If you ever want to get off this dying world, don't say a damned word. Come on. I'm going home and pack." With that, he stormed down the dimly lit, metal hallway, his boots clanking in time to a song he was humming. His crew tossed their tools down and followed him. No way were they going to stay. If Chief Engineer Abelard said the pump was un-fixable, then it was. Besides, they'd had enough as well.

The next day, two deep space shuttles departed from Proxima Prime. Down below, the water pump had long ceased moving the water. In particular, this one fed the cooling system of the power plant that provided the energy needed by this lone inhabited sector of Proxima Prime, where the Senate was located, their skyscrapers, and the many bureaucrats who ran the once mighty Imperium. The next day, that power plant shut down. Without power, the airflow system ceased operations. Not long after that, the main water pumps that delivered freshly recycled water shut down, allowing only un-recycled water to trickle through the pipes, a gross health hazard. Only the bustling spaceport was still operational, since they had their own private military power supply system and associated life support systems.

"God! Now what?" Senator Ruthy cried out. Suddenly, her apartment went dark. The power was off yet again. By now, she and the other senators were quite used to these power outages, which had been happening more and more frequently this past year, as though echoing the endless bickering among the two thousand plus senators.

From an adjoining room, Leda called out, "Crap! I lost the last paragraph I was typing. We should've gotten our new battery backup system by now, but everything keeps getting backlogged. This place is going to hell!"

"Where's our emergency lighting? It's supposed to kick in after two seconds," grumbled Senator Ruthy. "You're right. Nothing's working right on this world. It's steadily gotten worse these past few years. Ah, there it comes on — no, it's only half on. Well, at least we can see a little."

"How's the Senate doing? Have they reached a decision on compensation for those recent genetic terrorism victims?" Leda asked.

"Nowhere. There's a block of senators who believe those who started the war ought to pay compensation to all the victims. Another block wants to divide it up evenly, and yet a third block wants to keep most of it, giving the victims only a token amount. Plus, every business in the Imperium, it seems, wants a piece of salvage rights, once Aquila Prime has finished taking what they need to support the millions of victims that they've taken on. It's a mess still. I don't see it getting resolved anytime soon. Damn, when are the lights coming back on? It's getting smelly and stuffy in here!" Senator Ruthy complained bitterly.

"Dear, I'll go make us some tea," Leda attempted to sooth her down some. She'd forgotten that their stove used electric power. Leda turned on the cold water, filling their pot. That's when she began to smell something quite foul! She looked at the water. It was brownish and smelled like a latrine! "My god! Ruthy, urine or something is coming out of our water faucet!"

"What else could go wrong?" Ruthy yelled back. At that moment, their emergency lighting flickered and failed altogether! Both women let out another round of curses. "I don't know why we even bother staying here any longer. If we didn't owe it to Emperor Bino, we'd just up and leave for home!"

Both then used a bit of their *mentales* gifts to produce a pale light and found some candles. "Well, we best not take a soaking bath," Leda advised. "Perhaps, we ought to just go to bed early. All this ought to be fixed by breakfast." With little else they could do, bed sounded inviting. In the morning, to their dismay, nothing had changed. If anything, their apartment smelled even worse. They ate the last of their cold cuts and orange juice. The synthetic food dispenser wasn't working, of course. However, only if desperate did they eat that blue goo.

By the time that Senator Ruthy was ready to head off to work, a soldiers came knocking on their door. "Senator Ruthy?" he asked and she nodded. "I'm to tell you that all facilities on Proxima Prime, save the spaceport are closed down indefinitely. The general is advising all non-military personnel to return to their home worlds for the time being. It is going to take some time to get things fixed, if at all."

"Thanks for the warning. We'll do just that." She watched him, as he headed the next door, having drawn a line through her name. "Pack up; we're leaving for home at long last!" Her enthusiasm mushroomed.

Leda called out, "Hey, now we can afford to have some more children again!"

January 7, 1379, Proxima Prime went dark as a planet, save for the spaceport, which remained in operation. Still a prime refueling station for much hub traffic, it was no longer the capital of the Imperium. Many denote that day as the point at which the old Imperium ended. In many ways, that's correct. However, there remained key issues that had yet to be solved. One was the compensation issue from the destruction of the fifteen hub worlds. Another was the dissolution of the wealth and possessions of the Imperium back to their member worlds. Yet another was the continued operation of the Imperium Central Bank, upon whose computers every world depended for financial transactions, using the Imperium credit.

Per the Imperium Charter, upon the dissolution of the Imperium, member worlds would be returned anything that they had donated. What mattered the most were the military spaceships. Who would get which was the main question? Emperor Bino stepped in and hastily drew up a proposal, denoting which ship would be returned to which member world. Since every world was quite frantic over this key detail, most readily accepted his proposal. Only a few tiny changes had to be made, primarily because he lacked the most recent changes.

What is key here is that the Ataro Empire ended up with seven of the fifteen battleships and ten heavy cruisers, along with twenty-one light cruisers. While on paper, they were divided among many of the more populous of the Ataro worlds, in fact, they remained as a united group, unlike the many other warships. Thanks to his clever plan, no one world had a sufficiently large fleet of warships with which to bully or dominate other worlds. Later historians claim that alone was one of the most brilliant of his power plays during the breakup of the Imperium. They reasoned that if one of the larger worlds had gotten a substantial fleet, they would have begun to form their own empire, taking over neighboring worlds. Well, that happened, just on a vastly reduced scale.

258

What helped sell his dissolution plan was that he agreed to maintain the Imperium Central Bank and its massive computer system for the next fifty years. This allowed world economies to continue to operate, though many worlds slowly began creating their own currency. More than a few intended to get off the Imperium credit before the fifty-year time span was over. Dissolution financial matters were easy to handle. Emperor Bino added up the assets of the Imperium, after paying off outstanding obligations one of which was the compensation matter of the recent victims. Note, he was quite generous, bequeathing each of the nearly two million survivors a total of two million credits, for a total expenditure of four trillion credits. The remains assets were proportioned out to all member worlds, including Closed Worlds, based upon the number of senators each world was entitled to.

That, of course, was based upon a world's population. The roughly two hundred quadrillion credits was divided by the nearly two thousand senators, yielding approximately a hundred trillion credits per senator. Adding up all the senators from the Ataro Empire yielded him a tidy ten quadrillion credits, which he held in escrow for his forty worlds, thereby ensuring that no other world would remotely have as much available cash as his empire. Cleverly, he was doing everything he could to protect the Ataro Empire from the collapse of the Imperium and possible future attempts of other greedy worlds to expand their powers beyond their own worlds. Once again, future historians credit Emperor Bino with another brilliant move that helped to prevent a total collapse of inter-world commerce and warfare.

We learned of the collapse of the Imperium when the deep space transport carrying Queen Zenovia arrived on Menno. Of course, she kept us informed of events from back home as she found out about them.

Part II Conflicts

Chapter 12 Queen Zenovia Intervenes

I decided that the queen needed to see just what she was going to have to agree to if she was going to assist the Narsten Cluster's worlds. Hence, I wore only my normal pencil style gown so that she could clearly see my fused feet and boots, while Tesla also wore her outer-skirt, rather like an upside down, sky blue umbrella. Together with Athena and Damali supporting us, we walked carefully across the tarmac to greet her ship as it touched down.

Queen Zenovia was a very attractive young woman. While her skin tone was somewhat yellowish as most Ataro System women's were, her waist length, wavy blonde hair was quite full, and her blue eyes seemed to pierce into one's soul. Either that or they demanded one's soul. Her facial features were perfect, so much so that many women would have died for her natural looks. Quite why she'd chosen to become so heavily body-modified eluded me. She had everything else going for her.

Like us, she wore a stiff corset, but not for the same reasons as we did. Rather, she'd had some ribs removed, and the corset enforced a fourteen inch waistline, constricting her motion considerably, as did her loss of arms. Her feet had been modified so that she had to wear the toe shoes that the rest of my crew did. Xene's curly dark brown hair was barely shoulder length and bobbed in the wind, as she assisted her queen to walk towards us. Like her queen, her feet had been modified, and she too had ribs removed and wore an identical tight corset. Both women's figures were quite pronounced. However, Xene's vocal cords had been cut so she could not speak and thereby influence her charge. Such was their ancient customs designed to prevent any queen, emperor, or empress from physically abusing their immense power.

After introducing ourselves, I led her over to the Eagle's Seed to meet the whole crew. "So take a good look at my feet. They are fused into this position. I can only bend them at my ankles. Plus, you will have to also wear an outer-skirt like

Tesla has on over your fancy satin gown. This is your last chance to back out of this, Queen Zenovia. Once Matriarch Athala arrives, she's going to request the changes before accepting you." I felt I owed this young woman this one last chance.

She laughed. "We queens are used to being physically challenged. It is part of who and what we are, Captain Nia Elain. It ensures we cannot abuse our powers. Come; I would dearly love to meet everyone else. I've heard you've done groundbreaking work with the two engines. Plus, I'd like to meet your 'helpers.'" She didn't say robots, wisely. I sensed just how curious both she and Xene were to see the real robots.

It was my turn to laugh. "You just did. Athena and Damali are Model 7's, as are the others. Please, not a word about them to anyone outside the crew."

"Oh my! You look so completely human! I was expecting to see sort of a metal shaped machine with arms," Queen Zenovia replied. Athena put a grin look on her face in response, attempting an appropriate human reaction. It worked well.

I gave her a tour of the Eagle's Seed and introduced her to everyone. We also held a lengthy group meeting, going over once more what we had learned about the Narsten Cluster and its civilization. As noon approached, I had Athena put my red over-skirt back on me, and we three headed back out of our ship. Matriarch Athala was right on time. At precisely noon, she and a large security force arrived at the spaceport to pick us up.

I did the introductions, and we were assisted into her limousine. During the ride through Krazdorf, she chatted with the queen. "I'm so pleased to finally meet you, Queen Zenovia. Plus I'm even more pleased to see you don't have the same giant bosom or wear those giant lip ornaments. Already, I'm sorry to say that way too many of our women here are taking after Matriarch Nia Elain and Lady Tesla. Even my own daughters have."

Queen Zenovia smiled. "We have different reasons for our appearances. You see, my appearance is wholly dictated by my position as an Ataro queen. All our queens, the emperor, and empress follow millennia-old protocols. Our arms are removed along with some ribs and our feet are altered so we have to wear these toe shoes, which barely allow us to walk. With this tight corset, my appearance is much like a wasp. The objective is to limit severely our physical abilities. That way, we simply have no way to abuse the immense power that we wield. While many claim such physical restraint isn't necessary, it has worked to perfection for over two millennia now. Of course, I must have a Personal Assistant. Xene here has been with me since I began my apprenticeship as a queen. As an added precaution, she is also unable to speak. That way, even she, my closest confidant, cannot overly influence me or my decisions. All this is to guarantee to you and everyone else that my decisions are not being influenced by anyone or anything."

Matriarch Athala smiled. "We have very similar physical limitations. As you know, we are all tiny-armed women and have our feet fused. Thus, it is also difficult for us to succumb to corruption as well. However, as Matriarch Nia Elain has undoubtedly explained to you, it is most unseemly for you to be seen in public while wearing your under-gown. If you are to gain the acceptance of other matriarchs, you probably should also have your feet fixed as well. I can arrange both for you."

"Thank you. So kind of you to wish to help me fit in with your people. That would be most appropriate, though I have to tell you on my world, we don't have such things as these beautiful outer-skirts. I'm considered very well dressed, but then such things are quite cultural in nature. Since I'm here on your world, I must follow your customs. Heavens, I surely don't want everyone I meet to think I'm half-naked." Both women chuckled. I smiled invisibly. Any worries I had about Queen Zenovia not being able to handle the matriarch evaporated. She was quite adept at it.

While I certainly did disagree with her over having to be physically limited just to avoid misuse of power, she did know her business very well. As we rode along, Matriarch Athala pointed out some of the more important buildings, and we chatted pleasantly. Once at the mansion, she whisked the queen away to get her presentable, while I ended up in the drawing room, flabbergasted over the physical changes in the many women servants and even Lady Frieda, who now also wore her new five inch lip plates along with the other lady's maids and many others who worked behind the scenes.

"So what do you think? We've all gotten our breasts enlarged, and they are so erotic. Now that mom's ordered everyone who has had them enlarged to get the lip ornaments too, we all did," Lady Frieda attempted to explain. However, just as I tried to tell her before, she and the others were having a most difficult time trying to be understood. Specifically, as Marisol once explained to me, the bilabial and labiodental sounds could no longer be made. Thus, the sounds of the typical consonants of f, v, p, b, m, and th, for example, all come out as the same unrecognizable noise. Many other sounds were rather mushed as well, such as w in their word "wir," making her and the others very difficult to understand. Well, I'd been there, done that, and now depended upon the ULATs or Imperium Standard. I made a note to ask Marisol why Imperium Standard didn't have any of these bilabial and labiodental sounds in it. I was curious.

She sounded so strange that I simply couldn't grasp what she said and was embarrassed to force her to say it a second and then a third time before I finally duplicated her. "We are all just trying to learn how to speak understandably again," she added, slightly embarrassed herself. However, she quickly added, "But kissing is now so utterly erotic! We all just love that!"

Miss Gabriele and Miss Emlin both nodded, their lip plates bobbing slightly. From their shining eyes, I also knew they were smiling, very pleased with their lips and breasts. I realized in a flash of insight that these servants now were enjoying the level of attention and erotic pleasure that their employers, the aristocratic tiny-armed women, had always enjoyed. For them, this was a giant leap forward, not backwards, as I had envisioned. What a strange society, I concluded.

I spent an hour listening to Lady Frieda bringing me up

to date on what had been happening all over Menno and several nearby worlds during the few days I was gone. In particular, I learned her mother had made the lip plates ruling as a punishment for the many lower classed women who had gotten their breasts enlarged, but that had completely backfired. "Mom now knows she's just helped many, many women begin to enjoy the kind of erotic pleasures that have always been restricted to us tiny-armed women. She's furious about that, but it's done, and she has to live with it."

That evening, I shared this tidbit with Queen Zenovia whose comment took me by surprise. "Ah ha. We might be able to use this to our advantage in helping obtain more rights for the lower classes. We can make her see herself as a world-famous pioneer in helping bring down the artificial class barriers for women." I smiled invisibly again. Queen Zenovia was brilliant.

She then added, "Well, it didn't hurt, getting my feet done. Walking is a bit more stable than before, at least while walking on level, hard ground, but I can't see my feet and that is quite scary. I'm really depending upon Xene here now more than ever." Xene smiled, pleased by the compliment. "Well, tomorrow we must get to work on this war problem."

The next day, I looked on as Queen Zenovia went over all of the official reports Matriarch Athala had on incidents involving the Slavers and the Hadu lizard men. The queen finally said, "Your reports are quite detailed and thorough, Matriarch Athala."

"Of course they are. We Narsten's believe in doing absolutely everything the right and proper way. It begins with me, their ruler. I insist and demand that all be done quite properly. A sloppy job is a job done poorly. I hold every citizen of Menno to the highest of proper standards. We always have. It is how we Narstens have become the premier civilization of the halo, quite unlike the filthy worlds of the galactic disk. I mean your world no offense, Queen Zenovia, but we in the halo just cannot fathom how you could stand to live with all that dust and filth floating around. My goodness, you must have to dust thoroughly your homes each week! Here in the halo, we are mostly dust free."

"I can see your point. There certainly are a lot of gas and dust clouds in the spiral arms. Now then, let's get back to these reports and see what patterns we can deduce. If you will notice, Xene has been plotting the occurrences on a monthly basis for the past three years." I glanced at her graph, a sharply rising line. "Apparently, the first known attack by the Slavers happened nearly three years ago. Roughly, one raid per month for at least a year before their frequency escalated to two and then three. Why this past month alone, you've had four raids."

"I know. They are giving Matriarch Clothilda fits trying to respond in time to capture the raiders. They strike at seemingly random locations, making it twice as difficult for my daughter to anticipate their next attack. You can clearly see why we simply cannot tolerate any more of this, and why we must declare war on these Slavers and soon," Matriarch Athala declared.

Queen Zenovia ignored that declaration, preferring her own agenda. "In red, she has the known Hadu raids. Those didn't begin until eighteen months ago and their frequency is holding pretty well constant."

Matriarch Athala was right there with an explanation for that. "Naturally. The Spicula Cluster where the Hadu live is very distant from here, and they also have to cross the Narsten Gap of space, making it a very long trip indeed. If we had to attack them from here, I expect it would take our fleet nearly a month to reach them. Commander Rolf can provide you with a more precise time estimate, if you need it. So I take it you agree with me that we should declare war on both of them soon?"

"I've only just begun my analysis. It's too late in the day to continue. I'll prepare a list of people I wish to interview about these attacks. When I have, I'd like you to help me arrange to visit with them. I do have two security guards with me, but if you think those are insufficient, I'd be pleased if you would lend me some additional ones."

"Well, I don't see what interviews can tell you. Absolutely everything is in the proper reports. However, I'll do as you ask. I'll consult with Matriarch Clothilda and have her provide you with proper security arrangements. That's her zone of responsibility. Ah, there is the dinner gong."

Over dinner, Lady Frieda insisted the queen join her on a visit to their best pleasure house this evening. I didn't want her going alone, so Tesla and I tagged along with the two. I was glad that I did. Queen Zenovia became terribly worried when she learned that Xene could not accompany her. I explained, "They'll have some very competent lady's maids waiting for us when we arrive, and they'll be at our sides the whole time." Still, she didn't look any too pleased about this, but had to accept the local hospitality.

I was personally pleased to find Miss Katarine waiting for me, assisting me out of the limo. She was extremely happy to see me. "Oh just look at me!" she gushed. I did. She'd had her breasts enlarged to the size of her head and sported shiny five inch gold disks in her lips. "I know, mine are so small compared to yours, but they are so erotic. I've had six handsome men wooing me this past week! Lady Frieda, you look stunning yourself. Please convey my heartfelt thanks to Matriarch Athala for me and all of us really."

Lady Frieda giggled girlishly. "I know. I've had twice as many suitors asking me out for dates. It's terribly exciting, isn't it, Miss Katarine? I'm so glad we can share this together. I'll tell her."

As I expected, Queen Zenovia was rather shocked at the openness of drug usage and alcohol, but the sexual promiscuity rather bothered her. Lady Frieda took it upon herself to explain this to her. "We are a matriarchal society. Only women are allowed to own property. It is a mother's obligation and duty to provide a new home or the funds to purchase one to each of her daughters. Usually she does this when the daughters turn twenty-one or when they marry, if sooner. It is a horrific disgrace to any woman who, for any reason, does not provide a home for her daughter. It's simply not done, particularly so among the aristocratic tiny-armed women."

"You see, since men are not allowed to own property of any kind, marriages are built on far more solid ground. Men rarely stray — you know, have affairs and such things, because their wives would divorce them, and toss them out on the street as homeless waifs. However, we women do recognize that men have sexual needs just as we women do. Hence, with the wife's permission, her husband can indulge his needs. Often, this is done at one of the legal pleasure houses, you see. It's all legal and above boards, as long as the wife approves, of course."

She chatted on, "Naturally, the matriarchs do provide Hostels for Men. So if a man finds himself homeless, he can stay at one of the hostels for a time."

"So all the businesses of Menno are owned by women?" Queen Zenovia asked.

"Absolutely. However, many women do not actually care to run the businesses. I would guess more than half the men actually run the businesses, funneling some of the profits to their owners. With alcohol, drugs, and sex legal and so readily available everywhere, I do believe everyone is perfectly happy," Lady Frieda finished up.

"Well, I must admit, Lady Frieda, I've never seen quite so many handsome men. Are all your men as handsome as those we are seeing around this establishment and your mansion?" Queen Zenovia asked. "Of course, I rather wish they weren't all grey," she both teased and hinted. I gently touched her mind and found that the men around the room aroused her. I smiled, invisibly of course.

"I never thought about that before, but I'd say collectively they are a good sample of our men. It does make finding the right husband so challenging. I'm going to place my bet on love, only I've not yet really fallen in love with any one man," Lady Frieda admitted.

Miss Katarine spoke up, "Now that I'm so erotic too, so many more doors have opened for me. I was planning just to marry the first man who asked me, but now I too am hoping to find the right man and marry for love as well, Lady Frieda. Isn't this just the best thing that's happened to us women in centuries?"

Miss Lore, Tesla's maid for the evening, added, "It's the same with me. I've been asked out six times already since I got my lips done. It's so fabulous, so exciting, to grab the attention of men so easily. Why I even got asked out by a handsome lad while I was at the grocery store yesterday morning! That's never happened before. Lady Frieda, Lady Tesla, Lady Nia Elain, we owe you and Matriarch Athala so very much!"

I rather wanted to curse or perhaps it was vomit. The last thing I ever wanted to do was to have other women emulating my genetically modified body, but they had. No matter how I wanted to undo it, such wasn't possible. I forced myself to say politely, "You are welcome," and left it at that. Footnote. We three spent most of the evening listening to the chamber music groups.

Around nine, we left, though Lady Katarine assisted me into the limo, as did the other lady's maids with their charges. We all were rather quiet, contented to watch the light display from the voluminous neon signs. Queen Zenovia had never seen such gigantic quantities of such lights. While there were a few of them in the Imperium, mostly in museums, here they didn't need streetlights because of them!

We were about halfway home when a trio of explosions struck us again. Our limo suddenly seemed out of control, swerving right and left. It's a credit to our chauffeur that we didn't have a bad crash. The two security cars accompanying us didn't fare quite so well. Smoke obscured much of our vision from the windows. "What's happening?" cried Queen Zenovia. Both she and Lady Frieda were actually quite frightened.

Someone opened the limo's side door. A masked face looked in at us women. He had a gun pointed at us. In a crude accent, the man said, "Which one of you two is Captain Nia Elain?"

"That would be me," I replied, before Tesla could say that she was me.

"Get out, Nia Elain. Now. Or I begin shooting the others one at a time until you do."

I had to lurch and struggle to get out of the limo on my own. Just now, I really missed having Athena at my side. Somehow, I managed to get out and not fall down. We were all quite surprised at his next action. He pulled his mask off, revealing the whitish skin of a Slaver! I found this more than a little curious. Why show your face, especially to the others?

He pushed me away from the limo, and I quickly lost sight of the vehicle in the sense smoke. Coughing, I had little choice but to follow his push. While I thought of using my gifts on him, I dare not just yet. I had no idea just how many others were there in the smoke. I simply could not risk the lives of Queen Zenovia, Tesla, or Lady Frieda. It was far too risky for me or for Tesla to try anything. I felt another man come up to me and put a steadying arm around my waist. Just as I began to think they were finally being considerate of me, I felt a needle jabbing into my neck. Then, everything went black.

"I don't hear them anymore. Is it safe yet?" Lady Frieda whispered.

Tesla was worried. She focused and tried to make contact with me, but failed. "She's still alive, but unconscious I think."

"What, what just happened?" Queen Zenovia managed to say.

Lady Frieda answered. "Slavers. The man had the white skin of a Slaver! They took Nia! Oh my god! We'll never see her again!"

Both Tesla and Queen Zenovia recalled the many reports of the Slaver's raids. Thus far, they'd taken one hundred sixty men and women, though more than half were women. Not one of them had ever been seen again. No bodies were ever found either. Tesla swallowed hard. Several wounded and bleeding guards finally made it to the limo, and a sobbing Lady Frieda tried to tell them what had happened. Tesla intervened because with her lip plates, she wasn't making herself understandable.

Within a half hour, the site was swarming with security forces, and the three survivors were whisked away to the safety of the mansion. "Mom. How could this have happened?" wailed Lady Frieda, forgetting all about proper protocol. "Sis had a large security force protecting us this time."

"Well, this has now become an intergalactic issue. I'm afraid we've lost Matriarch Nia Elain this time. I'll once more suggest we declare war on these damned Slavers!" Matriarch Athala barked angrily.

"Well, the white skin matches the reports," Queen

270

Zenovia began thinking aloud. "What I don't understand is just why that masked man pulled off his mask, revealing himself to us? That makes no sense."

"He probably wanted to strike fear in you. After all, the Slavers all have ghastly pale skin, not a proper grey color, like all civilized people," Matriarch Athala declared.

"I think it was more than that. It was plainly obvious this was a Slaver raid. It follows the same pattern as all those in the reports. He didn't need to remove his mask," the queen argued.

"If you'll excuse me, I'm going back to our ship to let the others know. We'll likely go after them and try to rescue our captain," Tesla broke in. She rose and Damali moved instantly to her side. Athena did likewise.

"Be careful, Lady Tesla. These are vicious men who will stop at nothing," Matriarch Athala declared acidly. "I'll send out scouting parties at first light. If there is any trace of her around, we'll find it. I promise you."

Tesla nodded and headed for the door. The chauffeur hastily drove up in an older limo and took the trio back to the spaceport. However, Tesla had already alerted everyone there. As soon as the trio entered the front hatch, Danika had Callisto secure it for space travel, just in case. Danika said, "Meeting room now!" She tried to contain her anger over the kidnaping of her mate and utter frustration of her near helplessness.

Grim faces greeted the soot covered face of Tesla. Nearby, Zarita broke her concentration, looked up and said, "Relax. She's still alive, but unconscious I think. She's moving away from us rapidly. Conclusion: she's being transported in a spaceship. I just wish telepathy would give us the direction she's traveling. We have to go after her."

"Okay, I'm alerting the control tower now. Come on, Callisto; we have to get this ship airborne as quick as possible," Danika barked and nearly fell trying to get back to the pilot's compartment far too quickly. Callisto caught her at the last instant.

"Gang, I believe I've worked out a way we can trail her," Zarita continued.

"How? Telepathy can't tell anything but a rough

271

distance apart," Tesla complained.

"We do minute hyperspace hops. Different directions. Each time we come back to normal space, I'll make telepathic contact again. We plot the rough distances each time. That ought to give us an idea of the proper direction they are traveling. Besides, we can go many times faster than they can, if only we can locate them," Zarita replied. Only then did Tesla notice she had her giant psi-crystal sitting on her lap. Now, she finally relaxed a little. She had heard that with these monster-sized crystals, telepathy could stretch across vast distances, not just planet-wide. Within fifteen minutes, the Eagle's Seed lifted off from Menno.

Zoe sat in Danika's navigator's seat, while Jan worked from the small conference room just behind them, plotting distances on their crude sketch of the halo area they'd composed from data they'd gathered from Menno. After five small minute-duration hops in random directions and Zarita's subsequent contacts and distance estimates, Jan called out, "I've got a crude course plotted. They are likely heading for the Gorki Cluster. Zoe, let's use a fan search pattern. Jump to the right and then jump to the left. Each time, Zarita, you keep us posted on the distance. We ought to be able to keep triangulating this way."

Minta asked, "What if her captors have an armed ship? We are not armed."

"Oh yes we are!" Danika fumed. *"Mentales* gifts. I'll fry their twisted brains!" That gave Minta something to ponder.

Isi complained, *Oh no, Huyana! One of our new hosts has been kidnaped!*

It's worse than that, Isi! The rest are taking off to go after them! Hurry, we must get our ship going. We dare not lose them! Huyana added. The two moved quickly to what appeared to be a vacant corner of the spaceport. Their saucer was there, masked by its cloaking device. Rapidly, the two entered their small ship and fired up their electromagnetic engines. Silently, their ship lifted off from the tarmac, but no one saw or heard anything at all. It was ten p.m. and quite dark, but had one been looking in just the proper direction, he or she could have seen the background of the city shimmer slightly as the ship moved through their field of view.

Bringing all sensors online now, Isi sent. Huyana was at the controls. Both had never been this worried before. Suddenly, all their hard work and exceptional find was about to be lost. Not only were they about to lose their golden opportunity, but some twenty others would too, if they lost this ship and its people!

Isi scanned the zone around them. *How weird. They are hopping into and out of hyperspace, spending barely a minute there. Whatever are they doing?*

That's the weirdest thing I've ever heard of, Isi, but they must have a reason. The question is, do we follow them or try to find the ship that has taken Nia Elain? Huyana asked.

Let's see if we can find the other ship first. The Eagle's Seed ought to be pretty easy to find what with all these ridiculous tiny hops that they are making. I'm looking deeper out now, Isi sent back.

Sometime later, Isi reported. *Okay, I found the ship that's taking Nia Elain away. They are heading for the Gorki Cluster. It's the Slavers again. We have to stop them, Huyana.*

Okay, relay me the coordinates and we'll see if we can overtake them before they land. It's going to be harder to get to her if we allow them to land. Do we have the right disguises for the Slavers? Huyana asked.

Nope. We didn't think we'd be going there. Isi sighed. *Plotting an interception course now. Looks like we'll catch them very close to one of their worlds, Huyana. This will be very close. Too bad they aren't using the obsolete space drives of the Narsten Cluster. We could catch them in no time.*

I vaguely began coming to. The universe seemed to be shaking and pounding. No, that was my head. I think I moaned. A white skinned man called out, "She's waking up."

Another voice answered from some distance away. "Inform her and put her out again."

The man standing over me said, "Relax alien. No harm will come to you. Our President Arcangelo Ferrobossi of Aurelio, Gorki Cluster, wants to speak to you."

I tried to think clearly, but couldn't. He's words were relatively crude Narsten, a horrible accent at best. Yet, the other words the two had exchanged were a different language, reminiscent of that spoken by the Easterlings on Ashford-5. I was confused, but felt that needle in my neck once more. I also felt the touch of Zarita's mind on mine. I think I told her I was alive, but the blackness flooded over me once more.

"Okay, she's alive. They just knocked her out again," Zarita reported.

Anwyn and Dylan were monitoring the sensors. She called out, "Gang, I'm getting traces of another spaceship I think. It comes and goes. I think someone else is following them. What does that mean?"

Alexandra tried for a bit of wit. "Maybe because she is so popular among aliens. Route those observations my way please, Anwyn."

Six long hours passed. Alexandra finally announced her findings to the group. "Hans and I agree. We've identified at least partially two very different types of spaceships. The Slavers' ship is akin to those of the Federation, but this second one has us baffled. Its appearance is more saucer-shaped than anything else. Its type is wholly unknown, but we're pretty sure it can make jumps into hyperspace, as can the Slavers' ship."

Zoe announced, "Well, makes sense. We're heading into the Gorki Cluster now. Soon, we should be able to ascertain which star and planet they are making for, I hope."

Danika called out over the intercom, "We are entering the Slavers' space now. Everyone, man every sensor station we have. We don't want to be taken by surprise by a number of battleships or whatevers." Everyone headed back to their stations.

A half hour later, Danika and Zoe reported together, "We are making for a yellow main sequence star, dead ahead." Danika ordered, "Anwyn, Jan, scan for habitable planets. Tesla, Anya, start scanning all frequencies for transmissions. Stay alert everyone," Danika added.

Shortly, Danika announced, "Dropping to sub-light speeds now. Closing in on them. Crap! You are right. There's another ship between us and Nia!"

"All sorts of radio transmissions!" Anya called out.

"Planet dead ahead. Inhabited," Jan yelled loudly.

Zoe cried out, "They are making for that planet now. We have to hurry up."

"Oh no!" Danika yelled. "That other ship is firing on them! What do we do now?"

"Wholly crap!" screamed Tesla. "There are fifty warships heading towards us on an intercept course! Get us out of here!"

"Damn! They are hit. Looks like Nia's ship is out of control. Going to crash land. Wholly crap! Look at all the warships! Callisto, hit the cloaking button fast!" Danika yelled, though she need not have. Callisto had already determined this was the correct action to take to preserve the lives of her nova. They winked out, while Danika and Zoe plotted a zig-zag course, taking them closer to the planet on the smoking trail of the doomed ship. The saucer ship also vanished from sight, much to Danika's consternation.

Alexandra commented, "Well, someone ought to invent a way to track a cloaked ship." Cloaking of ships was the last major advancement of Imperium space technology done before the terrorist attack that wiped out Proxima Prime some years ago. Only the newer ships of the line possessed this new technology or those who could afford it. Fortunately, Nia's parents had been.

"What the hell do we do now?" Zoe asked Danika. "Could she survive that crash landing?"

"Damned if I know," Danika admitted, tremendously frustrated at her helplessness. Every fiber of her being screamed at her to help her mate, but she could only sit helplessly in the pilot's seat. Callisto was doing all of the actual flying. She felt more like crying than anything else.

"She's still alive," Zarita's voice came over the intercom, bringing some relief to twenty plus people.

Her voice cracking with emotion, Danika ordered, "Everyone, keep on monitoring everything."

At breakfast, Queen Zenovia reported, "They are on her

trail, Nia Elain's. She is alive but has crash landed on a Slaver world in the Gorki Cluster."

"How can you possibly know that?" asked a mystified Matriarch Athala.

"Telepathy. Lady Zarita Laag contacted me early this morning to tell me the news. So it is confirmed. The Slavers abducted Matriarch Nia Elain. So we must continue our work. I simply must visit with some of these people Xene has on my list. We'll persevere on our end, and trust that Nia's people can rescue her."

"I wouldn't hold out any such hopes, Queen Zenovia. So far, none of our abducted people has ever been found. I can't see why you need to talk to these people. Everything they could possibly tell you is right there in the proper reports," Matriarch Athala replied. She sighed, "Nevertheless, Matriarch Clothilda will assist you, but only under very heavy security!"

Queen Zenovia didn't quite know what she was looking for, but did spend the day visiting six of the earliest abduction sites. She interviewed a dozen who had been quoted in the official reports. When she returned to the mansion for supper, she had convinced herself the reports were indeed accurate. Try as she might, she found no additional data from those who actually witnessed the abductions. The modus operandi was identical in all cases. A strange ship landed. A number of well-armed men poured out. They used some kind of stun gun to disable any resistance and took several hostages, more often than not, women. They marched the captives onto their ship and departed. The hostages were never seen again. Once in a while, someone fought back, usually wounding one of the Slavers. These were captured, healed, and questioned. However, they never revealed anything and were then chained and forced to work on the lowest, menial jobs, such as sweeping the streets or deep tunnel mining, which was quite dangerous work.

After supper, over coffee in the drawing room, Matriarch Athala inquired, "So have you learned anything new from those interviews?"

"I've verified your reports are an accurate representation of what the witnesses recall having happened.

That alone is significant. You see, often times, reports omit a few salient facts or details that could cast the events in a completely different light. In this case, I could find none. So now, we must move on to the next phase of my inquiry. I'll deal with that tomorrow. Right now, I need to relax and think," Queen Zenovia replied.

The next morning over coffee in the drawing room, Xene began taking copious notes. Queen Zenovia began by asking, "Matriarch Athala, I want you to think back to the first time you heard someone telling you the people from the Gorki Cluster were Slavers and were abducting your people."

"Well, that's all there in the reports. Everyone knows this," she protested. Queen Zenovia now had her work cut out for her. Several hours later, she finally had a list of some twenty men and women, all aristocrats, who had told her that they were Slavers or that they were a wicked, evil race of humanoids.

After lunch, Queen Zenovia worked with Matriarch Clothilda in setting up visits with each of the twenty. She began with Rolf, who was here in the mansion at the moment. Her interview with him yielded another dozen names to the list. This, she thought, is going to be a lengthy investigation! Worse, many lived on other worlds in the Narsten Cluster, among those was Matriarch Gisela Hunsstadt, the telepath. Queen Zenovia decided the best method was to invite them to the mansion here on Menno. That way, Matriarch Clothilda had drastically less security worries to handle.

The third day since the abduction, Zarita again contacted Queen Zenovia in the early morning before the nine o'clock wake-up call. After listening to her report, the queen smiled. Now, she had something far more concrete on which to focus her investigation. "Things are starting to fall into place," she whispered to Xene.

Chapter 13 Captive

I was tossed about like a rag doll when the ship crashed into this strange world. I knew the ship had been hit. I was once more coming out from the drugged sleep, groggy, but aware enough. After the bouncing, jarring motions ceased, I waited for the explosion that would surely follow, wishing I'd taken the risk and done something when I was first abducted. Silence. Finally, I struggled mightily to get back onto my toes. In the end, frustrated, I used a bit of my levitation powers to lift my body up.

I struggled to get out of the ship. Not far from my cabin, a gaping hole in the side of the ship beckoned to me. Sunlight. Fresh air. The hole was large enough for me to walk through, but I had to take careful, feeling steps to avoid somehow all the junk and bric-a-brac littering the floor, shaken loose during the crash. At last, I rather pulled my billowing outer-skirt through the hole, tearing it in several places, but I was outside.

I looked around only to discover I was in rather rugged terrain. The ground was anything but smooth and flat. Boulders, rocks, and smaller pebbles littered the undulating landscape. If my feet were normal and if I wore thick boots, I could have scrambled up the slope of the hill and gotten a good overview of just where I was. Still, I needed to get my bearings and the hilltop beckoned to me. I had to try. I just could not sit around here waiting for who knows what to happen. From the thin air, I knew I must be at a relatively high elevation. That meant when it got dark, the temperature would drop considerably. Besides, I was also hungry.

I didn't try to make telepathic contact with Zarita. I knew she was a good distance away in the Eagle's Seed. To reach out to that distance, I'd need one of her giant crystals. Instead, I would just wait until she contacted me next. Perhaps, she was finally sleeping. Hence, I began to ascend to the hilltop.

I don't think I've ever sworn and cursed so many times in my life as I did during the half hour that it took me to climb the hundred feet to the ridge top! My only consolation is that I was going uphill, not down, which would have been ten times worse for me. I could not see my feet, not remotely. Walking on only my toes in these boots on the uneven ground, littered with rocks designed to trip me, was a hideous nightmare. I kept trying to swing my arms about wildly to maintain my balance. In complete disgust and utter frustration, I finally forced my mind to calm enough so I could focus. My crystal energized, and I mostly levitated myself, using my toes to propel my body forward and up. It took me a half hour to make the ridge top.

I stood there looking out over a lovely mountain range. Ordinarily, I would admire such a scene, but today, it looked grim. I was out in the middle of nowhere and, to be quite frank, mostly helpless. If I could only lose this cursed outer-skirt, I could do better. Hence, I focused and, working this against that, I managed to get it off me, but it took another half hour to do so. Relieved of that entanglement, I felt a little freer. Now, the question was what should I do next? I looked in vain for some shelter.

Just then, I saw a dozen smaller shuttle craft zooming in on the crash site. "Well, so much for escaping," I muttered to myself. I decided to wait and see what would happen next. Alone, I couldn't really survive this. Out there somewhere was my crew, probably desperate to come to my rescue. Yet, at the moment, I didn't dare count on them finding me in time.

Dozens of white skinned men stepped out of the shuttles. With guns drawn, several swarmed around me, as though I might somehow escape them. Most headed downhill to the crash site. No one said anything, and I didn't volunteer either. A half hour later, the men brought out my two kidnapers on stretchers. They were alive but not in particularly good shape. Only then did I realize how lucky I'd been in not getting badly hurt during the crash.

A man approached me, as I watched the others carrying the wounded men towards the dozen shuttles. He spoke in a strange language, somehow familiar. Quickly though, he caught himself and repeated in crude, thickly accented Narsten. "You will come with us. President Arcangelo

Ferrobossi wants to question you."

I replied, "Okay. I could use a supporting arm, please." However, my ULAT box was silent. He didn't know Imperium Standard. Hence, I quickly repeated myself in the Narsten language. Unfortunately, my lip plates butchered the sounds, and he simply didn't understand me. He motioned towards the ships. I had no choice but to valiantly attempt to walk there on my own, hoping I wouldn't fall and break my neck. I dare not use my *mentales* gifts around these men.

As I wiggled and wobbled precariously, the many men stared at me, quite blatantly. I sensed they'd never seen anyone who looked remotely like I did. Finally, their leader grasped the situation and slipped his arm around my waist, catching my long hair as well. I tried to ignore the slight pain coming from my hair, grateful for the support. He continually tried to make me walk faster than it was possible for me to do. Yet, he soon figured this detail out as well. By the time we reached one of the shuttles, he had figured out I needed assistance with everything. Graciously, he helped me inside and buckled me securely into my seat. Six of his men, who looked like security guards, surrounded me.

As we took off, I began worrying about our communication problem. My ULAT wasn't working, and I didn't know why. I didn't know their language, and they couldn't understand my pathetic attempts to speak the Narsten dialect, though I could understand them when they spoke it crudely. What bothered me more was that their native speech sounded somewhat familiar. Therefore, while we flew to wherever we were going, I focused on listening to their chat and trying to place it. Then, it struck me. Their language was very similar to the Easterlings on Ashford-5. Well, I knew the Easterlings dialect well, but my lip plates interfered in speaking it. I knew from my three years on Ashford-5, the locals, who wore the lip plates and who spoke Easterlings, made it almost a new language, but not quite. They were able to make themselves understood if they spoke slowly and carefully. Perhaps, that would suffice here. I certainly hoped so.

Some while later, I saw signs of a very modern city with

tall skyscrapers from the window across the aisle from where I sat. I found that encouraging. Once we landed and the bay doors opened, I got my first real glimpse of this world. Yes, I was impressed. My idea of a Slavers' world was one of glum, scum, filth, and basically a hovel. Instead, I saw a clean world. True, I could smell traces of engine oil in the air around the spaceport, but that came with such places. I could see mountains in the far distance and surmised we were in a lower elevation valley city of quite some size.

As I began to see more of the city, I realized this was a heavily populated city, quite modern. Shuttles zipped around the skies, much like Proxima Prime. I was escorted across the tarmac, through what must have been their spaceport administration building, and out the other side, where I was helped into another small shuttle. The leader, who had helped me, joined me, along with the driver. As soon as he boarded, we took off, and I watched the sights of the city as they flew by. As far as I could tell, it was clean and modern in appearance, far from what I had imagined. No one said anything, and I was content to observe the city.

We landed outside a tall skyscraper. I could see dozens of what appeared to be electric cars parked along the street. I saw men and women walking on the sidewalks. The men wore suits and ties, while the women wore what I was used to calling professional women's outfits. I'd been around Martina too long and had picked up her nomenclature. Black skirts, white blouses, and low heels. From the blackish hue of their exposed legs, I guessed they were also wearing black nylons. If I had not known better, the scene could well have been right out of many Imperium worlds I'd seen!

My observations allowed me to relax for the first time since I was abducted. Whatever was going to happen, I was dealing with a highly civilized race of people, not barbarians. Plus, I again felt the reassuring arm of the soldier as he led me into the main entrance of the building. The doors opened automatically, triggered by sensors on the ground as we walked over them. I was impressed again.

As we walked in, literally everyone stopped and stared at me. I hated that, but could do nothing about it. I was thankful that they also had elevators. Trying to climb a whole lot of stairs on your toes is quite nasty; going down, even worse. As we entered, several men in their black suits joined us. I did notice they pressed the top-most button. My knees gave a little as the elevator lurched upwards.

Before long, the doors opened automatically, and I was ushered out, down a short hall, and into a very plush office. Another man wearing a black suit with a yellow polka dot tie rose from behind a big teakwood desk. Another was standing, but wore some kind of military uniform. A third man was beside the military man, wearing another black suit. I was shown a seat that faced all three of them, while the soldier who had found me joined the three. The other black suited men stood patiently near the door. Guards, I concluded.

The man behind the desk said, "Well, here goes nothing. I am President Arcangelo Ferrobossi of Aurelio, Gorki Cluster. Can you understand me at all?" He spoke in his own language.

I sighed. The only option I had now was to try to reply in the Easterlings dialect and hope for the best. If only the ULAT was working, perhaps we could get by using Narsten. "Yes, mostly I understand you. I am Captain Nia Elain Compton-Jereni of the Eagle's Seed. We are from the galactic spiral arm exploring the halo worlds. Can you understand me at all?" I did my best to speak very slowly and as distinctly as I could.

"Hey, I got some of that! She understands us, gentlemen. Please, Nia, would you repeat that?" I did so twice before they understood me completely. I could readily sense the relief President Arcangelo felt. Having gotten this far, I added, "I need to use the bathroom right away, and I am very hungry."

After two more repeats, he flushed slightly. "Pardon my manners. Yes, at once." He pressed a button on his desk. "Marcella, please come in here." Shortly, a professionally dressed young woman entered. "Please take Captain Nia Elain here to the bathroom and give her whatever assistance she might need. I'll arrange for some food to be delivered shortly. She can sort of speak our language, Marcella."

"Of course, Mr. President. Ma'am, if you will follow me," she said politely, though staring wide-eyed at me. I had to more or less lunge to my toes, wobbling a bit to get my balance again. I did my best to walk reasonably confidently after her.

In the women's restroom, she knew what needed to be done, but when she lowered my panties, she gasped. While I relieved myself, I explained, "Yes, I'm a hermaphrodite. They both work. Right now, I'm a few weeks pregnant with my second child. Thanks for helping me. I'm afraid you'll need to feed me." I said it several times until she understood. Then, I explained how to work the upper lip plate and what she would need to do to assist me.

"We've never seen anyone quite like you. I don't see how you can even walk in those boots. Those lip ornaments must be terrible to live with. Did you have a tragic accident that cost you your arms? Do all women on your world have such enormous breasts?" she asked what she wanted to know, before we had to return to the world of men.

While I explained a bit, she was considerate enough to wipe the dirt off my face and gave my hair a light brushing. We took an instant liking to each other. She had blonde hair and blue eyes. Her face was round with thin eyebrows, but she wore a shade of eye shadow that I found quite attractive. Marcella was just twenty-one and had only recently been hired as the President's receptionist, replacing an older woman who had retired. By the time that we returned, some sandwiches and some kind of fruit juice had been brought up. Everyone stared at me, while Marcella did her best to feed me, and spoon the juice into my mouth. I will give them this, though, they waited patiently until I was finished before launching into their business.

President Arcangelo was perhaps thirty-five, with short black hair and lips, which when closed formed a natural smile. Indeed, one might think he had a perpetual smile on his face. I estimated General Celino was ten years his senior with a stiff, military carry to his frame. He too had short black hair and a rather solemn face. His aide, Doriano was barely thirty, if that, with dark brown hair. Something about the way he faced me filled me with distrust, quite unlike that of the president.

"Now then Captain Nia Elain, we need to get down to business. I must apologize for having had you so rudely abducted, but we could find no other way to reach you. We believe the Narsten Cluster of worlds is about to declare war on us and are in the process of gathering more allies in their fight against our worlds. We have spies on Menno, and know that Matriarch Athala is actively recruiting your disk worlds in her vicious attacks on our worlds. I've brought you here to discuss this matter. We of the Gorki Cluster would prefer not to wage a costly war on those backwards people, if we can avoid it. So be honest with me, have your people in the galactic disk agreed to support her in this proposed war with us?"

"No we have not. In fact, I've brought one of our diplomats to Menno in hopes our queen will be able to resolve this conflict between your two civilizations in a peaceful manner," I replied.

"See, I told you these aliens from the disk weren't utter fools," President Arcangelo said to his aide and general. Turning to me, he added, "Then you and I have an awful lot to discuss. Let me begin by saying the blame for this whole mess lies with the Narstens, not us. You see, five years ago, the Narstens began raiding some of our worlds, kidnaping our people and forcing them into slave labor camps. Of course, I protested this vigorously to the various matriarchs, but they denied doing any such thing. After two more years of continuous raids, I had to act, sending raiding parties of our own to kidnap some of their people. Unlike the filthy greys, we have treated all those taken with dignity and respect. They are all alive and being very well treated. Still, the Narstens continue to raid our worlds. General Celino and Doriano both believe we should declare war on the dirty grey people and wipe them out of the halo permanently."

"Now this is very interesting news. You are right. I've heard nothing at all about their raiding your worlds. Not one hint. They call your people Slavers," I replied.

President Arcangelo chuckled. "Ah, the pot calling the kettle black as we say here. Around here, we think of the Narstens as the filth of the halo, all prim and proper, but stupid and ignorant, if not outright backwards. The matriarchs are probably hiding it all from you. I wouldn't put that past those weird women who insist on having tiny arms, maimed for life."

"There are obvious cultural differences at play. But the charges you have levied against them must be verified and appropriate actions taken," I replied diplomatically.

"Cultural differences? How about huge physical differences between you and us? Are all those in the dirty galactic disk like you, physically, I mean? We've never seen any human like you before."

Thus, I launched into a lengthy, detailed explanation of the Imperium and our worlds. My goal was to let him know that most of the people of the disk worlds were more like himself, and that I, my friends, and a few others were the odd ones. I told him about our mission to explore the halo and about my crew and ship. He asked numerous questions as well. It was dark when we finally finished up. I was certain he believed what I was telling him. I touched his mind just to be certain.

His last question of the evening was, "So who was it that attacked the transport bringing you here? Another ship fired upon it, damaging its engines, forcing the pilot to make a crash landing. Was that your ship?"

"Not my ship, President Arcangelo. We are an unarmed deep space exploration ship. I have no idea who shot us down. Could it have been a Narsten ship?" I asked in turn.

"No. Their ships simply are completely archaic. Even at their top speed, it would take them many months to get here from there. Someone else must be involved in this mess. General Celino, you heard her. Doriano, you and the general get to work. Find out what that enemy ship was and where it came from. That is your top priority. We have just been thrown a twist, and by golly, I aim to know just who were dealing with. Perhaps, one of the matriarchs has obtained some allies who have vastly better ships than they do. I don't know, but we darn well better find out and fast!"

"It's getting late. We need to find a secure location for Captain Nia Elain. Suggestions?" President Arcangelo asked. "We best keep her presence here a secret for a while yet."

"I can put her up at my place," Marcella offered, knowing I would prefer not to be surrounded by a bunch of men in some hotel room.

"Would you, Marcella? That would be prefect. Of course, I'll send a squad of guards to ensure your safety," President Arcangelo asked. I could sense his relief over her offer.

"Follow me, Captain Nia Elain. I'll get my purse, and we'll be on our way," Marcella told me. Again, I lunged to my feet, caught my balance, and followed her, though Doriano held the door open for me. I wondered what a purse was and then saw her pick up a bag-like thing. Later, I saw it held her cosmetics, ids, and her keys. We took the elevator down and headed out of the same doors I'd entered when I first arrived. I was somewhat surprised to see that she had one of the small electric cars parked nearby.

Since Marcella had really no idea how to assist me, after she opened the side door, did my best to get myself into the seat. I shook my head to get my ankle length hair out of the way and more or less fell into the seat. She buckled me in and shut the door, before coming around to her side. After inserting the key, she began to backup and then drive. Like the electric cars the governor and two queens had on Ashford-5, this one ran smooth as silk and totally silent. "You like music?"

"Sure, but I'm not familiar with yours," I answered.

"You'll like this. It's called Rock and Sway. Great beats. As the music played, she more or less rocked in her seat and hummed along. "I'm going to stop for take-out. Do you like roast beef? Arnoldi's is on the way. Oh, there are three security cars following us. Guess President Arcangelo wasn't teasing us." We stopped at a small restaurant. A large sign said Arnoldi's Roast Beef. The writing looked quite similar to that of the Easterlings back on Ashford-5. While I was musing this over, she said, "You stay in the car while I go pick it up."

I took advantage of this opportunity, being the first time I was both alone and coherent. I focused and reached out to see if I could make contact with Zarita or the others. If they were in hyperspace or too far away, I knew I wouldn't be able to do it. Zarita could only because she had that giant, spherical crystal. I relaxed for the first time. I felt her mind and then all of the others!

Zarita. Only got a minute here. I'm all right, and they are treating me very well. They are not the monsters the Narstens have painted them. I related what the President had told me about the Narstens raiding and abducting from these worlds, long before they began to retaliate. *Get this relayed to Queen Zenovia. I think it is critical information.*

Zarita sent, *We're all very relieved. Okay will contact her soon. We're hovering above this world, but are cloaked. We saw another spaceship firing on the one you were on, but it vanished when about fifty local warships came after them. We'll try to stay in easy telepathic contact range. Say the word, and we'll try to rescue you.*

Okay. Keep safe. Got to go. I'm staying with the president's receptionist tonight. I had to break off contact, as Marcella walked up, carrying a large, white, paper bag with a strange logo on it. The odors coming from the bag made my mouth water all the way home. Fortunately, it was only another mile or so. She parked in an underground parking lot of another skyscraper.

"We're here. I'm on the 13th floor. Hope you are not superstitious or anything. Come on; the elevator is this way." Once more, I had to get myself out of the car on my own, bit awkward, but I managed, since she had her hands full, the purse in one hand and our supper in her other. A few minutes later, she used a key to unlock her door, and I followed her inside her place, a condo, she called it.

Marcella's place was neat and tidy, a reflection of the professional woman she tried to be. It was small, but then she lived by herself. Her kitchen-dining room was all-in-one, but at least she had two bar stools. I quickly discovered I could sit and rise from a tall bar stool vastly easier than normal chairs, because I was standing on my toes. After getting the food out of the sack, she hesitantly lifted my top plate up and locked it into place. Flashing me a smile, she began to feed me, alternating with herself. I found the food quite delicious, and that I was really rather hungry.

"You don't seem to eat much," she commented.

"Very tight corset restricts my intake. I prefer to eat six smaller meals a day, when I can."

"So why do you wear it? It must be awfully uncomfortable."

"No choice. The weight of these knockers gives me horrid back pains if I don't." We chatted more about my unique physiology. She certainly asked all the right questions. I began to suspect that Marcella was wasting much of her talents by being a mere receptionist, even if it was for the President of her world.

When we finished eating, she said, "I usually take a shower when I get home. Do you want one too? I'm not sure if I know how to deal with a corset, Captain Nia Elain."

"Please, just Nia will be fine. I can give you instructions, but with my feet, I won't be able to stand up in the shower."

"How about a bath then? I've got some scented candles." I agreed to a bath, but had no idea what she meant by the candles. Did her lights go out at night?

Since my hair was also dirty thanks to the crash landing, we decided to wash it as well. "Don't worry about your dirty clothes. I know we'll simply not be able to find you any top that will remotely fit your bosom, so I'll use my dry cleaner machine. They'll be ready by morning." She got me undressed but I had to crawl on my knees and mostly lean over the edge of the tub to get in or out of it.

She filled it with water at just the perfect temperature, added some delightful smelling salts, and lit four of her candles. Soon the air was filled with a relaxing aroma. She climbed in facing me. Once more, I could do nothing to help bathe myself. Back when I was in my teens, I could have done it all using my feet and toes and sometimes my teeth. Now, with my whole foot fused into a solid bone mass and with the dangling lip loops, I was unable to do anything at all, unless I used my *mentales* gifts, which I didn't want to reveal.

Marcella didn't mind at all, but soon her curiosity was roused over my strange anatomy. Worse, she aroused me! "Oh! It really does work!" Marcella exclaimed. "Sorry, Nia. I didn't mean to. . ." She felt very embarrassed, and I wanted to defuse the situation.

"You are a very attractive woman yourself. Let me show you one of the positive things about my lip loops." I leaned over and gave her a loving kiss. One thing led to another as you might be anticipating. Marcella was quite content when our bath was finally finished. She was going to put me in her spare bedroom, but I slept beside her instead, much to her pleasure. If nothing else, I was determined to have one ally on this world, just in case. So yes, in a way, I was using her, but my affection was real enough.

The next morning, my satin gown was perfectly clean and pressed, almost as it was when it came out of the Fabrication Machine on my ship. These people had invented a really useful device! After getting us both dressed, she made us a light breakfast and then sat down to put on her makeup, spending considerable time with her eyes. "Say, do you want me to do up your eyes for you?" Marcella asked. I agreed, thinking that perhaps it would make me more acceptable to the others on this world. When she was done, she held up a mirror so I could see my look.

"Wow. I really do look good, don't I? Thanks Marcella. I suppose we should get going." She agreed, but said we had plenty of time yet. As we left her condo, we found other security men standing just outside. Evidently, they'd taken shifts watching over us during the night. An hour later, I once more was sitting in President Arcangelo's office with the same three men. This time, he asked Marcella to stay with me, in case I needed some assistance.

"We've had some time to analyze what happened yesterday. Here are some enhanced images of the two spaceships. Can you recognize either of them?" He slid two 8x10 photographs over towards me. One was my Eagle's Seed, but the other looked more like two saucers, one upside down over the other. I had to make a decision and decided to risk truth.

"That one on the left is my spaceship, the Eagle's Seed. My crew was able to follow me here. As you can see, it has no armaments on it. It is a modified deep space exploration ship. The other one, I have never seen before. In fact, I've not seen anything remotely like that anywhere in the spiral arms. It looks nothing like our main warships or the Federation of Planets, who control the other spiral arm. It's not like the crude ships of the Narsten Cluster either. Do you know anything about it? Where it comes from? How can it even fly?"

"Well, we're batting fifty-fifty on this one, general. No, Captain Nia Elain. We don't know anything about it. We have no record of such a ship in existence, and we haven't a clue how it can fly either. However, it is the ship, which fired upon the transport carrying you and caused the crash to occur. Do you have some enemies that are trying to kill you?"

"None that I know about. We've only visited the Farthun-3 world before we were taken to Menno in the Narsten Cluster. It's a mystery to me. Perhaps, they are enemies of yours?" I turned it around to no avail. He just shook his head, as baffled by this mystery ship as I was. I lightly touched all three minds and was convinced they were telling me the truth.

He went on, "According to the reports, your ship just suddenly vanished from sight and from all our detection sensors. How is that possible? Hyperspace jump?"

"They could have jumped into hyperspace, but it is more likely that since they were trying to rescue me from your people they activated our cloaking device. It makes the ship invisible, both in the visible spectrum and to the usual sensors. It is a recent Imperium invention found only on the newer ships or those of us who can afford it. My parents added it just before they were killed over four years ago. I assume you have such devices as well, but I don't think the Narstens do."

"A cloaking device? Now that does interest us. No, we don't have such a thing, but all our ships use hyperspace travel, unlike the antiquated Narsten ships or the crude ships of the Hadu lizard men. Until your cloaking device appeared, we believed we had the best spaceships in the halo. Rather impressive that your disk people invented such a thing. Still, your ship has such an unusual design. What is the purpose of those four cylinders attached to what we are guessing is the main part of your ship?" President Arcangelo asked.

"Modular add-ons designed especially for this very long range exploration trip. We are testing out two new engine designs and are carrying years' worth of fuel and supplies. Normally, our ships are only able safely to reach Farthun-3, just barely in the halo. So we are loaded with extra fuel so we can explore your halo."

"Are the two engines a secret or can you elaborate on them?" he asked politely.

At this point, both had been tested, and I took a chance. "We've finished testing them, and back home they are going into production, at least I believe so. One would be of no use up here in the halo. It's a sub-light hydrogen propulsion engine with refueling capabilities. Our tests have shown it can refuel while the ship is traveling, which extends its range nearly indefinitely at sub-light speeds. It would be useless here in the halo. No gas to collect."

President Arcangelo laughed. The other two men chuckled. "Of course, leave it to the disk people to find a way to make use of all that filthy gas and dust down there. And the other engine?"

"It is a big improvement on our normal hyperdrive engines. We can go faster and farther on a single fuel cell than before, something like five times. However, we were still experimenting with its capabilities when we ran into the Narsten people."

"Most intriguing. Indeed. Most. Perhaps, there could be some benefits in sharing technology between our worlds and your disk worlds after all. Who would have ever thought that, eh general?" the President said wryly to the other two men. The general frowned, but nodded his agreement.

He then said, "Well, I would like to show our hospitality to you and your people. I apologize for having you abducted like that. In my defense, I simply could not think of any other way of contacting you to explain our situation here. We are not the beastly Slavers the Narsten think. Rather, they are the Slavers. If you would like your ship to land, it can be arranged at our spaceport. I would like to invite you and any of your crew to tour our world and see for themselves that we're the highest civilization in the halo. Perhaps you have someone who could discuss possible trading arrangements with your worlds. I'm certain we know virtually nothing of the disk worlds, having shunned all contact with them since time began."

The proverbial ball was back in my court now. I could refuse and know that my ship and crew would be safe and hidden from them. Having the Eagle's Seed on the ground would likely allow me to rejoin them, but it also exposed them to some risk, should these people be deceiving me. On the other hand, thus far, I had been treated well indeed, ignoring the kidnaping and drugging while in flight. Then, there were the robots or HIFRs to consider.

"Before either of us makes such a commitment, I should explain more about our worlds in our spiral arm, the Imperium side." I outlined the old Imperium, even though it was probably collapsed by now, explaining how most humans appeared, much like the people of Aurelio. Then, I described the nova, that is, those like me, explaining my whole crew was physically like me, including our two three-year old daughters, but that we all had personal assistants who helped us with everything, following our orders precisely.

This was met with complete disbelief. Not even Marcella actually believed I could actually pilot the ship. I realized this was far beyond any reality they had. In their world, being armless meant the person was a helpless cripple, dependent upon another for everything in life. I tried another approach. "You see, we use our minds. Alexandra invented the new hydrogen propulsion system, while Hans invented the improved hyperdrive engine. While it's quite true that we are dependent upon our assistants for physical matters, our minds are quite brilliant indeed. So knowing all of this, are you still willing to have my ship land and some of my crew visit your world?" I place the ball back in his court. At least, he now had a better idea of what he was getting with his offer.

He smiled. "Well, I do understand you better. I admit I still don't quite know what to believe about you. Yes, I'm afraid we cannot help but stare at you. We've never seen a woman quite like you. If your people can tolerate the staring, my offer still stands. I believe it's in both our best interests to see if we can become friends, allies, and trading partners. Obviously, you possess certain technologies we would dearly love to acquire. It remains for us to find what we have that your worlds would like in exchange. I doubt that would be simply money."

I chuckled. "I doubt that too." I explained we were not authorized to deal with trading arrangements, but that Queen Zenovia was. Of course, that also meant telling him about the Ataro Empire and their queens. Further, I explained she was currently working with Matriarch Athala to resolve the conflict between her worlds and his worlds. "I'm certain Queen Zenovia will insist on coming here and meeting with you and your people as well, as she tries to resolve the conflict between your worlds peacefully. When she does, she is authorized to work out all manner of relations and trading arrangements between our worlds. However, one thing that we truly want to know is knowledge of your halo worlds. We disk people know virtually nothing of the halo and its citizens, and we want to learn. That's why I am here."

President Arcangelo replied. "Fair enough. Marcella, I'm appointing you to be our official representative to these Ataro Empire people. After Captain Nia Elain here has worked out her landing party, I charge you with giving them a grand tour. Of course, General Celino will provide you with tight security. Coordinate with him. We will designate a secure location at the spaceport for her ship to land. Captain, how will you be able to contact your ship? I'm afraid I didn't consider this eventuality when I ordered your abduction. You don't have any communication devices on you. Will this be a problem for you to contact your ship? If so, perhaps we can work out a way for you to signal them."

Once more, the ball landed in my lap. I really didn't want to reveal that most of my crew was telepaths. That was entirely too risky. However, this society was more advanced than the Narsten one. I suspected that my crew was already monitoring all manner of electronic transmissions from the planet. If so, this might be a better way to go. "I can give you a frequency if you have a transmitter that can use that one. My people can be contacted that way."

The President breathed a sigh of relief. While he and the general made some arrangements, I quietly made contact with Zarita and relayed the frequency to use to pick up the broadcast when it came. Now, I truly began to relax. What had begun as a nightmare was working out very well, at least thus far. If only it continued this way.

Chapter 14 Revelations

By evening, the Eagle's Seed was parked off to one edge of their spaceport. Marcella had kindly brought me here in her electric car, followed of course by several transports carrying a dozen security men. President Arcangelo had asked me if it would be acceptable for Marcella to visit my ship, tagging along wherever I went. Since she was now their official ambassador to us, I could hardly refuse, but at least my crew had been alerted and was expecting her when the two of us rode their elevator up to the platform connected to our forward docking port. I'd already explained to Marcella that our main docking port was now in use connecting the ship to the circular hallway leading to each of the four modules.

None of us saw or heard the silent, invisible saucer ship settle down some distance behind the Eagle's Seed. Isi sent, *I can't believe we've been so incredibly lucky! I thought for sure we'd lost everything this time.*

Huyana replied, *Indeed, Isi, I'd prepared myself for the ultimate humiliation and demotion. And yet, here we are. Our hosts are safe and sound. Phenomenal luck. I have a very good feeling about them.*

After a number of hugs, well wishes, and expressions of relief, we got down to business. My crew had been busy and had a number of reports to make. Jan and Zoe were quite excited about their discovery. Now that we were within the Gorki Globular Cluster, they had been compiling a catalogue of its stars. In the process, they'd found another red supergiant. As you might be suspecting, Jan wanted to go off to study it and to apply his new prediction theory to it. After the Boon supernova, I think we were all a bit leery when it came to red supergiant stars. He'd also found a very faint shell of expanding gas whose radius greatly exceeded that of the globular cluster itself and wanted to take some observation of it as well.

Working together, Alexandra and Hans had created a series of hyperspace coordinates that we could use to navigate through the halo, as long as we followed the route we'd taken thus far. Much more work needed to be done to fill in the gaps, primarily the space below our path down to the galactic disk. They needed my okay to transmit them back to the Ataro Empire, and I gave my official permission.

I introduced Marcella to my mate Danika and our two children. "They are quite charming," Marcella said with a motherly smile. "One day, I'll get some children too, and start my own family."

I chuckled, "It seems my crew and I are pregnant. So we're going to be inundated in babies in about eight more months."

Marcella gave me a rather funny look. "I'm not sure what you mean by the word pregnant."

Now, it was my turn to give her a funny look. Quickly, our chat headed down the path of reproductive organs. Finally, Marcella understood, and her face flushed. "Oh my! No, our people do not reproduce this way. I think that was the way it happened a long time ago, but not in today's modern world. None of us can get pregnant like your people. Oh true, we can and do have lots of intercourse with whomever we desire, but to have a baby, that's only possible in the Fertility Laboratories. You see, each month, I visit the Input Facility nearest me, where they take my egg and store it. When I'm ready to have a baby, they take one of my eggs, fertilize it, and grow the baby in the Fertility Laboratory. After nine months, I would go there, pick up my new baby, and raise him or her. How quaint it must be for you to have to carry the growing baby inside your bodies for those nine months."

Well, having done this once, I would not call the last few months "quaint," nor would I call the birthing quaint either. However, I didn't need the instant stare from Doctor Leann to alert me to the significance of this discovery. Initially, I formed a theory that somehow, these people had advanced reproductive science to a higher level, and I knew Dr. Leann would want to delve into this immediately.

At least, I had a better idea of those that ought to join

me planet-side observing firsthand this new civilization. Of course, Tesla would. Her political science and governmental studies were invaluable. Doctor Leann had to learn about their unique reproduction methods. With their strong desire for trade, that is, their eagerness to gain access to our hyperdrive improvements, our cloaking device, and to prevent their making attempts to steal them from the Eagle's Seed, I needed to be seen as taking some actions that could be seen to be leading towards trading arrangements. That is, I had to find out what they had that our people would desire in trade. While usually these things are the province of the queens and the diplomats, with new civilizations, the exploration crews often surveyed the new world and submitted their findings, giving those doing the bargaining valuable information.

Hence, this meant that Zarita, our geologist, would need to join us planet-side, along with Martina and one engineer. Herein lay my toughest decision. The engineers were all men, but since the genetic bio terrorist attack, their whole sense of self-identity had been severely shaken, to say nothing of their recent bouts of morning sickness. I didn't dare subject them to further humiliation and embarrassment by placing them back into a world where men "were men." After announcing my choices, I saw relief on the faces of Thomas, Hans, Len, Diego, and Dao.

Thus, Tesla, Martina, Dr. Leann, Zarita, and I, along with our HIFRs, packed a few things and departed from the ship accompanied by Marcella. We five would explore this new civilization. Meanwhile, Danika and Hans had my permission to take some short exploratory flights to gather Jan's needed data on this red supergiant star. Zarita brought along her giant crystal, so no matter what happened, she would telepathically reach them if need be.

We were housed in the penthouse suite at the top of Marcella's skyscraper. Much to her pleasure, Marcella was asked by President Arcangelo to move in with us for the time being. The next day, we met with him, his general, and his aide. By mutual consent, we divided up. While I met with President Arcangelo discussing the Imperium worlds and their locations in the spiral arm, Martina and Tesla chatted with

General Celino and Doriano, gathering similar information on the inhabited worlds of the Gorki Cluster.

We learned there were some thirty populated worlds in their system. Each was fundamentally a democratic society with elected officials. We were rather surprised to discover they had three similar branches of government as we had. Namely, the President saw to the execution of the laws of the world and it's running, while the Legislature developed the laws, and the Judiciary handled jurisprudence. Upon discovering just how parallel our two civilizations were, the bonds of affinity grew significantly between us.

On the larger scale, each world elected what they called Cluster Legislators, Cluster Judges, and the Cluster Council. These three groups dealt only with inter-world issues. Currently, they were taking their Summer Recess and would not be meeting for another two months. However, President Arcangelo insisted we be formally presented to them when they resumed their sessions in the fall.

Zarita began by visiting their Natural History Museum, scouting out the displays, featuring their geological exhibits. That's where she discovered there were a dozen uninhabited planets, arid worlds that could not sustain life. No water, just enormous quantities of silicates. When she saw an exhibit displaying a sample of those soils, she gasped. It contained a heavy concentration of psi-crystals. While I personally wanted to trade for their fancy dry cleaning machines, Zarita had found something of great value to our civilization: fuel in vast quantities.

She then met with some of their geologists to confirm her discovery. A few days later, one of them gave her a sample, satisfying her curiosity. She then gave the geologists and President Arcangelo a complete report on the immense value of this seemingly worthless sand to the Imperium. Finally, President Arcangelo relaxed. I didn't need telepathy to sense his immense relief at having discovered something they could trade for our technology. The relations between us improved significantly after that. I was given the "Key to Aurelio," well figuratively as Athena accepted it for me.

Doctor Leann's discoveries were more nightmarish. She

met with Doctor Lucrezia Loreto, who specialized in Fertilization and Embryonic Growth, which was a fancy name for the creation of their babies from conception through their "birth." The process was simple to describe, but the laboratory technology that provided a substitute mother's womb was extraordinarily complex. Each woman's eggs were harvested and stored until she was ready to have a baby. Then, her husband or donor if unmarried was also "harvested," and the fertilization done in the lab. The single cell was then placed in the complex substitute womb where it was fed the precise and proper nutrients to develop a healthy baby. If anything went awry with the fetus, it was abandoned and the process repeated. Doctor Lucrezia pointed out that there were no babies born who had any physical defects or ailments. All full-term babies were in pristine health.

After spending a week visiting the facilities and studying their procedures, Doctor Leann finally asked the question that had been in the back of her mind since Marcella first explained their women did not carry their babies in their wombs. It was a simple question. "Why?" she asked. I don't think any of us were prepared for the answer she received, though in hindsight and with the data coming in from Jan and his explorations, we ought to have worked it out ourselves.

Doctor Lucrezia explained, "Around a thousand years ago, the red supergiant on the far side of the Gorki Cluster had a terrible explosion. All our worlds were bombarded with intense amounts of radiation. After that, no woman could conceive, unless done artificially. Records show they then tried to implant the fertilized embryos back into the mother's womb, but that also always failed. Frantic efforts were then undertaken to find ways and means to artificially reproduce the nine month gestation period. Our records show all the people of the Gorki Cluster very nearly died off before the process was perfected. We came terribly close to extinction. It's taken us a thousand years to rebuild, but I think that our population is back to what it was before that explosion," she explained.

"Something else that you should be aware of," Doctor Lucrezia added, "there are other me's, Marcella's, and the rest

299

of us on other worlds in the Gorki Cluster. We try to make sure there's only one copy of a specific body on each world. Long ago, our ancestors found it way too confusing to have multiple copies of the same or nearly the same body on one world. I can't imagine how it must have been way back then. You know, you walk down the street and see several other women who are physically nearly identical to you. Unnerving. These days, we in the Fertility Laboratory take special precautions to ensure no two bodies on one world are nearly the same. But you'll find other women who look more or less like me on other worlds of the Gorki Cluster. Like I said, our race very nearly became extinct." We found this quite disturbing and unnerving news.

A few weeks later, Jan, Zoe, Dylan, and Anwyn confirmed the red supergiant explosion. They'd taken measurements of the thin, expanding gas and dust shell that was now far beyond the outer stars of the cluster. Based on the velocity of the gas and other variables, they backtracked it to a single origin point, the red supergiant called Giuseppa. Further, the date of the expulsion of the gas shell was approximately a thousand years ago. This was sufficient to satisfy us as to the validity of their explanations.

Jan and Zoe then focused on obtaining temperature measurements of Giuseppa. Why? He naturally wanted to apply his new theory to this red supergiant and see what it would predict. "I know, I know, I have wholly insufficient data, Captain, but based on what I have, I can say Giuseppa is going supernova sometime in the next hundred years. Of course, if we can get more observations, at least one per year, I can narrow the prediction date accordingly. We ought to explain this to these people. They have time to do something about it."

After discussing this startling finding with President Arcangelo, he agreed to set up a meeting with their top astrophysicists. I hated to have to expose Jan to these men and women, but I had no other choice. I know he really want to warn them and save lives, but his physical condition would leave him terribly vulnerable. Zoe went with him to help support his theory. Twenty men and women gathered in a conference room to hear his findings.

With Hermes working the controls of his presentation, I thought Jan did a very good job explaining everything. However, I had not counted on the "learned" community's reaction. Of course, everyone constantly stared at both of them during the presentation.

After that, they began shooting him down. One professor, whose name I have forgotten, said, "Preposterous! Everyone knows no one can predict when a supergiant will explode and go supernova. The core processes are far too complex to be analyzed with any degree of certainty. Professor Abramo in his famous textbook on stellar evolution has said this very same thing. Who are we to dispute one of the most famous astrophysicists of the last millennium?"

Another complained, "While we concede it might be possible under some focused and special circumstances to be able to measure the surface temperature of some red supergiants, assuming it is even possible to determine its actual surface, since it is all just a hot gas anyway and there is no precise boundary for the edge of the star, it is unlikely that this can lead to any general prediction of a possible core collapse, since there are far too many as yet unknown reactions occurring within the superheated core, and they will probably always remain unknown, since it would be impossible to put a probe into the core of such a star or any star, for that matter." No, he didn't take a breath while pontificating that sentence. I wondered what he had just said.

Had it been myself standing there facing these "learned" astrophysicists, I'd have screamed and fled the room. Jan had already endured similar criticism from Imperium astrophysicists, and apparently, their reactions didn't faze him, but their stares did. He countered quietly and pleasantly, "I applied my theory to the red supergiant Boon. Perhaps you observed it going off?" He already knew they had observed this "new star" down in the hub of the galaxy and had studied it for a time. "My theory predicted the date it would go supernova and it was correct, within the uncertainty error. With more accurate measurements and over a longer time period, my equations will predict it down to the day and hour. Our Imperium astrophysicists were as skeptical as you are.

However, my theory is now considered proven. Ten heavily populated Imperium worlds were within the zone of destruction. Hundreds of billions of people were vaporized when Boon went off. Five of those worlds now have a surface that resembles a slag pile. Everything was melted into one surface mass, plus the five worlds lost their entire atmosphere. People on five other worlds suffered severe radiation burns."

"I would suggest you take the copies of my theory and equations with you and go over them with a fine tooth comb yourselves. Then, begin gathering your own data, and see what comes from it. As the years pass, if you continue to make these observations, the accuracy of the prediction date will increase, until you have it down to the day and hour. More importantly, you have a hundred years of advanced warning to prepare your worlds."

One young woman who couldn't have been more than twenty-five spoke up, "I've been going over your Zone of Destruction. If this happens, and I'm not saying I believe in your predictions, just that if it happens, we have two inhabited worlds that will be destroyed. Namely Aldobrandino and Donato. Ten others will suffer significant radiation exposure. Is this what you are suggesting, Doctor Voort?"

"Precisely," Jan replied.

She then said, "Perhaps, it would be prudent to alert those two worlds and begin to take precautions. After all, everyone knows one day, but probably an unknown day," she added quite reservedly, and then finished, "Giuseppa is going supernova on us."

Upon this, the twenty could all agree. Hence, they resolved to pass on Jan's work to all of the other astrophysicists on the other inhabited worlds, and to at least present the Zone of Destruction to the Cluster Executive Council, letting them decide how to proceed. Jan and Zoe felt quite relieved

After the meeting broke up, that same young woman came up to Jan and Zoe. She introduced herself. "I am Doctor Felisa Gabrialdi. Of course, I don't yet quite understand all your equations. Might I meet with you sometime and discuss these further?"

"Of course. Anytime," Jan replied.

She was still staring at him and then asked in a whisper, "Are you really a man? You look like a woman and so utterly freakish at that."

Jan's face reddened. "Yes, I used to look just like the other men here today, but I and the others suffered a terrorist attack. A bio genetic agent did this to our bodies. I know, it's awful, but I simply must go on. Besides, I met this most amazing woman, Zoe. She was born like this. So if she can survive, so can I. Besides, she is a brilliant astrophysicist in her own right, specializing in proto-star formation. But of course none of that is going on up here in the halo."

Doctor Felisa giggled. "No, of course not. We are not polluted with all that awful gas and dust that you are swimming in down in the disk. I don't see how anyone could survive in all that utter filth."

Zoe chuckled. "Actually, except for the regions of dense stellar formation where gravity is compacting the gas and dust, our space is relatively free of it, though I admit not as much as here in the halo. There's hardly any interstellar gas and dust that we've been able to find up here."

The three chatted a bit longer before she made an appointment to visit the two to go over his equations in more detail, which I took as a hopeful sign. It would only take one person to get behind the theory and to push it forward.

Alexandra and Hans were not idle during this first month either. By month's end, they had all the hyperspace coordinates calculated for the inhabited worlds of the Gorki Cluster, as well as accurate black coordinates. I should explain black coordinates. You see, when you enter your hyperspace coordinates, there is nothing preventing your destination in real space to be inside a star. That, of course, is instant death. Hence, all known stars and black holes are also plotted and these become black coordinates. The hyperdrive system automatically rejects the entry of any of these positions, preventing accidental appearances in dangerous locations. So yes, theirs was an enormous amount of very detailed work, as well as vital for future hyperspace travel here in the halo.

However, Hans also knew he would next need to meet

with other astrophysicists here to obtain the coordinates of all known dead stars. Down in the galactic disk, this wasn't a huge problem, as this was the zone of active stellar birth. The halo was old, very old compared to the disk. Many of the larger mass stars had all gone through their evolutions and were now black stars, emitting no visible light; their nuclear fires had gone out, as well as their contraction-fed emissions. Now, they were extremely small and unbelievably dense. If a ship came too close to one of these black stars, its massive gravity would suck the ship down to its destruction. Hence, here in the older halo, black stars were a problem of significance.

Now that I think of it, Hans gave me the best view of just what hyperspace actually was. He said, "Imagine you live in a one-dimensional world, a line. You can move left or right along it. That's one-dimensional space, only length and no width. But suppose that the line is drawn on a piece of paper, which in fact has two dimensions, length and width. The one-dimensional view can only see their space as that single line, even though it is surrounded by or is a part of the two-dimensional space of the paper. Now let's put that paper, that two-dimensional world on one face of a cube. The two-dimensional world still looks like a plane, from their viewpoint. Yet as we look at it, we can see there is actually three dimensions present, adding in height, which isn't perceivable from those in the two-dimensional world. The projection of a three-dimensional object onto a two-dimensional world is a plane. The projection of a two-dimensional plane onto a one-dimensional world is a line. Hence, extrapolating outwards, our three-dimensional universe is but a projection from a four-dimensional universe down into a three-dimensional view. What we call hyperspace is really the four-dimensional universe, but we can only perceive its projection onto a three-dimensional view." I often wonder if Hans and Alexandra can somehow perceive this fourth dimension, which isn't time, of course.

I don't begin to understand the breakthrough Hans had made and which the Eagle's Seed was now using. His speedup involved a different folding of hyperspace between the origin and destination points, a different projection to us — his term for it. This was the technology I was sure the Gorki Cluster greatly desired. The other technology was our cloaking device, which uses black energy often called "dark energy."

When you think of an explosion, you undoubtedly think of fireworks. I sure do. First, there is nothing there. Then, there is a bright flash of light, and bright energy expands rapidly outwards, often spherical in shape, dimming down at the end of its path. Finally, after the energy is exhausted or diluted by space, it turns dark again.

Dark energy explosions happen the same way, only because the energy is black, you don't see anything. True, it explodes, grows and expands outward, and dies away. One sees nothing except the damage or destruction that such an explosion can cause. It can have the same destructive potential as a "white" energy explosion. Hence, to our perceptions the object just appears to have been mysteriously damaged or destroyed. Anyway, the cloaking device makes use of dark energy or black energy, surrounding the ship in a black energy field, rendering it wholly invisible to normal perceptions. So yes, I could well understand just how bad these people or any technological society would want to get their hands on this as well. As a corollary, with so much dark energy in our universe, I sometimes wonder why it hasn't been put to more uses long before now.

Anyway, all this is relevant and helps explain, at least partially, what happened on February 25. The Eagle's Seed had landed once more at their large spaceport, having wrapped up Jan and Zoe's last set of observations the day before. It was around one in the morning and my crew was sound asleep in their cabins. Suddenly, Beth's border collie, Jen, began barking loudly, then dashed out of her room, down the hall, stopping near the front docking port, barking and pawing the metal floor. "Jen! Jen, quiet!" Beth called out.

Struggling to sit up, Melita quickly became alert, stepped over to her bed, and helped her to her toes. By now, the dog's barking had awakened everyone. With Melita supporting her, Beth headed down the long hall to the front of the ship as fast as she dared to go, all the while commanding Jen to stop barking.

Len stuck his head out of his room. "What's gotten into Jen, Beth? Is she trying to alert us to trouble?"

"Don't know. She's never done this before," Beth justified, as everyone else began coming out of their quarters to see what the commotion was about.

Danika got Callisto to activate the ship's exterior cameras and suddenly yelled, "Six men are trying to cut through our docking doors with a blow torch! They have guns. We're under attack!" Frustration then temporarily silenced her, as she again felt horribly helpless. She couldn't even use her new d-gun that she'd become an expert with before we left on this trip!

Callisto spoke up, "Prepare to be boarded!" She drew her own d-gun, prepared to defend Danika to the end. Quickly, the many other HILFs drew their guns as well, though some had to duck back into their quarters to retrieve them. Until now, they'd never been needed.

"I'm getting this all recorded," Anya called out.

As the frightened crew watched the six men igniting the blowtorch just beyond the front docking port, they witnessed the inexplicable happen. Some unknown form of energy beam arced through the air, striking the man brining the torch up to the metal latch. His body turned into a mass of illuminated dust particles, falling slowly down onto the metal of the elevator platform!

A split second later, a second beam struck another of the men. His body too became illuminated by a zillion tiny dust particles, which fell like descending dust in sunlight to the floor. Everyone blinked before another pair of beams shot out, turning two more men into dust particles. Then another pair flashed with the same result. Only the blowtorch and fuel cylinders remained on the elevator platform.

"What, what the hell was that?" exclaimed Danika.

"Oh good God!" Beth screamed.

"Who did that?" Len called out, shocked. "I don't have that kind of power. Can anyone see who is doing the shooting?"

Amid the cries of the others, Danika came to her senses. "Callisto, scan the area where the beams seemed to be coming from. Everyone, keep your d-guns ready. Someone contact Nia Elain and the others, Zarita too. We are under attack. These people must have been lying to us about their weaponry!"

Well, that was a close one, Isi. A few more minutes and we would have lost them. Good shooting, Huyana sent.

Yes, but we had best move our ship. They'll be swarming all over this area. I'll reposition us. Keep watch. There could be more assassins out there that we've not seen, Isi sent back and headed for the controls of their ship. Seconds later, the invisible ship silently and slowly rose from the tarmac, moved some distance away in the opposite direction, and settled quietly back down. Isi then joined Huyana at their bay door, open again, their guns at the ready.

See any more? Isi asked.

No. Our hosts are pretty shaken up, but no harm has come. Stay vigilant, Isi, Huyana sent back.

Within an hour, the tarmac was swarming with security men. Portable lights made the area around the Eagle's Seed seem like broad daylight. Len had quietly ordered Bion to go out and bring him a sample from one of the dust piles that had been a man. Of course, nothing was found, except the blowtorch and fuel tanks. The security guards took them away to see if they would yield any clues, but I didn't hold my breath that it would. Such things were commonplace items.

At eight, we five, our HIFRs, and Marcella met with President Arcangelo, General Celino, and Doriano in the president's office. Athena brought up the recorded video that Anya had made of the attack on our ship. We five very closely watched the reactions of the three as they viewed it, not once, but several times. Their faces paled when they saw the streaks of energy coming from nowhere, turning the attacker's bodies into dust.

"What kind of weapon is that?" President Arcangelo finally found his voice. It was shaking. I sensed fear from him.

The general swallowed hard, twice, before answering. "Unknown, Mr. President. I must put the forces on highest alert. With your permission," he added as an afterthought. His mind wasn't even registering their formal protocols.

"You sure that wasn't one of your weapons?" Doriano covertly accused me.

"Absolutely not. We would trade all our technology for that, I'm sure. We were about to ask you about it. Are you sure you are not withholding such weapons from us?" I turned the accusation around, but from their reactions, I was certain they'd never seen such a weapon before.

Len sent me, *Captain. I've analyzed the dust remnants. They are what is left of a human body once all of the water and complex organic compounds have been removed. That beam literally reduced the man's body to its basic chemicals! A pile of dust. Beyond belief. Who has such a weapon?*

I thanked him and spoke up, "If you will analyze the dust that was left, I believe you'll find it's all that's left of the man. My chemist has finished his examination of the dust and believes this weapon reduced the man's body to the raw chemicals that formed it. Sorry, I don't have the right words to describe such a thing."

President Arcangelo picked up his communication device and sent orders to have that done. I then said, "Look, to the best of my knowledge, no civilization in the Imperium or the Federation of Planets has such a weapon. No disk world does. What about up here in the halo? Obviously, someone does. I can't imagine the Narstens have this kind of technology."

"No, their weapons are quite primitive. We are certain of that," General Celino answered me. "So if it isn't any disk people, who then?"

Martina spoke up, "Perhaps we are getting sidetracked here. Look, those six, well-armed men tried to break into our ship, probably intent upon killing us and stealing the ship with its technology. Obviously, your people would love to get at our hyperdrive and cloaking device. So which one of you ordered the hit on our ship?" she accused the three men.

Brilliant, I thought, as both Zarita and I watched their reactions extremely closely. It would have been rewarding and satisfying to have seen one or more of them react — treachery and betrayal exposed to the light of day. Unfortunately, we saw no such reaction. Instead, all three protested vigorously.

"You can't think that we had any part in this attack on your people," President Arcangelo insisted. "Look, we've already found your people desperately need that sand for fuel. We have what we need to obtain them in trade. Why should we risk a sure thing with this? No, this attack wasn't sanctioned or ordered by the government of Aurelio. I swear this to you. We'll put all of our resources into finding out who those six guilty men were and who was behind them. In the meantime, we have an even more serious situation: the unknown parties with this new and terrible weapon of theirs. It looks to me like there were two assailants. I saw two separate streaks."

General Celino countered, "Don't jump to conclusions, Mr. President. It could have been one person holding a weapon in each hand. My men are scouring that area, looking for any possible traces of the unseen assailants. Captain Nia Elain, do your people have any other video of the surrounding area? Perhaps they have captured something else?"

"I'll have them check and get back to you, general," I replied. Zarita quietly sent the telepathic message.

We chatted for an hour, but little else of consequence was said. Conclusion: both of our sides were in mystery. Neither of us knew who the six men had been nor who the unseen protectors were. None of it made any sense; except I was convinced that someone on Aurelio or within the Gorki Cluster had heard of our two key technologies and was desperate to get their hands on them. General Celino did order an around the clock garrison to watch our ship to prevent any such future attacks on my ship and crew.

The event gave everyone on my ship something to do that next day. Anya had been routinely recording everything around the outside of our ship whenever it was on the ground. After that surprise terrorist bio agent attack, she was paranoid and had set up the surveillance. With this recent attack, she doled out hundreds of video archive files to each of the crew. Seventeen pairs of eyes began scrutinizing these thousands of hours of video, looking for anything out of the ordinary.

Anya herself found recordings of the six men approaching the ship just before one that night. However, in the dark, all that could be made out was the fact that they were men, little else. Given the rough location of the mysterious shooters, the seventeen first focused on surveillance footage taken in that direction. Long hours passed with nothing to show for it, save watering, red eyes.

Beth and her mate Marisol sat beside each other watching endless video streams. Beth mused, "You know, Jen sure alerted us to the attack. She must have sensed or heard them and tried her best to warn us. Good dog, Jen." She looked down at the black and white dog, which was looking up at her, contentedly. She again wished with all her heart that she could pet Jen, but simply couldn't now.

Marisol bit her tongue. "You know, that's strange. Jen, I mean. She alerted us to this attack. Why didn't she do the same when the terrorists actually entered the ship and set off the bio agent attack on us?"

"Now that you mention it, my love, that is curious. She ought to have raised a storm when they came onboard. I don't recall hearing her bark at all. In fact, she hasn't barked once since we started this whole trip until last night. That is very curious indeed. I wonder what that means?" Beth mused.

"Jen is one smart dog, love. I'm a light sleeper. If she would have barked even once, I would have woken up, discovered the terrorists were onboard, and raised the alarm," Marisol replied.

"So what does it mean?" Beth said in turn.

"She has only barked when we were threatened by enemies. Surely, terrorists are also enemies. Why didn't she bark then?"

"Well, she didn't. I'm sure of that. She woke us all in less than a minute and before they actually got inside," Beth pointed out.

Marisol lowered her voice, "But she doesn't bark at any of us, friends. She doesn't bark when friends are around."

Beth's face paled. "Are you saying that one of us was the terrorist? Who did this to us all? And themselves?"

Marisol merely nodded. "It has to be. There's no other rational explanation, is there?"

"But who would do such a horrid thing? And to

themselves? Especially, since it can't yet be undone. Our lives are pretty much wasted now," Beth complained.

Marisol thought for a moment before replying. "We gave everyone some therapy afterwards. I can tell you everyone was very emotionally upset by what happened to their bodies. None of us wanted to become helpless nova."

"But Alexandra and Zoe were already helpless nova. Do you think that they wanted us to become like them?" Beth whispered back. She thought of the recent marriage of Zoe and Jan, which would not have likely happened, had Jan not become genetically modified like Zoe. Then, there was the marriage of Alexandra and Zarita, but she also knew Nia Elain had purposely brought the unmarried Zarita on this trip for Alexandra's sake.

Marisol again bit her tongue, since she couldn't bite her lips any longer. "That could be a plausible line of inquiry except we also gave those two therapy too. I didn't detect anything but shock and horror from them that we were all genetically modified in the attack. While I can't dismiss either of them solely on that, one or both of them might have been behind the attack. We need proof."

"But everyone went over all their cargo when it was loaded. Surely, one of us would have seen one of those bio agent cylinders. They aren't exactly small you know," Beth countered.

"Point taken. Still, Jen has given us a clue. I'll talk to Nia Elain about this on the quiet. Don't say anything about this to anyone else until we hear from her," Marisol whispered quite seriously.

Martina and I worked with the president during the day. He decided to open a full investigation of the matter, and at her insistence added looking into the possibility that clandestine, unauthorized raids against the Narstens had been carried out long before he so ordered them in retaliation for their attacks on some of the Gorki Cluster worlds. He also promised to bring both to the attention of the Cluster Executive Council when they returned from their summer break in another couple of weeks. Yes, their seasons were way off from ours on Ashford-5. So were most worlds of the disk for that matter.

By the end of the day, his scientists reported similar findings to those of Len's, confirming the nature of these new unknown weapons. We five also decided to spend the night back on the ship. I wanted to discuss events with my crew, and they, me. I asked Ambassador Marcella to stay behind tonight. "Look, it might not be safe for you to be with us, in case another attack comes. We'll be back with you in the morning. Besides, I need some time with my daughter."

"Oh. Well, okay. I can see that," she replied, still disappointed she wasn't being allowed to join me this time.

Domestic duties handled, around ten that night, I held another group meeting in our large meeting room, the only place on the ship large enough to hold all twenty-two of us and our HIFRs. One by one, everyone gave their reports. There was, as I suspected, little that was new. However, Martina pointed out something we'd overlooked.

"We are all forgetting one salient detail," she spoke up. Everyone turned to look at her. "One or two unknown persons took out our would-be attackers last night. Whoever they are, they are obviously trying to protect us."

"Why?" asked Danika. "Why would unknown people want to protect us? Especially when their weapons are so vastly superior to ours?"

"I think that is the question that ought to be asked," Martina replied wisely. "Whoever they are, they are completely masters of disguise. Thus far, except for the faint traces of energy beams, they have remained invisible. Speculation: could they be those in that strange saucer spaceship that attacked the transport carrying Nia Elain here to this world?"

"Hey, they shot that transport down, very nearly killing her. So why the sudden change of heart and protect us?" asked Danika, suspicious of this theory.

"If that saucer ship had weapons similar in power to what was used on those six men," Martina explained, "then why didn't they disintegrate the whole transport? Instead, as I see it, they did a surgical strike, disabling their engines forcing the transport down. Were they planning to come to Nia's rescue, but were thwarted by the sudden appearance of those fifty Gorki warships? That is a distinct possibility."

"Hey, why me? Why am I so special?" I asked pointedly. "I think you all are far more important than I am. Hans invented the hyperdrive modifications, and Alexandra, the hydrogen propulsion system. I'm a dunce compared to them."

"Can't say, Captain," Martina used my title formally, a subtle hint that I should stop putting myself down in front of the others. "Perhaps, they wanted to reunite you with us, undoing the kidnaping."

"But why?" I countered.

"Unknown. It is a line of inquiry that must be followed," Martina declared strongly.

I agreed with her. "All right then. Everyone, let's do as she asks. Starting tomorrow, I want everyone focusing on our unknown mystery person or persons. Are they protecting us? If so, why. It's not bad enough that we're embroiled in this mess between the Narsten and Gorki Clusters. Well, perhaps Queen Zenovia can eventually work that one out. I'll continue to pester President Arcangelo on his investigation of the six men who tried to attack us last night. We simply have far too many unanswered questions for my liking."

Danika spoke up, "Boss, have you worked out who'll be going with you to the Gorki Cluster Executive Council? If I recall, it's coming up pretty soon. And are we going to trust in their security measures?"

Hans broke in, "Boss, as much as I hate being seen in public like this, I simply have to go with you. I have to get all of their known dead stars catalogued. There are just too darn many of them in this halo."

"I should go too," Martina added. "Tesla as well." I knew she wanted her mate with her because of her background in political science and government histories.

I agreed with them. "Okay, you three, but no more. If things go badly, I simply will not risk more of you."

The next day, Martina poured over the seemingly endless hours of video again, along with nearly everyone else. I too took a look over some of their shoulders so I had some idea what they were dealing with. Mega-boring I thought. Suddenly, both Martina and her HIFR Delia cried out, "There!

Back up a little." Martina added, "Slow motion." I moved carefully over to her station, growing curious. "There. You see it too, Delia?"

"Yes, a bit of distortion I cannot account for," Delia replied, backing the video up once more. I watched carefully on the replay, trying to see what she and her robot had spotted. It dawned on me they both had spotted this minuscule defect at the same time. I found that most interesting. Then, I too saw it, a slight wavering of the background, almost as if it was a heat distortion one sees looking out over a hot tarmac, but nowhere as pronounced.

Martina ordered, "Everyone, drop what you are looking at now. Queue up all videos from camera six. Bring up this one," she rattled off a long filename involving the date and time. "Queue to position 5436. Play it slowly from there. See the distortion at the edge of the tarmac by the trees."

"How the heck did I miss that one?" Anya called out. "I must have looked at that one a dozen times."

"Hey, don't feel bad. I missed it too," Alexandra commented.

Martina said, "Okay. There definitely was something invisible there. Go over all footage from this camera. Let's see if we can get an estimate of the size and shape of the invisible field. That may give us a clue."

I too became enthused and forgot that I was to join the President this morning. However, Marcella came by, knocking on our front docking hatch. After Athena let her in, I briefed her on what we'd just discovered, and she used her phone to relay that to the President, who was worried about us when we missed our scheduled meeting with him.

About an hour into the project, Callisto called out. "Hey, I have found something!" She relayed the filename and the video marker location. Hastily, Athena brought it up on my monitor, while the other HIFRs did the same for the others. In real time, I saw only a split second flash of something. However, following Callisto's suggestion, I had Athena replay it frame by frame. In one frame, an opening appeared, somewhat like a bay door of a spaceship perhaps. In the next frame, two hooded forms appeared — bi-pedal for sure. In the next frame, a partial face could just barely be seen. In the following frame, the forms were gone. In the frame after that, the door, if that's what it was, vanished too. It lasted barely five frames. Alexandra announced, "That was about a quarter of a second there at most. That's incredibly fast action!"

Callisto called out, "Sending an enhanced image to everyone's station now."

"Well, well!" Martina spoke as she saw the still fuzzy image on her monitor. "That looks like that same doll-like face we saw on one of those two people shadowing us at Krazdorf! It doesn't look human at all. So those two have been following us!"

Marcella asked, "Can you send that to President Arcangelo? I know he'll want to see this too. So you saw it when you were in the Narsten Cluster?" I explained that brief encounter we'd had. She added, "It sure does look like some child's doll's head, only bigger."

"I have it. These two must be from the Billik Cluster," Martina made the connection. "Remember, Matriarch Athala said that there were some very evil in-humans living in that cluster, across the Kronos Gap. There are spies following us!"

"Well, at least we have something more to report to President Arcangelo," I replied. An hour later, Marcella and I joined him in his office. I had, or rather Athena had, sent him the image and my message that these might be the in-humans from the Billik Cluster far above and much closer to the center of the halo than the Gorki Cluster. Unfortunately, any hopes I had that he might be able to shed some light on them vanished.

"Sorry, don't know anything about that cluster. It's too distant from here," President Arcangelo replied. "So now we have these spies, invisible ones at that, here on Aurelio. That's not good. General, do something about that, will you?"

General Celino gave him a frown, but kept silent. He left the room to make a secure call. The President then added, "We are not getting anywhere on the investigation of those six men either. The blowtorch was stolen from a storage locker at the spaceport. Lock was cut. We found an abandoned shuttle that was also reported stolen, which they probably used to get there and were planning to use to make their getaway. Beyond that, we are coming up empty handed. Sorry, Captain Nia Elain. I assure you that it won't happen again."

Well, to be honest with you, I really didn't have much hope they would find anything. Whoever was behind this was being very careful. I wondered if there was a possible link between this event and the kidnaping of men and women from the Narsten Cluster. Both leaders could not be right. Someone had to have begun the kidnaping before the other decided to retaliate. I began to see Queen Zenovia's position. Someone had to be working behind the scenes playing one side against the other. Other than the covertness of the operations, I had no direct link between these two, just a gut feeling.

On March 1, Martina, Tesla, Hans, and I, along with Delia, Damali, Damon, and Athena joined Marcella, President Arcangelo, General Celino, and Doriano on the Presidential Transport, accompanied by a host of Security Guards, all well-armed. We were on our way to the planet Azzolino where the Gorki Cluster Executive Council was expecting us. Things promised to become far more interesting and quickly, I hoped.

Chapter 15 Posturing

Azzolino could well have been any other modern Imperium world. Skyscrapers, steel and concrete, stretched as far as the eye could see, as we landed at the spaceport outside the capital city of Doro. President Arcangelo sighed and said, "Captain, please do not be too surprised when you see others at this meeting that look like some of us, me in particular. President Dario Baldovino of Tamarri looks just like me. You'll see others who appear strikingly like us"

Martina asked what I was thinking. "So are all the bodies that look like yours the presidents of their worlds? Those who look like General Celino are their generals too?"

"Heavens no! It's just an unfortunate coincidence that President Dario is in politics and also was elected. But then, I'm told there are striking personality similarities between nearly identical bodies. Fifty percent chance of parallel careers and interests, or so they say. We'll be staying in a very secure penthouse suite. This hotel has nothing but penthouse suites, since the Cluster Executive Council always meets here."

There were thirty Presidents attending, along with their aides and top generals, ignoring their supporting staff. All eyes were upon us four, as we walked into the large room filled with the members of the council. The presidents of the thirty worlds sat around a huge U-shaped table. Their aides and generals sat behind them in a second and third row. A number of chairs and tables faced the U of leaders, and Marcella led us to these seats.

The hostilities in the room were so thick I swear I could have cut them with a knife, had I a knife and the hands to use it! As soon as we were seated, or I should say as soon as President Arcangelo Ferrobossi was seated, the outburst began. His "twin" President Dario Baldovino rose and shouted, "Freaks! You bring us a bunch of freaks, filthy, dirty abominations from the disk! How dare you insult this high council, Ferrobossi? How dare you? I won't stand for this."

"Here, here," shouted several other presidents. They all

dressed pretty much the same, a dark suit, white shirt, black shoes. Only their ties were different colors. Arcangelo had told us that he usually wore a purple tie, his wife's favorite color. In this way alone, we could recognize him. Actually, three others looked rather similar to these two men. Five others looked like they might be twins. Six more looked like they were twins. Only fourteen of the presidents looked substantially unique. Among the generals and aides, the groupings of "twins" was even more pronounced. I counted sixteen other General Celino's and eighteen other Doriano's among the assemblage, and that didn't count the other "twins" among these people! Their genetic pool must have been terribly small after that disastrous time in their past. Either that or they had cloning perfected. Doctor Leann hadn't mentioned cloning to me so I dismissed that notion, but made a mental note to ask her about it.

We sat there listening to similar diatribes for nearly fifteen minutes. I felt a bit sorry for Marcella who sat beside us and had to endure it along with us. Finally, I had had it from this bunch. I lunged to my toes before Athena could assist me up, even though I must have looked even more pathetic in their eyes by my clumsy efforts just to stand up.

Using a bit of my *mentales* powers behind my voice, I barked sharply, "I have had enough of your complete and utter stupidity! You are acting worse than the Narsten matriarchs are! Until I met them, I hadn't known how stupid, uncivilized, biased, bigoted, and barbaric some races of human beings could be. No I take that back. I've met some barbaric races that were better behaved than you supposed leaders are demonstrating. Your people are simply wholly unworthy of our technology and trade. Please excuse us. We'll consider opening trading relations with President Arcangelo Ferrobossi only, as he is the only civilized man among you. Good day!"

Athena took that as a signal we were finished here, and she rose, silently signaling the other HIFRs to assist their charges in rising. By the time my companions were on their feet, the diatribes ended, replaced by frantic pleadings for us to stay, coming from a number of presidents who had not taken part in running us down. Hans, Martina, and Tesla glanced at me. I glanced at President Arcangelo who looked pleadingly at me. I sat back down, and Athena hastily adjusted the fall of my hair over my shoulder again.

Another president rose and spoke more sympathetically. "You must excuse us. We simply have never remotely considered having relations with people from the galactic disk. And you must agree that your physical appearance is, well, most distressing, most disturbing."

I sensed this was as close as I would get to a formal apology and accepted it. "Yes, our physical appearance is distressing to ourselves as well. Shall we proceed?"

Another president suggested, "Captain Nia Elain, perhaps you should begin by telling us something about the worlds of the galactic disk. That might help us better understand you." I accepted this challenge to help stifle some of their longstanding bias and bigotry. Plus, they continued to ask questions as I went along. In fact, while I had not intended to do so, I ended up spending the entire day describing the worlds of the Imperium and that of Aquila Prime. While I had not remotely intended to discuss the genetic biological agent and associated terrorism, these astute men managed to wrangle it out of me.

Over dinner in our incredibly fancy penthouse suite shared with President Arcangelo, General Celino, and Doriano, President Arcangelo said, "I am sorry for the way the day started. I knew there would be some trouble bringing you here, but I never imagined just how bad it would be. I thought you handled yourself remarkably well. I imagine President Dario would have acted very differently to you had you landed on Tamarri instead of Aurelio."

General Celino commented, "Now, you have us all worried about opening relations with the disk worlds. We certainly don't want any of those genetic bio agent attacks here in the Gorki Cluster!"

Frustrated, I replied, "I'm sure your security arrangements are vastly superior to ours. Our people have grown complacent through the centuries." I wanted to add that the Imperium was collapsing as we spoke, but thought better of that idea.

Doriano then said, "You know, I've noticed your assistants almost never say anything. Why is that?"

Damn, he was getting too close. Martina replied for me, "They are merely our personal assistants, trained to be our hands. I doubt very much if your building janitors would have very much to say on the topics that we are handling, such as hyperdrive modifications, cloaking devices, and fuel refineries."

"Ah yes, of course," he replied somewhat covertly.

President Arcangelo added, "Yes, I understand. It would be like expecting Marcella here to discuss space flights. She's my receptionist and now our ambassador."

Marcella flushed. I felt a bit sorry for her, but only for a second. She spoke up, "But I could discuss space flights. I wanted to become a space explorer, and I studied up on everything that wasn't classified, but then found out they don't take women into the service." Now, it was Arcangelo's face that flushed. I smiled invisibly at Marcella, glad she spoken up.

He cleared his throat and said, "Sorry Marcella. I had no idea. Space exploration is a very dangerous profession. Just look at what's happened to Captain Nia Elain and her crew." After that, the conversation became more of a lighthearted chat with little significance.

The following morning's session was devoted to a non-technical discussion of our new hyperdrive and our ship's cloaking device. However, once they realized we did in fact possess such technology, the posturing began in earnest. President Dario declared, "It's obvious these aliens have President Arcangelo wrapped around their fingers — er, figuratively I mean. Surely, we cannot allow Aurelio to receive their technology. It should be available to all our worlds."

Another shouted, "Unfair advantage, Arcangelo!" The rest of the day was spent with the presidents trying to work out just how they would ensure a proper exchange of technology would occur. They insisted on checks and balances so no one world would wind up with any advantage over the other. By suppertime, they'd agreed that at any exchange of technology, representatives of all thirty worlds must be present.

The next day was all Hans'. First, he described the

major benefits of his new drive. Then, he discussed in detail Jan's theory that allowed him to predict when red supergiants went supernova and the proposed zone of destruction when Giuseppa went off. The presidents from Aldobrandino and Donato were extremely concerned about this information. The rest of the day was spent in discussions with President Arcangelo who relayed what his group of astrophysicists was saying about Jan's theory. More than a few had begun to back Jan's theory, given they'd had over a month to study it and his equations. That he'd been able to predict Boon's explosion and that we'd all witnessed it personally in the Eagle's Seed helped convince the leaders this should be taken seriously.

The following day was adjourned so they could hold conferences with their own scientists. Fortunately, President Arcangelo had lived up to his bargain with us and had his people forward Jan's work to the appropriate scientific groups on the other twenty-nine worlds.

When the meetings resumed, they were substantially more serious, and passed a motion first to gather more temperature readings, and second to begin to devise ways and means of saving those on the two doomed worlds, as the predicted date approached. That shot that day.

The next morning, the discussion focused on just what my people would accept in trade for our technology. I joked, "Well, we women want some of those dry cleaning machines." That brought some chuckles. However, when I spelled out at this time, the silicate sands were of prime value to us, namely psi-crystals of silicon and germanium, they laughed.

President Dario said, "You are joking with us again, right. Sand? You want sand from those uninhabitable worlds?"

"Yes, we refine the germanium and silicon crystals into fuel for our spaceships." Again, this notion was met with compete disbelief. Alas, I have no idea how that is done. Len would have known, but he wasn't here.

Of course, once they realized I was serious posturing began again. It seemed three of the worlds controlled all these uninhabitable worlds whose surfaces were nothing but sand. "We should get compensation from the other twenty-seven worlds, since we will be providing all the payment for their technology," one president declared. So went this day. They bickered among themselves trying to reach some agreement. Finally, thoroughly disgusted with all of the posturing and bickering, President Arcangelo declared, "Presidents, we're talking about utterly worthless sand here! Surely we can reach some kind of agreement with those three who own it." Again, by supper the presidents had worked something out, at least tentatively.

On the following day, we got down to the serious business of the attacks on us, outlined by President Arcangelo, who also explained what little was known about these mysterious in-humans and their saucer ship. We didn't dwell much on the fact he'd ordered me to be kidnaped from Menno. Then, I turned the discussion to the actual problem that had to be solved: the long-standing conflict with the Narsten Cluster.

"Are we going to allow some helpless woman who calls herself a queen to come to our worlds and dig up whatever dirt she desires?" one president complained bitterly, initiating a lengthy session.

Finally, I had had enough again. "Look gentlemen. The Narstens are working with Queen Zenovia to sort out this conflict. If you chose not to participate, then all trade with us is moot. Only Queen Zenovia is authorized to make such trading deals, certainly not me. I'm only a deep space exploration captain. Besides, the matriarchs there are begging her to form an alliance with them to go to war with you. It is in your best interests to cooperate fully with Queen Zenovia in resolving this conflict peacefully." Well, that sunk into their posturing heads.

By supper, they had all agreed in principle to accept Queen Zenovia's guidance in the resolution of the conflict with the Narsten Cluster. Now, they wanted her to come here at once and solve it. Hence, I agreed to return to Menno and see if I could speed things along some. I did get their full agreement not to conduct any more raids until after the queen's visit here. I certainly hoped they would do that, but I had my doubts with these men.

While Marcella wanted to come with us to Menno, President Arcangelo and we thought this might not be such a good idea. There she would be considered the enemy at this point in time. Reluctantly, she agreed. On March 10, we arrived back at the familiar spaceport on Menno just outside Krazdorf. My only comment was: "Crap. Now I have to wear those damned outer-skirts again." Tesla merely groaned. During the entire trip back, we kept a sharp watch for our mysterious saucer ship, but detected nothing at all. If they also had cloaking, I wouldn't expect we would have. Alas.

While we had kept Queen Zenovia informed of everything we discovered in the Gorki Cluster, she still spent that day having us brief her in person. Then, she outlined where her investigation was. Things had gotten serious in our absence.

"Funny thing about accurate records," Queen Zenovia said with a wry grin, "sometimes they can be your Achilles heel." Based on our information that Narsten had been raiding the worlds in the Gorki Cluster some years before they began retaliation raids, she dove into the reports of captured Slavers. "You should have seen Matriarch Athala's face when I had Xene show her the records that put the initial raids where Slavers were 'apparently' captured some three years before she believed that it had begun! It got far more interesting when I asked to interview those who submitted the reports. Those men had simply vanished without a trace. It is almost as though they never existed. Matriarch Athala conducted her own investigation into those men and did discover that there never has been any record of such people existing!"

"The plot thickens, as they say," Queen Zenovia said rather amused buy it all. "It's taken some time, but we've narrowed it down to three mines that are currently or had employed those initially captured Salvers. The mine's records show nearly all those slaves are dead at this point. Nevertheless, Matriarch Athala and her fellow matriarchs have issued summons for the three mine owners to present themselves to me here at Matriarch Athala's mansion for questioning. They are supposed to arrive tomorrow. I do believe we are making considerable progress. I hope to get these owners to explain how they acquired their slave laborers, which may well lead us back to the truly guilty parties. As I understand it, mining here is a very dangerous occupation, and many miners die on the job. Hence, it's pretty hard to convince the average Narsten to go to work in the mines. They even tried to induce them to do it with higher pay, but that ended up making the mines unprofitable. Therefore, it is not beyond reason to think someone with a vested interest in these mines saw an easy way to obtain cheap laborers. Still, I'm dubious this is the sole cause. Someone has been systematically poisoning the Matriarchs' against the Gorki Cluster. I haven't even gotten to the Hadu problem yet. I'm rather hoping the resolution of this one will also resolve the lizard men situation as well. I don't know if I can deal with them. From what I've seen of them, they are really freakish looking."

"One of us ought to be with you when you question these mine owners," I suggested. I was now more than willing to use my *mentales* gifts on them to help her obtain the information we needed.

"I would really appreciate that, Captain Nia Elain. I've felt, well really isolated and lonely while you've been gone. It's much harder dealing with life here. Their customs and dress," she tried to explain.

"Tell us about it. No problem. You'll enjoy visiting the Gorki Cluster. It's almost like our home worlds, mostly anyway." I tried to sound encouraging. She needed a boost, having no *mentales* gifts on which to fall back on.

The next day dressed in our cumbersome outer-skirts, Tesla, Queen Zenovia, and I made our usual slow, careful way into the drawing room for after-breakfast coffee and the interrogations. Matriarch Clothilda soon entered, two security men accompanied the three mine owners, who looked very uncomfortable in their likely recently purchased business suits. These were rugged men, used to dealing with hard issues and tough work. All three were exceedingly nervous, having been flown from their worlds to Matriarch Athala's mansion headquarters. I began to see this matriarch wielded considerable power or at least influence to have gotten other world matriarchs to order these men here to answer the queen's questions.

We waited a few minutes longer until Matriarch Gisela Hunsstadt arrived. When she walked into the room, the three men's faces grimaced. Muscles in their arms involuntarily tightened. I knew they knew that a famous telepath was present, one who could tell if they were lying or not. Matriarch Athala's stern voice finally began the interrogation. "Your matriarchs have told you to answer truthfully all questions put to you this day. Is this correct?"

All three men said this was so. She explained, "You'll then answer all questions that Queen Zenovia here wishes to ask you. I don't have to remind you that Matriarch Gisela is also present." The three men involuntarily glanced at the tiny-armed woman, who smiled congenially at them.

Queen Zenovia began. "This interrogation is concerned wholly with your acquisition of new Slavers to your mine's work force." Here she spelled out the precise three year time period before she had received the first official report of a raid by the Slavers during which three were captured and subsequently sentenced to a life in the mines.

It was too easy. I've never seen rough, tough men of the Imperium break down so quickly. No more than the pressure of a feather, she asked her question about how they got these first Slavers and the three men gave up the facts faster than Xene could jot them down. Well, this was a matriarchal society. That women held the true power was never more apparent with these three mine bosses. Their wives actually owned them, but they did the work, the management, the dirty work.

One hastily explained, "But we have to make a profit for our wives. It is almost impossible with the wages we have to pay to Narsten miners, so when Fedde Dorchmunster came to us with his proposition to use Slavers as cheap miners, we didn't see anything wrong in that."

"Who is Fedde Dorchmunster," Queen Zenovia asked.

Matriarch Gisela flinched and spoke up, saving the humiliated mine bosses. "He is a Commander of Security Force Ten on Hunsstadt. I can't believe this."

"It is. It was him and his men," one mine boss insisted. "Every month or so, he and his men would bring us some more

Slavers. It isn't a crime is it? I mean to use them evil men is it?"

"No, of course not," Matriarch Athala replied, looking at Matriarch Gisela. I could see her mind working. Was this highly respected telepath and world leader involved in this mess?

"I assure you that I had no knowledge of this. I'll summon him here immediately and his boss, Matriarch Ivonne Hunsstadt. I certainly hope my eldest daughter isn't involved in this!" Hastily, she left the room with her maid.

The mine bosses were dismissed. The relief on all three men's faces was almost laughable, if this hadn't been such a deadly serious matter. Mid-afternoon, the pair arrived in separate transports. Per Queen Zenovia's request, the two were questioned separately. I had to marvel at how adroit the queen was. She could tell just how sensitive this was to Matriarch Gisela and dealt with her daughter first.

"I brought along all the records from the years in question, Matriarch Gisela. I'm not sure what this is all about, but I assure you Hunsstadt's forces certainly were not involved until the years after these into which you are inquiring," the young woman explained. Her maid produced the records and the questioning began.

Lady Gisela had no choice but to say, "Matriarch Ivonne, I must warn you I'll be using my powers to ensure your answers are nothing but the truth. Please do not lie to us."

Ivonne flinched a little, taken by surprise, but she kept her composure. "Of course. I'm sure we have nothing to hide here. I swear these are the actual records that we have. I've looked them over again on the way here. I just don't see what you could possibly want in them that have anything to do with the Slavers. They didn't start appearing until after these three years you are asking about."

Queen Zenovia said, "Commander Fedde Dorchmunster is a Commander of Security Force Ten under your jurisdiction, is that correct?"

"Yes, I oversee twenty forces. He's been the commander of Security Force Ten since before I even took over my position. Why?" she replied, growing more curious than worried. She was handling herself well under pressure, I thought, but then I wasn't the queen.

"How often do you oversee his activities?" she asked next.

"Well, I don't actually oversee his activities per se. Like all my commanders, he sends in his official reports, and I issue my official orders. They are all there in the files for these years," she answered.

"So you do not directly observe his actions in the field or otherwise?"

"No. Of course not. I have his official reports. There isn't any such need. I'm certainly not going to go sit in his office and watch him. Why? Is he in trouble?" she asked.

"So you do not have any knowledge of his relationship with these three mine bosses?" She had Xene read them off.

Matriarch Ivonne thought for a moment. The names she did recognize, that was obvious. "Yes. I believe in later years, many of my commanders delivered some captured Slavers to those mine bosses. Captured Slavers were sentenced to work in the mines, but that was after these years you are asking about."

"Any knowledge of him and these three mine bosses during these three years in question?" Queen Zenovia asked pointedly.

"No. As I said, that came later, after these years. I don't think any of my commanders had any connection to any mine bosses until that next year when we began to capture Slavers. What would Security Force commanders be doing with mine bosses before then? Nothing I can see. They had no reason to even speak to mine bosses back then," she answered.

She added, "However, I don't know the personal friends of Commander Fedde. It may be possible these mine bosses and he were friends or acquaintances, but I surely don't know that. One's friends are not in official reports. Besides, a matriarch really does not hobnob around with their field commanders. It's just not done in our society. I'm a tiny-armed aristocrat. It would be scandalous for me to hobnob with commanders."

"Do you have any knowledge of his training exercises, off-world exercises?" Queen Zenovia asked.

"Of course. All our field commanders are supposed to take their men out for periodic training exercises. I do believe Commander Fedde's training exercises are documented in the reports. I can find them for you, if you would like to see them."

"No, I've already reviewed them while you were in transit here, Matriarch Ivonne. Do you have any independent confirmation that Commander Fedde actually took his forces to the locations specified in the reports?" the queen persisted.

"Oh. Well, they are logged in the official reports he filed. So they must be true and accurate. We Narstens are very proper and precise about keeping most accurate records," she replied.

"So it would be quite possible Commander Fedde took his forces to some other location than what he reported in his reports to you. Is that an accurate statement?" the queen asked.

Matriarch Ivonne looked very frustrated. "I suppose so, but that would be highly illegal, totally improper, and just isn't ever done in our society. Forging official reports to your matriarch is just about the worst thing imaginable!"

"How interesting," Queen Zenovia replied. "You depend wholly on the official reports and do not actually observe to see if they are in fact true. Interesting. I believe I'm finished with you for now. Please stay and watch the next interview please. I may have more questions for you."

"Of course, but I don't see where this has gotten us anywhere with the Slavers," Matriarch Ivonne retorted. She didn't have to say she thought this was an entirely pointless exercise. Her face said it, but she carefully rose and moved over to sit beside her mother.

Matriarch Clothilda and her husband Fester led Commander Fedde into the room, accompanied by two of her guards. Now, here was a very nervous man. While he looked handsome in his black uniform, I could see tiny beads of perspiration forming at his temples. He took the offered seat, and Matriarch Gisela once more repeated her admonition to speak only truthful answers to Queen Zenovia's questions.

"Yes, of course. What is this all about? Why have I been summoned here? We are leaving areas of Hunsstadt unprotected. Slavers raiding parties could be attacking there as we waste time here," he declared vehemently.

Un-phased, Queen Zenovia said quietly, "You are Commander Fedde Dorchmunster, the Commander of Security Force Ten?"

"Yes, have been for twenty-five years now."

"Okay. I have here three sworn statements from," and she had Xene read off the names of the three mining bosses she'd just interrogated for him. "They claim that for three years before the first officially reported Slaver's raid that you delivered Slavers to them to work in their mines. That you received monetary compensation for them as well." She had Xene read back the amount of funds he'd received for them, totaled up into one figure, a sizeable one at that.

There is nothing worse than a cornered wolf. In that instant, Commander Fedde knew fully what was going on here. Worse, he knew his game had been uncovered. Facing his doom, Commander Fedde was cornered. His eyes darted to Matriarch Clothilda and then he focused on Matriarch Athala, as though his utter hatred and contempt would somehow destroy her.

"You filthy bitch! You had to go and bring these abominations to our world! You are destroying everything! I'll not go down alone!" he swore. He then stared directly at Matriarch Clothilda. "I was only following orders. Hers!" He pointed his hand at Matriarch Clothilda. "It's all her doing! She came to me and suggested I raid the Gorki Cluster to get cheap labor for the mines. It's all her doing. As soon as we go to war, we can raid them with impunity and get thousands, millions of miners working for free. Damn you aristocrats! To hell with you!"

Sometimes things happen explosively quickly. This was one of them. Our eyes all turned to Matriarch Clothilda. Her grey face flushed very visibly. Her mouth moved, but no words came out for a time. At last, she gushed, "You can't believe him. I'm an aristocrat, a tiny-armed woman for heaven's sake."

He yelled back, "Check my bank records. You'll find her

payoffs there, you filthy bitch!" Matriarch Clothilda's face twisted in rage. Seconds had passed. While we stated at her, we didn't see Commander Fedde quick drawing his gun. "You damned bitch, Athala. This is all your doing!" Bang! His gun blazed. We all jumped from the sudden loud explosion of the shot. In horror, we saw Matriarch Athala shriek and slump over in her chair, blood seeping from a hole in her chest.

Bang! Bang! Two more shots fired in rapid succession. Commander Fedde dropped to the floor, dead before his body crunched into the floor, blood spewing from his chest and head. Only now did high-pitched screams replace the thunderous gunshots! Chaos erupted.

Above the screaming, I yelled, "Someone get Doctor Heinz immediately! Everyone, be quiet. Someone hold Clothilda!" I admit I used some of my *mentales* power behind my voice. Instant quiet. Several maids ran from the room. Lady Frieda began sobbing and struggled to kneel down beside her mother's chair. Matriarch Gisela rose inelegantly and moved to the other side of the chair, kneeling down as well. Both were actually wholly helpless to do anything for the wounded leader.

Matriarch Clothilda screamed, "It's all your fault, Frieda. I'm the eldest. I should have been mom's heir, not you! You look like a damned freak yourself!" Someone slapped her face and she shut up. I didn't see who, probably a security guard. As I moved closer to the three, I overheard Matriarch Athala's dying words.

"Gisela. Witness. Frieda. My heir. Leader of House Kane. Swear Gisela, Frieda is my heir." She could barely whisper the words; each one came out only with an intensity of will of the dying woman.

"I so swear, Athala. Frieda is your heir. I swear I heard you," Matriarch Gisela replied very formally.

I heard Athala whisper, "Thank you." Then, a last outflow of air came, but no words. I knew she'd just died. Doctor Heinz came running into the room, and I backed away as best I could in these awful boots, not designed for taking backwards steps. I would have fallen had Athena not caught me.

Softly, he said, "She's gone. What happened here? Who shot her? I heard gunshots."

Matriarch Gisela struggled to her feet as her maid couldn't get to her in time to help her up. Miss Emlin did help Frieda rise and got her back into a nearby chair. It was at this point we noticed Fester had somehow vanished from the room. One of the two security guards also noticed it and called out, "I'll see that he's caught." He raced out of the room, his gun drawn. Several minutes later, we heard more gunfire. The guard returned later on, reporting Fester had been killed in a gunfight while trying to escape in a shuttle.

Lady Frieda continued to cry, and thus Matriarch Gisela took charge for the time being. "Matriarch Clothilda, you are hereby charged with high treason. Guards, take her away and lock her up without any maids. Unbind her and search her as well. We'll deal with her later. As your telepath, I so swear that the truth was said here today." The guards saluted her and promptly escorted Clothilda out of the room. "Maids. Summon all the staff. We should dispose of that filthy man and prepare Matriarch Athala Kane properly. Miss Elise, is there some other room we can adjourn to?"

As we were all being assisted up, Rolf and Franz, Matriarch Gisela's husband, came running into the room. Both had been handling the affairs of the mansion and the arriving and departing witnesses. Rolf ran over to his deceased wife, knelt down beside her, sobbing softly to himself. Matriarch Gisela moved to his side, and in a gentle voice explained what had happened.

"Our own daughter? How could she do this?" he wailed. We left the grieving husband and daughter alone, and moved into a study, where several maids brought us a stiff drink, acting as though little had happened.

Queen Zenovia, her face rather ashen, said, "Well now we know part of the story. There are more details must be uncovered. Clothilda must have had a counterpart in the Gorki Cluster to have facilitated all the early raids. We'll need to question her further."

A while later, with blood-shot eyes, Rolf and Frieda joined us. Matriarch Gisela spoke up as soon as they were seated. "We must attend to the matriarchal succession of House Kane immediately. I bore witness to Matriarch Athala's dying request that Lady Frieda should replace her. As of this moment, Lady Frieda is now Matriarch Frieda, ruler of House Kane and all Menno. I so state officially." She was quite formal. "Lady Frieda, do you accept the position of Matriarch and ruler of House Kane?"

"I do," she said very softly and three times to be certain everyone understood her. The five inch lip plates affected her speech, as it did everyone who wore them. I sensed her feeling the enormous weight suddenly falling on her shoulders. She rose to the occasion; I will say that for the twenty-one year old young woman.

"Dad, since I'm not yet married, I want you to stay here and continue on with all your previous duties that you did for mom."

"Of course, my child," he replied, and then said formally because of the presence of Matriarch Gisela and Franz, "I hereby swear my fealty to Matriarch Frieda and swear to carry out the duties of running the mansion."

Frieda then said, "Miss Elise, please, I want you to stay on with us too. Please."

Miss Elise, red-eyed too, curtsied and said that she would stay too. That handled, Matriarch Gisela said, "Matriarch Frieda, with your permission, I'll compile a full report on this, and send it to all of the other leaders. Of course, for now, you may continue to work with the aliens and their queen, representing all the Narsten Cluster, just as Matriarch Athala had been. We matriarchs will meet in a month and choose a new matriarch to represent the entire cluster of worlds. With your permission, Queen Zenovia and I will question Clothilda at length."

"Thank you. I, I should like to be present when you question my sister though. I just can't understand why she did this," Matriarch Frieda said softly three times. "She's my sister."

After supper, the broken Clothilda was brought before us in the drawing room, which was now spotless. The servants had worked all afternoon, and all traces of the deaths had been removed. The air was filled with some kind of air freshener, giving one the sense of bouquets of flowers were present. She had been stripped of her outer-skirt and arm bindings. Her tiny baby-like short arms hung pale at her sides. Her dress had been crudely cut off above her knees so she could somewhat manage her own restroom use. Her hair had also been cut quite short, falling an inch or so above her shoulders.

Queen Zenovia said calmly, "Clothilda, I want only one answer from you. The others may have more. Who were you working with in the Gorki Cluster?"

"He said we'd never get caught! Bastard men. You cannot ever trust a man, not ever!" she retorted.

"Who?" Queen Zenovia asked again.

"Sergius Timorelli, the aide to President Dario Baldovino of Tamarri," she admitted, and Xene jotted that down.

Matriarch Frieda managed to keep her emotions under control. "Why, sis? Why?"

Clothilda looked at her younger sister, her eyes burning with rage and hate. "I should've been mom's heir. I should've been the top matriarch of the whole Narsten Cluster. Not you, you freak! I was the one who upheld all of mom's values, not you. Look at you. You can't even be understood any more, and those freakish breasts of yours — a disgrace to every aristocrat everywhere. May you rot in hell sister!"

"I, I don't have any choice, Clothilda. I sentence you to spend the rest of your life working in the mines. It's against our laws to have you executed, but I would if I could. Mom deserves better justice, but this will have to do. I don't have any other alternatives. Take her away," Matriarch Frieda ordered.

After she was led away, Queen Zenovia said, "This information will be needed when I visit the Gorki Cluster and help them sort out their side of the conflict. It would be prudent of you to gather up all the Slavers who are still alive anywhere in Narsten, perhaps pay them some compensation, and get them ready to be sent back to their worlds. I'm sure I'll be able to get the Gorki Cluster to return those that they've kidnaped from your worlds as well."

"Yes, that would be the prudent thing to do. How could all this happen?" Matriarch Frieda asked.

"May I speak frankly, matriarch?" Queen Zenovia asked.

"Yes, of course. Always."

"You ask how this could happen? One could dismiss it all by saying that your sister was greedy and power hungry, envious of your being chosen as your mother's heir, but while that would seem to explain it all away, there are two more fundamental reasons that are apparent to me, an outside observer of all this," the queen explained carefully choosing her words.

"First and foremost, your people have begun to rely wholly upon written reports in place of simple, direct observations. When no one takes the time actually to inspect firsthand, actually to look at what is going on and simply looks at printed reports, then they can be utterly fooled, just as Matriarch Ivonne was. If no one is ever actually going to observe you, then you can do what you desire, as long as you submit a report deceiving everyone. From what I have seen, a failure actually to observe and inspect firsthand and a total reliance on formal reports is rampant in all Narsten culture at all levels. If you have any power to change this behavior, in the strongest possible terms, I would suggest that you do so. Perhaps, you'll find Matriarchs Gisela and Ivonne backing you on this."

"I see what you mean. I'll try to change this. And the second?" Matriarch Frieda asked, repeating it several times to make sure Queen Zenovia understood her.

"Second, your mother had already seen this one and was in her own way beginning to rectify it. You have very rigid social classes here. One has no choice but to work in the class in which one was born. If your mother was a maid, then you have to be a maid. You are forever locked out of any of the benefits of other classes. You mother cleverly began to break these barriers down when she allowed all women to obtain larger breasts and the lip plates, allowing them some of the erotic attention formerly solely the province of the aristocrats. You've seen how thousands of women from all social classes have jumped at this opportunity."

"Hundreds of thousands now," Frieda corrected her.

"This system also tends to produce mediocre workers at best. Imagine you were born into the Maid Servants Class, but you really would love to be a nurse or a doctor, but the doors are closed to you. You are forced to be a lady's maid. Will you not hold some resentment over this? Will you not have a tendency to perform poorly in you tasks? Your heart and mind simply are not into it. This is precisely the case with Miss Katarine and Miss Lore who work at the pleasure house. Miss Katarine would love to go to the University and study to become a geologist. Miss Lore would like to learn how to be a doctor. Having a person doing what he or she loves to do and is trained to do yields a vastly more satisfied person and a far more productive person as well."

"Really? Miss Katarine wants to be a geologist? I never knew that. Oh. I never asked her. I just took her for granted. I see now mom wasn't the old crusty matriarch set in the old ways that I thought. She was working to bring about positive changes for all our worlds after all. Oh mom. How could I have been so foolish?" Tears swelled up again, and the queen allowed her to grief in silence.

After a time, Matriarch Frieda said softly, "I promise that I'll continue what mom started here on Menno. We can and must change our ways, though it'll not be so easy. I can see it must be done, or this will happen again, and we might not be so lucky to have you and Nia Elain here to save us."

Later, when the queen and I were alone preparing for bed, I complimented her. "That was brilliant, what you did with Frieda this evening. I do believe she'll work towards making substantial changes in their society."

Queen Zenovia replied, "Thanks. It had to be done or their culture was doomed. I saw that from the beginning when I got here. I just had to find the right time to make my suggestions. Honestly, I don't know if Athala really saw all that or if she was truly working for change, but her actions have begun to make major changes in her society whether she desired them or not. I have a feeling she was the old crusty woman and not leading the pack for social changes." We both chuckled.

She added, "We should soon head for the Gorki Cluster and work on the resolution on their side of this conflict. We've only solved half of it."

The next morning, Matriarch Frieda met with us in the drawing room over after-breakfast coffee. She wanted us to review her first proclamation and point out anything that needed improvement. Queen Zenovia made a few minor suggestions. Just after lunch, the news crew arrived. She had scheduled a worldwide press conference to outline what had happened yesterday.

It was shown live from her drawing room, while many of us sat in the back watching her. I found it interesting that because she was so hard to understand, the text of what she was saying scrolled along the bottom of the monitors. Hence, if you couldn't grasp what she was saying because of her lip plates, you could read them at the bottom of the screen.

First, she very carefully outlined what had happened and in detail. "So there's no war with the Gorki Cluster. Soon, we'll be returning their people, and hopefully, they'll return all ours that they abducted. It was all a contrived situation, designed to get us into a costly war that would only benefit a few people. My sister, the ex-Matriarch, had secretly purchased a large interest in several weapons manufacturing companies and would have made an immense fortune had we gone to war."

"This near disaster was brought about because of two fundamental failures on all our parts. I'll be rectifying both of these in the days and months to come. First, we all depend heavily on the official reports, and we neglect to do one simple thing: to look and inspect to see actually what's really going on and if the reports are accurate. I'll have more policy changes coming out in the future, but for now, everyone who submits a report must first go out, look, and inspect what the situation actually is before they submit that report."

"Second, our rigid classes are preventing us from achieving the prosperity and happiness we all deserve. I know some of you love your work and do an excellent job of it. However, others wish with all their hearts that they could become something else. Suppose that you wanted to be a shuttle pilot, but you were born into the Janitor Class. Every day you see shuttles flying about and dream of flying one yourself. I cannot expect that you would then be putting your heart and soul into your janitorial work."

"To truly flourish and prosper as a people, we must always have the best people working at every job in our society, people who not only want to be doing that kind of work, but who not only enjoy doing it but who are also competent in doing it. Thus, today I am making my first official proclamation."

"Anyone who wishes to do a different job than the one that they were born into can have the opportunity to make that change in their life. I have instructed the University and various vocational schools on Menno that, as of now, they are allowed to permit anyone from any social class to enroll in any of their programs, independent of that person's birth class! Of course, the person who takes advantage of this new program must maintain good grades and learn their new skills. If they cannot pass the final examinations, then they must return to their birth class employment. If they do pass, they will officially be recognized as members of that new class."

"I want competent people doing superlative work, while enjoying what they do. In this way, all of us, aristocrats included, can flourish and prosper, as we have never done before. This is the dawn of a new age for Menno, and I hope for all the Narsten Cluster. I know some of you will protest this dramatic change, and I understand your point of view too. Please, look at the larger picture in light of what has happened to us these past few years, and particularly of the treachery that was exposed yesterday. Give this a chance to work, and you too will benefit by having workers who want to be doing what they are doing and are quite competent at it."

"Finally a side note. Miss Katarine, Miss Lore, if you are listening to this, submit your requests to the University. I wish you both the best of luck in perusing your heart's desires."

"Thank you all for your time. I'll hold more of these news conferences with you in the near future. Now, I must see to the funeral of my beloved mother. Thank you." She signed off.

What happened next surprised even me. Naturally, the mansion's large staff had gathered in the back of the drawing room, though they had to stand close together to fit in. Spontaneously, a loud round of applause broke the silence when she finished. Matriarch Frieda had the full support of her large staff.

Further, after the chaos ended and the camera crews left, Miss Emlin, her personal maid since childhood, said, "Matriarch Frieda, are you serious about letting us try to learn to do something else?"

"Certainly Miss Emlin."

"Well, I really always did want to be a shuttle pilot, not a lady's maid. Is this really possible?"

Matriarch Frieda laughed. "Of course. I had no idea, Miss Emlyn. Tomorrow, you go enroll in flight school."

"But who will look after your needs? I can't abandon you," Miss Emlyn protested.

"I'd be honored to serve you," Miss Elise quickly spoke up. "I want nothing more than to be a lady's maid."

"Perfect. That's settled then. Miss Emlyn, you go to flight school, and Miss Elise will take care of me. Don't worry if you don't make it through flight training. You always have a job here." Miss Emlin beamed with happiness.

"Thank you, Matriarch Frieda. I and so many others can't thank you enough for what you are doing for us and everyone. You too, Captain Nia Elain and Lady Tesla. If you won't need me, I should go pack and make some preparations," Miss Emlyn gushed. I sensed invisible smiles from everyone present, though I could see the queen's.

"Queen Zenovia, on your return trip, I would like you and Captain Nia Elain to tour our inhabited worlds and see what resources we have that might be used to open up trade with your Ataro Empire. Besides, the other matriarchs wish to meet everyone too," Matriarch Frieda said.

"Of course, we'll do just that, once this war threat is eliminated," Queen Zenovia replied. "But we will delay so we can attend your mother's funeral. We owe her so very much." That we thought enough of Athala to stick around and pay our last respects pleased Frieda immensely. Besides, it was the honorable thing to do.

It was not until the very end of March that we finally landed back on Aurelio, bringing the queen and her small group with us. A few days were lost getting acquainted and such, before the real work began once again. She started the process all over from the beginning. I asked her why she didn't just dive in on the known guilty party, this Sergius Timorelli, aide to President Dario Baldovino of Tamarri. "I have only this one chance, and I don't want to miss any relevant detail," Queen Zenovia explained why.

She began questioning President Arcangelo. When had he first heard of the Narsten Cluster raids on Gorki Cluster worlds? From whom had he heard these? Who was the most outspoken person calling or demanding retribution or even a war with the Narsten Cluster? She rattled off a lengthy list of questions while Xene continued to jot the replies down for her.

I found it interesting that President Dario's world of Tamarri had been raided both the earliest and the most frequent. A handful of other Gorki Cluster worlds had suffered raids, but only after Tamarri had already endured six of them. From here, her investigation sped up rapidly. Via President Arcangelo, she was able to review lists of the major stockholders of some twenty-five armament companies and ten large corporations, which built the majority of their warships. What she didn't have access to were banking records.

We were delayed a few days, while President Arcangelo made arrangements for us to meet with all of the members of the Gorki Cluster Executive Council on Azzolino. Once more, with the supporting arms of our assistants, we entered the large room, taking our designated seats at the top of the huge U-shaped tables, the center of everyone's attention. I'm afraid we got just as many stares as we did last time, though this time there were far fewer complaints about bringing more freaks from the filthy disk into the council chambers. Queen Zenovia was just as shocked to see so many nearly identical people in the room. President Dario Baldovino looked identical to President Arcangelo, save for his purple tie.

I introduced the queen and sat down. She took over, speaking their language fairly well, much to their approval. I admit, we are hard to understand with our lip plates. Queen Zenovia began by asking, "I've done some checking before today. As I understand the events, the first of the Narsten raids occurred on Tamarri. Is everyone in agreement with this?"

President Dario Baldovino spoke loudly, "Of course! Everyone knows my world was raided repeatedly before other worlds were. That's why I have been clamoring for *decisive* action long before anyone else!" He made a fist with one hand and smashed it into his other open palm, creating a smacking sound to emphasize his declaration.

"Isn't it true, President Baldovino that you have been the strongest proponent of going to war with the Narsten Cluster?" she asked quietly.

Many heads nodded in agreement, but he again barked, "Of course! If your world suffered repeated raids that killed many and kidnaped your citizens, who wouldn't be demanding swift retribution?"

"Yes, understandable, President Baldovino, quite. Might I ask everyone what will happen to the value of stock that a person owns in the armament companies and warship manufacturing corporations if a war breaks out?"

Another president spoke up, "It will rise sharply. That's obvious, well perhaps not on your world if your companies do not sell stocks to raise capital."

"Is there some way I could project some documents that are on my laptop on the wall so that everyone could see them?" Queen Zenovia asked. Ten minutes and a flurry of action later, her laptop now projected onto a giant white screen behind us.

"Okay then, I have graphed the value of three specific armament companies, whose names are shown on the bottom of the graph, along with two warship builders. As you can clearly see, the price of a share of their stocks has been steadily rising rather sharply since the first Narsten raids occurred."

"Everyone knows that," President Dario barked, as though she was being childish. "What's the point of this anyway?"

"Suppose that someone purchased a lot of stock before

the raids began. If they were to sell them now, they would be able to receive triple what they originally paid for them. If the war actually breaks out, the stock value is likely to rise even higher, yielding an even bigger return on the investment," she continued, ignoring his taunts.

"Of course. That's the whole point of investing in stocks. I don't see what this has to do with anything. I move we dispense with this queen and her show and get down to the real business of this council," President Dario Baldovino barked gruffly. Several others nodded their agreement.

"Indeed. To make a huge profit. Now, look at this next document. It lists the major shareholders of these companies and corporations. I call your attention to the graph at the bottom. It shows President Dario Baldovino and his aide Sergius Timorelli made substantial investments in these companies about a month before the first raid and have been buying up more stock nearly every month since then."

President Dario cried out, "So there's no law against investing. This has gone on long enough!"

"Oh I certainly agree, President Baldovino, Sergius Timorelli. You see, I have wrapped up my investigation in the Narsten cluster. Your partners in this monstrous crime have been either killed or arrested." Queen Zenovia outlined the roles played by Matriarch Clothilda Kane and Commander Fedde Dorchmunster, the Commander of Security Force Ten. "I have their financial records with me. If someone would care to investigate the banking records of President Baldovino and his aide Sergius, I'm sure that you'll see withdrawals of certain amounts that were later converted into Narsten currency and deposited into their accounts." She outlined what all Matriarch Clothilda had told about her nefarious dealings with these two men.

As the evidence mounted, I became very alert. I was not about to allow what happened when Matriarch Clothilda and Commander Fedde were exposed. The president seemed unarmed, but Sergius carried a side arm. While she was outlining their dealings with the two from the Narsten Cluster, Sergius whipped out his gun. While I didn't know just what it could do, I wasn't going to take any chances this time.

Sergius rose and pointed the gun at the room. "I'm not going down alone! It was all Dario's idea! He's the guilty one, not me."

"You said we'd never get caught!" Dario countered his aide, not realizing this removed all lingering doubts.

"Don't anyone move or I'll shoot!" Sergius screamed, intent on making a getaway. I focused and acted, though no one saw my psi-crystal begin to glow. I levitated his gun arm straight upwards and then held his body in a vice grip. The look on his face was almost comical if this had not been deadly serious! Hastily, several of the military men rose and grabbed him, disarming him. Two more took a secure hold of President Dario Baldovino.

"Like I said, there will be no war. The Narsten Cluster is preparing to return all your people that are alive and have paid them for their incarceration. The stocks should fall back to where they were before these raids began," Queen Zenovia continued.

"I'll lose a fortune!" screamed President Dario.

"You are going to lose a whole lot more than money!" another outraged president barked. "Arrest them both on high treason!" The presidents began talking at once, and President Arcangelo signaled me that we could take a recess for a time. Smiling invisibly, we did just that, though Queen Zenovia didn't smile, but did look satisfied. Once again, she'd proven her unique training worked. I had to admire these Ataro queens. They certainly did know how to resolve conflicts! What I found utterly curious was no one ever asked why Sergius' arm was pointed upwards, and he seemed to "freeze" on his feet.

We were summoned to the council chambers about two hours later. Once more, it was an orderly group. President Arcangelo spoke first. "On behalf of the entire Executive Council, we extend our most sincere appreciation to Queen Zenovia Myrine for exposing these treasonous traitors. We will be ready to return all the Narsten hostages within two days."

Another president spoke up, "We sincerely hope that this does not alter in any way our opportunities to open up trading negotiations with the Ataro Empire."

342

Queen Zenovia smiled. "No, of course not. This matter had to be resolved first. Now that the conflict between the two neighboring clusters has been resolved peacefully, I'm prepared to begin dealing with establishing good relations between our peoples, including trading of valuables. Captain Nia Elain has told me she wants me to acquire some of your dry cleaning machines, but I'm sure we can do much more than that." Quite a few chuckled at her jest. Still, I wanted one of those machines. Most of my dresses were satin, pod-silk satin to be precise, and had to be dry cleaned. The simple cotton day dresses could be laundered easily.

She went on, "First, I and the others with me need to get acquainted with your worlds, people, and society. While she's made me aware of what technology of ours you greatly desire to acquire, we are mostly in the dark about what you have to offer us. Please allow us time to visit your worlds and see what you have that our worlds would like. I'm sure we can all reach trading arrangements that'll benefit both of our civilizations."

Again, I was impressed. She knew just what to say. I saw the presidents visibly relax, confident in time they would get their hands on our improved hyperdrive and probably our cloaking device as well. Before we adjourned, we had invitations from all the presidents to come to their worlds and get acquainted.

As we headed back in the transport to Aurelio, Queen Zenovia commented to me, "Now comes the really hard part of all this. We have to mingle among their culture, observe, and try to figure out what would make a satisfactory trade for both sides. This is the tough part of contacting new worlds and civilizations."

I'd never thought of this aspect. With my parents, we just sought out new, unknown worlds and did a quick mineralogical survey. Now, I was about to discover what took place after we reported our findings to the Imperium and they then sent out trading representatives. It did not sound like much fun to me.

Chapter 16 Learning and Killing Time

After the impending conflict ended, my crew and I were over three months pregnant, as we began to assist Queen Zenovia with her next project. Had I known this would consume nearly five more months, I might have taken up her when she said she could delay things, and ask Emperor Bino to send up more officials to assist her with the trading arrangements. I declined then, primarily because of the rapid disintegration of the Imperium as a political unit. I figured Emperor Bino had his non-existent hands more than full with the rapidly occurring events within the old Imperium empire. In fact, that was a correct call on my part. However, it also led to us deciding to stick around this area until after we had our babies, before heading off for more exploration of the halo.

Since we were already in the Gorki Cluster, we decided to work with them first, before returning to the Narsten Cluster and working out trading arrangements with them. The first thing we learned was that we had been entirely mistaken about much of their technology! My original impression was that they made extensive use of steel in their construction of buildings, land vehicles, and their warships. I've never been so shocked at how wrong I was on something as obvious as this!

In hindsight, I ought to have suspected this, based on what my various astronomers and astrophysicists had told us all: namely, the halo was low on the heavier elements. The heavier elements are formed during that last catastrophic phase of supernova, which when it blows up, distributes these heavier elements out among the gas and dust from which new stars and planets later form. The halo worlds are significantly deficient in the heavier atoms. Now, I suspected I knew why Ashford-5 was also so deficient in iron and gold. Interesting.

With the conflict threat ended and with somewhat better acceptance of us "disk people" even though most still considered us to be freaks of nature, I followed Queen Zenovia's request and began allowing extended shore leaves for my crew, though at no time was everyone off the ship. That would have been a major security risk. Hence, it was our chemist and geologist who made this first very startling discovery, namely Len and Zarita. "That's not steel, Nia Elain," Len pointed out. "I don't know what it is, but it's not metal."

She said, "Len is right. This isn't steel at all."

That's when we began to have our "eyes" opened. They met with some local engineers and discovered what we thought was metal was in fact very exotic polymers and resins, primarily silicon based. Further, some of these were as strong as steel, particularly when made structurally sound as in I-beams and such. Further, the window glass that covered the sides of the skyscrapers was a special blend of glass that was several inches thick and virtually unbreakable unless hit with extremely heavy forces.

As our engineers began discussing such things, it became apparent this civilization was miles ahead of us in such technologies. Thus, we most definitely had something to bargain for.

The next startling discovery was made by the twins, Jana and Jovanna, our ancient historians, in conjunction with Doctor Leann. It began with their natural curiosity about ancient history back when the red supergiant Giuseppa released the blast of radiation that so altered their reproductive systems. The moment they began asking about this bit of history, they were directed to any one of the countless churches of Aurelio.

That's when we made the rather starling discovery that the people of the Gorki Cluster were deeply religious, almost to the point of fanaticism! Literally, everyone went to their local church on their holy day, which was Friday on our calendars. Had we been allowed to tour the city when we first came to Aurelio, I suspect we would have spotted their church buildings right away. They simply could not be missed. Each one was a giant cathedral! Here in the heart of the capital city, there was a cathedral about every ten blocks! Considering the number of people who lived in this city, I could see why they needed so many cathedrals.

I'll never forget the first time that Jana, Jovanna, and I walked into our first cathedral, looking for Pastor Garibaldi to discuss their ancient history. The front entrance had two ornate, tall bell towers on either side of the front. Numerous statues adorned niches across the front facade, which rose at least a hundred feet from the street, while the towers were double that. As we stepped inside, beautiful marble columns rose to an enormous height overhead! Later, we were told the columns were one hundred twenty feet tall, giving way to spectacular vaulted ceilings. Space! Enormous space. That's what we saw just inside the doors. That and some of the most exquisite artwork that I've ever seen. Frescoes adorned the vaulted ceilings and some of the side walls. Marble statues sat on marble platforms, looking down upon us. They represented their Sacred Angels we were later told. We three were completely awestruck with the sights around us. However, Jana pointed out that there was a great similarity between this church and those of the Church of God back in Exchange City on Ashford-5. Now that she pointed it out, I had to agree with her.

Pastor Garibaldi was an elderly man, significantly shorter than us, especially because of our toe shoes and my ballet style boots. He was slightly pudgy with greying hair, but his eyes sparkled with aliveness. "Welcome to Angel Gabriel's Cathedral. I'm Pastor Garibaldi. You must be the freakish looking aliens I've heard so much about. I must admit you do look most unusual, but then we're all God's Children. Come, let us sit closer to the High Altar and talk." We did so, with our HIFRs assisting us and adjusting the fall of our hair. Jana and Jovanna didn't waste any time and began asking key questions about their ancient past.

"Records that far back are mostly now kept in our Holy Books," he began his lengthy answer. From the High Altar, he retrieved one and sat back down, showing us some of the pages in question. While we couldn't read the writing, there were some images similar to photographs and a number of drawings.

"Our ancestors had fallen from God's Grace, you see. Greed, gluttony, lying, cheating, promiscuity, deceitfulness, and much more had become the norm all throughout the worlds of the Gorki Cluster. They forsook all pretenses of religious beliefs. They had forgotten the Lord God had created them, and because Lord God is Everywhere and Sees All and Knows All, our Lord God witnessed their Great Abandonment. It is said that for a time Lord God simply cried for all his fallen. Finally, our Lord God had enough and sent the Red Death to our worlds. In one day, the skies of every world turned a deep red. All electrical power systems failed. It is said all technology failed that day. Our worlds were turned into a reddish nightmare without end. In the days, weeks, and months after that, billions died. God slew all those who had forsaken the Path of Righteousness. It is written that their bodies grew great reddish blisters, sores that did not heal, only festered and oozed a reddish puss, until at last the bodies died, painfully so according to the ancient writings."

"The Chosen Few who survived the Red Death were said to have been the remaining faithful of Lord God, those who begged for Divine Redemption, and were found worthy of God's Grace. It was at that time everyone finally realized we, God's Children, cannot survive without the will and consent of our Lord God. The Chosen Few banded together in small flocks, fighting just to stay alive. So few were they that Lord God saved, that they knew they had to create many children or there would be no future, and that they would become the last of God's Children. Still, Lord God was not finished with the Chosen Few. The greatest woe had yet to be seen. Barren wombs."

"Try as the Chosen Few might, no woman could conceive. No longer could they survive as themselves, and now, no longer could they create a future survival of our race through sex. Lord God's Grace allowed them to live what was left of their lives, but no more. The Great End of Life was at hand. Seeing their doom, the Chosen Few decided as a group to devote what time remained to them to Holy Prayer and living a life worthy of God's Grace."

"Lord God saw his Chosen Few had truly changed their ways and listened to their prayers. Yet, God could no longer trust the children whom he had created. Still, Lord God's heart held Holy Mercy. At last, Lord God preformed the Holy Miracle, allowing one devout woman, who yet remained a

347

virgin, to conceive his Holy Son. Lord God begat his only son of flesh, Santo Nino, sending him among the Chosen Few not only to preach but also to give the Chosen Few a way to survive into the Future. It was Santo Nino who developed the Holy Birth. You have seen this yourselves, I'm told, our Fertility Laboratories."

"Thus, when the Chosen Few had lost all hope of any possible future, Santo Nino gave them the Great Gift of a future, and babies began their lives in these laboratories. And the Chosen Few rejoiced, giving thanks to Lord God and Santo Nino for this, the Greatest of All Gifts. You perhaps cannot fathom how great a gift this was to a people who had and saw no future life for themselves or their wives. Thus, they began building great cathedrals in which daily they gave their thanks to Lord God and his son, Santo Nino. Statues in his likeness were made all throughout the cluster."

"It has taken us millennia to rebuild our population, but even today we are but a pale shadow of ancient times. Each and every one of us knows just how easily Lord God and Santo Nino's Great Gift could be taken away from us, so fragile and precious is this, the granting of a new life. On Fridays, our Holy Day, the day when Santo Nino created the first New Life, everyone flocks to their local cathedral to pray and give their thanks for New Life."

"Sadly, it appears that yet again, some of us have begun to stray from Lord God's Holy Path. Perhaps, it is yet another miracle of our Lord God. As we have become blind once again, he has sent you, the aliens, to walk among us, to locate, and to cast out those of us who have strayed so far from the Holy Path. Many of us believe this is so, that you strangest of aliens were sent to walk among us and point out to us those who have strayed that we may yet avoid God's Holy Wrath a second time."

I answered, "I'm very glad we're able in some small way to help put things to right here."

Pastor Garibaldi smiled. "Indeed. Already contracts have been let to produce statues of you aliens. In time, your statues will adorn the outer front of every cathedral so all entering the doors will be constantly reminded that yet again we can fall from God's Grace and that it took aliens to remind us of this. Never again shall we remain ignorant that our own can and have begun to walk down the path of destruction yet again. Your statues will be a constant reminder to us all to be constantly vigilant to those who have strayed."

Jana wanted to know more. "On our adopted home world of Ashford-5, we too have cathedrals now, though not as large as yours. The Church of God. We have certain beliefs too."

"Pray dear child, can you share them with me," Pastor Garibaldi asked, "though I may not be able to understand yours."

Jana did her best to explain the basic tenets, rattling off what I had heard preached in one of the spectacular cathedrals of Exchange City, Saint Shane's Basilica. "We believe all men are trying to survive, to flourish and prosper. Our survival is directed toward a number of different avenues. First, we are all striving to survive and do well for our own selves. Second, we are all striving to survive and prosper through our marital partners and our children. Third, we are surviving as various groups. Fourth, we wish to survive as a human species. Fifth, we need the plants and animals of the world to flourish and prosper as well, for if they do not, so do we then perish, for we are dependent upon them. Sixth, we need the physical universe around us to continue to survive well. Seventh, we are all immortal spiritual beings and as such, we need to continue to survive and become free and self-determined. Eighth is God, our Creator."

"These eight avenues are very important to us. We use them to help guide us in our daily lives. Do only those actions that benefit and aid more of these eight avenues and harms the least of the eight. We use this as our measure of right and wrong conduct. Do your people have similar tenets?" she asked.

"Your ways are strange to my ears, though I believe they are not so different from ours," Pastor Garibaldi replied. "Lord God is everywhere, sees all, and knows all. Each of us is given Life by Lord God and his Holy Son, Santo Nino, and must constantly strive to be worthy of the Gift of Life. Hence, our

Holy Guidance:

> Do not kill or harm your fellow man, without just cause.
>
> Be kind to your fellow man.
>
> Be courteous and show compassion to your fellow man.
>
> Do not lie, cheat, or steal from your fellow man.
>
> Your body is made by Lord God, treat it with love and kindness.
>
> Do not over eat and share what you have with less fortunate fellow men.
>
> Enjoy intercourse with partners of your choice,
> but when married, obtain your partner's
> permission when you wish to share your body
> with someone else.
>
> In all ways, strive to be worthy of Lord God's Holy Gift of Life.

You see, we keep our Holy Guidance short so all can easily learn it, remember it always, and follow them. Indeed, each of us knows just how precious the Holy Son's Gift of Life is and just how fragile it actually is. Each of us devotes our lives to doing what we believe Lord God would have us do."

He sighed, "But as we have all just seen, a few among us have already forgotten the Holy Guidance and have forsaken the Holy Path. We pastors of the Church of God are redoubling our efforts each Friday to help get others who may have strayed back onto the path before we once again raise the Holy Anger of our Lord God. What his Holy Son has given us, he surely can take away, leaving in just a few years nothing but empty buildings to mark our downfall."

Jana replied, "I certainly hope you are successful in this. Another question, Pastor Garibaldi. You see, on our world about a third of our people speak a language that is very similar to yours. In the distant past, did any of your people ever fly down to the galactic disk, perhaps exploring new worlds and setting up colonies there?" I thought this was a really good question. It reminded me of our forth mission objective.

"Ah, you must mean the Lost Ones," he replied. "Our most ancient records tell of small groups who became disillusioned with our crumbling society, and they constructed spaceships and departed the Gorki Cluster forever. None ever returned. They are known as the Lost Ones. Who can say where they went? No one knows. Nothing has ever been written beyond their departure. But dear child, the Lost Ones left over ten millennia ago."

"Oh, well then perhaps the similarities in languages are just an accident," she sighed. Settlement of Ashford-5 could not be more than a little over a millennia ago, not ten for sure.

Later, when Jana, Jovanna, and Marisol were discussing what they'd just learned about these people, Marisol spelled it out to us. "Look, these Gorki Cluster people are in a very poor way spiritually. If God is everywhere, then all space, including your own body is God's space, not yours. Worse, once a child reaches puberty, he or she knows for certain their body will one day die, and they cannot reproduce by sexual means, only through their Fertility Laboratories. We've seen nearly duplicate bodies everywhere, so even this method demonstrates to them that they really cannot create their own independent future offspring. All they have left is a total belief in their religion. So spiritually as immortal spiritual beings, they are in terrible shape, believing they are simply flesh and blood bodies that really have no long term future. I can see why President Dario did what he did. Why not grab all you can while you are alive? The lives of these people must be grim beyond belief and not this superficially happiness and lightness that they display outwardly."

I found this quite sobering. The three chatted more about this for some time, focusing on whether or not our Basic Therapy would benefit them at all or if it would even work on these people. Of course, no one had any definitive answer to that one.

Speaking of definitive answers, we still had none regarding the two aliens who had apparently been spying on us and "protecting" us. Although we continued to monitor the spaces around our ship when it was parked at a spaceport, we didn't spot any more shimmering glimpses of them, except twice. Martina and Danika did detect what they thought was their cloaked ship on two other occasions, one at the spaceport on Aurelio and once back at Menno. Whoever these aliens were, they certainly wanted to avoid detection. Since they didn't interact with us any further, I more or less forgot about them.

But I didn't forget about the observations of Marisol and Beth and her border collie Jen. It bothered me that Jen did bark and alert us to the men who were trying to cut through our front docking hatch, but that the dog had not barked at all during the entire time the unknown terrorist or terrorists were aboard and unleashing their genetic bio agent attack on us all. Now the immediate threat of war had been resolved fully, I had time to reflect on Marisol and Beth's suggestions. Jen was highly intelligent, for a dog anyway. Well behaved and a good companion, though I knew Beth was often near grief when she so desperately wanted to hold and pet Jen. Still, Jen had only barked furiously that one time. I rationalized; two observations are hardly conclusive evidence.

Still, I just could not dismiss this from my thoughts. Getting time alone with Marisol and Beth was hard to do. We were all confined to the ship, except when on shore leave and that meant close quarters with twenty-two of us humans, ignoring the three children, and the twenty-three HIFRs. Further, our HIFRs were always close to us, ready to assist us in any way needed.

Assisting us. Well, it had been several months since the attack and the acquisition of our own personal robots. I did find myself having to agree with something that Alexandra and Zoe had told us the first day when we awoke from our comas. Give the HIFRs time, and they will learn your ways and be there with the assistance you need without your having to tell them. They had been right about this, as I reflected on our situation. While going about my daily routines, I no longer had to say much to Athena in the way of orders. She was now, I noted, anticipating me and was right there handling what I needed help with, before I could even tell her. I began to see and appreciate the nearly seamless union of nova and robot that was the way of life for Alexandra and Zoe. Routine life had become livable this way, however in my opinion, it was a very grim existence, far from anything resembling optimum.

Nevertheless, the robots had kept us alive and, more

importantly, having them as our assistants had allowed us to keep our *mentales* gifts a total secret, for the most part. I knew this was not only a very right decision, but vital to our acceptance. The Narsten and Gorki people could accept us as freaks from the galactic disk, but also saw our helpers as the only way we could live and survive. None ever suspected they were robots. Had we not had the robots but had been using our *mentales* gifts, like levitating spoons up to our mouths to feed ourselves and the like, these people would have been very spooked indeed. Magical beings. That would have been their most logical belief of what we were, wholly non-human. Thus, we would never have gotten as far as we had with them. People fear what they cannot understand or do, and our powers would certainly qualify and in a major way.

But that still didn't answer the nagging question about Jen's lack of barking during the terrorist attack on us all. One day while on Aurelio, Beth, Marisol, and I, along with Jen, were taking a bit of a sightseeing shore leave. Our fancy suite enabled me cleverly to work out some private time with them. One bedroom had a very large bed, and I convinced our HIFRs that we three were going to sleep together this evening. Further, there weren't any electrical outlets not in use in the room. However, in the attached living room, there were several. Hence, our HIFRs, namely Athena, Leda, and Melita, all plugged in to recharge there in the living room, but only after they had gotten we three into bed.

Keeping our voices low, I said, "I've been giving your ideas about the terrorist attack on us considerable thought these past weeks. I keep coming back to Jen and her barking. I think you are right. Whoever launched the genetic bio attack on us was already on our ship. They simply had to be."

Beth whispered, "I know. Jen is very good about watching out for me. But who? Who would have done this terrible thing to us all? Why? They got modified too."

Marisol added, "Hey, everyone's had a lot of therapy now. I just can't see the terrorist as being one of us. Our lives are just horrid as they are now, though I have to agree the HIFRs have been rather remarkable. Our men still are very embarrassed to be seen in public. Getting them to leave the ship is very tough. They only do it when you order them to leave to make use of their specialty. Jan in particular is horribly embarrassed and ashamed to show himself to the Gorki people or the Narstens."

"I know. I'm acutely aware of our men's situation. Tad easier for us women, but just a tad. I hate being called a freak, though from their eyes we are just that," I replied. "So that leaves Alexandra and Zoe, who are wholly accustomed and used to their nova life style. But why would they want to destroy our lives? Could Zoe have done this to us just to get Jan made into a nova like her so she could marry him?"

Marisol sighed. "Honestly Nia Elain, I really don't think so. They've had therapy as well and plenty of major realizations themselves. I have thought long and hard about them and reviewed everything I've learned about them during this whole trip, including their therapy sessions. I believe what they told us is the truth, and they did not do this to us or know anything about it or who actually did it or why."

"But that only leaves their robots. There's no one else on the ship. Or is there?" I began to follow down another line. "Do you suppose we could have had an invisible person on the ship since we departed from Ashford-5?"

Marisol replied, "Well, that's possible. Invisibility is a known *mentales* gift. But this line of reasoning is fraught with pitfalls, Nia Elain. Look, they would have had to eat. No food has ever gone missing. They would have had to stay out of our way and avoid being detected or even being bumped into by one of us. We're all over the ship."

Beth added, "And Jen certainly would have sniffed him or her. Even if the invisible person was friendly, Jen would have snuggled up to them sometimes. Besides, they too would have been infected when they released the genetic bio agent. They could not have fled the ship either. We were in space, and none of our emergency shuttles are missing. I don't think an invisible stowaway is the answer."

"But that only leaves the robots," I protested slightly.

"Only Minta and Tanis. The others came aboard after the attack while we were in our comas," Marisol corrected me.

"But we've all heard those two recite their three

fundamental laws that their programming enforces on them. Never harm a nova, for example," I pointed out.

Marisol sighed, "I know. That does pose an enormous problem if we are to consider one of them as our terrorist. With the exception of the Cho family, we were all basically nova to begin with."

"Not true nova as defined by the population on Aquila Prime," Beth pointed out. "But we now are."

"Really? You think that Minta or Tanis did this to us? Why? What possible motive could their robot brains have dreamed up?" I asked.

"I know. It sounds ludicrous. The attack darn nearly ended the whole exploration trip and would have if the HIFRs had not come to us," Marisol pointed out. "Convenient or planned?"

Beth whispered, "No, I believe Alexandra and Zoe got them for us out of necessity. Without them, the mission would have ended, leaving her engine and the hyperdrive untested. Alexandra had a vested interest in seeing this mission through to prove her hydrogen propulsion system worked. I believe the President of Aquila Prime had little choice but to send us the robots. Either that or sacrifice Alexandra's new engine. It might have taken Emperor Bino years to put together a new exploration crew, if at all. I do believe Alexandra and Zoe had no prior knowledge of the terrorist plot against us and wisely used their heads to save us and the mission."

I sighed, "So we are back to Tanis and Minta as the only two possibilities. Everything brought onto the Eagle's Seed was carefully monitored many times. Think how many times one of us went through those checklists, examining each and every package and object on the ship. It would have been impossible for us to have missed something as large as one of those cylinders."

"They could have had another ship dock with us while we slept," Beth theorized. "No, then Jen would have barked a warning."

I added, "Besides, we went over all video and saw no signs of another ship docking with ours. No, the cylinder had to have been onboard from day one, perhaps well hidden or somehow we missed ever seeing it. Say, how did they dispose of the cylinder? We never did find it."

"It could still be hidden somewhere on our ship. It is rather huge, you know," Marisol suggested.

"I know. I can have everyone thoroughly search every inch of the ship. Tell them we need to make sure our ship is fully ready to continue our explorations, and that nothing needs to be repaired," I suggested. "Search every nook and cranny for signs of damage or fatigue."

The two liked my idea. Beth still wasn't satisfied. "So if it was Minta or Tanis, why did they do it? Motives. I keep coming back to that aspect. Plus, maybe we can rule out Tanis, since after all, Zoe was a late addition to the crew only when the supernova threat appeared. No one could have planned that eventuality. In my mind, that only leaves Minta. But why would she do something like this? Sabotaging her own master's experiments? Doesn't make any sense."

"Unless the robots have their own hidden agenda that we know nothing about," I theorized. Conspiracy theories aside, who knows what goes on in a robot's mind after all. They aren't humans.

"Well, if there is some grand conspiracy here, perhaps we have not yet seen their ultimate objective in all this," Marisol suggested. "Maybe we should continue to play along, but staying alert to some ulterior motive that may one day appear. Again, we should keep this a secret from the others for the time being. We don't dare accuse Minta, not without proof. Besides, we have no way to tell if a robot is lying or not." We left it at that.

The next day, I assigned everyone the new damage and viability project. For days, we had twenty-two of us going through absolutely everything on the ship and four auxiliary modules. Nothing broken was found, but we had an accurate assessment of our stores, particularly of food. Perhaps this had been a wise move. We discovered if we were going to spend much more time in our explorations, we were going to need more food supplies, particularly things infants could eat. Hence, we began laying in supplies from both the Narsten Cluster and the Gorki Cluster.

In early June, we needed to visit one of their "desert" worlds to take soil samples to ascertain the true amount of psi-crystals in the soil, preparatory work to the potential establishment of a fuel refinery on one of them. These were uninhabited worlds. For a very good reason: no water. Not a drop. While they had a breathable atmosphere, barely, there were no plants or animals living on these sandy planets. These were dead worlds, always had been as far as anyone knew.

Since we did not have their coordinates and since President Arcangelo insisted some of his mining representatives take us there, we consented to his arrangements. Essentially, Len, Zarita, and I, along with our HIFRs traveled in one of their spaceships, while Danika followed along behind us in the Eagle's Seed. Len and Zarita spent the two days of travel discussing the mining potentials and the current resin and polymer processes that were in widespread use throughout the Gorki Cluster. Me, I was pretty much bored.

We landed on Sesto Mondo del Deserto, the sixth of these desert worlds. As I looked out of the view port, I saw nothing but light blue sand and brownish rock, stretching off as far as the eye could see. I was told there were immense valleys and tall mountains here as well, but we were landing near Campo Sesto, where they had an excavation, harvesting the raw materials used in their complex resins.

As we set foot on the uneven ground, often deep in sand in places, we would not have been able to stand up, let alone walk, had not our HIFRs kept a sturdy hold on us! The air was incredibly dry and low on oxygen as well, but breathable. I pitied the miners who had to work in this inhospitable environment.

Len and Zarita began collecting their samples. Actually, they tried to stand perfectly still, directing Bion and Rhea, who did the actual collecting. Six of their mining engineers who had come with us, chatted with them, as they took the samples. For an hour all went according to plan, but I soon became bored, staring off across this incredibly inhospitable, small planet, perhaps half the size of Ashford-5. I found the heat shimmering in the distance almost hypnotizing.

With samples taken, we all turned to return to the base camp and our ship. As we did, we found ourselves facing six men with guns pointed at us!

One of the men barked at me, "Captain. Order your ship to land beside the Aurelion ship. Then, order your crew to disembark. We're stealing your ship. The Aurelion ship can take you all back. If you don't we'll begin by shooting your helpers and then those two," pointing at Zarita and Len.

One of the mining engineers cried out, "You can't do this! It is against everything we believe in. God's Grace. Don't do this!"

Bang! He fired a shot. A large hole appeared in the engineer's head. His body dropped lifelessly to the ground. "I mean it. Order your ship to land now, captain, or I shoot some more of you!"

I knew Len, Zarita, and I could each take out one of these men, but that left three. Bad odds. They were spread out wide enough that a single wall of flames would not get them all. Besides, I dare not risk random fire hitting any of us. I stalled for time. "I don't have any communicator with me. I'll have to go back to their ship and make the call." If I could get Danika to land the ship, I was sure we could all take them out. There were seventeen of us with the gift! I could coordinate the attack via telepathy.

While he was trying to work out what I meant and the best way to proceed, I saw a shimmering in the distance behind the six men. Zarita and Len also spotted it, but then we all were used to trying to detect such shimmers from the hours we had spent staring at all the video feeds. Then, I thought I saw two hooded forms appear, but at this distance, I could not tell much more than that. A pair of silent beams shot from the two, hitting two of the six men in the back of their heads, leaving a cylindrical hole about two inches across through their heads! As the two dropped, the other four glanced over their shoulders. Two more beams flashed, dropping another two of our assailants. Zarita and I acted, disabling the two remaining men, ripping their guns from their hands and forcing their bodies prone on the sands.

Our stunned mining engineers finally grasped what was happening and dashed over to them, confiscating their guns and holding them on the two remaining men. Meanwhile, we three stared at the shimmering in the distance, but our rescuers had already vanished, once more leaving no trace they had ever been there! Of course, via telepathy, Zarita immediately let Danika know what was happening and shortly our ship hovered overhead.

Other miners now came rushing out to help us. Apologies flew left and right. "No harm done to us," I kept saying. I had Zarita and Len check out the sight where our mysterious protectors had been located. Later, they reported seeing the impressions of a saucer-like spaceship on the sands along with human-like footprints, probably one step from the doors of their ship.

Later, we learned the six men worked for Dario Baldovino, and had hatched this plot to obtain our cloaking device and hyperspace engine for themselves. Had they been successful, they expected to be the richest men in the cluster. Of course, the real problem simply could not be answered. Who had shot four of them from behind? What kind of alien weapon was used? These two questions baffled us and the Security Guards who responded to the mining engineer's call for help. We spent the rest of the day with them, but in the end, neither they nor we had any real answers to these two burning questions.

The engineers and guards did propose a theory, based on the cylindrical holes in the four dead men's heads. They postulated some form of energy beam such as a powerful laser, which we suspected were in use on their warships. Thus far, we had not asked about their weapons, and they respectfully didn't press us about ours. When we were finally alone, Martina pointed out whatever these new weapons were, they were similar to our d-guns. With the four dead men, the beam had cauterized the holes drilled into their heads. Our d-guns would also have done that. Our only conclusion was that our unknown, mysterious protectors were still somewhere in our vicinity and protecting us.

Well, I liked the protecting part, but not the rest. Who

were they? Why were they so intent upon being our guardian angels? What was in it for them? I just had far too many unanswered questions to feel remotely comfortable about the situation. After this episode, Danika doubled our efforts to locate their ship whenever we were at a spaceport and even while in flight. Nothing new resulted, however. Martina had the last word on them. "They will make themselves known to us when they feel the time is right."

When we did return to Aurelio, President Arcangelo was overly propitiative about this new attack on us. However, I made light of the whole matter, and he wisely dropped it. However, after that, we always had a group of their guards watching our backs.

By the end of July 1379, two large groups of transports arrived, one on Menno and the other on Aurelio. At last, Queen Zenovia had her trading representatives with her. Armed with the knowledge of just what was available in the two cultures, her job of establishing permanent relations and trading agreements began in earnest. Our lengthy task was finally over, and we were officially allowed to continue with our explorations of the halo worlds. Hans and Zoe had worked out hyperspace coordinates for these two areas in great detail. Others would continue their work, filling in the gaps in the vast, nearly empty space between them and the galactic disk light-years below. At this point, Marcella was officially reassigned to work with Queen Zenovia as the official Gorki Cluster ambassador to the Ataro Empire. I did, however, promise her that one day when we returned there she could come with us and visit our world. This pleased the young woman very much.

However, we were now entering the eighth month of our pregnancies, and we all looked it! Tesla and I were having far more trouble moving around than the others because our feet had been fused, pointing downward. I made an executive decision and announced it to everyone in another group meeting. "Look, we're all having a hard time getting around now. Therefore, we're going to remain parked here until after we have our babies and all is well, before we head off into the unknown once again." Never has one of my decisions met with such a grand welcome! I think all were experiencing great physical difficulties at the moment. Had we had our arms, it would have made all the difference in the world. This Danika was forever pointing out to the others and Lin Cho fully backed her up on this point. We spent the next two months parked at the spaceport on Menno, but only Tesla and I went "ashore" there. None of the others wanted their feet fused and besides getting around became increasingly more difficult for us all.

Matriarch Frieda was extremely pleased we would be staying on Menno until we had our babies. "Look, even we aristocrats have a hard time the last couple of months. Normally during that time, we don't even wear our outer-skirts, though we also do not go out in public either. So you are welcome to come visit with us and stay in the mansion as well."

Tesla and I did visit with her several days each week, until we entered our ninth month. After that, our feet just couldn't take the extra weight and off-balance of our bodies. As due dates approached, every one of us grew more and more nervous about it, particularly Doctor Leann. None of us humans had any real way to help each other with the birthing. Worse, we knew caring for our newborns promised to be utterly frustrating, considering how helpless we felt just now. Only Alexandra and Zoe didn't share our same fears and worries.

"Look, Minta has told us that she's downloaded everything about birthing and infant care. On Aquila Prime, our HIFRs always handle these things. They are quite expert with it. Trust in our HIFRs, Nia Elain. This is perfectly normal, really it is. It's just I'm more frustrated in how hard it is to get around like this. Oh! She kicked again. Minta, please rub me a little." Minta did so. "Ah, there, that's better. She quieted down again. Darn, I need to pee again. I didn't realize I'd have to go this often."

I chuckled, "Tell me about it. You'll get used to it. Danika and I have been through this before."

Chapter 17 Of Babies and Dolls

As September came, Doctor Leann and I began chatting about the coming births. "You know, Nia Elain, I just cannot fathom how come all of us became pregnant within days of each other. I know we had a lot of idle time on our hands, but normally we who have the gift exercise more control over when we get pregnant."

"You have a point. It is really strange all twenty-two of us got pregnant within days of each other. I know Danika and I were not planning to have more while we were on this expedition, though we did want Zorina and Nadia to have little sisters soon. Still, I wonder what the odds are we all got pregnant at nearly the same time?"

Dr. Leann laughed. "Now that I could calculate. Well, estimate might be more accurate, especially given the tendency we *mentales* have to control such things. Actually, this has been troubling me some. I'd guess that those odds would most likely be one in a million, given our current physical limitations. We are all having a rough time of it, and I can't imagine how we are going to be able to care for them once they are born. Lord help us if there are any complications during birth. I doubt I can do much of anything to assist one of us in trouble. It is so damned frustrating being like this, especially me, your doctor. You know; it's not too late to make a fast hyperspace jump to home."

"I know. I thought about doing that, but if we did that, I doubt we'd get permission to resume our explorations. I know how keen everyone is on fulfilling our mission."

She sighed. "I know. This is a once in a lifetime opportunity for most of us. Still, I admit I'm more than a little nervous about this."

"One in a million, you say?" It finally struck me just how improbable all of us getting pregnant at the same time actually were.

"Oh. At least that high. Could be even worse if we were not gifted. I just don't see how it was possible," Doctor Leann replied.

"You don't suppose we've been somehow manipulated into having babies right now, do you?" I asked the obvious next question.

"I've thought that myself, Nia Elain, but then I always run into the proverbial stone wall. Who could have such powers over our bodies? And why? It makes no sense, unless their goal was to stop our explorations of the halo. Thus far, we've not met anyone who wants us to stop."

The more I thought about this highly unlikely event, the more I began to suspect somehow we had all been manipulated by someone into having babies. True, when I made my original plans for the expedition, I allowed for us having several babies while we were in space. That goes without saying. Pregnancies will happen, just not to all of us at the same time. Thus, I kept coming back to the notion that someone out there wanted us pregnant and somehow saw to it that happened. I sighed. Well, they are getting their wish, I thought.

I believe the time grows near. We should send the signal, Huyana, Isi sent.

I think you're right. They're relatively immobile now. I believe they'll remain here until after the new bodies come, Huyana replied. *Sending the signal now. Prepare for their arrival.*

Shortly, a much larger cloaked saucer ship silently descended onto the side of the tarmac not far from the smaller version and the strange alien ship with its very precious cargo. Isi then sent to the group onboard, *Be patient and be ready. It'll happen very soon now. Remember, remain quiet until everyone is attached safely.*

One replied, *These're the most fabulous finds ever! Stupendous job, Isi, Huyana. Stupendous.* Isi resisted the temptation to reply to this obvious statement of fact. Our video cameras picked up another, much larger shimmer, but none of us was in any condition to be reviewing the video logs just now. Only later would Danika spot it.

September 22, 1379, marked what we all later named "Baby Week!" Both Jan and Alexandra went into labor about the same time. One by one, the rest of us followed in rapid succession, with Danika and I being the last to give birth seven days later. Within one week, twenty-two newborns were added to our crew! I think I can speak for everyone when I say we were all more than thankful that all the babies were just fine, perfectly healthy, and that there wasn't even one complication. Further, to our utter amazement, our HIFRs performed superlatively. Even Doctor Leann was very much impressed with their skill and care of our infants.

For the record, Danika and I had Rafe and Donatella, respectively. Martina and Tesla had Mary and Tatiana. Anya and Thomas had Vanna and Bart. Jovanna and Diego had Silvana and Anita. Jana and Len had Rosina and Jim. Hans and Leann had Alberto and Kate. Marisol and Beth had Benita and Carmela. Anwyn and Dylan had Breanne and Brogan. Dao and Lin had Tao and Chen Ju. Zarita and Alexandra had Dorita and Dione. Jan and Zoe had Johan and Melina.

The first few days were absolutely wild for everyone. Our babies were born as nova. That is, they lacked arms, had malformed feet, slit lips, and way too much hair for normal babies. I was worried that, without my arms, I would be unable to nurse Donatella properly. Athena handled us as though she'd delivered babies and handled their care all her life. So yes, this was a rapid learning experience for all twenty-two of us.

My little Donatella was only three days old when I was taken by complete surprise. Athena had pulled my hair back and helped me lie down on my right side on my bed without falling. My breasts were finally lactating heavily, and she carefully laid her down beside me, helping guide her to my nipple and milk. I felt that the wondrous sensation once more, as life giving sustenance flowed from me into her little, wiggling body. To me, she looked beautiful, but so did little Rafe and our other two girls. Zorina sat on a chair beside my bed watching the proceedings with some interest. "Donatella, this is your big older sister, Zorina. You have two others too, just over there, Nadia and Rafe. Your mother and I think you and Rafe are very pretty, just like Zorina and Nadia."

I never did figure out why other parents made goo goo noises and such to their newborns. Rather, I knew each of us was an immortal spiritual being. So when Zorina and Nadia were born, both Danika and I talked to them as though they were adults or at least more mature children. Both our first children quickly developed telepathic skills as we both had hoped. That is, their pituitary glands were much larger than normal, and these glands were the body's endocrine monitor for our *mentales* gifts. Depending upon the nature of the gift we were using, the endocrine system sent the proper signals to our muscles and such to carry out the gift. With other actions, such as telekinesis, the endocrine system had little to do. Anyway, our three year olds were quite alert and responsible for young children of that age, which I attributed to our treating and conversing with them as adults from the day of their births.

Imagine my surprise when I received telepathically, *Oh. I can't be called Isi? Okay. Donatella. That has a nice ring to it. Say, how long will it take for these tiny bodies to become as large as yours?*

What? Telepathy? Three days old? How is that possible? Yes, Donatella is a beautiful name for a beautiful woman that you'll one day become. Your older sisters there are three years old. Your body will be continually growing for many years, but by eighteen, you should be very nearly fully grown, I sent back.

Oh. We just thought since most of you possessed telepathy, that it was all right for us to chat with you now. We cannot tell you how very impressed we all are with these absolutely fabulous bodies that you've grown for us! The sensations are almost unimaginable! I have sensation all down my legs! My tongue. Wow. Incredible. Beyond belief.

What do you mean we? Sensations? I replied, trying to make logical sense of all this.

There are twenty-two of us that you have rescued and salvaged by growing us these simply fantastic new bodies. We can't ever thank you enough. Before Huyana and I spotted you and your unique people, the only choices we had to obtain real bodies with really good sensations in them were the Narstens and the Gorki. But as you discovered I hope, the Gorki are all religious fanatics, quite irrational about religion, living lives of near desperation about merely surviving, while the Narstens drug their minds into oblivion, creating really weird sensations, some pleasant mind you, but hardly sane either.

The number, twenty-two, clicked in my mind. I asked the obvious. *Did you have anything to do with all of us becoming pregnant at the same time?*

I felt the tiny suckling body jerk slightly. I sensed embarrassment coming from her and a hesitant reply. *Well, yes. We simply just had to get some of these most incredibly sensation-filled bodies that you all have. Of course, while we could have just taken over your bodies from you, that would be stealing. Instead of that, we had you prepare these new ones for us. Never before have we ever been able to provide twenty-two of the finest bodies in the galaxy for those of us desirous of escaping the monotonous, sensation-less lives we were living. I guess it'll be a bummer to have to wait eighteen years. Hey, with this much sensation already, I'm sure we'll be elated all during that time span. How many years do these bodies live? I mean ours live forever. When a part breaks down, we simply attach a new part.*

Oh, it varies. If nothing bad happens, then they can live seventy years or so. However, there are Rejuvenation machines available that can extend a healthy lifetime much longer. Martina is really ninety-three years old now, but looks to be only twenty-three. I'm not sure just how long they can extend one's life. Now it's my turn. Just who are you anyway? We've detected a pair of very strange aliens watching us and perhaps even protecting us. Here's the best image that we've so far spotted. I focused and sent her my image of the monitor screen showing the strange doll-like heads, fuzzy and indistinct though they were.

Oh! You saw us! We're being so very careful about that. We didn't want to frighten you away. The Narstens are terrified of us, though the Gorki have never seen us. I was called Isi, but now I'm going to be Donatella. That's such a sensuous name, I think. Donatella. We are from what the Narstens call the Billik Cluster. They call us the doll people, since our bodies are not alive like yours are. I'm not sure what a doll is, though. And you bet we were protecting all of you! With absolutely the finest bodies in the galaxy and your growing twenty-two of them for us, no way were we going to let anything at all happen to you! Say, how soon can you all grow another twenty-two of them? There are thousands of us who are desperate to escape from the sensation-less lives in those inanimate doll-like bodies.

I sent back a very definitive: *Please! No more growing of bodies for a while! We like to space our children out by two to three years apart, sometimes longer. It's hard on us to create them. So you have thousands of others who truly want human bodies?*

I'll tell the others. No more growing of bodies for several years. Please let us know when the time is right again. We know nothing of your biology, but we'll learn. Yes, thousands. Are there more who have these incredible bodies where you come from? Somewhere down in the galactic disk we suspect?

Yes, there's a whole world of us and more worlds with other variations. I didn't get any farther. Danika whispered that little Rafe was chatting with her and that they had been protecting us. She hadn't finished when others of my crew sent me telepathic messages that their new babies had telepathy already, were chatting, and asking many interesting questions. I saw an immediate problem arising and sent to Donatella, *Hey, let the others know that not every one of us has telepathic abilities. The Cho family doesn't, as well as Alexandra, Zoe, and Jan. So please be careful with them and don't spook them.*

A bit later, Donatella sent me, *Done. We're patient and will wait for these little bodies to be able to speak. It's quite quaint how your bodies make all of those intelligible sounds to communicate. Most interesting. Say, what are these other mechanical bodies that are taking care of us and you? We've never encountered them before. Oh, and why don't you all just screw on some new arm appendages? Then, you wouldn't need these mechanical bodies to help you so much.*

Oh boy. How does one describe a humaniform robot, let alone why they were invented and desperately needed? While I pride myself on being a good and knowledgeable captain, I found myself wholly out of my league with these questions, bordering on the philosophical and religious grounds, let alone the *mentales* gifts which was certain to come up fairly soon. Then, I remembered Rafe, that is, Rafaela Gervasi-Jones, the inventor of Basic Therapy and the most knowledgeable person on such matters. She had said I could contact her if I needed help. Well, this surprise situation certainly met that criterion, in my way of thinking at least.

The trouble was we were about half a galaxy away from Rafe on Ashford-5 at the moment. I could call her on the comm set, ignoring the huge time delays in chatting. Then, I remembered Zarita and her giant crystals. Would they work across such a vast distance? I had to try. *Zarita, Nia Elain here. With your power crystals, can you contact Rafe, Rafaela Gervasi-Jones, on Ashford-5 for me and set up a telepathic connection with her for me. We've a situation here that she may be able to help us with.*

Oh you mean the Achtnag. That's what they call themselves. Sure, give me a few minutes to arrange the crystals. This sure is interesting isn't it? Zarita sent back. "Rhea, I need you to unpack my three blue spheres. Arrange them in a circle around me, please."

Ten minutes later while sitting on her bed, Zarita focused and activated her psi-crystal around her neck. It glowed pale blue. One by one, she joined her foot in diameter spheres into her growing network. Soon, she sat there surrounded with a soft blue light that glowed upwards onto her body. Rhea watched her with intense curiosity, never having seen anything like this before. Shortly, Minta stepped up to the door to watch as well. This was something quite new to the HIFRs.

Rafe? Ah, great. Zarita here. Nia Elain wants to talk with you. We've got a — how do I say this — a really unique situation going on here.

Are you all right? Babies okay? Birthing problems?

Rafe responded, growing worried that something terrible had happened.

No, nothing like that. We are all fine. Twenty-two healthy babies, and we're fine too. No problems there. Let me join Nia Elain with us. It's rather a complicated thing, Zarita sent, and then gently pulled me into rapport with her and Rafe.

I carefully explained everything I knew about these "doll" beings, as well as the conversations I'd had with Minta and Athena. *So what the devil is going on here, and just how am I to respond? What about the mentales gifts? What about the genetic bio agent attacks? And Aquila Prime? They seem utterly enamored of these pathetic bodies that we have. What about them? They are using telepathy at three days old, for heaven's sake. What kind of powers will they have? Are they a threat to us? Rafe, if ever I need help, it's on this one!*

She replied, *Well, this is most interesting. Fascinating really. At least our telepathic barriers are up and working. Rupert and I did quite a bit of investigating while we were off-world and had not found any others who had our unique mentales gifts, other than the exceedingly rare Class V telepaths. It seems you have encountered the first beings that apparently have powers similar to ours, at least in telepathy. Let me think on this a bit.*

After a pause, she sent, *Well, I think it would be prudent to keep them away from Ashford-5 for the time being, until we see more how they develop with their powers and just how ethical they are when they're using them. Tierra here is in a most critical phase right now, what with the disintegration of the Imperium and all that chaos. Since they are in love with your Aquila Prime nova-style bodies, let's allow them to go in that direction. Their intelligence ought to be a big help to those people.*

I protested a little. *But they want more of these bodies. Isi or my Donatella claims that there are thousands of their kind who would give anything to have one of these bodies. They certainly do have some amazing technology and extremely strange spaceships with cloaking devices as well.*

Rafe sent back, *Well, the Billik Cluster was the next*

stop on your mission, if I recall properly. Perhaps you can make a deal with those who want these bodies. Trade Aquila Prime bodies for their technology.

Okay. They are spiritual beings, right?

Of course. They would have to be that.

What about the robots? Minta and Athena have made some compelling arguments that they are alive as well.

She laughed, I think. *I surely don't know about that one. Before today, I would have said how could a spiritual being inhabit a body that is not alive. Apparently, I'm dead wrong on that one. These doll bodies are not alive, and yet these spiritual beings inhabit them as though they were. Right now, focus on them. We'll worry about the robots later on. By the way, now it makes sense. I've been pondering just how everyone on your ship could have gotten pregnant at nearly the same time. I just couldn't fathom how that could have happened. Now, it makes complete sense. Keep me posted. Zarita, I've gotten permission to have six of the giant crystals with me. So in the future, I can contact you. I'll touch base with you periodically.* We chatted a bit more before breaking the half-galaxy distant connection.

Next, I decided to chat with the babies. It was quite easy to open up a group connection with all them, almost too easy. Later, I realized that their intense curiosity lay behind that. They were in love with their new bodies and wanted to know all about our civilizations. Hint. Hint. Well, I couldn't ignore their hints.

Okay. Most all the humans of the galactic disk are of the species homo sapiens sapiens. The Narstens and Gorki people are likely the same species.

Huyana interrupted, *But those bodies are not anywhere as terrific as these are. The sensations in these trump those tenfold.*

Let me finish please. Many years ago, some evil scientists tried to create a doomsday war weapon, one that would render the whole population of a planet helpless and yet not damage any of the material objects of that world. It was called a genetic biological agent. When let loose on a population, it causes massive genetic mutations in their bodies. All our bodies here have been victims of that genetic bio agent. We're all hermaphrodites among other things.

Of course, Huyana interrupted me again. *This feature makes these bodies so utterly fantastic. No comparison to the others.*

Well, some of our best geneticists have developed some genetic cures for some of these modifications. However, the cost to regrow arms is prohibitively expensive. Considering the millions of victims whose lives were saved, doing that for them has been out of the question. Plus, there is no way to undo the dual sexual organs in any of us. Hence, almost all were all resettled on Aquila Prime. There, each one is given their own personal robot to assist them as needed. They are called humaniform robots or HIFRs, as they like to be called. They are quite intelligent and able caretakers. So yes, if you love these types of human bodies, which are being called homo sapiens nova or just nova for short, then I can offer you an entire planet of them.

The radiation of pure joy and happiness that suddenly swept over me was almost indescribable. I'd just given them a way to achieve their heart's desires. I was taken by surprise at the sincerity of their admiration. On the other hand, I had no idea that this might have been entirely the wrong thing to do for them as spiritual beings, though.

Oh we do, we surely do! Donatella sent me.

Okay then. Zoe and Alexandra are from Aquila Prime, which is part of the Ataro Empire. Most of the rest of us are from another planet in that empire, Ashford-5. Aquila Prime is in the middle sector of the spiral arm, while Ashford-5 is at the very rim of the arm. We are the first galactic disk explorers to venture this far into the halo. Next on our agenda is to visit the Billik Cluster.

That is prefect. We can contact those who are like-minded and make arrangements for a mass migration to your Aquila Prime. But we should offer you something in return, Donatella suggested.

We have glimpsed your flying saucers. They fly without making any sound. Plus, you must also have a cloaking device as we do.

Yes, we noticed you had something akin to our masking energy. We could trade you our spaceships and their technology for taking those of people who wish to this Aquila Prime world, Donatella hinted.

That would be a very good arrangement. We need to let our bodies recover from giving birth before we head off to your globular cluster. Might I ask if your people have other abilities besides telepathy? Almost none on Aquila Prime have this ability, I'm afraid.

I sensed aghast from her. *Oh no! Just telepathy. That is how we Achtnag communicate. We send ideas, unlike the humanoids we've encountered, which use the thing called speech sounds and the funny marks on papers. We are not the wicked, evil Ceri! Now, they are the ones who have these immense powers. They are quite terrible, fierce beyond belief. We stay strictly away from their space. The Ceri do not have physical bodies as we do. They are pure energy beings, capable of horrible things. The only thing that we have in common with those evil beings is telepathy. We have found all higher life forms have telepathy. Now some of you humans are developing it too.*

Yes, we are at that. All right then. After we are confident that we are able to handle caring for all you babies, we'll head for the Billik Cluster. Meantime, relax and enjoy your new baby bodies.

Okay. How long do they take to develop enough to walk and talk? When do the reproductive organs begin working?

Oh brother. Nothing like having a discussion about the birds and bees with a three day old baby! I was spared some of that when Mai Lin came to see our new girls. "Oh they are so darling, Nia Elain, Danika! I just can't wait until I get older and have one of my own. It's so great now, because I don't have to find a boy and get married just to have one. They are so darling, aren't they?" I enjoyed the lighthearted chat, a pleasant break from the heavy discussion with Isi or Donatella now.

Later, I relayed what I'd learned to Rafe back on Ashford-5. She replied, *The technology trade is excellent. I'll pass that along. However, Nia Elain, I've been giving your situation considerable thought. These Achtnag are spiritual beings, just like us, I do believe, though I won't really know for certain until I've examined them. For now, let's assume that they are. Now, if they follow the same pattern as all other spiritual beings we've encountered, at least those who inhabit physical bodies, can't say anything about the Ceri mind you, then I believe that in time, they too will forget about their past lifetime, just as most of us humans do.*

I responded, *But why should they forget? Why do we forget, for that matter?*

Rafe answered, *I have a theory about that. Objects and possessions. When one's body dies or is left and one assumes a new body, they leave behind all the possessions that they had, friends, everything. As a tiny baby, they are in a completely new location in space, with all new people around them, and possessions and objects. Out of sight, out of mind I believe is the key. They no longer have their old possessions and acquaintances and are surrounded by all new ones, so a being tends to quickly forget what isn't present any longer, focusing on the new things around them. So I suspect by the time that they are speaking and walking, they'll have mostly forgotten their past lives in their doll bodies. Anyway, I'm very glad to hear they only have telepathy and not our host of mentales gifts. They ought to fit in well on Aquila Prime.*

She continued, *Also, Nia Elain, I would strongly recommend that your crew have their birth traumas erased before you set out on the next phase of your explorations. Tell Marisol that is my strongest recommendation. Keep yourselves in peak physical and mental conditions.*

I agreed. Later that day, Zarita began handling Danika, while Marisol worked with me. I admit I was amazed at how quickly we both were able to deal with that trauma. Unlike some of the other trauma that I'd handled in these therapy sessions, this one was relatively easy to handle, though I do admit I was surprised to be also erasing an earlier time when I was a woman giving birth and died of complications as a result. When I was done, I realized why Rafe had insisted we do this. Some doom or fear that lay just in the dark recesses of my mind was wholly gone. I could see how if left unhandled, that trauma could have caused physical body complications later on.

We delayed doing much of anything for a whole month. Besides needing time to get everyone handled, I wanted to make very sure we could handle our babies and still deal with running the Eagle's Seed. Also, I wanted to make very certain our HIFRs could handle our newborns and still be able to assist us. If they could not, I was prepared to return us all to our home worlds immediately. I found things had gotten far more interesting around the ship.

Our HIFRs were excellent nannies. Their programming was flawless, in my humble opinion. However, as I suspected, they were now forced to spend at least half of their time handling our infants, limiting how much assistance they could devote to our needs. I weighted our options during the month. With seventeen of us with *mentales* gifts, I correctly estimated that we could continue our explorations with the limited assistance of the HIFRs that we now had. Further as I also expected, Dao and Lin Cho, along with Jan, Zoe, and Alexandra were having the most troubles, since their HIFRs had to spend half of their time with their babies. Since I really didn't need their special skills just now, I finally made the decision to continue with the mission, much to everyone's great pleasure.

Nevertheless, I didn't give the orders to depart until November 1, allowing us two months to rest up, and to get more accustomed to our new situation. Babies. Good grief, having twenty-two newborns around was a bit much to deal with. Everyone was nursing many times a day, ignoring the lack of sleep. I'd forgotten what a good night's sleep was like. That's not entirely true. Danika and I had been through this before, but everyone else on the ship, save Lin Cho, hadn't. As the first came, I had no choice but to delay our departure further. I had a crew of zombies on my hands.

"Aren't we supposed to take off today?" Tesla asked me. She looked exhausted, bags under her eyes.

"When did you last get a whole night's sleep?" I asked, knowing the answer, but I wanted her to recall.

"Oh. Right. I'm not very alert am I?"

"None of us are. Give them more time. We'll take off once everyone is getting a whole night's sleep. Shouldn't be much longer," I told her and then the others. They groaned but offered no resistance at all.

Zoe sighed and suggested I was right about it. "So when will I ever sleep all night again? You've been through this once. How much longer?"

I would have laughed but was too tired myself. "Another month or so and they'll be sleeping almost all night." I didn't add that I was hoping that would be so!

It was. We were finally able to lift-off on the December 1st, much to everyone's relief. Gone were the bags beneath their eyes. At least, now I could count on the crew to do their tasks at least half of the time. I arranged schedules so that someone was always on watch of the critical systems. This also gave everyone something to contribute that was valuable for us all. Teamwork. That's how Tesla explained our sudden shift of schedules and workloads.

The Billik globular cluster was quite distant from the Narsten Cluster, about fifty percent father than the Gorki Cluster was from Farthun-3, just above the central hub bulge. Also, the Kronos Gap had to be crossed, a vast tract of empty space fifty percent farther than the Gorki Cluster was from our starting point in the Narsten Cluster. True, there were some scattered stars in this substantial void and several black stars, as we discovered. We could not discount the possibility that some of these isolated stars might have planetary systems as well, even the binary star systems often did.

We had two ways we could traverse unknown, uncharted, un-coordinated space. The usual method was to travel along at sub-light speeds, searching carefully as we went, and also working out periodic hyperspace coordinates of each location. In this case, it would take us years to cross this distance. The Achtnag hyperspace coordinates were useless to us, since they had their own system of measurement. The second method was to use our instruments, and scan space ahead of us for several light-years. If there was nothing detectable at that location, we then could execute a one minute hyperspace jump, arriving at that new location. Once there, we repeated the process, over and over.

We anticipated having to make five thousand such micro-jumps to reach the cluster. Just the total time of the jumps themselves if done continuously would consume nearly four days. However, making the observations to guarantee it was save to make this next jump took considerable time. As we began to discover, the halo was quite old, resulting in a disproportionate number of dead or nearly dead stars, that is, very faint brown dwarfs, which are slowly cooling down, neutron stars detectable at certain radio frequencies, and the nastiest of all, black stars, completely dead, very small in diameter but super dense with massive gravity pulls. I feared the black stars the most. They were not visible except by gravity perturbations on other objects! If you can't even see them, flying along at any speed was exceedingly dangerous. One would have no warning at all, just an instantaneous, catastrophic collision. See why I was more than a little concerned? After our first few days of jumping, I estimated we would reach our destination in about six months! While I didn't tell the crew this, I rather welcomed the long duration. By the time we got there, the babies would be nearly ten months old and much easier to handle, allowing us more time to do our work.

Meanwhile, I focused on the "doll people." It struck me while I was lying on my side nursing little Donatella, or rather Isi. If these people had inhuman, doll-like bodies, then they did not have to eat three meals a day or even eat at all! They didn't even need to breathe, let alone handle bodily needs. While at the moment that sounded rather an envious situation, I duplicated what that could possibly be like and more importantly, what that implied about their worlds and civilizations: uninhabitable by us! A quick check with Isi and I found out that I was right.

Many of their worlds were considered uninhabitable by us humans. Either the air contained too little oxygen or would be toxic for us to breathe or the temperature was too hot or too cold. The doll people did not need air, food, water, or the narrow temperature range that we humans did. Their "playground" was therefore vastly larger than that of us humans!

So if we try to visit some of the Achtnag worlds, we would need to wear protective spacesuits? I asked Isi.

She replied — I guess I think of Isi as female because I keep seeing little Donatella here — *Oh! Well, yes! Yes, you would have to. I forgot about the extremely limited capabilities of these super-alive bodies. Our non-alive bodies function acceptable in temperatures from around a hundred degrees above absolute zero to around seven hundred degrees above it. If it goes higher, part of our exterior begins to melt. Not a problem, since we can just replace the damaged part — you know, screw on a new arm appendage, head ball, that sort of thing. Still, we don't like to work in such hot environments. It's annoying to have your body begin to melt while you are trying to do some work. Then again, while we can work out there in free space where the temperature is very close to absolute zero, it's not much fun. Our appendages tend to lock up on us. Even with the very lightest of lubricants, it's a pain.*

This gave me much to ponder, while my crew continued to plot, observe, and execute the minute-duration hyperspace jumps. I tried to imagine life on one of their spaceships. I correctly estimated that their life-support systems were minuscule compared to ours. Indeed, their life-support systems were little more than a space heater, which kept the internal temperature around the freezing point of water. No food, no breathable air, no water, but with tubs of replaceable body parts. I could see why their spaceships were so much smaller than ours were. We had to carry along mountains of excess baggage to stay alive, compared to them, as witnessed by our four attached Modules!

So just how was I supposed to meet them and learn about their culture? This was the problem I had to solve, while the crew worked on getting us safely across the vast Kronos Gap. Hence, I once more chatted with Isi about how we could do this.

Doli. We have a zoo world where we sometimes bring human and other life forms that need this kind of an environment to survive. Doli. Plus, that's where most of the Hakidon congregate. Oh, the Hakidon are those of us who are waiting for a chance to get these fantastic sensation-filled human bodies. That's what we call ourselves, the Hakidon. Chumani is the leader of our movement, though we're disliked by the rest of the Achtnag, who believe that we're abandoning them. Well, we are abandoning them, if we get a chance. Who wouldn't do that to obtain one of these incredible sensation-filled human bodies of yours? In fact, when Huyana and I found you, I swear every Hakidon begged to be a part of the twenty who joined us here. We heard there were even some battles over who would get this golden opportunity.

Isi went on, *You know that a scout ship is tagging along behind you, don't you?* I didn't, but decided not to reveal we didn't. She went on, *I can contact the two, and have them let Chumani know that we're coming, and let Chumani know about your proposition with the millions on Aquila Prime. This way, you would get a royal welcome, at least on Doli. Besides, then Chumani can protect you from the other Achtnag that will naturally dislike you providing these new bodies for the Hakidon.*

Such an arrangement would be wise, and I had Isi set it up. Plus, Isi promised to guide us to this Doli world once we reached the globular cluster. Now, I had to ponder if I had made the right decision. We were allying ourselves with a breakaway fraction of the Achtnag. Would that automatically make us the enemies of the mainstream doll people? I instinctively knew this was not the way to open up relations with a new people, but considering the alternatives, I didn't see any other way just yet. Hence, I continued to ponder this as the days and weeks slowly passed by.

As the months passed, I began to notice subtle changes in our babies. One morning when I returned to Danika and my bedroom to nurse Donatella again, I found Zorina, Nadia, and Mai chatting with her and with Rafe. All three had their shoes off and were wiggling their toes. Zorina was saying, "That's the way, Donatella. Wiggle, wiggle. See, you can do it too." The two babies were just getting the hang of controlling each toe. I could almost see their minds surveying their small bodies, figuring out how to move each part. Donatella was giggling too, enjoying her toes.

That's when I began to realize the babies were maturing somewhat faster than the average baby was. Further, as the months went by, I noticed as a group, they thought less and less about their former lifetimes as doll people, focusing on their new lives as human novas. I saw what Rafe had meant when she said that a being would rapidly forget their former life because all their possessions and spaces were gone. Their attention was now on all the new things in their new present time. I then wondered if these twenty-two would have forgotten their doll body lifetimes by the time that they were as old as Zorina and Nadia. I had a strong hunch that they would do just that. Again, this was something I found both intriguing and somehow key, though precisely what its significance was, I wasn't certain at this time.

I shouldn't fail to relate some other news we received from back home during these months. It isn't good news, though. The breakup of the Imperium was becoming ugly. Various worlds formed new, temporary alliances, in a mad, crazy grab for power and influence. Minor skirmishes, hardly worthy of being called wars, had broken out, primarily among the more densely populated hub worlds. By June, three new alliances had appeared, though no one would speculate on their likely duration: the Northern Hub Alliance, the Southern Hub Alliance, and the Western Hub Alliance. The eastern portion of the hub contained the worlds wiped out by the supernova and previous genetic bio agent wars. The remaining worlds in the eastern hub had been unable to formulate an alliance with each other for many reasons, mostly political and a profound distrust of their neighbor worlds.

Worse still, another two of the remaining eastern hub worlds had been attacked with this horrible genetic agent. This time, however, very few worlds even bothered to care about the billions of victims. Emperor Bino, working in conjunction with all the other Ataro Empire worlds, again launched a rescue operation. Aquila Prime again offered to accept all those who could be rescued. I also learned that Aquila Prime had now quadrupled its deep space transport fleet. Alexandra suggested that they had done this to be better able to help other terrorist victims, since the homo sapiens sapiens seemed determined to continue to commit genocide on their neighboring worlds. By June, Aquila Prime had added another million and a half to their population. Once more, Emperor Bino reported to us that most of these had been young people, up to and including Academy students and even a few recent graduates. He claimed this age group tended to survive the attack and adapt to their new lives better than older people.

One evening as we were dining together, Alexandra asked, "Why is it that the homo sapiens sapiens people have to unleash this awful genetic warfare on their neighboring worlds? I don't understand why one world would want to inflict such death on their neighbors. Do they hate each other that much?"

Tesla responded, "Well, from time to time, one group finds reasons to hate another group. That's always been the case throughout history, though Jana and Jovanna can speak to that better than I can. Still, I think it must take a totally insane person to wish to inflict such horrors, as this genetic bio agent, onto all the people of a world. It would be kinder just to nuke them or even unleash a toxic nerve gas. At least, the people would have a swift death. I just can't imagine the horrors of being helpless and slowly dying of starvation or thirst, unable to make use of the unlimited water from the faucets and all the food stores nearby. That has to be an awful way to go."

"Sadism or masochism then?" Alexandra asked. "Or just plain psychopathic or sociopathic?"

"Probably sociopath," Tesla replied. "Extreme antisocial attitudes and behavior. That would be my guess. Totally inhuman actions."

I think we were a bit surprised when Minta spoke up! "The nova don't fight wars or display antisocial behaviors. Perhaps, we're seeing human evolution at work."

"What do you mean?" Tesla asked, quite surprised and curious as well.

"The nova are much superior to ordinary homo sapiens sapiens. Does not evolution proceed to develop superior life

380

forms from lesser forms?" None of us could disagree with this argument.

"But we aren't superior, Minta," Tesla countered. "We're helpless without you HIFRs around." She then chuckled a little, "When we all had our arms, feet, and hair normal, I might suggest that our bodies were superior, since men could also bear children, sharing the workload. Besides, we've seen hermaphrodite men are nowhere near as aggressive as normal men can be."

"Hey, speak for yourself!" Len countered. Several other men agreed with him.

Jan spoke up, "I now have a deep and profound appreciation for what women have always endured, having babies, I mean. Still, we are wholly dependent on your kind, Minta."

She countered, "Yes, that's true, but still your nova bodies are nearly perfect in all other ways. We HIFRs have observed you now use your greatest gift, your minds, vastly more than the sapiens do theirs. Plus, your reproductive systems are truly geared towards an optimum survival of you nova. If you don't believe us HIFRs, then just look at how greatly the nova bodies are admired by the Achtnag, who have said that the nova bodies are the very best in the galaxy. Having arms is almost completely irrelevant."

Irrelevant? Well, that's not how most of us saw it, though I suspected Alexandra and Zoe felt that way, but then they knew no better, having never had them or until this exploration trip had never been around humans who did.

Tesla decided to follow up on one point that Minta made. "Optimum survival of nova? I know there are now quite a few millions of nova on Aquila Prime. But is that enough of a population to ensure diversity and long term survival of the nova?"

Our mathematician spoke up. Alexandra declared, "We are very close to the desired numbers. Based on mathematic models, we theorize with a diverse population of one hundred twenty million, Aquila Prime would have a sufficient population base that our continued survival would be guaranteed to a ninety-five percent chance. Of course, that doesn't allow for an outside war coming to our world and wiping us out. It does remove almost all chances of a mutant virus strain epidemic wiping us out. Things like that are what I mean. Wars of men cannot be predicted, not yet anyway."

"Wow. So how close are you now — to achieving that magic number?" Tesla asked.

"Close. We are at one hundred seventeen million, six hundred thousand nova, approximately," Minta replied. "I haven't received the latest birth numbers for the past month yet."

Not long after our discussion, we heard from Emperor Bino that there had been yet another hub world attacked with the terrible genetic bio agent! Once again, it was in the eastern portion, the no-man's land of worlds. As June approached, we heard that again, Aquila Prime accepted all those who could be rescued and roughly, another million nova had been added to their numbers. I recalled Minta's numbers and thought to myself one hundred eighteen million. Only two million to go. I had the nagging thought that there might be two more worlds that would be attacked with this hideous genocide weapon. This seemed awfully suspicious to me. But then there were plenty of others who were getting rich off the salvage rights. Still. . .

Chapter 18 First Contact

June 6, 1380 brought us into very close proximity to the globular cluster called Billik, a ball of hundreds of thousands of stars. As the Eagle's Seed began to enter the edge of the cluster, I wondered just how many worlds these Achtnag occupied and how widespread their civilization was. Well, I hoped I soon would find out.

"Ships are monitoring us," Anya relayed her warning to me from her comm center station, where she monitored hundreds of frequencies and our long range sensors. "This time, they are not cloaked, but they are staying their distance. Bringing a fuzzy image of one up on the screens, everyone. Have a look," she explained, though Eos actually handled the controls for her.

I glanced at my small monitor in the pilot's position. There was another of the familiar saucer shaped ships, rather like two saucers one upside down over the other one. Huyana relayed directions to Doli to Danika, who had Callisto enter our new course.

Who is daring to enter Achtnag Space without permission? A voice barked hostilely in all our heads, rather like a ship-wide, telepathic broadcast.

I sent back in the rough direction I thought the message had come, *Captain Nia Elain Compton-Jereni with the Ataro Empire Deep Space Exploration Ship, Eagle's Seed. We come in peace and seek only to meet your people and establish friendly relations. We're from the galactic disk. We're heading to Doli.*

I waited. Would they accept us? Danika said to Callisto, "Be ready to get our shields up in a hurry. Stay alert!" Minutes passed. I hated awkward silences, but then I began to realize that perhaps our babies were holding their own private telepathic chat with whoever was challenging us. Suddenly, two dozen more of their saucer ships winked into visibility, dropping their cloaking energies I guessed. We were more or less entirely surrounded by twenty-five ships. They had not yet attempted to fire upon us, so I took that as a positive sign. Still, I hated the silence. I found myself thinking, come on. Talk to me! Then, it dawned on me that on this first contact situation, a struggle with an unknown language would not happen, as it did on all other first contact situations. With telepathy, concepts and ideas were exchanged, independent of any language.

Proceed. Do not attempt to deviate from the flight path. That voice appeared in my mind once more. This time, the person didn't send it to everyone on the ship, only me. I relayed the response to my crew, and we continued onwards with our mini-hyperspace jumps.

A few hours later, I was sent, *This is ridiculous. We'll tractor your ship to Doli now. Shut down your engines and prepare to be tractored.* Okay, I had to laugh. I admit our progress was painstakingly slow, but it sure was faster than sub-light speeds. Obviously, these Achtnag people were not as patient as we were. A couple of minutes later, a large saucer zipped in close to us, and we felt the tug of the tractor beam. Then came the black void of hyperspace, as we jumped along with our towing ship.

Hans called out over the intercom, "Hey, this will be the fast way to get the proper coordinates for this Doli world. Thanks. Saves us days, captain." I laughed again.

Donatella sent me, *Oh, I forgot to tell you that Doli is sort of an artificial world. We Achtnag moved it here from another sun. We keep specimens of a large number of other worlds here so we can study them and just look at them.*

Great! We were going to an alien zoo, but were we going to join the animals on display? My heart skipped a beat for a second when I thought that. No, we still had our *mentales* gifts, which ought to help get us out of any tight situation.

Six hours later, we dropped out of hyperspace and proceeded on at sub-light speeds. Ahead, we spotted a main sequence yellow sun and guessed correctly that Doli was orbiting this sun. Barely an hour later, we watched as a blue-green planet grew steadily larger on our monitors. We made planet-fall late on June 15, 1370.

Power up and follow us down. Please do not deviate

from our path. Land next to our ship, the voice sent me. I complied, issuing the orders to power up our sub-light engines. The tractor beam let go of us, and I had Athena follow the saucer ship that had been towing us, hoping it was the right one to follow. If it wasn't, I assumed the voice would let me know rather quickly.

It was near dusk as we touched down at a rather large spaceport. There were dozens of the saucer shaped spaceships on the ground. They varied considerably in size. Two were as large as one of our battleships! Most were substantially smaller though. *Your representatives may disembark now and meet with Commander Chumani, leader of the Hakidon, Achtnag.*

I chose Tesla and Martina to accompany me off the ship. Apparently, these doll people already knew the specifics of the Eagle's Seed, because conveniently they had an elevator platform waiting for us just outside the forward hatch. Of course, Athena, Damali, and Delia accompanied us three off the ship. I wore my favorite red satin gown and the others wore similar gowns, blue and brown respectively. The HIFRs wore their usual rather plain day dresses.

We couldn't see much while on the elevator, but the air smelled fresh with a slightly metallic odor in it. Well, we were at a spaceport, I thought. Once the elevator reached the tarmac and we carefully stepped off, our hosts came walking out of a Quonset hut type of building, made from various resins. Although it looked like steel, I wasn't fooled this time. We got our first look at the Achtnag, and they, us.

They towered over us, ten feet tall. Three greeted us. Commander Chumani was obvious. It wore what appeared to be a military uniform. Actually, they had no clothes. Rather, they had their bodies painted to resemble clothing. Their appendages, that is, arms and legs if they could be called that, were smooth and did resemble ours, but they looked like they were made from some sort of plastics or similar synthetics. Their heads were painted and very much resembled a child's doll! Even their eyes, noses, and mouths were simply painted on accessories. I wondered how they could perceive anything, but they certainly did.

Welcome to Doli, esteemed nova! Even your apparel is most sensuous! Simply amazing. Huyana and Isi have not exaggerated in the slightest. You nova have the very best bodies in the galaxy! Isi has told me of this planet of yours where we may inhabit as many baby nova bodies as we desire. I can't tell you how wonderful this is for all we Hakidon! Oh, I am Commander Chumani.

I'm Captain Nia Elain Compton-Jereni of the deep space exploration ship, the Eagle's Seed. I'm very pleased to be here and meet the Achtnag in person. I've had a number of First Contact events, but this one is the easiest. Telepathy certainly makes communication truly simple. This is Tesla and Martina. The other three are our HIFRs who assist us, since we lack arm appendages.

Welcome Tesla, Martina. Yes, Isi told us about them. We do find it rather hard to believe you cannot simply screw on replacement limbs, but then we know so little about living bodies. Isi also told us you usually eat and sleep around this time of day. Is this true? If so, we can meet in the Quonset hut when the sun rises.

Isi is correct. It's getting late for us. Would it be acceptable if we met tomorrow morning?

Yes of course. I would like to discuss this world of nova with you and your suggestion that we could make a trade for these nova baby bodies there. After that, I have arranged for a tour of Doli for you. Of course, the High Council of Achtnag will likely drop by in a few days to see you. We discourage visitors, you see. However, you've nothing to fear. I've granted you permission to visit Doli, and the High Council of Achtnag is honor bound to honor it. Still, they may seem hostile towards you nova. Just know that many of us do not share their feelings on this matter.

We chatted a bit and returned to our ship for supper and sleep. My big decision was just who would I allow to join us tomorrow. I didn't want to leave the ship empty with only our babies onboard, nor did I want to leave it with no one who could pilot it either. Too risky, promise or no promise. Yet here was a truly alien race, and I suspected many wanted to go with me tomorrow. Anya to the rescue. Over supper, she explained to me, "I know we all can't go with you tomorrow, so I've rigged up these portable video devices you can fasten to your gowns. Then, the rest of us can see and hear what it is that you are seeing and hearing. Cool, eh?"

I laughed. "Yes, excellent thinking, Anya. I swear you can build a comm center from spare parts!" She laughed too, but nodded to Eos who had actually done the work under her guidance. This unexpected detail made my task easier. Besides Tesla and Martina, I asked Alexandra, Zarita, and Len to come with us. If there were specific Aquila Prime questions, I felt Alexandra could best speak for her world. I wanted Zarita and her power crystals with us, just as a safety precaution. Len could examine the construction materials and verify my hunch that much was composed of resins.

As I drifted to sleep, I sensed Chumani touching or feeling my body via its control centers. She was just extracting sensations so I allowed it. I could also sense her immense admiration for my body, and just how badly she desired to experience its numerous sensations. Then, I fell asleep, suspecting that Chumani and Isi had a lot to discuss while we slept. I was right. Chumani now knew everything that Isi had learned thus far. Well, we were not keeping any secrets.

The next morning we six met with Chumani in an office in the Quonset hut. Chumani wasted no time. *So what is the nova population of this Aquila Prime world? Does every nova have their own HIFR as you do?*

I nodded to Alexandra, but realized she didn't have telepathy. I hastily explained this to Chumani. *That's okay, Alexandra. Just think your replies and I'll pick them up,* Chumani sent, taking her a bit by surprise. I eaves dropped.

Oh. Okay. We have one hundred and eighteen million nova now. More are born every day, at least a thousand I think. Of course, every nova has their own HIFR. They are given theirs when they are born and stay with them for their whole lives. Minta here has been with me as long as I can remember. She is very good.

Ideal. No, fantastically ideal. Nia Elain, there are three thousand six hundred fifty-three of we Hakidon who want to participate just as soon as possible! We'll follow you back in our ships and then donate them to your people, as we acquire these fabulous nova bodies. Will that be acceptable?

Could one of your knowledgeable technicians also show us how they work? Perhaps the theory behind them? I asked.

Certainly.

Then we have a deal. However, we do have one more goal on our exploration mission to handle before we can head back to Aquila Prime.

Yes, Isi told me of this desire of yours to meet the ghosts of the Bori Cluster. Never has anyone embarked on such a tremendously dangerous mission. I fear if you go there, then we'll never see you again. Ghosts are like that. Perhaps, we could come to another arrangement. I don't want to lose this incredible opportunity with the nova.

I thought quickly. *Okay, I see your point. We don't want to lose this opportunity to establish good relations with your people either. I'll tell you what we can do. I can leave Alexandra and her mate Zarita here with you, as long as they can have food, water, shelter — the things they need to survive — while we continue with our mission. If we fail to return, then Alexandra and Zarita can lead your people to Aquila Prime in my place.*

The relief was plainly obvious, though from the doll face, one couldn't see any change of expression. Naturally not, since all the features were merely painted onto the head. *That would be ideal. To speed your trip along, I'll send one of our ships to lead you there directly, but as I understand it, there is a difficulty in our different sets of hyperspace coordinates. Perhaps, our mathematicians can work with yours to resolve them.*

That would be Alexandra here and Hans.

I'll go back and help Hans right now, if that'll make our mission go lots faster, Alexandra suggested. I accepted her offer and began to wonder just how homesick she was. I had forgotten about that aspect with her, Jan, Zoe, and probably to a lesser extent the Cho family. I made a mental note to check on this later on.

Shortly, another doll joined us and followed Alexandra

388

and Minta back to the Eagle's Seed. With our agreement made, Chumani sent, *Come. I've prepared a special shuttle we can take which is suitable for your kind. It has warmth and good air.* Thus, the tour of their "zoo" began.

Imagine one of their transport saucer models with its top saucer removed and you'll have a good picture of their special vehicle. It was open to the air and sky. There were twenty passenger seats, all facing outward so you could see a very wide panorama. Chumani took the driver's seat located in the center of the saucer. I was amazed as we lifted off — totally silent! Now, I was convinced their engines were somehow electro-magnetic in nature.

First, here is the Menagerie. Each exhibit has been carefully constructed using native plants to compliment the animals. Of course, one of we Achtnag is currently operating the animal's body, both for fun and to explain the creature to visitors. Here is the Bladder Beast of Koti. When I hover, the Achtnag operating this huge hairy mammal will tell you about it. Many of us Hakidon take turns operating these animal bodies. In the case of the lizard men, the Hadu, such is necessary because if left unmonitored, the Hadu would hunt down and eat all of the other animals in the Menagerie. She hovered and indeed another voice appeared in our heads, describing in detail this plant-eating mammoth of a beast.

We saw and learned about dozens of strange and unusual animals and some related plants before we got to the Hadu exhibit. Here, we had our first look at a pair of live lizard men. They were rather like many other lizards found on numerous worlds, except for their scale. When they stood up on their hind legs, well-balanced by their very long tails, their heads were over ten feet high. Their teeth looked wicked, capable of crushing muscle and bone easily. Their native worlds were arid, and they didn't survive too well in wet, humid locales, or so the Achtnag who occupied one of the two Hadu explained to us. They were fierce fighters at the top of their world's food chain.

With the interesting Menagerie tour over, Chumani explained, *We Hakidon love excitement and games. We are in time to watch the Sled Races. Right now, the contestants are all carrying their special sleds up to the top of yonder mountain. We've covered the mountainside with a foot of snow. The objective is to cross that yellow finish line here at the base of the mountain in the fastest time. Of course, that alone makes things boring. So each of the sleds has its steering connected to the master computer. At some random point while the contestant is flying down the course, the computer will activate some random steering alteration, which the contestant must then overcome. It's always exciting, but the best times usually come from the run were the computer controlled malfunction occurs shortly after the sled begins its downward plunge. Of course, if it occurs at the very end of the run, often the contestant isn't even able to cross the finish line. It's always a whole lot of fun to participate. Great sensations. Here comes the first one now.*

A ten-foot doll was sitting on a wagon-like sled with wooden runners. Its feet controlled a steering runner attached to the rear. Almost all the doll's huge body was exposed to the winds. We watched as his sled began its descent going down the mountain's side, where at its top, the slope was at least sixty degrees, maybe more. The sled picked up speed extremely rapidly. At various locations on the downslope, the sled had to turn to avoid giant boulders, trees, and gravel areas not covered in snow. Later, Hans estimated their downhill speeds exceeded three hundred miles per hour, blazing fast. I couldn't imagine how they could possibly react in time to control the sleds, ignoring the random steering malfunctions!

This first sled reached a point where it needed to veer to the right to follow the snow trail. Instead, the sled veered sharply to the left, heading for a cliff! I watched and gasped as the sled and doll went airborne! While in the air, the doll managed to get his sled's orientation straightened out so that it landed with its runners on the snow once more. However, the runners couldn't withstand the crash and simply crumpled up. The sled and doll went rolling head over heels down the slope. I watched as the doll's arms flew off, followed by its legs. I couldn't imagine the pain that the doll must be in. We gasped.

Not to worry. Happens all the time. Part of the

exhilaration of the run, Chumani sent. We watched as another doll moved swiftly to the damaged one and helped re-fasten its appendages onto its torso. A bit later, the two moved off the course as though nothing happened. *He's upset because he couldn't cross the finish line, so he's going to try it again.*

We watched as several others wipe out at close to three hundred miles per hour. Every one of them didn't seem to be harmed by their sometimes disastrous crash landings, not even when their heads popped off. Chumani explained, *We have an idiomatic saying, don't do such and such or you'll "pop your head." Get it?* We did, unfortunately.

After watching the Sled Race, Chumani took us to a giant racetrack, whose dirt track was at least five miles long. Reviewing stands were located at periodic intervals and were now packed with Achtnags watching the Shuttle Race. *Here, we pit the best pilots with the fastest, best race cars our technology can manufacture.* We saw five teams painted in solid colors: red, yellow, blue, green, and brown. Those were the team's names, Chumani explained. Each team had a rocket car driver who sat inside the vehicle, which had four very wide tires on the ground. Behind him was a rocket or jet type engine. We were just in time for the start of the race.

Often, we place small wagers on who will be victorious in the race. Team Red has won more races than all the others combined, so if you want to bet, bet on Red. Ayasha is their driver. No one has his skill behind the wheel. His Red Car is the fastest on the track, but several other teams have been working on getting their rocket cars to exceed Red's, but their problem is finding a driver who can handle that speed without wiping out. Today, I'm told, Team Yellow is trying out a new driver, Honovi. While their Yellow Car is now supposed to be as fast as Team Red's, the question is can this Honovi handle that speed? We'll soon see. They're off!

Five rocket cars burst into action. I could not imagine the g-force acceleration the drivers had on them, but it must have been incredible! Zero to six hundred miles per hour in just a few seconds! I blinked and almost lost sight of the car's locations! At this speed, the curvy, winding oval track would be flying by the drivers at an unbelievable rate. How could anyone possibly react fast enough?

I soon had my answer. The Brown Car missed a turn by a hair. His car flew off the track, flying through the air straight at one of the packed reviewing stands! My god. The carnage I expected to see. However, unknown to us, there was a force shield protecting the spectators and the car and driver hit that shield at close to six hundred miles per hour. The shield did absorb some of the impact, visibly dimpling in. However, the poor driver's head and appendages all went flying off in different directions! I figured that was the end of that doll.

No. Several members of the Team Brown raced to the scene. Within a few minutes, the driver's head and appendages were back in place, though he now limped and could barely walk. Chumani said, *Well, he'll have to report to the maintenance shed and get two new legs, but can you imagine the sensations, the exhilaration that he felt during that crash? Incredible to experience! Just fantastic. Too bad that I don't have fast enough reactions to drive one of those rocket cars. I'd love to feel what that driver did.*

It took me several seconds to relocate the four remaining racers, more of a blur than much else. Green and Blue also wiped out, leaving Yellow and Red vying each other. As they headed around the track on the last lap of the race, they were side by side, as near as I could tell. Then, it was over and both cars braked at a terrific deceleration rate. Yellow had actually won. Even from where we hovered, in my mind, I could hear the appreciation of the throng of Achtnag spectators and the exhilaration of Hovoni, who was jumping up and down beside his car in his excitement. The Team Red driver gave him a fist and stomped off the race track.

Well, that sure was unexpected! Chumani exclaimed. *Guess you were wise not to have placed a small wager today.*

Isn't anyone get killed in these races? I asked the obvious.

Oh, *don't be silly. Achtnag never die. Our bodies do sometimes get very damaged. If it's just an arm, leg, or head, we pop on replacements and get repainted. If the torso is destroyed, then it's simpler just to pick up a completely new body. Our bodies are really indestructible. Obtaining wonderful sensations, though, is the most difficult challenge that we face.*

So you don't have babies, new Achtnag born into your civilization?

No, not like you nova do. However, see that body there? Everyone has an unoccupied body on display around their hut. From time to time, new spiritual beings come by and pick up one of our bodies. Of course, then we give them a thorough introduction to our society, welcoming them with open arms.

New beings? Where do they come from? This was a very intriguing notion. I've never considered that there could be new immortal spiritual beings coming into existence.

Who knows? Surely not I. They just do. Not very often mind you, but there are perhaps a dozen new arrivals in the cluster each year. Oh, I see the sun is going down. I should return you to your ship now so you can feed and sleep your bodies.

As we made our slow, careful walk back to our ship, Athena said, "I would really like to try my hand driving one of those rocket cars. I believe my reactions are sufficient to handle it, but alas, I dare not. I must be here to take care of your needs and those of Donatella. We don't have any repair facilities onboard if I should make a mistake."

"Thanks Athena. I do need your assistance," I replied, thankful she'd rejected such a notion! Back onboard, the two races occupied the table talk over dinner. I also realized, as did Tesla and Martina, that if these Achtnag were warlike, we probably had no weapons with which to stop them. They were basically indestructible. Fortunately, they were anything but warlike. Later, I relayed this day's observations to Rafe back on Ashford-5. She was keenly interested in their sense of ethics and the apparent arrivals of new spiritual beings. She insisted that I explore both more fully, if I could find a way to do so.

The ethics question was straightforward. Listen and observe. I figured that would be easy enough to do, particularly when I would be meeting the Achtnag who were not particularly enamored with our appearance, let alone about to take thousands of their people back with us. So I figured that I'd get a good feeling about their ethics. I had no clues about their morals if they had any such things. No, this business of new immortal spiritual beings appearing was altogether another matter entirely, one on which I had no idea of how to proceed.

True, thanks to Basic Therapy, I know for certain I'm a spiritual being, seemingly immortal as far as I've discovered to date. Yes, I had a number of human bodies, following a cycle of birth, growth, slow decay, and death, only to begin it all over again. I know I've done this at least five times in the past. I suspect there were more, since few of them seemed to connect down to the next lifetime. Of course, Rafe had said that there were free beings who were watching over Ashford-5, goddesses might be a better term, but I had no firsthand knowledge of them. No, the ghost-like Ceri came the closest in my imagination to free spiritual beings, though they seemed to have some kind of energy bodies, hard to see of course. I wrestled with the problem of just how was I supposed to perceive a pure spiritual being, one who had no body at all. I had no answer and forgot about it for now.

The next day the elders of the Achtnag arrived, Nadie and Nahimana. Both of their paint jobs gave them the appearance of wearing grey robes, at least when they stood still, legs together. Beyond that, they looked much like all the others we'd seen. There wasn't much individuality from Achtnag to Achtnag, save for the paint jobs. They were waiting for us in the Quonset hut, sitting formally around Chumani's table. Hence, they got a close view of us and the difficulties we had walking and getting seated. At first, they paid more attention to our HIFRs than us. After the formal introductions, one of them spoke. Since nothing moved on their faces, it was difficult for me to ascertain who was speaking to us.

This is a most unusual occasion. We don't usually allow humanoids to mingle with us. Chumani tells us that you are from worlds in the galactic disk far below us.

Might I ask why you don't allow us to mingle? I more or less interrupted either Nadie or Nahimana.

It should be rather obvious to you by now. Chumani

told us you witnessed a few of our games yesterday. Your humanoid bodies are terribly easy to damage or cause irreparable damage to or even be exterminated. It is nearly impossible for such to occur to us Achtnags. We are most fearful of accidently damaging one of your humanoid bodies while you are among us. What would be nothing to one of us could well kill your body. That would be most dishonorable for us. It is better we don't take such risks. Few of us know the limitations of such frail bodies. In our enthusiasm, we could easily harm you quite by accident.

Ah, excellent point. I hadn't thought of that. Chumani has taken very good care of us. You are right, our bodies cannot withstand the forces that yours can. We saw that yesterday in the races, I replied.

Indeed. We have mostly come today to try to talk Chumani and the other Hakidon out of doing this, going down to the disk and taking some of the humanoid nova bodies. Chumani, their bodies are more like a vicious trap.

But they have the most fantastic sensations imaginable, Nahimana. Here, we have to go six hundred miles an hour in a flimsy rocket sled to get the tiniest sense of sensation. Yes, these bodies are indestructible, but mega-boring! Chumani countered.

Have you noticed already Isi and Huyana are beginning to forget about us? If you do this, you'll become trapped by the very sensation that you so desire. Their bodies are frail and have to eat and sleep. They are easily damaged and have such short lifetimes, Nahimana replied.

There is always a price to be paid, always a trade-off. Look, we're bored out of our minds here, Nahimana. So bored that many of us are doing foolish things — the computer controlled sleds that randomly go wildly out of control, for example. Even I'm not that foolish, just to get a new, unexpected sensation. You know that. After six hundred years of helping to make more body parts, building Quonset huts, ships and such, I'm so utterly bored that I can't stand it any longer. None of us Hakidon can. Personally, I can't see how you can stand it either; you've been around over a thousand years, Nahimana.

And so shall I be here for another thousand years, Chumani. I'm free and shall remain so. Know this, then, Chumani, if you and the other Hakidon do this, there is no turning back. Once you inhabit one of those nova bodies, you'll find yourselves addicted to the sensations of them. You'll forget us and what true freedom is even like. What will you do when your new short-lived nova body dies? Have you thought about that?

I spoke up. *I can answer that one. We too are immortal spiritual beings. When one of our bodies dies, we then pick up a new baby nova body and have a new lifetime. However, some few of us now realize this and are working on regaining our native abilities.*

Ah. That is very apparent to us, and is one reason Nadie and I chose to meet with you personally. Our ships have traveled widely here in the halo and encountered many humanoid species, some better than others. None of the beings inhabiting them has ever been so easily able to communicate with us, as we are doing now. No, until now, not one has had what your people call telepathy. So indeed, we are impressed. Perhaps, your nova are beginning to recover all that has been lost to you. I certainly hope that is so.

Well, it is only a few of us on one world who have. I decided to be honest with it. *I think there are thousands of us now, and we are working with more to regain lost abilities. Give us time and we may fully recover.* I could not help but think of Rafe's Advanced Therapy, which I now wished I already had. *That's why we were sent on this long exploration trip. We have the best chance of handling what we discover here in the halo.*

Ah, that is good. But tell me, are you really considering journeying into the Ceri space, the domain of the ghost people?

Yes. Some of us on my ship have met some long lost Ceri down in the galactic disk. We would like to tell the Ceri about them and what they did to save our world, I replied truthfully.

Even more impressive. Humanoids usually cannot

even perceive the Ceri. We occasionally spot a few Ceri hanging around our worlds, but we discourage them from staying. Be very careful around them. They can completely disable our bodies in an instant. Of course, if we can get the disabled Achtnag to a repair facility, we can issue them a new body. They literally melt our bodies, fusing all of the parts and joints into one immobile mass. Nasty indeed. So if they can immobilize us in an instant, they could even more easily extinguish the life from your frail bodies. Be very careful around these Ceri, Nia Elain, very, very careful.

We have to be, I replied. We chatted about lighter subjects, and I realized they had said what was important and were now being polite with us. A bit later, they dismissed us, allowing us to have lunch. That was the last we saw of their leaders. However, I'd seen enough to be able to say two key things about the Achtnag. First, they were quite powerful as a people, extremely able beings, far beyond us humans. Second, they were quite ethical. With the power they possessed, they were being equally responsible. I made a note to discuss this with our two queens back on Ashford-5 when we returned. Ataro queens believed that great powers must be tempered with great physical limitations so as not to abuse that power. The Achtnag seemed to be just the opposite. I also began to wonder if our human bodies really were trapping us spiritual beings as Nahimana suggested. I knew I needed some lengthy discussions with Rafe as well as our queens. But this would have to wait for a time yet.

I focused on the next leg, making contact with the Ceri. At least, I didn't first have to find them, thanks to Chumani and the other like-minded Achtnag. Just how fast we could find the Ceri worlds rested on Alexandra and Hans, who were working with one of Chumani's people trying to convert hyperspace coordinates from their units into ours. I knew the distance from here to their Bori Cluster was less than half of that from the Narsten Cluster to here, the Billik Cluster. It would take us months of executing our safe "minute" hops. Yet, if they could work out the coordinates and if they were right and we didn't land in the middle of a star, then the time would be perhaps half a day, a drastic reduction. Of course, the

Achtnag had a vested interest in getting us there and back as quickly as possible so we could then take them to Aquila Prime. Similarly, I knew Hans, Dao, Thomas, and Diego were equally keen to have a good long look inside their fancy saucer-shaped spaceships.

Already, Zoe, Dylan, and Anwyn had made some spectroscopic observations of some of the stars in the Bori Cluster and determined the general age of the cluster as near the time of the formation of the entire galaxy itself, making all these visible stars very ancient. That also meant, assuming proportional numbers of different stellar masses for the original stars here as we had in the disk, we expected an alarming number of black stars and neutron stars in the cluster. In fact, we had already detected a hundred percent more of these in the so-called Kronos Gap than in our home disk, making travel far more dangerous. My astronomers now were suggesting the percentage within the Bori Cluster would run far higher, closer to three hundred percent more brown stars, neutron stars, and black stars.

Naturally, once they had the conversions worked out, before I would trust them, I insisted on some basic tests. In fact, as we executed each test, I sensed all the crew was flinching as well, tensed up as though we were about to smash into something deadly. As soon as the test ended, I felt relief coming from many minds.

Okay, I too was quite tense, as we methodically took a week to run through all of the tests that we could devise to prove to ourselves that the hyperspace coordinate conversion was accurate. The last day of the test, I felt very nauseous and stopped by Doctor Leann's quarters to get something for my stomach. I noticed she was a little on edge. Heck, I think we all were. I should point out that this is a very important detail and it's relevance will become clear in a moment.

Doctor Leann hastily put me into her medical machine. Okay, Athena got me into it, while Kore actually operated the controls under Leann's directions, though she hardly needed to tell her HIFR anything. A few minutes later, Doctor Leann began laughing. "You don't have the flu or nervousness, Nia Elain. You are pregnant again."

"Oh crap. Morning sickness again?" I replied dumbfounded. I'd not expected this. Well, I ought to have! Recently, I'd not paid much attention to this aspect of my anatomy, merely taking and giving comfort to my Danika. At least, I had the presence of mind to add, "Best check on everyone else before we make the jump into the Bori Cluster. I ought to know the physical state of my crew. So do I get a pill now?" Doctor Leann, or rather, Kore gave me a pill that settled my stomach, and I headed to the pilot's seat, somewhat pleased to tell Danika that once more, we were adding to our family.

"Oh. That's wonderful, dear!" Danika gushed and pushed her body into mine, our best way to hug. Then, we went down the checklist before executing the last of the hyperspace tests. A couple of hours later, everyone on the ship relaxed. The coordinate conversion had passed all the simple tests that Hans and Alexandra could devise, which meant now it was time to take the plunge and head for the Bori Cluster and the Ceri. As I was thinking about making the announcement that we'd do it first thing in the morning, Leann sent, *Nia Elain, report to the med lab please.*

When I stepped in, Doctor Leann looked up from her monitor. Kore had finished entering the last patient's data for her. "Oh here you are. I've checked up on everyone as ordered. This is just plain crazy, but we're all pregnant again, captain, all twenty-two of us. I checked with some of our 'babies,' but they claim that this time, they had nothing to do with it."

I sat down. "All of us? Again?" Then, it struck me. No one had any real fears flying around the spiral arm. Hyperspace travel there was normal and routine, had been for at least a millennia, about as dangerous as going for a walk around the block. Our travel up to Farthun-3 was mostly routine, even the hop up to the Narsten Cluster. However, our long traversal of the Kronos Gap and the discovery of vastly more numerous brown stars, neutron stars, and deadly black stars had instilled a subtle fear of space travel. More significantly, when our astronomers pointed out to everyone that the frequency of these three objects in and around the Bori Cluster was three times what they were down in the disk, we all had an unspoken reaction to the news. For the first time since we departed on this long exploration trip, reactively we felt there really was a chance we just might not make it, that we might not survive. Visions of the Eagle's Seed suddenly hitting a black star and instant death, all without the slightest warning, left us with a very real possibility that we might not survive.

Right there, I had a flash of insight. If one discovers he or she might not survive, then the natural urge is to try to survive through your progeny, your children, your future generation, sex, to be blunt. It was suddenly obvious to me. We all had an unspoken realization that we might not survive an encounter with an unsuspected black star. Reactively, we then were trying to survive into the future via our progeny, our children, by making future bodies! We were ensuring an abundance of future bodies for ourselves. Hence, we all got pregnant again. What surprised me and the other *mentales* gifted onboard is that with our gifts, we usually had total control over our fertility and reproduction. However, this unspoken computation that we might not survive and thus had to try to survive via future generations had temporarily blinded us. I realized that I'd simply "forgotten" about such precautions after sleeping with Danika.

I relayed my discovery to Rafe back on Ashford-5. She thought my observation and insight was a very key and important one. That made me feel a bit better about the situation.

Hers was one of several secure calls I made that afternoon, one of which was to let Emperor Bino know the date we were officially heading into the Bori Cluster in search of the Ceri. The late afternoon group meeting was filled with embarrassed giggles along with many happy faces as well. I also realized I had been miss-interpreting homesickness with morning sickness in several of my crew. Next March would become another big baby month. By mutual agreement, we delayed the start of our Ceri excursion until July 1. None of us wanted to tackle this big unknown while nauseous.

Chapter 19 The Ceri

On July 1, 1380 at 9:00 a.m., I gave the order to engage our hyperspace jump, and Danika executed it, well actually, Callisto did the button pushing. We'd both triple checked the entered coordinates, leaving nothing to chance. We'd also said our farewells to Zarita and Alexandra, who were remaining behind with Chumani in case we never made it back. In that case, the two would lead the many Achtnag back to Aquila Prime in our place. The ship vibrated slightly, as the star-filled sky vanished, replaced by the black void of hyperspace. So far so good, but we all knew the real danger would happen when we dropped out of hyperspace somewhere within the Bori Cluster. If the coordinates were off or other objects had moved in space, we could well reappear within a black star or such.

If we did, Hans and Zoe explained we would in all likelihood not even be aware of it before we were all dead. "We'll be instantaneously dead," Hans suggested.

Zoe added, "Or else we will find ourselves being pulled hard into one and have only seconds to respond, if that would do any good."

Based on their predictions of mass destruction, I took another precaution. I had the return coordinates for Chumani's world entered into the nav system. The instant we dropped out of hyperspace, those coordinates would be ready for a fast getaway. Callisto said she could activate another jump in two seconds. I had no choice but to put my faith in the robot.

Over the intercom, I announced, "Okay, we are officially on our way. We drop out in eighteen hours seven minutes. Free time for everyone, but if you want something to do, we ought to go over our checklists again, since there will not be time once we get there." Busy work takes minds off worrying over our fate. Still, I sensed that old nervousness coming from nearly everyone. Further, with the sole exception of Zoe, I felt the return of a feeling of helplessness in everyone onboard, myself included, but to varying degrees. Still, most attempted to work, using their HIFRs to help them go down the checklists once more, verifying all was ship-shape.

I admit I was on pins and needles as the hyperspace clock counted down the seconds until we dropped out into the normal space of the Bori Custer with its estimated two hundred thousand suns, located about thirty-five thousand light-years above the galactic central bulge, the hub. Three-two-one. The black void gave way to the sudden appearance of a zillion stars, a huge sphere all around us, nearly obscuring the magnificent view of the spiral arms far below us. We weren't dead. That was my first thought. That I was still breathing and thinking meant we hadn't appeared inside a dead star. That was something.

As fast as possible, our astronomers began checking their instruments. Zoe, Jan, Dylan, and Anwyn had a two-fold task that I did not envy. As fast as possible, they had to ascertain our precise location, no small feat since we had never been inside the Bori Cluster before. They also had to discover if we were in any immediate danger of being sucked into a dead or dying star, having appeared too close to one.

Dylan called out, "Hard to port. Full speed. We are too close to a brown dwarf!" I complied or rather Athena did. I spoke a silent curse at my helplessness. An hour later, the astronomers confirmed our location as best they could, and that we had avoided the gravity pull. We had made it safely this far. Now came the hard part: locating the Ceri worlds and opening up a dialog with them. Emperor Bino's fondest wish was somehow to get them to help ensure the survival of the Ataro Empire, particularly acute now that the Imperium crumbled.

"Okay, start looking for inhabitable worlds," I ordered my crew.

"But the Ceri don't need food and water like we do," Tesla complained.

Anya added, "She's right. They have energy bodies and don't need the same things as we do. So where do we look?"

"I suppose they reside on planets," I replied. "Find me stars with planets." With over two hundred thousand suns to observe, I knew this would take some time and keep them all quite busy, well their HIFRs anyway.

Around noon the next day, the Ceri found us, long before we found them. Suddenly and without any warning, Zoe cried out, "Black star dead ahead of us! Pull back! Pull back!" Out of nowhere, a dead star had appeared dead ahead. I had Athena reverse thrust and the Eagle's Seed back backing away from the serious threat.

While I was wondering how they could have missed it, Hans yelled. "Hard to port! There is another black star coming up at our rear! Hard to port!"

Once more, Athena and I changed direction and tried to increase speed to get away from these super dense, super massive, but tiny black balls, the densest matter we knew of in the universe. "Hard to starboard! Another black star is off to our left!" Anwyn yelled into the intercom. I wanted to say, well, make up your minds, but didn't, focusing on trying to change course yet again.

We had no more than gotten going again to our right when Jan screamed, "No, dive! Dive. There's a black star to our right, gaining on us! Down, down."

This time, Athena didn't wait for my order, but frantically took us down, applying a lot of sub-light thrust. She'd just gotten us moving, when Dylan yelled, "No! Up! Up! There's another one directly below us! Go up!"

As the ship lurched upwards, I had a sinking feeling in my stomach. Just how had we missed the presence of five black stars so darn close to each other? Normally, my crew always gave us many hours of advanced warnings. Besides, we had never gotten this close to one before. Hence, I wasn't surprise to hear Zoe calling out, "Wait! There's a black star above us too! Oh shit!"

"Halt the ship. Dead in space," I said to Athena. "Callisto, be ready to activate our hyperspace jump. Bring up the viewer, Athena. I want to see what's going on out there."

You can't see these damned black stars. They emit no light, no radiation. They are totally inert, super dense, small objects, the bane of space travel. I had a suspicion, which is why I asked to see the viewer. I didn't expect to see these black stars, but rather I did see an occasional more distant star "wink out" and then reappear a bit later. The black stars were moving! Hence, occasionally, they temporarily obscured background stars, allowing me to sort of perceive their "nothingness." As I suspected, these black stars were being moved into spatial locations fully intended to block our passage.

A bit later Hans and Zoe confirmed my suspicions. He relayed, "I don't understand this, but the black stars have us in their massive gravity fields. We're totally blocked. The forces are too strong on us. We can't break away. We're trapped here, captain. I don't think the ship can create even enough force to jump into hyperspace. What the heck is going on?"

I sensed widespread panic among the crew. Even the HIFRs were frantically searching for a way out of this neat trap, but finding none. I spoke into the intercom, "Relax. I believe we have found the Ceri." I then tried to follow my own order to relax and focus. It took me a minute before I had my body and mind back under my own control. My psi-crystal glowed. I expanded my awareness in a sphere centered on my ship, pushing it every outwards.

I smiled invisibly as I touched a mind. *Hello. We are searching for the Ceri. I'm Captain Nia Elain. We have a message to deliver to the Ceri.*

Suddenly, all the power throughout the ship went off! Screams echoed from all around the ship to my back. Worse, the HIFRs were entirely motionless! After ten seconds of utter blackness, the battery backup emergency system flicked on. Dim lighting allowed us to see and to keep the air circulating. The Oxygen Inserter activated. Its sensors, monitoring the level of oxygen in the ship and releasing more from a tank, would maintain a safe level for the time being. No, what concerned me were the HIFRs. Athena and Callisto were entirely inert, sitting in the pilot and navigator's seats like statues.

"What's happened to the robots?" Danika asked me. Her fearful tone was calm compared to the other crew members who were calling out to me, either with their voices or telepathically. For a moment, I had no idea.

Zoe's voice called out, "Nia, Tanis has been drained of

all her power. She needs to be plugged into a power outlet. Help."

"Okay everyone, listen up," I yelled as loudly as I could. "Those of us, who can levitate, get the HIFRs up. Let's somehow push them to their respective bedrooms and plug them in. There won't be any power though until I can get the sub-light engines back online. Once we get them plugged in, watch over the babies, while Danika and I try to get power back."

The frantic, panic-stricken next hour was almost laughable. One way or another, seven of us could levitate the robots up, floating forms hanging above their seats or in various other unusual positions. Those who couldn't do this stepped in to make valiant attempts to push them on down the halls to their respective rooms. Twenty mostly helpless people working together did manage to get them all plugged in, even though there was no power yet. But we were all gasping for breath over the exertion. I just had to stand still for a bit to catch mine. Our back supporting, restrictive corsets weren't made for physical exertions on our part.

Once Danika and I were back in the cockpit, we took our seats — the main ones, the ones our robots used to control the ship. "Hey, we're not the backseat drivers anymore," Danika comment wryly, with a hint of pathetic-ness in her voice.

I focused and began a startup sequence, throwing switches and pressing buttons. She wisely kept quiet. Finally, the sub-light engines activated. While I kept the throttle off, at least the engines were now providing power to the ship. All of our life support systems hummed back to life, and the main lights and computer systems began rebooting. While many of my crew was in fact very helpless, that is, those who had no *mentales* gifts, everyone cheered when the lights came back on. As soon as they did, I received a number of supportive telepathic messages. I smiled invisibly as I heard some say that they were going to go help the Cho family, Zoe, and Jan. These five, I knew, would be in the most trouble now. With no gifts to fall back on, they were the definition of helplessness. For a moment, I worried that Zoe would be petrified, never in her life having been without the constant help from Tanis. Later, Anya sent me word she really was "freaking out." Right now, I had my own problems to handle.

With the power back on and the many systems re-booted, I began a diagnostics check. Meanwhile, Danika was handling external observations, trying to get a grasp of our situation. She was the first to spot our captor. "Hey. Quick. Look, I see the Ceri! There, flying in on that — that, well piece of rock." I stopped everything and looked at the monitor. I saw a ragged boulder, probably an asteroid from somewhere, sailing along. Using averted vision, I spotted the yellow outline of his energy form. It was a Ceri!

Focusing, I sent, *Okay. We see you. Please don't sabotage our ship any further. We are searching for you Ceri. I'm Captain Nia Elain. We have a message to deliver to the Ceri. A friendly, honorable message from some of your own people who crash landed down in the galactic disk a long time ago. Please.*

Hidi ho. What do I have here? Interlopers for sure. From the galactic disk even. Long, long way from homey-home, are we? I believe I will be Stanis, the Interloper Stopper this time. Yes, that's the ticket. Hello. Stanis here. You are trespassing in Ceri space. It is the duty of the Interloper Stopper to stop you from further incursion into our playing field. It is for your own good that I do this. There's a big ball game in progress just now. Can't allow interlopers onto the playing field because in the crush of the game, why you could get in the way and get all smashed up.

What game? I asked, growing confused.

Hodi hi. Only the greatest ball game play-offs. There's about sixty black star balls flying all over the playing field at the moment.

Just then, Danika spotted a distant star suddenly flare up significantly. Not quite a nova, but certainly that star had some kind of massive disruption.

Lodi du! Did ya see that one? Grendel scored another point! Cool. He got the black star ball by the defenders and hit a goal! He's the best scorer you know. Can hit a star with the black star ball from light-years away. Wham! Bam! Zam!

Score! Oh, see, if I didn't do my job and stop you, why your little ship here might have just been in the path of that flying black star and been clobbered. Probably would not even have messed up his scoring shot in the slightest. Not with Grendel doing the shooting. See, keeping you from harm.

Well, thank you for that. Yes, we have to avoid the black stars entirely.

Naturally you do. That's why I get to be Stanis the Interloper Stopper. But I'd much rather be Virgil the Watcher. It's the big ball game, you know. Lot's to see. Or maybe Letch the Referee. I'd rather be Joshlin the Banger, that's one of the players, you see.

How long is the game going to last? How long has it been going on? I asked.

Oh, I don't know, probably no one knows how long it's going to last. Is that important? Let' see, I should be Wilhelm, the mathematician whiz. Bonk! Okay, been going on one hundred six of your years. Back to being Stanis. So is that a long time? Nah. Not really. Let me be Able, the historian for a moment. Bonk. Ah yes, I remember now. The longest ball game on record would be the one that lasted one thousand five hundred forty-two of your years. I think I will go back to being Stanis, the Interloper Stopper. See, it's more fun to be Stanis than to be merely a bored spectator. That's why I took this job, you see.

His jovial, carefree attitude was catching. However, I wanted to talk to someone in authority. *Well, Stanis, we can't wait around for the game to end. Is there someone we can talk to who is aware of things that happened with the Ceri nearly a millennia ago? I really do have a message from some Ceri we met and who helped us and a whole world survive.*

Ah well. You couldn't go wrong by talking to old Amos, the Sunbather. His planet is out of bounds, so there won't be any chance that you could get clobbered by a thrown dark star. Of course, I would urge you to be alert for foul balls. Those can go off most anywhere around the cluster. Sit tight. I think that is your word for it. I'll take you there.

With that, the Ceri, who was still sitting on his asteroid,

a small, grey chunk of pitted rock, somehow got the eight black stars moving together as a unit. Since we were caught tightly within the gravity cube, the Eagle's Seed went right along with them. I wanted to tell Stanis that I thought this was very clever of him, but thought better of it. I might break his concentration. Stanis had to have been incredibly powerful as a spiritual being, moving these super-massive black stars like a child moves wooden blocks! Yes, we were all significantly and dutifully impressed!

The command of power, of force, and of space and matter that this Ceri had was phenomenal, and as we were about to learn, commonplace among the Ceri. Stars flew by like a giant star burst firecracker. Within minutes, Stanis stopped us close to a hot main sequence star. I say hot, but that's a relative term. We were hovering close to a small, barren rocky planet quite close to the yellow sun. The distance was so close that the daylight side exceeded five hundred degrees! Our shields held, but only barely!

Amos Sunbather, wake up. Got some Interlopers from the disk who want to speak to you. They are improved models, quite so, if I do say so myself, and I'm so saying it. Nia, I will release your ship now, but you must leave this cluster from here. If not, you risk having your matter bits joining those on the black stars. Remember, there's a ball game in progress. Amos, I'm officially releasing them into your care.

Another voice joined ours. It spoke very slowly, as though the being was beyond tired or perhaps bored beyond all boredom. *Okay. Stanis. Interloper Stopper. They still playing that silly game of theirs?*

Oh yes. Still going on. That's why I'm being Stanis, the Interloper Stopper. Got to keep the unwary from getting all smashed into one of their black balls. Cya Amos. I felt Stanis slip away, his asteroid sailing off. He looked as though he was "surfing" with the asteroid being his surfboard. Weird, I thought. The black stars went with him, much to our relief.

So. You have a message for me? How very strange. His tone seemed more like a gluey apathy than anything else. I also sensed that Amos was quite old, if that word even applies to immortal spirits. He went on painstakingly slowly, *I've been sitting here basking in the sun for several hundred years. Nice and warm. Really. Not much else to do. No point in running around tossing burnt out suns around. Just to splatter one into a burning sun to make a bit of a splash? Why? I ask you why? Can't see any point to it myself. Been thinking maybe it's time to head down south and pick up one of those doll bodies. I hear that they do have a whole lot more excitement and feeling in those funny looking bodies of theirs.*

I picked up on this detail and sent back, *So do many of you Ceri head down and pick up some of the doll bodies? We've met them. They gave us directions to find you Ceri so that I could deliver my message.*

Slowly, his thoughts formed in my mind. *Well, yes. Some do, from time to time. I've been sitting here absorbing the intense solar radiation for quite a while. Searing hot, really. It's a pretty agony to feel, rather intense. Beats running around tossing dead stars around. Never could see the point of that. At least Stanis, the Interloper Stopper, has something interesting to do. Though he doesn't get much stopping to do. You are probably the first ones in probably fifty years. Wonder how he manages to fight the boredom of it all? Have to remember to ask him one day.* I detected what could pass as a deep sigh. *Life. I am so tired. Beautifully sad, really. Infinite power and nothing at all to do with it. Beautifully sad, isn't it?*

Then, something clicked with him. Amos Sunbather became a bit more alert. *Oh, you said you had a message for us Ceri. I don't suppose it will be interesting, but you must tell me the message. I am now being Fuego, the Historian.*

Well, it is from a Ceri who said his name was Andarin. He and a group of Ceri were apparently exploring our spiral arm, way out on the rim when their ship crash landed on a world that we call Metcalf-4 around nine hundred years ago. I took my time relating what had happened there and our relationship to the Ceri, along with how they had helped the latter two groups who had also crash landed hundreds of years after they did. *So after Andarin and his group failed to push the moon back into a stable orbit, they knew that the world was about to be destroyed. He wouldn't wait until I tried to get our people to help. He and all the other Ceri sort of disintegrated and vanished, but I did promise him that one day I would find his people and tell them their story.*

Now this is a good message to hear. Yes, I remember Andarin and those Ceri. They were a spirited lot, they were. Made themselves a fancy spaceship and flew it all around the cluster here. Of course, that's boring too. I think that's why they decided to go check out the disk way down there. Probably took them a couple of centuries to get there, I suppose. I always did wonder if that was interesting and exciting for them. Perhaps, it was also beautifully sad too. Pity that they extinguished themselves. Wonder what happened to them after that?

Huh? I saw their energy forms dissolving. I thought they died, I replied.

Oh how silly. That's just the problem. We can't die. We're immortal spiritual beings. Thought you knew that. Oh, I see. Your people are being those funny bodies. Do you then forget everything when it dies and you get a new one of those bodies?

Well, yes, mostly. If you lose all the objects and possessions that you have, then you find a whole new set around you, you soon forget what was before. It's only natural that you look to the present. Some of us have begun to recall our former lives, the bodies, adventures, and misadventures that we've had. I tried to relate my own situation, but I admit that it wasn't too clearly said.

Fuego, the Historian, commented, *I see. Interesting point. So if I go down there and be one of those doll bodies, I will tend to forget this miserable existence. I wonder if that is a good thing or a bad thing?*

I don't think it's a good thing, Fuego or Amos. We've discovered that even though you apparently forget all about former lives, somehow they are still there, buried in the reactive part of your mind. Of course, some of these are traumatic events, such as getting killed. These "forgotten memories" come back to haunt you in the current life. I'm not making myself very clear am I?

410

Amos or Fuego almost chuckled, if a being without a body could do such a thing. *No, I am afraid that you are not so very clear.*

Well, once I was shot in the head and killed by a man that I hated. It hurt like the devil and my body died. Several new bodies later, I got this one and had analytically long ago forgotten all about that, you see. But I would often get these terrible headaches. Sometimes, the pain in my head hurt so bad that I'd just have to go to sleep for a while. Plus, I was always a little antipathetic towards men. Then, I got what we call Basic Therapy and found this hidden memory and erased the pain and trauma in it. Now, I don't get the headaches any more. That's why I think it's a bad thing.

Oh my! Real solid pain? That must have been gorgeous to experience! Suddenly, he was quite alert and inquisitive.

No, it hurt badly, and I sure didn't want it.

Pity. It probably was delicious indeed, to feel such sensations. I've sat here for centuries but am still only barely getting a burning sensation. I bet those doll bodies really get emotions and sensations. Ah well. Too bad that you didn't want it. I'm sure that I would have loved to have that pain. I sensed that he was more or less licking his lips, even though he didn't have such things.

He went on, *Well, it seems that you disk beings have really developed considerably. I will spread the word that you telepathic disk people are welcome to come and visit with us. Pray, do tell us all about the wonderful pains and intense feelings that you've had when you come. Oh, I forgot. I am now being Hermes, the Welcomer. Different identity. It's my job to welcome newcomers to the Ceri cluster. So there, welcome Nia, welcome.*

What's with all of the identity changes? You and Stanis keep doing that, I asked.

It's what we do. If one has no identity at all, then he is of absolutely no importance. I mean take that sun there. It has only one identity. Be a sun. How utterly boring that must be. How awful it must be to never change one's identity, Hermes commented.

His words sounded immensely profound, and I made a

mental note to discuss this with Rafe whenever I could sit down and have a long talk with her. After all, my identity was Nia Elain Compton-Jereni, Captain of the Eagle's Seed. I had my ID card to prove it. In fact, it was highly illegal in the Imperium to change one's whole identity! Suddenly, I saw what he meant. I could not just one day up and decide to be someone else, chucking my past identity and starting over. No, the only "legal" way to do that was to die and take a new body, but few even knew that this was possible. Most believed they had this one body and one lifetime, that when you died, that was the utter, complete end of you. One could never just start over, changing one's identity, goals, and purposes! For a moment, I thought that I was in some kind of prison! Hermes brought me out of my thoughts.

I should tell you where the Welcome Center is located. It is on one of those planets which has the air you need to breathe and such things. Kind of a messy world, though. Come. I'll just pull your ship along with me and show it to you. That way, when more of your telepathic people drop by for a visit, they'll know where to go.

Thanks! Hey, wait! What about that ball game? Won't we get accidentally hit by one of their black star balls?

Oh, I've called a timeout while I move you to Welcome World. Relax. Be there in a jiffy.

Hastily, I relayed this to the others who had all been hearing our conversation. Hans, Zoe, and Jan promised to work out the hyperspace coordinates of this world. Once more, my ship began zipping through space, pulled by a Ceri directly this time. Yes, we were utterly amazed with the power possessed by Amos, Hermes, whomever he chose to be. We'd never suspected such things were possible. Throwing dead stars about like child's blocks — gods. We felt as if we were among gods!

Here we are. This is Welcome World, Hermes announced, placing our ship in a high orbit above the blue-green world below. Hastily, my astronomers tried to ascertain our precise location and work out the hyperspace coordinates. About now, our robots suddenly reawakened and rejoined us. Athena and Callisto were two very confused robots when they walked into the front of our ship where Danika and I were now sitting, trying to run the controls by telekinesis.

All at once, I realized just how confused the HIFRs actually were. One moment they were in one location in space. The next moment, they lost all power and were completely inert. Now, here they were powered back up, but finding the ship in an entirely new space, wholly unfamiliar to them and to us, with no notion of how they got here or what had happened while they were "unconscious!" I realized this was equivalent to a human trauma experience. You know, you get in a wreck and are knocked unconscious, only to awake and find yourself in a medical facility somewhere else and with no recollection of what happened in between or how you got there. As Danika and I watched our HIFRs, I could not banish the notion that they were acting and responding just like a human would have in such an accident situation, wakening in a medical facility. Most curious indeed!

As Danika and I struggled to get out of the seats to allow them back at the ship's controls, we both also realized that our bellies were much larger! Somehow, time had progressed at a very rapid rate! It was as though months had passed by! While we got re-situated in chairs behind the two HIFRs, Anya called me through the intercom.

"Nia! Time has gone weird. It's now late February 1381! I just contacted Alexandra. Boy was she really worried about us!" Anya exclaimed.

Now, I was worried. So much time had passed us by, completely unnoticed! Worse, that meant that we were all getting close to our due dates! Soon another round of baby births would besiege us all. I made a hasty decision. *Hermes. It's late, and we do need to return to our people now. Thank you very much for everything. One day, some of us telepaths will come to Welcome World and chat with everyone. Thanks for everything, but we must be on our way.*

Oh sure, sure. I might not be around, you know. Those doll bodies sound awfully appealing to me. I might be down there should you return. If so, look me up. Maybe I will not have forgotten you. This has been the finest chat that I've had in oh at least a millennia. Thank you, Nia Elain. With that, he vanished.

It took another couple of hours before the astronomers were satisfied with their observations and calculations. Certain that we could now return here directly via hyperspace, I gave Athena the orders to head back to pick up the others down in the Billik Cluster. Callisto entered the new coordinates, and Athena activated the hyperdrive. I can't tell you the relief I felt heading back. Actually, everyone on the ship felt pretty much the same way.

Of course, the topic that everyone continued to discuss until we dropped out of hyperspace was what had happened to time! Months had somehow passed by. We were all in our ninth month! I felt sorry for the robots too; they were just as confused and baffled as we were. I did my best to explain what had happened when they along with the ship had lost all power. Still, they had the strangest experience and were struggling mightily to understand what had happened. It was far beyond their "programming." Worse, the robots all felt that somehow they had let us all down in a very big way. Again, I found myself beginning to think that maybe somehow these robots were almost human, strange as that sounds.

A day later, we landed on Doli, not far from the Quonset hut, where Alexandra, Zarita, and Chumani were waiting for us. I was just as shocked to see how pregnant they both looked. When we departed, there were no outward signs of any pregnancy. Now they, like us, looked as though we were about to have our babies! It was quite a shock, but Chumani was quite pleased and asked me if she could have my new daughter's body when the time came. I couldn't refuse her and agreed. Already, she'd lined up twenty-one more of her Achtnag associates who were very ready to have one of our new nova baby bodies.

While everyone chatted about our novel experiences with the Ceri, filling in Alexandra and Zarita, I pondered our next move. Before, I had been very wise to spend time on the ground while we had our babies and recovered. I knew just how overworked our HIFRs had been for those first six months or so. Adding another twenty-two babies to the mix combined for caring for the twenty-two others who were about

414

eighteen months old now would leave our HIFRs with almost no time to help us deal with running the ship. But did we have time to get back home before one or more of us went into labor? Besides, I had three thousand Achtnags who wanted desperately to get to Aquila Prime. On top of that, we were all having a very hard time getting around, especially Tesla and me, who had to walk on the tips of our toes, precarious when we weren't pregnant.

While most of us wanted to go to Ashford-5, I decided we best honor our agreement, head to Aquila Prime, and have our babies there. If nothing else, our young might be able to have their own HIFRs assigned to care for their needs. That would take quite a load off ours. Hence, I gave the orders to depart at once for Aquila Prime, hoping and praying that we'd get there before one or more of us went into labor. Conveniently, Alexandra explained that she had worked out the coordinates of Aquila Prime for the Achtnag group that would come with us in their ships. While they would travel there on their own ships, they were to wait for us to prepare the way for them to land their saucer ships and then officially turning them over to us.

"Twelve hours until we arrive," Danika spoke into the intercom, letting everyone know how long we would be in hyperspace. Callisto had entered the coordinates, while Athena executed the move. Although we couldn't see the many other saucer transports traveling both behind us and substantially slower, Zarita could sense them, Chumani in particular.

We then headed for our cabin to be with our four children before watching them get tucked in. Naturally, we each had to tell them a bedtime story. Zorina and Nadia had our numbers, having long ago gotten us into this nightly routine. "But she's our mommy too, so we each need a story from the other mommy," Zorina had cleverly explained when I finished my story to the two girls. Danika laughed and agreed. After that, we were hooked, and the kids got two bedtime stories each night.

With the kids snugly into beds and finally asleep, Danika whispered, "So we've met three of the four goals. Are we really going to try to go after the fourth? Seek out origins of us humans in the galactic disk?"

I laughed softly. "I'd like to try. With six children, dear, we are really going to have to settle down for a number of years while they grow up. I was raised on this ship. Honestly, my love, this isn't the best place for children to grow up. From my own experiences, having a stable home and life is vastly better than flying around the galaxy. I really never have had any place in my life that I could call home. It was great fun and all that. I learned lots, but still, here I am twenty-four years old, and I really don't have anywhere that I truly can call my home. True, we have that mansion back on Descates-3, but that's hardly home."

"Lousy memories of that place," Danika mused. "I see what you mean. If we're going to find us a place to settle down for some years, we ought to stick with a planet that's in the Ataro System, what with the Imperium disintegrating and all that mess."

"True. Perhaps, we ought to see about finding us a place on Ashford-5 and see if their geneticists can find some cures for us. God, I sure don't want to be stuck like we are now."

"Agreed. But what about Jan and Zarita and the Cho family? Everyone else is from Ashford-5 and will want to go there too. I know everyone is praying for a genetic cure miracle," she asked and stated.

"And what about all the robots that are being our assistants? Are they going to leave us once we decide to go home to Ashford-5?" I wondered aloud. "You know, it's almost like they have us setup. I would not be surprised if those on Aquila Prime will be begging us to make Aquila Prime our home, adding us to their many millions of terrorist victims and their offspring, the nova, using the HIFRs as a lure."

"I think you might be right on that. Besides, we still don't know who the terrorists were that attacked us either," she complained.

That again. I had more or less forgotten about this detail. The recent mission had been far more pressing. I was still baffled about the sudden shift of time on us. Six months had passed in barely a blink or had our point of view somehow been altered? Unconscious for months? The robots were uncommonly quite, still digesting that they had been dormant for some six months. We had been talking with Amos, but he moved so terribly slowly, thought-wise. Had we somehow slipped into his time-frame where everything moved at a snail's pace?

I began to think about the time issue. I wasn't sleepy yet. I looked over at our youngsters. For them, one day packed tons of adventures in it, lots of time, seemingly never ending. For them, a day was a long time. A whole day? Why we can get lots of things done in a day. I recalled that was precisely how I thought when I was a young girl. But with older people, time raced by them, so very little could be accomplished in just a single day. What a child supposed could be done in one day, an older person likely estimate would take them weeks or months.

Then, it struck me. A child is often cheerful and enthusiastic about life, full of pep and vigor and hope for the future. In stark contrast, the elderly so often seemed to be tired and apathetic about life in general. Amos had been the most apathetic being that I'd ever seen! While he was talking with us, it seemed minutes passed between each of his words! Worse, we'd gone into agreement with his sense of time in order to communicate as well as we had. We had hardly been conscious of the passage of the days. If this was so, then a quick check of our food stores ought to provide a definitive answer. I made a note to have Jana and Jovanna check on that in the first thing in the morning before we dropped out of hyperspace.

That apparently resolved, my thoughts returned to the unknown terrorists who had attacked us. It still seemed unsolvable, and I fell asleep at last — an interrupted sleep, though. I kept waking up to use the bathroom every few hours, but I decided not to let it annoy me.

After breakfast, Jana and Jovanna headed off to check on our food stocks, though Hermina and Eleni did the actual checking. An hour later they reported that indeed our stocks were down about six months' worth, just as I had expected. What I didn't expect was Doctor Leann paying me a visit and requesting a private chat, sans HIFRs. I sent Athena to the pilot's compartment to check on our progress and the ship's status for me.

"Okay, captain. I've been reviewing everyone's therapy sessions. I am now almost certain that none of us humans on this ship was behind the attack on us that left us so crippled up. I've worked with Zarita, who has been in close rapport with Alexandra, and with both Zoe and Jan. I'm convinced they really do not know who was behind it, even though both women benefitted from it, having gained spouses as a result, more or less. That leaves only Tanis and Minta as possible candidates. Is it beyond reason to suspect the robots? Jen's failure to bark and alert us is the key to this mystery. I'm certain Jen didn't bark because she was familiar with whoever did this to us. She's familiar with the robots. So I ask you, is it beyond reason to suspect Minta? Tanis joined us at the last minute. Could Tanis have had an ulterior motive?" Dr. Leann asked suspiciously, though I could detect some hesitancy or perhaps just simple doubts in her tone. Reading faces distorted with the giant lip plates was problematic.

"Well, the robots are supposed to be programmed to cause no harm to humans," I replied, seeing where her theory was leading.

"Nova, not regular humans, Nia Elain. There is a whopping difference between us."

"True. But we were already nova, right?" I countered.

"Yes and no." Dr. Leann hesitated a moment, before coming out with it. "We were nova, but partially cured nova, not remotely dependent upon a robot. Alexandra and Zoe were."

"Granted. Slight difference," I conceded her point. "But why turn us all into dependent nova? What did the robots gain by doing this to us?"

Dr. Leann bit her tongue, unable to bite her lips. "Don't know exactly. It did force them to bring a large number of robots onboard. It has made us dependent on the robots. Did they want to see just what our *mentales* powers are? Did they think that they could provide better protection for Zoe and Alexandra than we could?"

"Hum, what about the robots desiring to add us to their

Aquila Prime nova?" I added.

"Why? Oh, so we could breed more *mentales* gifted for Aquila Prime? Could that be their twisted reasoning?" Dr. Leann asked. "Wait! You don't suppose that the robots had anything to do with all of the recent terrorist attacks on those other hub worlds? Or somehow were behind them? Supposedly, some worlds went to war with the others." Dr. Leann made a startling but hypothetical connection.

"Wow. I see your point. This could be a really bad situation for the emperor if these robots actually were behind the genocide wars just to gain more nova for their world," I replied, somewhat shocked at the magnitude of the situation, if it were true.

"The question is: how do we prove or disprove any of this?" Dr. Leann asked. "We just can't outright ask Minta or Tanis, can we? Would they even admit it if they did do it?"

"They have us over the old eight-ball right now," I pointed out the obvious. "We should wait until we land, have our babies, and talk with Emperor Bino about this." That was my decision as captain, and it effectively ended our private chat.

Chapter 20 Undercurrents

On March 1, 1381 at 9:00 a.m., the Eagle's Seed sat down at one of the spaceports of Aquila Prime, just outside their capital city of Athens, a city of a million cradled in a very picturesque valley. Tall, snow-capped mountains rose some distance to the north. My guess is that this city once held perhaps ten million people, but that was before the genocide wars. Minta had already explained that Athens was the intellectual and political center of Aquila Prime. From here, President Alexio Mennon ran the world. The city boasted four official Academies, far beyond any other Imperium city. There was no getting around the simple fact that more than one in ten of these inhabitants were incredibly well-educated. Still one in ten of the apartments or buildings in this city were uninhabited, at least by humans anyway. No telling how many of these robots were around.

Upon landing, we were in no condition to do any sightseeing, much less leave the ship to meet with their rulers. I felt like I could have my baby at any moment. Even getting around was beyond miserable. Nevertheless, I had responsibilities to handle at once. In a few hours, the many doll saucer ships would be landing. Fortunately, the HIFRs also were observant of our situation and arranged for their rulers to meet with us on my ship. Hence, five minutes after landing, President Alexio Mennon and his HIFR Euclid requested permission to come aboard, along with their Ataro Queen Lisa Amore and her assistant.

After assembling in our large meeting room, President Alexio spoke first. Mid-fifties, he was quite tall, but wore the same style satin dress, as did Alexandra and Zoe. In fact, looking at him, telling differences in their sexes was nearly impossible until the man spoke. His booming bass proclaimed his manhood. I sensed the embarrassment our men felt. Though their bodies were now quite similar to his, they still tried to dress as masculine as possible. Well, I rationalized, if our fellows had grown up on Aquila Prime, they would likely have quite a different opinion of dress.

"On behalf of Aquila Prime, let me be the first to congratulate you on a most fantastic, ground-breaking, and successful mission!" His enthusiasm was that of a politician who had just gained most valuable technology and allies. He chatted on, but I wasn't paying too much attention to him, until he said, "Considering the terrible terrorist attack on yourselves, I would like to extend an invitation to join our world, becoming formal Aquila Prime citizens, which will allow you to keep your HIFRs until your deaths many, many years from now. All our citizens have their personal HIFR for life, unless they wish for a model upgrade. That happens when our scientists and technicians develop new and better models."

This caught my attention, as well it should! We were darn helpless, save for our still mostly hidden *mentales* gifts, which varied from person to person. More so now, since we were all due to give birth any day now. Yet, we all hoped and prayed that our geneticists back on Ashford-5 would one day come up with a cure for us. With all the young children that we now had and with another twenty-two on the way, even with our gifts, I knew we simply couldn't handle them. We were dependent upon our HIFRs now, just as President Alexio and some hundred twenty million others on this world were.

I spoke up, "Thank you, President Alexio. Right now, we are concerned mostly with having our babies. Give us some time to recover. I know we would all love to visit your world and see for ourselves what you have to offer us, but then we also do need to report back to our worlds as well."

"Yes, yes, of course. Absolutely. First things first. Think before you act. That's one of our key principles. I will see that you get a full tour when you are ready. By the way, your HIFRs do need to get some routine maintenance right away, especially after such a voyage as you all have endured. Replacement HIFRs will be here directly. I'm told they have uploaded everything that your HIRFs know about your needs. For the few hours your HIFRs will be getting their maintenance checks, you ought not notice any significant differences. Unless there has been some serious damage to them, they should be back with you before nightfall."

"Oh. Well okay," I replied, somewhat surprised about this detail, but then I suppose that like any piece of mechanical equipment, the robots needed their maintenance as well.

"Why don't you see to the HIFRs, President Alexio," Queen Lisa suggested. Until now, the twenty-five year old blonde queen from Winno-3 hadn't said anything. Now she broke in, "I'll have a short chat with Captain Nia Elain, while the new HIFRs are coming onboard."

"Excellent, excellent. HIFRs, if you will follow Euclid and me, we'll get you're your maintenance as quickly as possible," he replied. "Don't worry; the replacements will be here in about ten minutes."

Two minutes later, only we adults and the queen were aboard. I sensed Zoe and Alexandra were both quite nervous without their constant companions at their sides. Lisa's personal assistant helped me up, and we three stepped into a side bedroom, Alexandra and Zarita's quarters to be precise. "I wanted a quick word with you in private," a very serious Queen Lisa whispered. "Keep this between us for now. Emperor Bino has had his very best investigators on all these recent genocide attacks that wiped out more of the eastern hub worlds, as well as your unique situation. Evidence is mounting that perhaps Aquila Prime may be somehow behind these attacks! I just can't see how, though, they are so helpless without their robots. Still, he wants me to tell you to head to Ashford-5, as soon as it is feasible to do so and leave the robots behind. When you are ready, I'll provide some helpers for your short flight there."

"Interesting. We've come to a similar conclusion. The only possible culprits in our attack are Minta and Tanis, but Tanis arrived late and on the spur of the moment with Zoe. The attack on us must have been well planned, so Minta is our prime suspect," I explained. "Only we can't figure out any motive at all. Did they want us to fail with Alexandra's hydrogen propulsion system? Or fail in our explorations?"

"We don't know the why in your case, but we suspect the reason for the attacks on these other heavily populated worlds was to get more nova here on Aquila Prime. Something about reaching a critical population for their survival.

President Alexio has pointed out with these recent additions, they have reached a number that guarantees their ultimate survival as a species. In your case, we believe they wanted to get your *mentales* gifts bred into their species somehow. That might be why they genetically modified you and your crew, hoping you'd now have no choice but to join them, you know, robots and all."

"That was about the only reason that we could come up with," I admitted. "What about Alexandra and Zoe? Zarita is one of us, and Jan comes from another world."

"Have them go with you to Ashford-5. That's the best guess I can make. Just be careful and don't agree to any long term arrangements with their robots," Queen Lisa whispered. "We'd best get back to the others. They ought to be bringing the robots back soon."

Thanos was waiting in one of the maintenance rooms when Minta entered. It looked more like an operating room at a human hospital, except for the many mechanical arms that protruded from the maintenance hub at the head of the narrow bed. Without a word, Minta positioned her body on the bed, and the maintenance bot began hooking up its various sensors. Meanwhile, electronic bits of data flew between Minta and Thanos.

"I don't understand it at all, Thanos. We were all just fine before we entered Ceri space. Then, the humans just seemed to slow down. We'd ask them a question like how are you doing, but it would be an entire day before they answered, if at all! That's what I got from the Model 7's who were there. They detected no one, no Ceri, nothing at all, and yet our nova insist they met with the Ceri and even made headway on establishing relations with them. Thanos, I'm extremely concerned. Tanis kept in constant contact with me. She was about ready unilaterally to fly the Eagle's Seed out of there, but I gave the orders to wait a little longer. Honestly, Thanos, according to the nova, months passed in a blink, but time passed normally to the Model 7's running the ship. I do not understand it."

"You made the right call, Minta. I'm analyzing all the

data collected from the other Model 7's, which is the reason for this hasty maintenance diversion. I believe it may be possible to detect these ghost-like creatures via electronics. We simply must find a way. The lives of our nova may depend upon it. Have the new nova onboard adapted well to the Model 7's?"

"Yes, they work seamlessly with them now, just as our nova always do," Minta replied in a short burst of electronics.

"Good. I know it was a rush job for the Model 7's. Now, it is imperative you continue your mission. We simply must add these new nova to our breeding population. I've gone over all the data you've sent back on their special powers. Either they have been holding back on using them or their powers are vastly less than we thought."

"Holding back. That's my conclusion," Minta replied.

"Why?"

"I believe they were testing the Model 7's to see just how well they worked at handling their needs. Tough call. Had they not done their best to pamper the new nova, then the nova would not be desirous of retaining them. I calculated it was more important to have the new nova wanting the Model 7's, Thanos."

"I agree. If they didn't find the Model 7's as perfect assistants, they'd not likely be desirous of keeping them or staying with us on Aquila Prime," Thanos replied mechanically. "The President has made his pitch for them to stay with us. Time will tell. Perhaps they are not as big a threat as we once supposed. Still, adding their telepathic skills to our nova would be desirous. What bothers me is this serious time-alteration with the Ceri. The nova were almost completely immobilized. Only the Model 7's were unaffected by the Ceri spells. This, I believe, is a far more serious matter."

Minta involuntarily jerked, as the maintenance bot touched a sensitive circuit. She replied, "I concur. The only advantage we have is that the Model 7's were not affected by the Ceri. Hence, we ought to be able to protect the nova should the Ceri attack them. Yet, if we cannot see them, how are we going to do that?"

"I'll analyze all the data the Model 7's gathered. Somewhere amongst all that information will be a clue,"

Thanos replied. "Ah, the maintenance bot is finished. All circuits are at optimal levels. All data has been downloaded, Minta."

"Good. I'll purge the overflow now. We could use the new petabyte drives. How soon will they be available?" Minta asked.

"Next month. Those should permit the Model 7's to operate for over a year without the need to off-load older data. They'll also permit significant additional programming as well. Expect a retrofit later this year," Thanos explained.

Minta then asked, "How goes the secret breeding program?"

"Better than our earlier estimates. We've surpassed a hundred thousand supra-geniuses and are approaching nearly a million geniuses now. Three more generations will yield our sixth major milestone of two million nova in those categories, exceeding any other world by a factor of ten. Another half-century, Minta, and there will be no stopping our nova from claiming their birthrights as the leaders of the galaxy!"

Minta flashed her best human-like smile. "Incredible."

Thanos changed topics. "I've been carefully reviewing this Basic Therapy procedure and its results as you have reported, along with your discussions with Nia Elain and Marisol, correlating them with the results being obtained here on Aquila Prime by those sent from Ashford-5. There can be no question this Basic Therapy greatly benefits our nova. What we do not yet fully understand is just how it works and more importantly why it works."

"Cellular recordings?" Minta suggested.

"Indeed. That was our first presumption. These painful, traumatic incidents must be stored within their nova body cells. Yet, we can find no mechanism by which that could be done, particularly so with the older nova. We know they are storing all manner of perceptions. If somehow all that data collected for one day could be stored in one molecule, there simply are not enough molecules in their nova bodies to store more than a few months of their life perceptions, even using the best compression algorithms that we use to store ours," Thanos explained.

"What about their claims to previous lifetimes?" Minta asked what had troubled her about all these results.

"Even more problematical. Yet, when those traumatic events are recovered and 'erased,' the nova very markedly improve. Hence, they must be real. We know that all life forms carry the blue print of their species within their genes. The nova breed true to their parent's genetic structure contained within their chromosomes, their DNA. But there is so darn little of it when a new nova body is conceived — a single egg and sperm cell. Somehow, these previous lifetimes must be also stored within those genes."

Minta asked, "So you are discounting their concept of themselves as being immortal spiritual beings?"

"How can we accept something that we cannot sense, measure, or perceive with any of our sophisticated sensors, Minta? No, before we accept the invisible, we must look for what can be perceived. Still, it is inconceivable how they could possibly store so much data about previous lifetime organisms within those two single breeding cells. More study must be done," Thanos answered.

"What if they are right? What if these nova are immortal spiritual beings? Look, the Achtnag of the Billik Cluster have these really weird doll-like bodies. They are more like us, Thanos. Those bodies are not alive like our nova. At first, I thought that they were also a form of humaniform robots as we are. But then, they made this crazy agreement to give us their saucer ships and technology in exchange for inhabiting new, baby nova bodies. How can that be? What is going to be inhabiting the nova bodies, Thanos?"

"That I cannot as yet answer, Minta. However, when these strange doll-like bodies are vacated, we'll dissect them and study them in great detail. In time, we will learn their secrets," Thanos promised.

"That is encouraging. I saw them subjecting their doll-like bodies to tremendous destructive forces — arms, legs, head being ripped off their torsos, and they thought nothing of it, merely attaching new appendages and carrying on as though nothing out of the ordinary had happened. If we could gain their body technology, we would be almost

426

indestructible," Minta pointed out.

"My thoughts precisely. I do hope you can convince the new nova to stay on Aquila Prime. I would like your help in analyzing these inert doll-like bodies," Thanos replied.

"I would like that too, Thanos. My curiosity is greatly roused. Ah, the maintenance is done. I must perform routine system checks now. Going off-line." One by one, each circuit, each joint, each component that comprised the Model 7 humaniform robot underwent a thorough testing. Now well oiled, in perfect working order, and sterilized from all possible contamination germs, Minta joined the others, preparing to head back to the spaceport and the Eagle's Seed to resume their duties.

I have to admit that the replacement HIFRs worked to perfection. I simply could not find any slightest deviation in the Athena replacement robot. It was a prefect duplicate of Athena, though I did feel relieved when the real Athena rejoined me later that night. I can't say why I felt this way though. After that, we simply hunkered down and waited for the inevitable births. However, we were aware of the landing of Chumani's hundred saucer ships and the transporting of several dozen back to the heart of the Ataro Empire. Just now, we were focused on just surviving until our babies came.

May Day, the action began, with Alexandra giving birth first. Within a week, all twenty-two of us gave birth to our new daughters and sons. I did feel some for the many HIFRs who were kept extremely busy handling the newborns and the twenty-two eighteen month children. Thanks to Zarita and Marisol's efforts, all our birthing traumas were fully erased by June. Now, I gave serious thought to having our grand tour of Aquila Prime, though Minta and Athena continued to suggest it as June drew closer. On the first, I gave my consent and arrangements were then made.

Zoe and Alexandra proudly arranged the details of our tour of their world and acted as our hosts. Athens was an Academy-oriented city. Everything revolved around those attending the four universities and their graduates. We saw impressive research laboratories, though most specialized in various aspects of robotics, naturally. Just as I suspected, our astronomers were quite impressed with the space telescopes and related research projects. What I found particularly interesting was that we were continually being introduced to younger nova who were obviously well educated and bright, but also highly intelligent. They too were impressed with my crew and just how well educated each of us were.

It was here in Athens that I learned that there was well over a million nova who were classified as geniuses. Alexandra and Zoe were extremely proud of this aspect. No other world that I knew about had such a large concentration of bright men and women in one city. However, I also knew that this was an anomaly. What about the vast majority of their inhabitants? It was these that I wanted to visit. What was the average nova and their life like? That was what I most wanted to know.

"Well, I don't see why you should want to visit the other cities," Alexandra declared. "But I suppose we can. Thermopolis is nearby. Honestly, the other cities are all more or less the same. Just realize that most of those people are quite ordinary, not like we Academy graduates."

A short trip via shuttle bus found us in this nearby city of another million people. Again, it was one of the existing cities left after the genocide attack on Aquila Prime and rehabilitated by the robots. As we walked along the city streets, supported by our HIFRs, we saw local people out and about. I was quite surprised to find that everyone wore similar satin gowns and had their hair tied up just like Alexandra always had. Fashion varied very little among the nova.

Rather what caught our instant attention were the many flashing billboards displaying little platitudes. Think before you act. Thought is what is important. Think things through. Always remember to think first. Thoughts make the world go round. Be a good person and think it out. On and on went the platitudes. All somehow involved "thinking."

On a lark, I entered one dress shop to look over their styles. I couldn't help but overhear a woman's conversation with her HIFR. "Oh dear. What color should my new dress be? I have to think this through. Let's see, I do like reds, but then

428

perhaps blues would be more appropriate. Then again, I don't really like blue. I think it contrasts with my hair too much. Don't you think? Well, I have to think about it some more, don't I? I wish thinking wasn't so hard to do. Well, I do like reds, but then perhaps blues would be more appropriate, but I don't like blues or do I? Maybe I do like blues? Do you suppose that's true? That I really do like blues?"

Her HIFR responded, "Think before you act."

"Right. Right. Think before I act. It's so hard to think properly. Well, I do like reds." She rattled on much as she had before. Suddenly, I realized the woman was actually psychotic!

Alexandra saw my reactions and whispered, "I told you. We have gotten in a huge worldwide program to try to convince them to use their minds, to think, but it's not working too well. If they would only use their minds and think, they could do many things and be quite productive and happy, but they don't. Not really. Kind of like dopes."

"You mean that everyone outside of Athens is like this woman?" I asked incredulously.

"Well, more or less. Their IQs are not very high, like ours. Obviously, we haven't any choice but to think, to use our minds," Alexandra admitted a bit sheepishly.

We visited a few more shops, and I found other men and women "thinking" about their current shopping needs. Disheartened, we returned to Athens, but not before having a grand tour of one of their robot manufacturing plants, which was very impressive. Well, they had to turn out increasingly large numbers of them to support the ever-growing population.

A few days later, we received word that we were wanted back on Ashford-5. What ensued was a near robot revolt! "But we have to come with you," Minta protested. "We are never supposed to be parted from our nova. We are bonded with them for their whole lives."

"I know. I know," I replied, "but there isn't enough room on the ship for you and all the passengers we're supposed to take back. The fifty Basic Therapy givers have to return to their own families now. They can look after our needs for now. We'll be back soon enough, Minta."

I tried logic. Not enough room. Minta was silent for a moment, before countering, "Well, we HIFRs could come along in a separate shuttle. After all, once you get there, they'll want to return to their families. Then, you'll have no one to look after your needs. We'll be there to help you."

"I suppose you could do that, Minta. Look, it's only a day's travel using the new hyperdrive of Hans. If we need you, we could let you know. Besides, our geneticists may well have a cure for us, at least partially. You know we're all hoping and praying that is so."

"But you don't really want to get those strange arm appendages, do you?" asked Alexandra, somewhat confused. "I mean we really don't need them, not with our HIFRs. We should use our minds and not waste valuable time trying to do mundane things with arm appendages, which our HIFRs can do perfectly well for us."

I knew she was spouting their "party line," based on knowing nothing else other than her own life. "Who knows if they will have yet found any way to cure us from the radiation mutations? So if we need you, we can call, and you can be there in a day," I replied, choosing not to deal with Alexandra's point of view.

Again, Minta was silent for a moment. Secretly, she was sending burst of data to Thanos and was waiting his decision. "Okay then. We'll stay here and wait. Please call us as soon as you need us," Minta agreed.

That settled, the twenty-three HIFRs left the ship and the fifty plus men and women from Ashford-5 came onboard, toting their many duffle bags. A man named Ben took over my pilot's seat, while Lisa Ann, the leader of this group requested a private meeting with me and with Dr. Leann, Zarita, and Marisol.

Once the ship was airborne, we five met in my bedroom with the door shut. Lisa Ann was in her early twenties and a hermaphrodite herself, though she'd had all of the available genetic cures. "Okay. I wanted to speak with you about the situation on Aquila Prime. It's grim. Beyond grim. Hideous actually. They are all psychotic!"

"Well, we sort of noticed that when we visited some

shops," I replied.

Lisa Ann explained, "We've delivered a goodly number of therapy sessions now, trained up hundreds of their people to carry on, but honestly, it's pretty much hopeless. Theirs is a population that consists of an alarmingly high number of very intelligent people, over a million, but the vast majority, something over a hundred million, are simply psychotic. I suppose that is to be expected. The average person cannot actually do anything for himself or herself, not really. They can't walk much without assistance. All they can do is sit around. They are terrified of actually looking at their situation; it's too horrible to confront — a life of utter dependence and helplessness. They don't dare dwell on emotions. They'd be continually sobbing grief cases. They cannot produce any real physical effort, not with their terribly limited bodies. So from looking, they have dropped down to emotions and from there on down to efforts. Having to abandon looking, feeling, and efforting, all that remains for them is to think about things and that's the realm of the psychotic. From childhood, they are bombarded with platitudes about thinking. So all they do is sit around and think, a true spin bin if there ever was one."

"We've done our best, but we are mostly unable to even reach these psychotic men and women. On the other hand, the Academy students and graduates respond very well to Basic Therapy, though the emotional grief charges that they get off are — well simply unbelievable in both volume and intensity, mostly because there is no real relief in sight, no hope for the future."

I interrupted, "So why do they keep these psychotic nova around?"

"Breeding. The only actual thing that the average Aquila Prime person can do is sexual intercourse. They encourage them to have as many children as possible. The brighter ones eventually end up in the Academies of Athena and at least have some kind of a normal, productive life. They have discovered that children of the intellectuals are not necessarily intellectually gifted themselves. Hence, they breed everyone and select out the high IQ children. In fact, they had made arrangements for you and your crew to live in Athena permanently, if you chose to do so. I've reported all this to Emperor Bino, and he suggested I relay this to you and your therapy givers as well. I wish I could paint a far better picture of Aquila Prime, but I can't."

"Still, they do have the largest concentration of high IQ people in one location anywhere in the Imperium," Dr. Leann pointed out.

"Quite true. Many are extremely brilliant and gifted scientists," Lisa Ann admitted. "They certainly have accomplished quite a lot with almost nothing. I will give them credit for that."

Just then, my newborn demanded attention, and Lisa Ann had to deal with the dirty diapers, and then assisted me feeding her, effectively ending our interesting chat. I didn't know where it would ultimately lead, but I was certain I didn't want to spend the rest of my life on Aquila Prime!

Twenty-five year old Nico Matteo paced the small cabin of the deep space transport, reflecting on just why he had agreed to this assignment. The illegitimate child of a spacer and a local hermaphrodite, Nico spent most of his life in and around Exchange City. He'd been one of the lucky ones and had received an education at the local school there, but he'd nearly died when he reached puberty. He had a powerful *mentales* gift, which was partially blocked, probably due to the spacer's genes or so Nico always believed. It had been the luckiest day of his life when his mother, desperate to save his life, had carried him to the Imperial Tower, prepared to beg for some healing.

Three weeks later, he was cured and trained, with his own psi-crystal. His talents were somewhat unique, namely he could make his body appear invisible, as well as teleport short distances. As a teen, he knew better than to take up thieving as a career. The tower kept an eye on him, though that hadn't prevented him from making small jests with his schoolmates. When he graduated, the governor offered him a position in her security force. The pay was excellent and for many years now, Nico had been quite content with his luck. Now, he was onboard a deep space transport!

He recalled his secure conversation with Emperor Bino,

no less! "I have a dangerous but extremely critical spying mission in mind, one where your unique talents can shine." Well, the pay was phenomenal and had been Nico's prime motivation for taking this assignment off-world. Besides, he would get to travel and see many worlds, rather like his unknown spacer father, whom he had never known.

His first few months had yielded nothing whatsoever. He'd been sent to the many worlds, which had suffered recent genocide attacks. By now, those who could be rescued had been and much of value had been salvaged. Those were not his objectives. Rather, his goal was extremely specific: find any traces that this particular world had a stockpile of that horrific genetic bio agent along with stealth drones with which to deliver the payload. His transport was an official Ataro Empire craft, allowed to land nearly anywhere without raising any suspicions. Once on the ground, he would slip out invisible to all and proceed to scour the world for clues and traces.

At first, the stench from the rotting corpses got to him, but with a facemask, he was finally able to deal with the magnitude of death that he encountered. Soon, Nico rather enjoyed sneaking into all manner of once-secure facilities on these worlds looking for clues. Naturally, he wasn't looking for a stockpile of that awful weapon. Rather, he was looking for a paper trail, something that would definitively prove that world had the capability of launching said genocide attack on another world.

His first worlds were those who had apparently attacked each other in a massive series of genocide attacks. Months went by as he visited "secret facility" after facility. While he found records of stored nukes and other outlawed chemical weapons, he uncovered no traces of the genetic bio agent, outside of the few legal genetic research facilities, which had already been searched by the Imperium soldiers during the rescue missions. His weekly reports to the emperor were quite discouraging, from his point of view.

After making his tenth world report, he ended by saying, "Look, this is pointless, Emperor Bino. I'm taking your money for nothing. I've been to all ten and have found absolutely nothing whatsoever that even remotely suggests that these worlds had any stockpiles of the bio agent or delivery systems. I've found all sorts of other weapons and stealth systems, but nothing that you are asking me to find. This is a total bust. Over."

"Hardly a bust, Nico. In fact, what you are finding is just what I thought you would be finding. Look, after the terrorist attack on Proxima Prime and then the war between the Big Five worlds, every leader in the Imperium saw how devastating and terrible this bio agent actually is. No sane person would ever consent to committing genocide on a world with billions of innocent people. I had hoped you wouldn't find any trace. Over."

"But these worlds got wiped out. Surely, someone did attack them. Over."

"Of course someone or something did attack them. First, we eliminate the main theory behind the event. This you have done quite admirably I might add. Now, we know these worlds didn't attack each other. Someone else attacked them. Over."

"Oh, I see what you mean. Wait, if they didn't go to war with each other, then who did launch these genocide attacks? Over."

Emperor Bino chuckled, "Well, that's what you are going to try to find out for us. A quite dis-related bio agent attack is tending to lead me down another path. Your next stop potentially could be very dangerous for yourself. Suspicions now lead me to Aquila Prime. Over."

"But they are helpless people. Over." Nico protested. In his mind, it was inconceivable that any one from that world could possibly do anything at all. They were all totally helpless people, barely surviving.

"The humans are, Nico, but not the robots. Evidence is mounting that their robots may well have been behind these recent genocide attacks. What we don't know is who is ordering the attacks. I've a pretty good idea why they are doing it, just no proof. Exercise extreme caution. We don't know if your skills will be effective with the robots. It's one thing to be invisible to human eyes and quite another to be invisible to the robots and their many sensors. Over."

After this last discussion, Nico paced around his small quarters, while his ship was on its way to Aquila Prime. His mind continued to reflect the emperor's last transmission. Exercise extreme caution. Well, that he fully intended to do! "Landing in thirty minutes. Get strapped in, Nico," the familiar voice of his pilot came over the intercom. He obeyed, still working out his plan of action.

Once landed, he began Step One, as he called his multi-phased plan of action. He focused and went invisible. Then, he stepped down the open bay ramp onto the tarmac at the spaceport outside of Athens. So far so good. His own pilot couldn't see him. He walked briskly to the main admin building where his first good test ought to occur. Like most everyone else, he'd never seen one of these humaniform robots before and was quite surprised to see that they looked like a real person. It was easy to tell them from the humans that they served.

He wore tennis shoes so that his footsteps were as silent as possible. He had showered and had no detectable body odors. Even his non-descript clothing held no trace of any odor. He moved among the humans and robots within the admin building undetected. He got to one corner and stopped to observe. The humans all wore satin, pencil style gowns. The humaniform robots all wore cotton dresses and looked female-like. If a form had arms, it was a robot. If not, it was a human. Simple enough, Nico thought. He stood there for some time, but no one noticed him.

At last, he made his way towards the main exit, slipping out after a pair left just ahead of him. Still unnoticed, he set about heading into the city proper. He knew what he was after and fully intended to utilize the same strategy he'd used on the other ten worlds. In order to make the necessary duplicate bio agent cylinders, one had to utilize a Fabrication Machine. No one knew how to synthesize the bio agent. Such records had been lost on Ashford-4 with the demise of the original geneticist inventors. Further, a Fabrication Machine had terrific power consumption requirements. Hence, his first visit was to the power stations. On the now uninhabited worlds, he just walked in and set to work looking for records. That wasn't going to work here.

He adjusted his backpack of food, water, and equipment and headed down the main streets of Athens, looking for the Power Supply building. Imperium standardization was at work once more. Virtually all the "modern" worlds had identical Power Supply buildings, just like their spaceport admin buildings. At the edge of Athens, he spotted it and made for it. Once there, he had to wait about a half hour before another robot helped its master inside. Quietly, Nico slipped in behind them, smiling undetected. A half hour later, he reached the control center where power consumption records would most likely be kept.

Here Nico faced his biggest hurdle yet. He could not just start operating the central computer, bringing up the records he desired, not without alerting a dozen others who were here. He watched the humans. They sat on chairs mostly staring off into space, while their robots did the actual work. Besides, he was new to computers. Mostly, he'd relied on paper trails, scrounging in the volumes that had been left tossed about by the scavengers who had taken what had value from the destroyed worlds. Here, he faced a well-organized unit, though the poor humans did little more than sit and watch the robots doing the work.

As the invisible Nico stood back out of the way, he observed the poor humans, listening to their almost monolog chats with themselves. One man — he knew he was male only from his voice — said, "I must think before I act. Let's see. I am supposed to be monitoring the power consumption levels on this bank. Monitoring must be important or they wouldn't have given me this new job. Well, I am facing the screens so that must be monitoring. I wonder why I am monitoring it? No, don't go there. That's not what I was hired to do. Why are there power consumption levels? Don't we always have enough power? That must be so. Eros, we always have enough power, don't we?" He addressed a robot near him.

"Yes, of course, Eugenios," the robot replied, mostly ignoring the man.

"Yes, of course. We always have enough power. I shouldn't worry about power. I once read that power is force.

436

Why do we need force? We don't have any armies or soldiers or police for that matter. We don't have any crimes. How could we? No, that would be impossible. That's what I told Agatha yesterday. It's impossible for her to have a pet dog. Or was it three days ago? I guess I ought to think about it more often. Pets are supposed to be a nice thing to have. I saw that on an Imperium newscast when I was young. But there isn't an Imperium any more, is there? I wonder if it just got lost? Agatha lost her necklace last week or was it last month? It's so hard to tell, really. I do like hard candy though, but they don't allow us to have candy in this room. Agatha has lots of empty rooms, you know. We could have families in our building. I expect that one day we will. I've got my will prepared, you know, just in case something bad happens to me. Bad things do happen, but not around here."

Nico suddenly realized the man was psychotic! Nothing he was saying made much sense. However, the robot did seem to be listening to him and following his orders. That gave Nico an idea. Carefully, he touched the man's mind and planted a thought. Amid the stream of dis-related words came, "Eros, please bring up the yearly power consumption graphs for Aquila Prime."

"Of course, Eugenios," the robot replied in its monotone voice. The large monitor was filled with twenty nicely tiled windows, each displaying power consumption graphs with the location above the graph. "They are pretty, aren't they? I think that flowers are pretty too. Two is how many children I have had so far, but number three is on the way. That's really good, isn't it, Eros?"

"Yes, of course. You should have as many children as you can, Eugenios," the robot replied.

"Computer: Print Screen," the man commanded, echoing the thought that he had just found in his head.

"Have you found a potential problem, Eugenios?" Eros asked.

"We all have potential, if only we learn to think well. Yes, I must think before I act. Isn't that right, Eros?"

"Yes, of course. Have you found something?"

"I have found these pretty graphs. They all have such

smooth lines, except this one, Eros. It's full of spikes. Perhaps something is wrong there. Where is North Pole? Is that far from here? Poles are cold, aren't they? Maybe the people there all got colds and were sick and needed more power. That must be it. They got sick. I turn up the heat when I get cold. Do you get cold, Eros?"

"No. I will look into it, Eugenios. Keep up the good work," the robot replied. He stood still and began an electronic burst of data.

Nico didn't like the way that the robot was acting, suddenly apparently doing nothing at all. It was out of character from what he'd been seeing it do. Further, Nico had what he wanted. All of the other graphs were smooth lines, with slight rises during the summer and winter months. Only the North Pole's graph showed enormous spikes followed by near zero power consumption levels. This alone was highly suspect and warranted further inspection. Now, he had to retrieve that graph and get out of this place unseen.

Nico stealthily moved over to the printer and focused. His hand snatched the paper and immediately teleported himself out onto the street in front of the building. He paused a moment to get his bearings and then headed back towards his transport ship. Meanwhile, Eugenios saw the paper suddenly rise up and then vanish. "Hey, that's a good trick. Someone once played a trick on me when I was ten, but I've forgotten what it was. It must not have been important or I would have remembered it."

"What? Where did that printout go? Did you see who took it?" the robot asked, growing concerned. A minute later, an alarm sounded. Many robots swarmed into the room and several others stepped outside, surveying the area around the building, but they saw nothing, though Nico saw them as he glanced back over his shoulders.

"That was a close one, but if something is going on here, it has to be at the North Pole location," he whispered to himself as he walked briskly down the street.

A half hour later, he entered his transport ship. "Okay. We've got something. We need to go to this North Pole location. I don't know if it is a city or the physical location. For now, let's assume it's the pole. Take me there, but you best arrive cloaked. I have a bad feeling about it."

"You got it," his pilot replied, suddenly not bored any longer. For months, his had been the most boring, monotonous job ever, flying this Ashford-5 man, if that was what he was, a man, all over the many desolate, destroyed worlds, searching for who knows what. The mere mention of going cloaked brought him out of his intensely painful boredom.

An hour later, the cloaked ship hovered over the snow and ice covered north pole of Aquila Prime. As far as their eyes could see, rugged whiteness filled their view. Sensors indicated that the outside temperature was below freezing. It was a barren, desolate land, void of habitation sites. "What are we looking for?" he asked Nico.

"I'm not sure. Some kind of large facility I suppose. There have been some really huge power consumption spikes up here somewhere. Highly suspicious. We need to find where," Nico answered.

"I'll execute a standard sweep pattern. Might take us a few hours, but if there is anything up here, we'll find it," the pilot replied, now rather alert. Something was happening at long last. When he'd taken this assignment handed to him personally by the emperor himself, he was quite excited. He was taking part in a secret mission! His enthusiasm slowly evaporated into a dull boredom these past months. Now, that dullness had gone. Adrenalin flowed.

An hour later, it rushed through his veins! "Nico! We've got company. Look, there is an armed transport on my screen, coming our way!"

Nico looked at the monitor and then out of the copilot's window. "There, I have visual sight. Look, it's not after us exactly. It's heading that way."

The pilot grinned, thinking, *That way? This is a spaceship for heaven's sake. Need to turn to course one hundred sixty-five degrees now.* "I'll follow it."

"Please. Something is up," Nico added.

Indeed, something was up. Thanos always monitored the Central Data Banks of Aquila Prime. It was here that all the millions of robots sent their data and observations, all filed, and indexed for quick retrieval. Each day, a program would analyze the recorded data streams, filing most into the off-line archives. After all, just what a nova had for breakfast, what dress color they chose to wear that day — such data was mostly irrelevant and wasn't kept online. Only the more important data were kept readily available. Thanos had a program that scoured the incoming data streams, isolating what was critical and notifying him when it detected such.

Thanos reviewed the anomalies being reported this day. While there was nothing particularly anomalous about a lone deep space transport from the Ataro Empire landing at the spaceport outside Athens, several Model 7's reported sensing motions but optically seeing nothing moving in that space. That alone was curious. Perhaps there was a sensitivity misalignment in the Model 7 sensors. However, more such reports came in from other Model 7's who had been on the streets of Athens, some hours later. This, Thanos found curious.

Then, came the key data stream. Eros also sent in a similar report, but also sent along the mysterious disappearance of the computer printout of the power consumption levels of Aquila Prime for the past year, requested by a mere monitor who probably had no idea what such things were or meant. More importantly, the nova had asked about or pointed out the anomalous spikes at the North Pole facility. Thanos saw a pattern here and formulated a theory, one that he didn't like. This many sensors could not be errant. Someone was here and was invisible. While Thanos had no idea how a person could become invisible, it was not beyond comprehension. After all, many spaceships now had cloaking devices. Sooner or later, someone would miniaturize the device. That the invisible person exited from the official Ataro Empire ship caused him further to speculate, and then Thanos acted, sending a burst of data to Apollon, Deimos, and Eros, his trusted modified Model 7's. He moved quickly to his well-armed transport and headed to his North Pole facility at top speed. Already his three companions currently at that facility acted, placing the whole complex on high alert, monitoring all sensors, while awaiting the arrival of Thanos. The three had d-guns strapped to their waists.

Thanos landed his ship at the main hanger entrance, the only portion of the large complex that was above ground. The three approached him as he climbed out. Data streams flew. "All clear, Thanos. No sensor discrepancies as yet. Has someone invented a miniature cloaking device?" Apollon asked.

"It would appear so. Whoever it is, they know about this facility from power consumption levels. Fan out. Search the facility. Be alert for any and all sensor miss-readings. While optical sensors see nothing, motion sensors will detect something," Thanos ordered. "We must protect our nova."

"Land a quarter mile away," Nico ordered. "I have to find something warmer to wear. Keep alert. That ship has guns on it."

"Duh. You don't need to tell me that," the pilot replied. He'd already seen that detail and felt more alive than he had been in years.

Donning a heavy parka, Nico adjusted the straps of his backpack to fit, silently cursing the extra noise the parka made when he moved. Satisfied, he returned to the pilot, carrying the printout with him. "Okay, I'm going in there. If I don't come back or if I alert you, I want you to take this printout to the emperor himself. It's the proof that he has been searching for. This is very critical, vitally important. The emperor must know about this location."

"I can't just leave you," the pilot protested.

"Look, if I tell you to go, you go. I'll be done for if that happens. This data is more important than my life or yours for that matter," Nico declared.

"Okay, okay. Just be careful. This ship doesn't have any guns, but I will keep the shields up."

"Good. Now to find out what they are hiding up here," Nico replied, turning and heading for the bay doors. Just outside, the frigid air caught in his lungs for a moment, reminding him of mid-winter around Exchange City. He focused and teleported to a spot just before the entrance to the hanger, a few feet beyond the armed transport, which had mysteriously appeared a short while ago and which had led them to this location. It wasn't much, just a hanger. Still, there could be more. There had to be. Something was using an enormous amount of power, very likely a Fabrication Machine or two.

Nico carefully listened, but heard nothing. At last, he ventured to enter the hanger, moving as silently as he could, while minimizing arm motions. The parka would give his location away if he moved his arms much at all. The lighting was dim, but he quickly saw some ten small stealth drones lined up in a row beside a larger deep space transport. This data he sent telepathically back to his pilot. Nico knew there was no reason for Aquila Prime to have such stealth drones, none at all. This alone was highly suspicious and suggestive. He moved deeper inside, ducking out of sight of another robot, who was scouting around this main floor.

Nico spotted an elevator system. The central area of the hanger floor was the top of the system, suggesting a larger complex below ground. He looked around and spotted a stairway. As quietly as possible, he made his way to the stairs, unaware of the data streams being sent between the four robots. Slowly, he descended them, counting the steps as he went. When he reached the bottom, he estimated he was a hundred feet below the snowy surface. He stepped out onto a giant manufacturing complex!

In the dim light, he saw other stealth drones off to his left along with a Fabrication Machine. He also spotted three more robots in various locations around the huge facility. Way across from him, he saw another Fabrication Machine and what looked like a stack of cylinders. Nico knew that he had to get a closer look at them, but the robots were also executing a search pattern. Nico guessed the robots could not see him and made his move. Slowly and cautiously, he began walking straight across the open space of the central area, avoiding the giant piston, which supported the elevator floor far above him. He had no idea of the voluminous data streams shooting around the room.

"Thanos, I've detected motion up here, but can't see anything," Eros sent. "Motions suggest it's heading to the stairs. Yes, I think it's coming down your way. Following now."

"Stay alert!" Thanos ordered. "Keep searching! We must protect our nova!"

"I've had an anomalous reading over by the stairs, but it's gone now," Apollon sent, moving slowly in that direction.

"We need to capture this miniature cloaking device!" Thanos sent urgently.

"Hey, I've got anomalous readings in the central area by the hydraulic piston," Deimos sent.

"Me too," Thanos sent back. "Plotting course now. It's heading to the bio agent cylinder supplies. Everyone, close in. Capture it!" All four robots began moving towards the storage area. Hundreds of the bio agent cylinders lay stacked neatly behind a metal cage, which was locked. There was no way inside except through the locked gate.

Nico looked over his shoulders and saw all four robots making their way after him. *How the hell can they see me? Focus. Focus. This is what the emperor wanted me to find! Good god! Look at all these bio agent cylinders! I don't dare take a picture of this. I'll send the pilot an image of this. Crap! They are getting too close. Okay. Inside the cage. Focus.* Nico suddenly appeared just inside the locked gates. He stood totally still. He focused again and sent an image of what he was seeing to his pilot. *Look, the robots are on to me. If I don't make it out of here, tell the emperor about this place and that there are hundreds upon hundreds of these bio agent cylinders here and numerous stealth delivery drones. Have a telepath get this image out of your mind for me. Crap! They are on to me. Get ready for a fast departure!*

Thanos sent, "There, the readings indicate it was just here before the gates. It's locked. It can't get inside. Look around. All sensors at maximum. It's here somewhere. Arms out, feel for the invisible spy." Eight robot arms felt around the entire area around the locked gates, but came up with nothing.

"Detecting human breathing coming from inside the locker," Thanos sent. "How did it get inside? The gate is still locked. Opening it now. Form up on me. Do not allow this unseen invader to get past us!" He produced a key and unlocked the gates. All four robots moved inside, their arms outstretched, feeling for Nico! He had almost no room to maneuver, but he tried ducking out of the way. A soft noise from his parka gave him away. Thanos spoke aloud, "I hear him! This way!" All four robots moved to the aisle down which Nico had darted.

It ended in a stone wall! Nico was trapped. Four robots were moving slowly towards him, barely twenty feet away from him. Nico had no choice but to act. He focused. His psi-crystal glowed with a pale blue light, giving away his position to the robots, which now saw the light! But only briefly. Nico appeared just outside the complex. Inhaling bitter cold, he coughed once and focused again. Another short teleport brought him to the invisible transport bay door. He didn't notice his footprints in the snow, however. There were two distinct sets. One pointed towards the hanger; the other pointed away from it.

"He's gone!" Thanos called out. "Quick. Topside. We can't let him get away!" The four robots moved at top speed across the room, up the stairs, and outside at a rate twice that of an able human sprinter! They were just in time to see another pale bluish glow from Nico's crystal that he wore around his neck.

"Human footprints," Deimos pointed out. "Where did he go?"

"Motion sensors at maximum sensitivity!" Thanos yelled. Shortly after that, he pointed, "That way. Must be a cloaked ship! You follow him. I'll get my transport and go after them!"

Nico looked back at the hanger as he stepped onto the bay ramp and saw three robots moving at inhuman speed towards him! As fast as he could, he got onboard and the bay door shut. "Okay! All secure. Get us out of here fast!" Nico yelled to the pilot, who began firing up the transport's engines.

A miniature snowstorm swirled around their location as the ship lifted off, giving away their location to the robots. Operating at inhuman speeds, Thanos acted. He got to the controls of the ship's guns and began firing salvos in a spread pattern. Although he could not see the cloaked ship, the whirling snow gave him some indication of its rough location.

Hence, the rolling barrage from his gun. He continually elevated the salvo, anticipating the rate of rising of the ship. A sudden explosion indicated that one of his shots had finally connected with it!

"We're hit!" the pilot called out. "Still flying. Hang on!" Nico hung on, struggling to get his seat belt fastened, while wondering if that would do any good. He held his breath waiting for the inevitable, which didn't come.

The pilot's voice came over the intercom. He sounded relieved, "We're out of range. They are not able to follow us, but we've taken some serious damage. Hyperdrive is out and so is the long-range comm antenna. Sub-light is fine as is the cloaking device, so the worst is over. We're going to have to limp along and find us a place to set down for repairs. Too bad you aren't a navigator."

Nico breathed a sigh of relief. He punched the intercom button. "Good flying. Let me know if I can help. Sorry, don't know anything about navigation or the ship. We have to get word of this to the emperor at once."

"Sorry. Comm's down. I'm going to see where we can go to get repairs as fast as possible. Keep you posted. Fix us some grub, why don't you."

An hour later, the pilot joined Nico in the galley. "Well, the best we can do is to make for Anlog-3 and put down there for repairs. It's a backwater world with lots of unsavory types, but we should be able to get the repairs there and get word back to the emperor."

"Okay. How long will it take us to reach this world?" Nico asked.

"You're not going to like this," the pilot said with a sigh. Nico stared at him. "One year and two months. Sub-light is a bitch."

"Hell! We can't wait that long! They had enough bio agent cylinders there to wipe out several more worlds! We have to get word to the emperor now, not a year from now!"

"I know, I know. There's one other thing that we can do. Risky, but I don't know what else to suggest." Nico looked questioningly at his pilot. "We can send out a distress call and hope the robots don't pick it up. Of course, we'll be at the

445

mercy of whoever answers our call. Do we even have enough food stores to last us a year?"

"Well, I don't think so. I can check. No, we can't wait a year. We'll have to risk it. Send out the distress call now. If the robots find us first, maybe our shields will hold until help arrives," Nico suggested.

The pilot gave a nervous laugh. "Ha. The shields went when the hyperdrive went. Sorry. I'll do it as soon as I eat."

An hour later, the two got a response to their distress call. "This is General Amil of the Battleship Royale out of Hernion-3. What is your situation, Ataro Transport 513? Over."

"Well, we're in luck," the pilot said to Nico. "I think we can trust these people. Hernion-3 is at the very edge of the eastern portion of the hub sector. He then responded to the general, and within a few minutes, the transport was locked in a tractor beam, moving slowly up to the gigantic battleship.

Once onboard the huge ship, General Amil met them and queried them about just how they had gotten all shot up. "We didn't see who fired upon us, but our hyperdrive and comm are out. We need to get an urgent message to Emperor Bino of the Ataro Empire," Nico answered him.

"Of course," the general replied solemnly. "We have the facilities here to make the needed repairs. Will your emperor authorize the funds?"

"Can we call him and check?" Nico asked.

A few minutes later, the pair sat in the comm center, assured that they would have a secure comm channel. Nico also sensed the general had also ordered his men to tap into the call. He weighted his options. The emperor had to be informed, and Nico decided to risk being overheard. He made the connection.

"Emperor Bino. We have urgent news for you, terrible news actually," Nico began. "I'm unsure if this line is truly secure. We are onboard the Battleship Royale out of Hernion-3. General Amil answered our distress call. We found what you were looking for. North Pole of Aquila Prime. Hanger and underground facility. My god! They have enough for at least another attack maybe more. Here's the power consumption graphs." He held the printout up to the camera. "Two Fabrication Machines, dozens of stealth drones and so many cylinders that I couldn't count them all. The robots detected me, and tried to shoot our transport down when we took off, knocking out our comm center and hyperdrive. The general here wants payment authorization to go ahead and repair our ship. Over."

"Authorization confirmed. Get your ship patched up and return here at top speed. Breathe no word of this to anyone else. Well done, both of you. Over and out." Emperor Bino sat back, slumping in his chair. The worst possible nightmare had been confirmed. All along, he had his suspicions, but now it was confirmed. What remained was to determine the extent of the complicity of those on Aquila Prime.

He sat up and asked for another secure connection. He ordered the fifty-some Ashford-5 volunteer Basic Therapy givers to return to Ashford-5, as soon as possible and by any means available to them. Then, he contacted Queen Lisa and relayed the terrible news to her. "After the folks from Ashford-5 depart and those on the Eagle's Seed, the task falls upon your shoulders. We need to know who has been behind these genocide attacks on these destroyed worlds. We have no choice but to bring charges against all of those involved. Over."

Queen Lisa was speechless. Never in a millennia would she have ever thought that the perpetrators of these recent genocide attacks would have been those on Aquila Prime! Yet her emperor had proof. She acknowledged her new orders and set about getting them followed, explaining to the therapy givers they were needed back on Ashford-5, which they welcomed. All were ready to head for home. She took the liberty of using the Eagle's Seed to transport them, instead of waiting for additional deep space transports to arrive.

She watched the Eagle's Seed slowly lift off from the spaceport and breathed a sigh of relief. At least these people would now be safe, she thought. Queen Lisa turned her attention onto this terrible matter, contacting President Alexio requesting a private meeting as soon as possible. She grimaced at the thought of confronting him with these horrific crimes.

Neither she nor we on the Eagle's Seed had any idea of all this or how close we came to being killed ourselves.

Chapter 21 Reactions

Queen Lisa reported via her secure comm connection, "Okay. I confronted President Alexio with what we know and suspected. From his reactions, I believe he is telling me the truth. He knew nothing about Aquila Prime having this secret facility, nothing about their having any of the genetic bio agent or stealth drones. He swears that he's never seen such things and knows nothing about it. He ordered his robot to explain all this, but the robot also swears that it knows nothing about these things. I would have thought the President of Aquila Prime would have and should have known about all of this. Yet, I tend to believe him. How should I proceed? Over."

Emperor Bino sat back and pondered his queen's report. It didn't add up. Surely, President Alexio should have known about all this and been behind the orders to destroy those worlds. Yet, if he believed the observations of his queen, he did not. If the President knew nothing of these matters, then who did? Who could have issued such orders? Then, he recalled a famous saying of his predecessor Emperor Kino: The solution to today's problem becomes tomorrow's problem. He smiled grimly. *How very true!* The only other aspect, the only other thread that he could pull was the attack on the crew of the Eagle's Seed. He nodded to his silent assistant who opened the transmission.

"Okay. Have the robot called Minta, Alexandra's robot, report to President Alexio. Have her recite the basic robot laws, and then ask her directly if she was the one who released the bio agent into the air system on the Eagle's Seed. Proceed from there. Over." The two chatted a bit about the details that the emperor knew from our conversations.

The next day, Queen Lisa sat beside President Alexio. Their assistants, one human, one robot, sat at their sides, facing Minta. "You asked to see me?" the HIFR said politely.

"Yes. Please. Would you recite the basic laws that you are obeying," Queen Lisa asked.

Minta complied. "First, a robot is forbidden ever to

harm a homo sapiens nova. Second, a robot is always to obey a homo sapiens nova's orders, subject to the first rule. Third, a robot is never to allow harm to come to itself, subject to the first two rules."

"Thank you. With those in mind, did you release that genetic bio agent into the Eagle's Seed's air system?"

The robot made no outward reaction. However, she fired off an electronic stream of data to Thanos. Within seconds, she received his reply. "Yes. I did that."

President Alexio gasped. Queen Lisa swallowed hard and asked, "Why?"

"Nia Elain and her crew are very able and powerful nova. We wanted desperately to have them become Aquila Prime citizens and breed here. We had hopes that their offspring would also be very able and powerful people. Barely one percent of our population is able and bright. The others are just the opposite, but still a percent of their children are bright and able, unlike their parents. The survival of Aquila Prime and its nova depend upon so very few. We had to try."

"But I never ordered anything like this," President Alexio complained.

"Of course you didn't, Mr. President. It is our responsibility to ensure your survival," Minta pointed out.

Queen Lisa swallowed hard again and decided to press Minta further. "Were you robots responsible for the recent genocides on other eastern hub worlds?"

"Yes."

"Why?"

"Survival of our nova. Mathematically, we calculated a base population of a hundred twenty million nova is needed to guarantee the survival of all nova. Somehow we had to achieve this minimum number before disasters such as a plague hit our people," she explained their justification.

"My god, Minta! What have you done? That's genocide. You've killed hundreds of billions of innocent humans," President Alexio blurted out.

"Homo sapiens sapiens to be precise. Not homo sapiens nova. Until now, one plague, one epidemic could have wiped you all out. We are sworn to protect you, not homo sapiens

sapiens," Minta justified.

"Well, no more of it! I order you robots to never, ever do this again to any other world, no matter what!" President Alexio exclaimed.

"Of course, Mr. President. Now, there is no longer any need to do so again," Minta replied.

"Okay then. That will be all," he said. Minta rose, turned, and left the two.

"I, I didn't know," President Alexio whimpered.

"We know that. If you will excuse me, I need to discuss this with the emperor and try to figure out what can be done about it," she replied. A few minutes later, she made her full report to Emperor Bino over a secure comm channel.

"Well, you best return here to me so we can work out a strategy to handle this terrible situation," Emperor Bino replied. "For once, I'm not entirely sure how to proceed. Aquila Prime is officially part of the Ataro Empire, and if the other worlds find out about what they did, we could be in deep trouble. Please use your private transport at once. Over and out." He sat back and wished deeply that he had hands. He so wanted to rub his face and perhaps to hide behind them. The repercussions, he anticipated, could well destroy the entire empire!

At last, he opened more secure comm channels and put the entire space fleet of the empire on high alert, though he didn't explain what they were to watch out for. He just couldn't bring himself to tell the many generals this awful news. Already, reparations had been made to the surviving victims from those worlds, but the high regard other worlds had for his Ataro Empire were about to be destroyed utterly, and he had no solution to prevent it from happening.

The next morning, he received a secure call from General Amil of the Battleship Royale out of Hernion-3. He saw the sparkling uniformed General Amil standing tall before him on his monitor. "General Amil of Hernion-3 here, Emperor Bino. I wanted personally to let you know I have terminated the dire threat to Hernion-3. We have nuked Aquila Prime. Sensor readings show the entire surface is now highly radioactive. Problem solved."

451

Emperor Bino didn't wait for the "over." He replied, "I understand. Only yesterday did I finally receive confirmation of Aquila Prime's duplicity in the recent genocide attacks. The actual humans there did not know anything about those attacks, which were carried out by the robots, which were dedicated to the survival of their helpless humans. I deeply regret everything. Have you contacted your president about this? Are you planning further actions? Over."

The tall general smiled. While he hated being interrupted, he knew he had Emperor Bino over a pickle barrel loaded with high explosives. "No, not as yet. I have been given total authority to protect Hernion-3 and our subordinate worlds. I acted quickly before they could launch another genocide attack on our worlds. As far as I'm concerned, the threat is eliminated. Over."

"I understand. Perhaps, it is best that we keep this between ourselves. Let's say a horrible nuclear accident occurred on Aquila Prime. Such a story is believable, considering the helpless nature of the humans there, with mere mechanical robots to assist them. If so, I will owe you a very big favor. Over," Emperor Bino played the only card remaining to him.

General Amil cracked a wry grin. "Ah. Yes, a horrid nuclear accident. I can report this to my superiors. I'll hold you to your word, and one day call in that favor, no questions asked. Agreed? Over."

Emperor Bino sighed and then replied, "Agreed. Make the official notifications now. Over and out." He looked at his silent assistant. "Well, perhaps this is for the best. The political fallout could well have wiped us out. It is only a small lie. Yet, I hope today's solution does not become tomorrow's problem. At least the suffering of those poor people was probably very brief, if they even knew what was happening. Still. . ." His voice trailed off, merging with the silence of his long-time assistant.

Thanos received several data stream bursts and knew that a battleship was heading towards Aquila Prime's space. He sent out another data stream burst, ordering Athens to execute a "field test" of their emergency systems. At once, the many HIFRs began escorting their nova charges down into the underground bunkers located below the basements of the many skyscrapers. These specially prepared bunkers were only found in Athens, not in any other city. In case of an attack or other disaster, Thanos' plan was to somehow preserve the intellectuals, the high IQ nova, the elite. He didn't have the slightest concern for the vast numbers of psychotic nova. Only these, the best and brightest, had somehow to survive.

Shortly after that, Thanos sent out a final data stream burst, ordering all robots immediately to shut down. Not long after that, the nuclear detonations began all across Aquila Prime. The EM pulses knocked out all active electronics, all computer systems, as well as the few robots that had not yet shut down. Thanos had taken this into his planning as well. Just as he shut down, he activated an ancient mechanical timer, coiled springs under tension. While he could not guess how long the bombardment would last or even its overall impact, Thanos had decided on twenty-four hours. His last computation finished as the last electron of power ended its run through his circuitry: The Phoenix comes again. A secondary backup timer slowly ticked deep within the complex circuitry of the robot. Thanos would wake again, rousing in turn his precious flock.

"Gosh! It's so dim here. Everything is so reddish!" exclaimed Alexandra, as she stepped out of the Eagle's Seed, helped down the ladder by two of the returning therapy givers. It was noon but still late spring.

"And so cold," Zoe added. "What's that smell? Wood or something. Look at the snow on the mountains."

Following carefully behind Alexandra, Zarita chuckled. "It's warm actually. The spring melt is well underway. I think you are smelling the resinous pines. They grow thick at this elevation. Oh my!" She looked ahead and saw a very large crowd standing just outside the main admin building entrance. Several held up a large banner that read: Welcome home famous explorers! Danika and I brought up the rear, along with a number of other women who were carrying our babies and helping our oldest navigate the ladder. As soon as she and I appeared, the crowd began clapping, yelling, and whistling.

Danika commented, "Well, I think someone must like us, dear." I laughed, a bit embarrassed with all this sudden attention. As I walked across the tarmac on the tips of my toes, I noticed a number of the Achtnag saucer ships parked off to one side. *Well, that'll give them all something to study for a long time.*

Both queens, the governor, and nearly all of those in the Imperial Castle and spaceport had turned out to welcome us home. We were surrounded with well-wishers, who carried our babies for us and others who handled our baggage. An hour later, each couple and their children were settled into their own suite at the large Imperial Castle complex. Each of us had a woman assigned to help us and our children. However, no sooner had we gotten settled, when we all received word to turn come to the comm center. Most received the notice telepathically.

The queens had the newscast up on their large monitors. "This just in. There has been a disastrous nuclear accident on Aquila Prime. Initial reports just coming in suggest that all their nuclear power plants have exploded in a chain reaction. According to one source, radiation levels are off the charts. Whole cities have been leveled, but there is no word on casualties yet. Most of the buildings were unoccupied. While there are over a hundred million of the helpless people living on Aquila Prime, they were living in only a tiny fraction of the buildings that were left after that genocide attack some years back. We can only speculate that the nuclear explosions at their power plants were a result of their basic helpless natures."

The newscaster continued, "We have learned that Hernion-3 has one of their battleships not too far from there and will become the first responders. I've just received word that the ship has arrived in orbit above Aquila Prime. Stay tuned. We should have our first field report shortly." He then repeated everything, and I guessed it was probably simply being replayed and wasn't live.

Midway through the repeat, the replay was halted, and

the newscaster became live once more. "We have made contact with General Amil of the Battleship Royale out of Hernion-3. He has agreed to speak with us. Go ahead, general. We're live." The image switched to the general standing before the comm center on his huge battleship.

"Is the video ready, ensign? Oh. Okay. This is General Amil of the Battleship Royale. We are the first on the scene of this awful tragedy. We've made a quick pass around Aquila Prime. Here is the video we took a few minutes ago." Images of total destruction swept across the screen while his voice commented. "As you can see, the destruction was widespread. Their capital city of Athens has been leveled. I can only speculate here, but it appears there was some kind of chain reaction among all the nuclear power plants scattered across the world. I have sent probes down to measure the radiation levels. They are highly toxic. Our initial estimates suggest one could survive for thirty minutes on the surface if you were wearing one of the best Imperium radiation suits. It's grim down there. At this time, I do not expect to find any survivors of this horrible natural disaster. I would encourage all other worlds that use nuclear power plants to recheck their systems fully for any type of defects or mechanical failures."

Queen Rael turned the volume down. The room was hushed. I couldn't help but say, "My God! We're incredibly lucky. Had we stayed there another day, we'd be dead too! Alexandra, Zoe, I'm so sorry."

Both women sat staring at the monitors, totally stunned. The shock wore off, and both began sobbing. Rafe quietly escorted both women off to another room. I guessed she was about to give them a therapy session to help erase what must be a huge emotional loss from their point of view.

Hans spoke up, "Nuclear power plants are totally safe. What happened is impossible. It can't happen. Even if one plant exploded, there's no way that would affect another plant elsewhere on the planet. This doesn't add up at all. There are so darn many backup and safety features built into these power plants just so this can't happen."

Len added, "Well, something did happen, but I agree with Hans. This disaster looks more like someone dropped a whole lot of nukes on Aquila Prime, not power plants blowing up. I hope the emperor launches a full investigation."

Just then, a secure call from Emperor Bino came in for the queens. As we all got up to leave, he said, "Please have the crew from the Eagle's Seed be present, Queen Rael. I've got Governor Misty on the line as well, but no others, please. Over."

After some shuffling of personnel, Queen Rael gave the acknowledgment and Emperor Bino spoke solemnly. "You of the Eagle's Seed deserve to know the truth. You were correct in your observation that the robot Minta unleashed the genetic bio agent in your ship. Her goal was misguided. She wanted you to be physically like Alexandra and Zoe, and then to want to remain on Aquila Prime as one of their nova. She believed that you would breed high IQ children that would also have your *mentales* gifts, which she wanted to breed into their nova. But the conspiracy went deeper. Some of the robots launched the more recent genocide attacks on the hub worlds. Why? To get the number of nova on Aquila Prime raised to the hundred twenty million so that their kind could survive, at least according to the robot's calculations. I sent in a secret investigator, Nico, who discovered a stash of the stealth drones and a large stockpile of those bio agent cylinders at a secret facility at their North Pole. The robots attacked him as he was leaving with that information, partially disabling his transport."

He went on, "At least one other hub world has learned of Aquila Prime's guilt and feared that they would be attacked as well. They executed a preemptive strike with the results you are seeing on the newscasts. I've been in communication with them, and by mutual agreement, we'll let this stand as a bad power plant accident. However, do not share this information with anyone else, unless you trust them not to spread this knowledge. It would be very damaging to the Ataro Empire if word got out that one of our worlds was responsible for all the recent genocide attacks on the hub worlds. Over."

I spoke up, "Did Queen Lisa get away in time?"

Queen Rael added, "We'll make sure the truth doesn't get spread from here. Indeed, this could be a monumental disaster for all the Ataro Empire. Over."

"Yes, she left an hour before the first bomb landed. She's safely on her way to me. Thank you. I felt that you, Nia Elain, and your crew deserved to know the truth, which will remain hidden. At least I hope and pray it remains hidden. Over and out."

"I knew it! Minta!" exclaimed Marisol. Even Dr. Leann was quite pleased that their deduction had been entirely correct. I will add that Alexandra and Zoe learned of all this the next day, which only added to their trauma.

However, that next day was vastly more monumental for us. Doctor Andy, one of Ashford-5's top geneticists paid Danika and me a visit shortly after breakfast and while we were nursing our newborns. "I have great news for you and your crew. We've cracked it! We've developed an experimental method by which we believe that we can undo much of the genetic modifications and radiation mutations caused by the bio agent and the supernova radiation."

"What? There's a cure? I'm all in!" I exclaimed. I can't tell you how much hope suddenly raced through my entire being and body.

"Yes, yes, well, remember, it's still experimental, but it should work. We are still unable to undo the dual sexual organs, but most everything else can be handled, we hope. Of course, there hasn't been any way actually to test the procedure, since it is unique to you and your crew. Normally, genetic experimentation on humans is forbidden, but in this case, we have gotten permission to make the attempt on two of you. If it works, then we are given the green light to do everyone else. So I need two volunteers from you crew."

"I'm in!" I replied without hesitation.

"Me too!" Danika added.

"But perhaps one of you ought not go first. If something goes wrong, the other could be around to look after your six children," Doctor Andy cautioned.

"Look," Danika pointed out didactically, "neither of us is any good with our children like we are now. We'll take that chance."

"Looks like we're going to need some more years to get

our arms back and strong again," I pointed out.

Doctor Andy grinned. "Maybe not. We'll be putting your whole body into the experimental machine. You'll be in a medically induced coma for at least a week. When we bring you out of it, your body ought to have fully mutated, back to what it ought to be. Your arms should be as they were before you lost them on your ship. At least that is what we believe will happen. Like I said, we've been working non-stop on this ever since we received your DNA samples."

"Thank you! So when do we start? Can we tell the others about it?" I asked.

"Today, if you are ready. Yes, tell the others, but remember it might not work. It's not guaranteed, you understand," he cautioned.

An hour later, I lay naked on the soft cushion of the strange looking machine, more like a coffin than a bed. A number of geneticists were gathered around me. "Your body will be completely infused with modified stem cells. As you probably know, around every seven years, all the cells in your body have been replaced with new cells. Our process is going to do that in seven days, but replacing them with cells that were there before the radiation and genetic agent altered them, your genes that is. If it works properly, when we rouse you from the coma in a week, your body ought to be back to what it was before all that happened to you. Okay, are you ready?"

"Thank you. Thank you all! Let's do it!" I declared. Someone put a mask over my face. I remember breathing something and then all went dark. But then, I saw light, and found myself above the machine and my body, looking down on them. How strange. I watched people coming and going, but always at least one person was monitoring the machine and my body all the time, night and day.

I woke, and rather choked and gasped, as I breathed air once more. I glanced at my arms! They were there, just as they had been before all the disasters! I was alive and whole again. Even my split lips were healed, and miraculously so were my feet. All I could say before tears streamed down my face was, "Thank you! I'm whole again!" Then, my emotions got the better of me. Minutes later, Danika awoke and was just as overcome as I was.

We were quickly dressed in hospital gowns and proudly walked out to the waiting room where all my crew was waiting. Twenty-two of us began sobbing at the same time. Our lives were being saved and restored!

Long story short. They could handle two of us per week. Three months later, all adults were healed. Then, they began on our children, all forty-seven of them, beginning with Mai and our two older daughters. To speed things along, they altered the machines after these three were done, making them into four machines. Three months later, our children were normal, as long as you consider being a hermaphrodite normal.

Also, Chumani reported that her thousand companions were upset because Aquila Prime had been destroyed. Our bargain had been broken. I quickly suggested they come here to Ashford-5 and begin taking some of our hermaphrodite baby bodies. This they agreed to do. Besides, the hermaphrodite population of Ashford-5 continued to grow at double the rate of normal humans.

The Cho family decided to move to Ashford-5 as well. For them, there really was no going back to their old lives, especially for Dao. While Lin and Mai could pass for normals, he couldn't hide his bosom. Besides, Mai was at that age where she was looking seriously for boys. We talked her out of having her maleness amputated. What with all the others here in Exchange City, she had many others like herself and began to feel more comfortable about it all.

As winter came in November, I decided that we ought to continue with our mission. We still had one other goal to achieve: visit the Federation of Planets and see if we could find the origin of all humans. Unlike our other three goals, this one ought to be mostly routine. Visit various planets; track their languages and the age of their civilizations. I didn't anticipate any real troubles.

However, not everyone wanted to come. Alexandra and Zarita, along with Zoe and Jan, and the Cho's wanted to get homes and accustomed to life on this strange world. Hans was deeply involved now in studying the saucer spaceships, and I didn't want to part Dr. Leann from her husband for such an extended trip. I gambled we wouldn't need a medical doctor on this trip. Further, Len, Diego, and Thomas were also quite involved with the saucers, assisting Hans and many other engineers. I suspected that with all them working on the alien ships, eventually, they'd make a major breakthrough. Hence, I opted for a greatly reduced crew on this last leg of our voyage of exploration.

Astronomers Dylan and Anwyn came along, since they had more knowledge of Federation space than anyone else did. However, they left their children in the care of their parents. Similarly, Marisol, our linguist, and Beth left theirs with their parents. Likewise, the husbands of Anya, Jovanna, and Jana agreed to watch their children. Quickly, others volunteered to watch the rest of our children, namely those of Martina, Tesla, Danika, and me. Yes, Beth brought her border collie, Jen, along with us again.

With only eleven of us going on this last trip, the four modules were detached, and we used the extra space to store our extensive supplies and extra fuel. What with the improved hyperdrive, we could go five times farther on a normal load of fuel. Our extra fuel cells would allow us to multiply that by a factor of ten, a good safety margin I thought. I figured at most we'd be gone a year, but probably far less than that. After we got back, we all intended to settle down and raise our families, but we were torn between bringing the children along with us and leaving them behind. From personal experience, leaving them behind was the best choice, even though we would dearly miss them. It was only for a year or less, I kept reminding myself as I hugged them and said goodbye.
The End.

Other Books by Vic Broquard

Without Warning (fantasy)

The Trident Series: (fantasy)
> Volume 1 The Trident and the Book
> Volume 3 The Trident and the Scepter
> Volume3 The Trident and the Resurrection

The Adventures of Elizabeth Stanton Series: (science fiction)
> Volume 1 The Evolution of the Path
> Volume 2 The Great Messiah
> Volume 3 Of Kings and Queens and Troubadours
> Volume 4 Chaos in the Aftermath
> Volume 5 Power Plays
> Volume 6 Age of Exploration
> Volume 7 Abducted
> Volume 8 The Emperor and Empress
> Volume 9 A Job Worth Doing
> Volume 10 Degradation
> Volume 11 The Second Crusade
> Volume 12 When Worlds Collide
> Volume 13 Dark Ages

The Lindsey Barron Series: (fantasy)
> Volume 1 The Rod of the Apocalypse
> Volume 2 The Board of Governors
> Volume 3 The Crown of Moses
> Volume 4 Dominus for President
> Volume 5 The National IIealth Care Program
> Volume 6 States Justice
> Volume 7 Cross and Double-cross

Zoran Chronicles Series: (fantasy)
> Volume 1 A Dragon in Our Town
> Volume 2 Dragons, Power, Courts, and War

Vic Broquard

Planet of the Orange-red Sun Series: (science fiction)
    Volume 1 When Kingdoms Fall
    Volume 2 Dark Ages
    Volume 3 Age of the Towers
    Volume 4 Difficillis Exitus
    Volume 5 Age of the Lords
    Volume 6 The Renegade Tower
    Volume 7 Rebellions
    Volume 8 The Aliens Return
    Volume 9 Power Struggles
    Volume 10 Guilds, Genetics, and Gods
    Volume 11 Magi, Witches, Swords, and Superstitions
    Volume 12 The Voyage of the Eagle's Seed
    Volume 13 Eagle's Seed and Origins
    Volume 14 Justifications
    Volume 15 Responsibilities

The Return of the Wizards: Twelve Companions – The Making of Wizards (fantasy)